22733

FORTUNE'S WHEEL

Books by Rhoda Edwards

FORTUNE'S WHEEL

THE BROKEN SWORD
(Published in the U.K. as *Some Touch of Pity*)

Fortune's Wheel

RHODA EDWARDS

Doubleday & Company, Inc.
Garden City, New York
1979

Library of Congress Cataloging in Publication Data

Edwards, Rhoda.
Fortune's wheel.

1. Richard III, King of England, 1452–1485–Fiction.
2. Great Britain–History–Wars of the Roses, 1455–1485–Fiction.
I. Title. PZ4.E267Fo 1978b [PR6055.D97]   823'.9'14

ISBN: 0-385-11582-2
Library of Congress Catalog Card Number: 78-7752

Contents

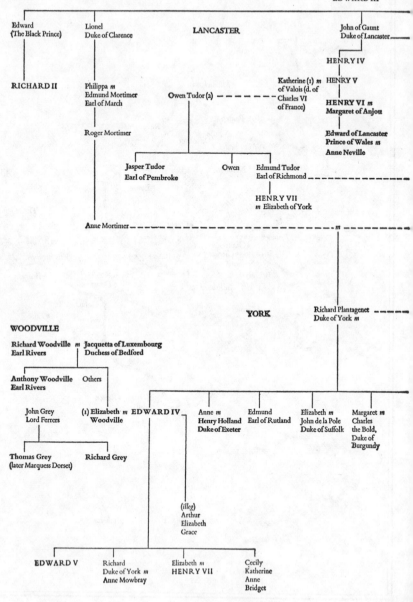

The Houses of York and Lancaster

Characters printed in bold appear in this novel

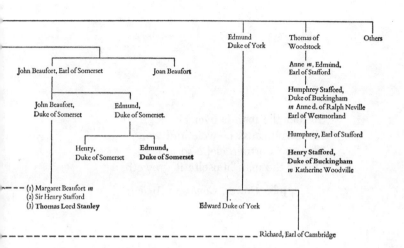

Edmund
Duke of York

Thomas of
Woodstock

Others

John Beaufort, Earl of Somerset

Joan Beaufort

Anne *m*, Edmund,
Earl of Stafford

John Beaufort,
Duke of Somerset

Edmund,
Duke of Somerset.

Humphrey Stafford,
Duke of Buckingham
m Anne d. of Ralph Neville
Earl of Westmorland

Henry,
Duke of Somerset

**Edmund,
Duke of Somerset**

Humphrey, Earl of Stafford

**Henry Stafford,
Duke of Buckingham**
m Katherine Woodville

- - - (1) Margaret Beaufort *m*
(2) Sir Henry Stafford
(3) **Thomas Lord Stanley**

Edward Duke of York

- Richard, Earl of Cambridge

NEVILLE

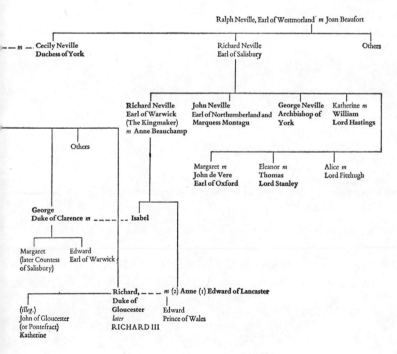

Ralph Neville, Earl of Westmorland *m* Joan Beaufort

- *m* - **Cecily Neville
Duchess of York**

Richard Neville
Earl of Salisbury

Others

**Richard Neville
Earl of Warwick
(The Kingmaker)
m Anne Beauchamp**

John Neville
Earl of Northumberland and
Marquess Montagu

**George Neville
Archbishop of
York**

Katherine *m*
William
Lord Hastings

Others

Margaret *m*
**John de Vere
Earl of Oxford**

Eleanor *m*
Thomas
Lord Stanley

Alice *m*
Lord Fitzhugh

**George
Duke of Clarence** *m* - - - - **Isabel**

Margaret
(later Countess
of Salisbury)

Edward
Earl of Warwick

**Richard,
Duke of
Gloucester**
later
RICHARD III

m (2) **Anne** (1) **Edward of Lancaster**

(illeg.)
John of Gloucester
(or Pontefract)
Katherine

Edward
Prince of Wales

So that the man is over al
His owne cause of wele and wo.
That we Fortune clepe so,
Out of the man himselfe it groweth.

John Gower, *Confessio Amantis*

FORTUNE'S WHEEL

Seulement Un

December 1468

W for Warwik, goode with sheld & other defence,
The boldest under baner in batell to a-byde;
For the right of Englond he doth his diligence,
Bothe be londe & watyr, God be his gyde!

R be the ragged staf that noman may skapen,
From Scotland to Calais there-of men stond in awe;
In al cristen landes is none so felle a wepen
To correcte soche caytiffes as do a-gayne the lawe.

Twelve Letters save England (c. 1461)

The December night was mild and damp as a dog's lick. Unmoving cloud hid the moon. As the barge rode the flowing tide, its oars dipped lightly, the rowers' muscles scarcely swelling. The prevailing smell was of Thames water. That this river should smell uniquely nasty was strange, because other tidal rivers cleansed other cities twice daily and still retained some tang of the sea or of the hills at their source. Many jests were current at Westminster concerning the properties of rivers, and their pernicious influence. The words of Pliny's *Natural History* became delightfully derisive when turned against that unpopular man Richard Woodville, Lord Rivers, the Queen's father. The rivers multiply and overflow the land—one of the chief resentments against Lord Rivers was that he had managed to multiply himself twelvefold. Richard of Gloucester had never repeated any of these gibes himself, and seldom had to stifle laughter; he did not find the subject amusing. He had learned while very young to keep silence. Nevertheless, rivers—and Rivers—stank.

The Thames below the City had more than a taint of Billingsgate, the shambles and public jakes on the Fleet. Yet it should be clean. It was deep, wide and dangerous on this stretch from Greenwich to London, far from human habitation, the dark hiding miles of winter-desolate marshes. The only friendly aspect the Thames offered to Richard was that of a bolt hole. You could row upon it out of sight and sound of the Westminster warren, into the tranquil Chelsea reaches—if you kept rowing long enough you would reach Sheen, or the first bridge, at Kingston. The Thames in summer had a smiling face, tempting you to swim in it for pleasure. One of the things that the Earl of Warwick had insisted upon was that boys under his tutelage must be taught to swim. This was an unusual demand from a sea captain; sailors usually refused because it prolonged a watery death, but too many men had been lost on land campaigns by drowning in assault or rout, and Warwick fought on land as well as sea.

Richard was travelling by river from Greenwich, where the court had gone to await the Christmas season, to visit the great Earl of Warwick at his house of the Erber, in the City near Dowgate. A year ago, he would have made this journey eagerly, with hope. Now the summons was received uneasily partly because of its long delaying, and partly because he was a year more experienced in suspecting the motive of such an invitation. During that year, the quarrel between his brother the King and the Earl of Warwick had gone from bad to worse. His thoughts took refuge from his anxiety in trivia; he wished himself there, and the thing over.

Because he had been taught in Warwick's household, Richard reckoned that he knew at least half a dozen more ways of killing a man in close combat than other young men of his age. That he had survived four years of Warwick's regime never ceased to amaze him, as it evidently did others, and his confidence in his own capacities after this training was only diminished by his apparent inability to grow. Having reached manhood at sixteen years, he remained the size of a fourteen-year-old boy. It put him at a disadvantage in every way. He saw no prospect, unless a miraculous shooting up occurred, of catching up with his fellows. If he had not such a crowd—five—of enormous brothers and sisters, he would not have felt his deficiency so deeply.

As the oarsmen took the barge round the curve of Cuckold's Point, Richard wondered idly why this name should have been given to a stretch of Rotherhithe wall, marsh and dyke, whose only inhabitants were the Abbot of Bermondsey's cattle; it would be more apt for the palace stairs at Westminster! His barge was a large one, with ten rowers, as necessary for the prestige of the King's brother, even if he were only a minor and perilously short of the King's coin. On close inspection the paintwork and gilding could be seen to be the last of many layers. It had been decorated in the York colours of murrey and blue, and King Edward's device of a white rose upon the sun in splendour, among which a few slightly misshapen examples of his own boar badge were now squeezed. It had been retired by the royal bargemaster but refurbished in the Lambeth sheds for his own use.

The barge speeding through the night seemed as insubstantial as a paper boat on fire, riding a sea of pitch, and it was surprising that the helmsman was not the dreadful Charon, but the Duke of Gloucester's bargemaster. The torches that lit it streamed tails of sparks like comets. Richard put up his hand experimentally to let the fire motes fly through his bare fingers, and they did not even prickle his skin; the rushing air extinguished them to nothing. He yawned, stretched his legs and hooked the toe of one shoe under the edge of the opposite seat. The shoe was of smooth red leather, one of the few pairs he owned as yet unscuffed. Though far from being a slovenly young man, he had not yet lost the boy's habit of maltreating his shoes. He waggled his foot back and forth. The tapering, elegant point of the toe was stuffed to retain its shape, and bent to and fro rather ridiculously. After a certain length of wear the peaks became shapeless and bulging and threatened to trip one up.

Aware that he was trying to divert his mind when he should be arming his defences, he jerked himself upright in his seat, shoved each hand up the furry sleeves of his gown and found that he was nearly under London Bridge. The rowers shipped their oars as they approached the middle arches, smaller craft

giving them the way. The widest lock was on the north side of
the chapel of St. Thomas, and then only allowed about twenty
feet of passage. They dived out of the light spreading from the
houses on the bridge, into a deafening roar of water, shooting
through the dark, torches gleaming on the slimy sides of the
starlings, and popped out into quieter waters on the other side.
One shot the bridge each time with a sense of relief, and a quick
thanks to St. Thomas, who allowed too many drownings under
his chapel.

A great number of Warwick's servants were assembled to meet
the young Duke. Their torches made the quay seem bright as
day. They had been sent to escort him the short distance up
Dowgate Hill to the Erber, a courtesy the Earl always afforded
his more important visitors. They had even brought wooden
clogs for him to wear, as the street was dirty. The men all wore
jackets of scarlet, a ragged staff as big as a man's forearm in gold
on chests and backs. Scarcely a soul in the kingdom would fail to
recognize that livery. Merely to put on Warwick's colours made
a man stand out from his fellows. The chest bearing the ragged
staff seemed broader, the swagger more pronounced, in addition
to which the purse probably hung heavier—Warwick paid better
wages, Richard suspected, than even the King, and felt disloyal
to his brother for thinking it.

The Earl of Warwick was taking a bath. He had returned later
than expected from riding, his servant apologized, but his Grace
of Gloucester must come at once and take wine with him. As
Richard entered the room, the Earl rose from his tub like Nep-
tune from the waves, water streaming off him, and stepped out
on to towels. He moved with youthful agility. He was forty years
old. The moment Richard set foot in the room, he knew the
Earl's presence was as arresting as ever. Warwick was a rare
man, and produced feelings in other men either of dazzled admiration, violent antagonism or riveted fascination, but never
indifference. This was something from which Richard desperately wished himself immune.

The Earl favoured his young cousin with his most spontaneous
smile. "Your Grace is the most welcome visitor I've had in

months! My dear Richard, I take the liberty of greeting only old
friends in this degree of undress!"

Richard smiled back; the informal friendliness was infectious.
He had removed his hat as he had walked through the door out
of politeness; it would not have occurred to him to do otherwise,
though his rank excused him the gesture. All was exactly as if he
had left the Earl's household only yesterday. He had witnessed
this scene many times. Warwick's squires were rubbing him
down as efficiently and ungently as ostlers. He enjoyed briskness
in everyone about him. Richard almost felt it should be himself
who fell upon the Earl with hot towels, retrieved the soap from
the water, poured him wine—never let a drip run down to the
foot of the silver flagon—and offered it as if to a king. But Warwick's squire, a boy with whom he had previously been friendly,
had hastened to pour wine, and in the roles of royal guest and
servant, they were too constrained to be caught exchanging
grins. On Richard's cup was engraved a motto: *Seulement Un.*
Well chosen; Warwick could bear no equal, and he taught absolute reliance upon one's self.

Richard realized that this familiar scene was probably a deliberate ploy to disarm him, and he had been momentarily hoodwinked by it. He felt afraid. This was not because he thought
that Warwick might force him to act as he did not wish, but because he knew that his affection for the Earl was still sufficient to
betray him. Warwick must know his vulnerability well enough.
Disappointment and misery reduced him to silence; before, he
had never found himself tongue-tied in front of the Earl. As
Warwick did not seem to find it necessary to begin a conversation at this stage, Richard watched while the servants finished
their work.

When one looked at him closely, Warwick did not have
strictly handsome features, but his person combined so many attractive elements that his overall aspect was that of a handsome
man. He was of medium height, with not an ounce of spare flesh
on him, a man still in his prime. His limbs were well made and
hard, as if carved from new wood; the gown of brilliant scarlet
and white silk into which his squires helped him undoubtedly
flattered him. Even his face, particularly in profile, had this

smooth, finished look, which prevented it from being too hawk-
ish. His head was startlingly well shaped, like a Roman general's
on an antique coin, with close-growing, crisp hair, neither
curling nor straight, dark nor fair, now a little salted with
white. Some said his eyes were like a predator's, and that he'd
have less influence on men if he could be hooded; he had the
awful, wide-open stare of a yellow-eyed goshawk. In fact, his
eyes were grey, exceptionally clear and light, like mirrors, or
water. That was his element, water. The sea—implacable yet irresistible. Proud as Lucifer, ill-wishers said. This arrogance was
not obtrusive, and so much part of his fascination that one condemned it reluctantly. Only when slighted did he choose to reveal it, then it scorched the beholder. Men did not easily forget
being singed. Warwick's Countess had once said that she could
see a look of her husband in Richard, which had secretly
delighted him. Warwick was his full cousin. They had the same
name.

When he had been dressed, Warwick said, "Now we are ready
to join the ladies." He selected rings—three only—and slipped
them on his fingers, flexing his hands as he did so. Hands for use,
not display, but shapely and well-cared for all the same. Then
the Earl stood aside and gave his guest precedence.

The servant who opened the door and announced their arrival
could not know that he revealed to Richard a nightmare spectacle. It was so admirably domestic. In the company of Warwick's
wife and two daughters, grinning all over his face like a cat with
a canary, sat Richard's brother George of Clarence. Richard tried
to keep an expression of dismay from his face, without success.
He felt as if he had walked straight into an ambush. George rose
to his feet, bowed with exemplary courtesy to the Earl—he had
natural grace and had been taught beautiful manners, though he
too often employed them only where or when the whim took him
—and said to Richard, "Ah, my prodigal brother. . . . We'd forgotten the colour of your coat here!" putting the younger boy in
the wrong from the first moment.

The women descended upon Richard and kissed him, the
Countess with nervous affection, Isabel without taking her eyes
off George, and Anne like a sparrow snatching a crumb.

"Dear Richard, we are always so happy to see you here. It must be a twelvemonth since your Grace was last . . ." The Countess's speech trailed off apologetically, as it often did.

"Madam, I hope not to be guilty of the omission in future," he said stiffly. Then, because he did not like to see this timorous little woman, who in past years had tried so hard to foster him, discomfited by his uneasy manner, smiled. The Countess's face flowered becomingly to genuine pleasure. Richard had noticed that ladies of an age to be his mother often reacted to his smile in this way. More wine was pushed into his hand. The family folded itself round him in welcoming comfort. He found himself seated near the fire next to the little girl, Anne. George was already beside Isabel, as if by right; he was evidently an established visitor. While making some effort to respond to their small talk, Richard hunted in his head to find an excuse for escape.

"Which of you girls has been playing?" Warwick was relaxed, and never an over-stern father.

"My lord father, Anne has a new song. . . ." Isabel would do anything to avoid being asked to sing herself, for she had no voice and did not like looking foolish, especially in front of Clarence. She was adroit, Richard thought, at passing tasks off on to her younger sister.

"Sing for us, little one," Warwick said gently. Richard had always suspected that Anne was the daughter he preferred. It would not have crossed either girl's mind to question their father's request, though Anne would clearly have liked to. She had always hated being pushed to the forefront in company. She was blushing. But she took up her lute obediently and began to pick out a melody. It quickened into a nimble tune, such as children dance to in the street. Her fingers flew, the music's gaiety giving her confidence. When she sang, her voice, like herself, was small and self-effacing, but sweet. She sang in French as easily as she did in English; she had spent several years in Calais when she was tiny, with French nursemaids, and had learned to talk using both languages at once.

George began to beat time with his toe, then to sing in part

with her. It was a song that he used to sing with his favourite
sister, Margaret; they had made it their special song.

> *Margot labourez les vignes . . .*
> *Vignes, vignes, vignolet . . .*

he carolled in his chiming tenor, like a golden bell. People, especially women, used to call George a golden boy. The egg-yellow
hair of early childhood had long ago darkened and dulled, but
he still had a glow of health and promise. George, his sharp and
disillusioned young brother thought, should at nineteen be showing signs of promise bearing fruit. The cooing and gushing
which had been lavished upon him as a child, but not upon
Richard, often had not survived the trials of longer ac-
quaintance.

George had done such appalling things; Richard never knew
how he'd escaped being skinned alive. There was the time he
had encouraged his dog to deposit a turd under the chair in
which sat his oldest and most formidable Neville aunt, and
worse, the incident of the ink in the holy water stoup at Foth-
eringay. It had been set in a dark place, and the congregation
had emerged each with a brownish cross on forehead, as if
branded by some mysterious agent of God, or the Devil. No
doubt it was still remembered as a miracle. Nothing had been
proven against the culprit and Richard had not told tales. Now,
he wondered why he had not; George would probably have
benefited from punishment.

The song ended, George flushed and laughing, Anne with eyes
modestly downcast. Compliments were passed. Richard noticed
Anne smiled at George but not at himself.

Of the two girls, Isabel, a year older than he, was the prettier,
at least everyone said she was the prettier. Yet he did not often
look at her, and if he did, she did not hold his attention. Anne,
however, who had always been considered plain, gave him cause
for thought. This was not merely because of the two little bumps
in the front of her gown—a year earlier they had not been there—
or because the gown was stylish, which had the effect of making
her seem more of a child when it was meant to add years, but
because they had once been friendly, and now she avoided his

eyes entirely. She had pecked his cheek so hastily he wondered
if it were his appearance she did not like. He was nothing to look
at, of course, but he was not spotty, nor was his hair unwashed
or uncombed, and his teeth were clean and in good order. He
had always thought Anne looked up to him a little, as a small
sister might, as his own sister Ursula might, who had died before
he was big enough to do more than poke his nose over the edge
of her cradle. He was sure that a great deal went on inside
Anne's head, of which no one but herself had knowledge. Her
head was bent now over the lute, which rested in her lap. A very
small head, the hair in two neat sections on either side of a pre-
cise chalk-white parting. Hair that lay sleek and flat against the
delicate skull, very smooth, very shiny, like a pelt. Well, mouse-
like, it had that sort of indeterminate colour. She was twelve
years old—add on half a year, her birthday was in June. The
eleventh, odd that he should remember.

Anne's mother, watching the self-contained young man and
her even more self-contained daughter, wished yet again that
Anne was not so childish looking. She knew her husband's ambitions with regard to these two, and desired a match even more
than he, for the additional reason of sentiment. Anne was of mar-
riageable age, though her immature looks might cause men to
think that she was not. Really, as she was now, it would seem
like a child violation; there was nothing yet to titillate appetites
with even hope for the future. She had an uneasy feeling that
matters with Gloucester should have been pressed two years ago,
when the match was first mooted. The King had squashed the
idea, which had then been dropped. Richard had been so much
more malleable then. Now, he was not the boy that she had
known, had wished so much was her own. She knew that already
he had a mistress—no one at court could keep secrets of that kind
—and he might turn out to be as heartily promiscuous as his
brother, the King. She was not a clever woman, but she was per-
ceptive enough to realize that such a husband would ruin Anne.

Warwick wanted a high match for each of his daughters. That
excluded any of the Queen's brothers—he would have seen himself hang before consenting to that—and also those desirable mi-

nors, heirs of Dukes and Earls, four of them, who were now married to the Woodville sisters.

More important was the securing of Clarence for Isabel. Because the Queen had so far borne only daughters, George of Clarence was the King's heir. Secret negotiations were in progress at the Papal Curia to obtain a dispensation for the marriage. George had bought a betrothal ring from a London goldsmith already. He was captivated by Isabel's blonde prettiness, her admiring glances and, though he did not know it, by her determination to have him as a husband. Warwick's task had been made absurdly easy.

Anne, sitting quietly enough to be almost forgotten, knew exactly what was going on. Now that her father had won George to his side, a stick with which to beat the King, she was the carrot dangled under Richard's nose, to lure him into the Neville alliance against the Woodvilles. She thought that for once her father had overestimated his influence. She no longer trusted his omnipotence. Richard would reject her. Even if she were older, and beautiful, it would make no difference; he would never put anyone before his brother the King. This certainly hurt her deeply, both in her awakening femininity and her family pride. Richard had been the one person whom she would not have minded marrying. Not that she imagined herself in love, not with anyone, except perhaps in dreams, and she was sure she never dreamed of Richard; he had been too much a part of ordinary everyday life for that. But she had always liked him; he had never frightened her with noise when she was little, or repelled her with boasting, and, until recently, she had never felt shy of him. She was shy with a great many people. Now she showed her resentment of Richard's desertion of her father and herself by ignoring him.

After not too prolonged an exchange of pleasantries, the Earl did what his wife knew very well he was going to do. He suggested that Richard should accompany him to the armoury, where he had something to show him. This implication that the Earl and the boy had interests in common would make sure the interview began on the right note. Richard took his leave of the ladies very courteously, but evading an answer to the Countess's murmurs about a next visit. Though he did not know how much it showed, it was evident, especially to his smirking brother, that he wore an armour of prickles. Warwick, as he steered the boy in the direction he wanted, allowed himself a little bleak amusement. In the armoury, he placed in Richard's hands his most recent personal indulgence, a hand gun from Germany. The stock was as elaborately decorated as the finest crossbow, with ivory inlays of hunted animals and long tassels of green silk hanging off it to encumber the marksman. It fired a lead ball the size of a nutmeg. Warwick tossed this thoughtfully in his open palm.

"I believe that one day this little pellet will render all armour useless."

"But not in our lifetime . . . ?"

"Not in mine. In your son's, maybe. I'd rather face cold steel, I think. This does the same sort of irreparable damage as the cannon shot."

"Is it cowardly to hope for a quick crack over the skull?"

Warwick gave a bark of a laugh. "No! No, merely acknowledging your kinship with the rest of men. I feel the same." He carefully put back the hand gun into its velvet case.

"Kinship. . . ." he said slowly. Then, "I'm sorry, Richard, that your Grace has ceased to regard my family as your own."

"I would never deny I am a Neville, my lord."

"Then why stay away from my house, avoid my company?"

"It has come to the point, my lord, where it is neither politic nor pleasing to do otherwise."

"Your pleasure," Warwick said, between his teeth, "is of no interest to me. Who has proclaimed it impolitic to be my friend?"

No answer.

"You have no more need to name them than I have to ask the question."

Silence.

"I see. You fear them?"

"Not them. They drop poison in my brother's ear."

"Ah! You think the King has begun to see all who are close to the Nevilles as his enemies?"

"No."

"Yet this is what the Queen wishes him to think?"

"My brother the King thinks his own thoughts and speaks with his own mouth. He is a Neville too."

"I used to be glad of it."

"Used! My lord, there is my reason!"

Warwick's in-taken breath made a sound like a knife being drawn. But he did not yet betray his anger.

"My dear Richard, I'd be only too glad to return to a happier situation. Most men wish at one time or another that the years would retreat. But it is not possible. The time has come when I can no longer endure the insults, or suffer the ingratitude humbly."

"My lord, my brother the King is a generous man!"

"And you know by this time as well as I that the whole Wood-ville tribe suck his generosity until it dries up at the fount. They are swollen with gain like a fungus on a tree, and the tree they batten on is the King. I tell you, Richard, it is time to lop them from the tree. If the King will not take action against them himself, then he must be forced to do so by others."

"No subject can force the King to any action. It is treason to talk of it."

"Do you champion the Woodville faction?"

"No, but I will not listen to treason spoken against the King!"

"I do not consider acting in the King's best interest to be trea-son. You are too young to realize that King Edward is himself still young and not above being led. Led—you can have my can-did opinion—by the prick, by the Woodville woman, and by that trio of whoremasters, Herbert, Hastings and Stafford."

"I am not too young to realize that you seek to lead my brother by the nose for your own gain!"

Warwick's temper unleashed at this, in a fury that swept away all reason and prudence. His hand lashed out and should have fetched the obstinate, defiant boy a mighty clip over the ear, but he was clumsy with rage, and his fist landed hard across Rich-ard's mouth. The weight behind it knocked the boy across the edge of the table, off which he bounced, staggering on his feet, realized he had swallowed one of his own front teeth, feeling the blood run. He got himself out of the room, and his servants out of the Erber, though they would willingly have stayed to brawl with Warwick's men.

The barge shot London Bridge on the ebb tide race in a fashion that caused the rowers to pray harder than usual. Richard, trying to disguise the evidence of Warwick's assault on his face, was not aware of any danger. The outcome of the encounter had been even worse than he had expected. As the Thames tide took him back to this brother's court, his loyalty to King Edward unbroken, he felt little satisfaction. At the back of his mind was the certainty that soon he might have the chance to become a real man and go to war. There was no joy in it.

2

The Sun in Splendour

January – June 1469

Sithe God hathe chose thee to be his knyght
And possesside thee in this right,
Thou hime honour with al thi myght,
 Edwardus, Dei Gratia

Oute of the stoke that longe lay dede
God hathe causede the to sprynge & sprede,
And of al Englond to be the hede,
 Edwardus, Dei Gratia

Edwardus Dei Gratia (c. 1461)

Gold, frankincense and myrrh—the three caskets were borne not before three kings, but one. On the morning of Twelfth Day, the King of England went in solemn procession to the Abbey of Westminster to offer these gifts to Christ as the kings Caspar, Melchior and Balthazar had done upon the first Epiphany. As a small child, Richard had wondered what frankincense and myrrh were, and whether they could be eaten.

King Edward wore his crown. In it, he stood about six and a half feet tall. He looked splendid beyond belief, his cloth of gold tissue, jewels, gilded embroidery and crimson velvet as magnificent as the copes of the Abbot and the bishops; even the three kings of Orient could not have looked so fine, and they had been Moorish, and probably much smaller. He strode along at a good pace—short legs always had to work hard to keep up with King Edward—and the January sun made of him a gilded reflection of itself, as if one could have warmed one's hands in his rays.

At the time of King Edward's coronation, Richard had been eight. His brother was nearly eleven years older. He could never, since, see the King crowned and splendid without experiencing something of that child's awe. The crown, the candles, the incense, the astonishing fact of his brother smiling down at him—it happened now, when he was old enough to have forgotten. But the promise of that June day eight years past had now been blighted.

The procession moved across palace yard; it was impossible to tell whether the sprinkle of whiteness which had been carefully swept from underfoot was snow or heavy hoar-frost. The Abbey roof was silvered in big patches melting into dampness; the pinnacles were rimed as if with powdered sugar. In the first hour or two after snow, the palace of Westminster could look like the towers of Camelot; at all other times it looked like a ramshackle tenement sprawling outside a city's walls. It was so crowded with people no one could relieve himself without all his neighbours knowing. From the look of the patched-up houses of all ages, shapes and sizes, the place could be the home not of the King and his court, but of all the thieves, pimps and whores in the kingdom. Sometimes Richard thought that it was.

In the crowd of lords all jostling for precedence at the Abbey doors, no one would have dared actually to elbow the King's brother out of the way, even if he were young and likely to be ignored by those hasty in their climbing into the royal favour, more especially by the ones who had chosen the ladder of the Queen's patronage. In the procession, behind the King and his crowd of attendants, was the Queen. At the banquet to be given that evening in the White Hall, Richard had been assigned the task of attending upon the Queen. He cursed the fact that he was still thought young enough for these duties; that he would be sharing them with his fourteen-year-old cousin, Harry Buckingham, did not comfort him at all.

After the divine service in the Abbey, Richard watched his brother walk among the press of court, greeting people constantly as he went, a nod here, a touch on the shoulder, a clasp of the arm there, and always a smile and a word. It was incredible how many of them he could recognize and put a name to. King Edward never forgot a face, or its name, and this extraordinary memory of his ensured much of his personal popularity.

He was still talking away to one and all, easy and friendly, in the evening when the company began to file into the hall for the Twelfth Night feast. Richard joined the group of the Queen's attendants and knelt before her. It was another in the list of minor purgatories he had been forced to endure at her hands. He would never, he thought, kneel to her in anything but grudging homage. It would not have been so bad if she had demanded a little less knee grovelling and reverential hand kissing—woe betide anyone who presumed to *touch* her hand with their lips. A queen was a queen, but before this one, her royal brothers and sisters-in-law looked like adorers at the feet of the Queen of Heaven. Only the Duchess of York, their mother, rose above her abasement and turned every humiliating act into one of gracious condescension. George of Clarence made every obeisance appear an insult, which was foolish and dangerous. Richard noticed that neither George nor the Earl of Warwick was present at the feast.

The Queen, while Richard was standing and kneeling in front of her, began to stare at his face. As he had not looked in a mirror, he was not sure if the damage Warwick had done was obvious and turning a horrible rainbow of colours. Probably the Queen thought he had been fighting and had taken the worst of it. He did not stare back at her; that would have been an unforgivable breach of manners. Many people, other than himself, thought she was made for staring at.

Elizabeth Woodville was close on thirty-two years old, but still men gasped at the sight of her. She dazzled the eye armed with nothing other than her silver-fair colouring, but it was not her habit to appear before her subjects unadorned. Heavy paintwork was not necessary; it would have spoilt the perfect skin, luminous and pale, like the inside of an oystershell, but she always wore enough gems to make Our Lady of Walsingham look a pauper. She preferred the colourless stones—and the most costly —diamonds and flawless pearls, as if she challenged them to outshine herself. She loved gowns sewn with crystal drops, shimmering cloth of silver and inappropriate virginal white. This did not mean that she disliked the fire of rubies, emeralds and sapphires, or despised amethysts, beryls or garnets, for, loaded with them, she could look like a queen from Byzantium. She was one of the sights of Europe, like a shrine; foreigners would gawp for hours, while she did not deign to give them so much as a look or a word. She looked as inviolate as the Madonna.

It was hard to believe that she had two sons by her first husband, one of whom was as old as Richard. When she had snared King Edward, she had been a widow five years older than he, with only a posy ring to deck her fingers. Now she was seven months gone in her third pregnancy. This last fact was extremely evident; she carried her babies high and jutting. For a woman with the rare delicacy of a pearl, she enjoyed robust health. Childbearing did not cause her to droop, and she did not retire to her rooms until the very last moment custom decreed. It was unfortunate that she had so far given the King no heir, only two little daughters. Richard thought that she was as tough as a camp-follower, and that it might have solved everyone's problems if she were not. It was wicked to wish her dead, but sometimes he did. He hated her. Not because she was more beautiful than anyone he could possibly hope to attain, or because she treated him with a mock-sisterly patronage, which he knew concealed a contempt for his youth, smallness and lack of manly attractions (or lack of response to herself), but because the woman behind the mother-of-pearl façade was merely a commonplace bitch. Because he loved his brother, he felt that Edward deserved better, and would not admit that what Edward had got had been acquired by his own wilful determination to have it.

The Woodville beauty could stun even himself sometimes, though it always left an after-chill. He could not, even in moments of wildest fantasy, imagine what she was like in bed—sinful to uncover his brother's nakedness in his thoughts—but she could not be so unsatisfactory as to make Edward reluctant to lie with her; he did so often. There were many others; Edward was demanding in his requirements, and he regarded variety as his natural prerogative, but he always came back to his wife. Their brother George, who never kept a hold on his tongue, said that

he would not have her or any of her sisters if he were given a
crown for the service.

Sisters, brothers—Woodvilles swarmed, lesser stars in her
firmament. Running his eye briefly along the tables in the hall,
Richard could see six of one and five of the other. All were now
provided with spouses they could not even have hoped for had
their eldest sister not captured the King. And there, right under
his nose, and responsible for the existence of the whole lot, was
the Queen's mother.

Lord Rivers' French wife, Jacquette, was usually known by
her more impressive widow's title of Duchess of Bedford. She
came of the highest nobility of France, daughter of the Count of
St. Pol, and had been made the wife of the Duke of Bedford,
King Henry V's brother and Regent of France, when she was
very young. After his death two years later, she had secretly
married one of his household officials, to the horror of her family,
for Woodville had been only a petty squire. The pair had to pay
an enormous fine to the King for daring to do it. But Rivers must
have been handsome, randy and on the make, like his sons and
grandsons. At sixty he still looked as brawny and virile as ever,
and as determined to climb ever higher. Between them, he and
Jacquette must have spawned about fifteen children, of whom
this ubiquitous dozen were very much alive. George of Clarence
called her the Duchess of Bedward, because this was the message her eyes still gave to the world.

It was largely due to the Duchess that the Queen received so
much grovelling and silent adulation; no one could do other than
emulate the woman's own mother. Jacquette Woodville was small
and coquettish, very aware of her Frenchness, and hard as a
mason's block. Her eyelash fluttering, eye rolling and waving in
the air of tiny, elegant hands disgusted Richard, and he was sure
her still quaintly accented English was an affectation. What he
found irritating was that she was not a raddled old hag of over
fifty, exposing too much flesh in unsuitable gowns, but a graceful
little figure dressed with exquisite taste in discreet colours, all
her wrinkles and sags covered. Worst of all was her manner towards himself. She called him *"mon cher Duc"*, and amused herself by making him glower. Richard had to admit to being a little

frightened of her. She had a reputation for dabbling in witch-craft and he always half expected to see a toad sitting on her shoulder.

Richard's head, back, shoulders and legs had all begun to ache with the strain of standing, kneeling and keeping a wary compo-sure before the Queen. The court had eaten itself into satiety, but there were the entertainments to endure.

A troupe of tumblers spilled out over the floor, turned them-selves upside down, stood on each other, carried a dwarf about on their shoulders, while a fool dodged around, trying to trip them up.

A disguising was enacted of the Judgement of Paris; it was no coincidence that the girl who played Helen of Troy wore a wig of blonde hair in imitation of the Queen.

Into the space left vacant by the mummers came a strangely attired figure. He was greatly hampered by the sheer size of his boots; they reached up his sides to meet the points of his hose and shirt, and the feet were big enough for Gog the giant. As if this were not grotesque enough, his doublet was so short that it ended just under his armpits. He tottered along, groping ahead and prodding the floor with a staff twice as tall as himself, his backside sticking out absurdly like a couple of apples. On his head was a hat the size of a cartwheel, an exaggeration of the hats pilgrims wore to keep off the rain. The lugubrious and un-jesterlike face under this was of Jack Woodhouse, one of the King's more witty fools.

His progress was made in silence and, because of this, the en-tire hall fell silent also while the freakish figure came on slowly, right up to the King's table. By this time everyone was craning for a view, and King Edward's own eye was caught.

Leaning forward, in the greatest of good humours, he said, "You look as if you're expecting a new Deluge, Jack—come on, tell us what you're up to!"

Making a great business of clinging to his staff, the fool said, "Why, your Grace, I've been journeying through every county in your realm, and in each of them I could find no fords, and with-out my good marsh pike, I'd have been drowned, for I could scarcely find the bottom of any *rivers*, they were risen so high . . . !"

Woodhouse's voice carried to all corners of the hall—the rivers rising high had been a trumpet call. One moment more of silence was broken by explosions of laughter from every side. It did not wait for the King to lead it; it could not be contained, having waited a long time for such a jest to let it loose. Richard felt a grin split his face before he could straighten it into a look of discreet aloofness. His chest began to ache with the laughter trapped there, which he dared not let out. The Rivers rise high! It was rich, and ripe, and it had been said in public by a daring fool. It was not as if it had been a very funny or clever jest, but it was a release of resentment, and Woodhouse had given it the proper ludicrous treatment. No one cared who saw them laugh. Richard heard his young cousin Harry Buckingham yelping like a delighted puppy dog; many of the older lords were clasping each other and laughing themselves into painful indigestion.

After a first quick frown, King Edward's mouth began briefly to twitch, and he let out a shout of laughter as loud as anyone else. It was a signal for even greater uproar. Then, defiant, dissembling old dog that he was, Lord Rivers himself began to laugh. The mirth of the skeleton at the feast, Richard thought, watching Woodville's valiant grimacing and apoplectic colour.

Lady Rivers—the Duchess of Bedford—however, took an unequivocal stand. Her comment shrilled over the guffaws, almost in Richard's ear. "*Cochon!*" she spat, like a little striking adder. Richard flinched, as if she had aimed the word at himself. But no one took any notice, they were enjoying themselves too much.

The fool, not one to press his luck, turned a somersault over his marsh pike and shuffled off as fast as his boots would allow.

The Queen, insulted in her presence by this jibe at her father, sat as if turned to marble, as if she had heard nothing. Her remote, perfect face made Richard shiver. I hope Woodhouse is well protected, he thought, and that his protector can prevent her from touching him.

Then, suddenly, he was sure that he knew who had paid Woodhouse to enact that particularly dangerous piece of impudence. The outrageous absurdity, and its direct insult to the

Queen, bore the mark of his brother Clarence. Warwick would never have trifled with such things. George was as capable as any fool at devising jests, and his patronage and payments were unlikely to be rejected even by the King's servants. It was an episode which should act as a warning to the King.

Yet the King was slow to heed the warnings of his brother's disaffection. George, who now professed no love for King Edward, had at one time been violently jealous if his elder brother had shown favours to others—to Richard especially. When they had been children Edward of March as he had been then, had never once neglected Richard for the brighter charms of George, and George's jealousy had been both unreasoning and permanent, staying hidden within him into manhood.

George of Clarence's temper did not sweeten with the coming of spring. This was noticeable on the few occasions when Richard saw him. Nobody ever seemed very sure of George's whereabouts. Richard suspected that he was dividing his time between his own estates and Warwick's, some of which conveniently converged, and that he had probably been on a visit to the Moor in Hertfordshire, the house of Warwick's youngest brother, the Archbishop of York. This was a bad sign, as the two Georges, Neville and Clarence, were likely to feed the vinegar of discontent in each other.

It was nearly two years since the King had deprived the Archbishop of York of the office of Lord Chancellor—two years in which discontent might ferment. Richard saw his brother briefly when the King and Queen's third child—another daughter—was baptized at Westminster. She was named Cecily, for her paternal grandmother. King Edward had hoped for a son this time but was not a man to grumble at what fate chose to give him. He was very fond of the two little daughters he already had, and, as he said, with a wink, he did not think as some did that the world was too full of women.

Clarence did not appear again at court until Ascension Day. He came to Windsor for a special meeting of the Garter Chapter, when the King's brother-in-law, the Duke of Burgundy, was elected to the Order. It was obvious, as the knights walked from the chapter house after their business was over, that George intended once again to demonstrate his alliance with Warwick and his dislike of the Woodvilles by indulging in Rivers baiting. As Richard walked behind him, he thought that this time Woodhouse the fool would have done better.

Immediately George was out of the door, he stopped in his tracks, leaving just enough room for Richard to squeeze out beside him, and there he waited for Warwick. When the Earl came up with him, he laid hold of Warwick's arm and launched into an apparently confidential and prolonged conversation. While this took place, one or two other knights were able to emerge past them, but Lord Rivers found his way well and truly blocked.

Richard, watching, had to admire his brother for having the nerve to try such tricks which it was not in himself to attempt. He twiddled the gold tassels on the long cords which fastened his blue velvet gown and waited. George had managed to spread the train of his gown around his feet so that it took up the maximum space, and even Rivers hesitated to tread on it. Warwick was smiling and nodding as Clarence spoke into his ear the words so clearly meant for him only. Rivers, stuck in the doorway, a high-coloured man in any case, was growing purplish in the face. Peering round his bulky shoulder, was the face of his eldest son Anthony, sharp with annoyance. After a minute or two of this, Richard found the suspense unbearable. A picture of an unseemly brawl among the Garter knights came into his mind.

"My lord of Clarence!" King Edward's voice rang out, pleasant, but with an edge of authority in it. His two brothers stood facing each other, angry, yet drawn to each other as by a lodestone, alike in the light blue Garter robes. George, when you looked at his face, was in fact the more handsome, but beside his elder brother, people tended not to notice this. Edward was both taller and broader, a focus for all eyes. Richard did not think of himself as resembling either of them, and would have been surprised to be told of similarities between his own face and the King's. He had long ago ceased to notice the slight amusement of onlookers when he was at his brother's side, or that he had to gaze upwards into the King's face. George did not have this disadvantage. Richard held his breath; if George did not move, a scene was inevitable.

But George moved. He still could not disobey the King to his face. If he had been drunk, he might have brazened it out, but at eleven in the morning he had not had the chance to give himself courage from wine. He moved aside, and Lord Rivers came out of the chapter house door with his head lowered like an angry, snorting bull.

Warwick drew back to let him pass with a gesture of exemplary courtesy, but Richard saw the Earl's face when Rivers' back was turned. His hawk's stare bored into the back of Rivers' head as if willing a headsman's axe to fall upon it. Warwick's face seemed pinched and aged; the intensity of his hate consumed him from within, coldly, like the icing over of water. Richard felt its chill within himself and was afraid.

When Warwick went over to speak to the King, no trace of anything other than an easy naturalness could be detected in his face. Because King Edward was never the first to pick a fight, it was easy for onlookers to assume that he was good-humored to a fault and easily hoodwinked. He was not.

"I hope, Richard," King Edward said to Warwick, "that the fleet is ready down in the Cinque Ports, to take to the sea against the Hansards. I should not like my brother of Burgundy to lose his ambassadors and his new Garter to the Hanse pirates!"

Warwick, who would feel personally affronted if the Hansards captured an English ship after all his precautions, would not have worried if Duke Charles of Burgundy strangled himself with his new Garter in one of his famous fits of temper. The thought of that bit of expensive goldsmith's work buckled round that over-muscled leg was galling. It was just as galling to see the collar of the Burgundian order of chivalry around King Edward's neck, with its pendant dead sheep—Toison D'Or, or Golden Fleece was a good name for it. The pursuit of the Burgundian alliance by the marriage of the King's sister Margaret with the Duke had fleeced the English of 50000 gold crowns, with 150000 yet to pay. The exchange of orders of chivalry between Duke and King was a sour reminder to Warwick of King

Edward's rejection of all his advice and labours in trying to bring about a rival understanding with France.

King Edward, who did not need to read Warwick's mind to know better than to dwell upon the subject of Duke Charles, said, "My lord, I have every faith in your preparations for the defence of the realm on the sea. It's one less worry for me. I hope your brother of Northumberland is as prompt to deal with this Robin-whatever-he-calls-himself, in the north."

"The commons in the north," said Warwick, "have never in my memory been anything but unruly. I can't calculate the number of Robin Mend Alls who have appeared over the years. They mend nothing. Hoping for a chance to rob the rich to give to the poor, no doubt, like the merry man of Sherwood. This Robin won't get away with it. My brother John knows how to deal with rebels."

"I rely on his talents, as I do on yours, my lord. I intend to go to St. Edmund's Bury and Norwich shortly, then on to Walsingham, to pay my respects to Our Lady. Then if this trouble in the north continues, I may go to York to look into things myself. I hope you will join me there if I should send for you. I also hope to see your brother the Archbishop of York there; it may help to pacify his see."

When the Earl of Warwick and his lady visited the town of Sandwich, they were always given presents. As the Earl was Lord Warden of the Cinque Ports, these visits had been fairly frequent. A special bond had been established between the Earl and the town, and he usually stayed in the house of the Mayor, or of one of the other Common Councillors. This time, Warwick received three swans, six gallons of Bordeaux wine and several basket-loads of oranges. A Venetian galley had recently put in at Sandwich, and the Earl and his family were loaded with small gifts of pretty goods from Messina.

The Kentish swans appeared on the table that night at Anne Neville's thirteenth birthday feast which, as usual, was shared with St. Barnabas. She liked roast swan, and she had been given a coral jewel from Sicily to hang round her neck. Though the occasion was Anne's feast, Isabel behaved as if it were hers. Anne had listened to her sister talk of nothing but her coming marriage to George of Clarence.

"The only thing," Isabel had said that morning, "about marriage which I don't like, is that I shall have to put my hair up under a cap all the time. I look better with it hanging down."

Anne was inclined to agree with her. There was nothing special about Isabel's face, though it was quite pretty, but her hair was lovely, very fine and straight and a pale golden blonde. Beside her sister, Anne always felt she looked washed-out, and thought that when the time came for her marriage and she had to put her own hair up, she would look positively plain.

"Do you really like him?" she asked Isabel.

"Clarence?" Isabel looked at her as if she had asked an odd question. "Yes, of course. He makes me laugh—I mean, he's witty and amusing. I couldn't endure a dull dog for years! He's good looking. He's the King brother. He's the King's heir. But you've seen nearly as much of him as I have, Anne. Mother never leaves us alone together. You don't talk to him much. Don't you like him?"

"I don't really know him," Anne said lamely. "He talks to you mostly."

"Good," said her sister. After that Isabel lost interest, and Anne did not have a chance to ask if she thought whether George would be kind, and not suddenly less witty and amusing if one were ill, or developed a pimple, or just felt bad tempered, or if one's family became politically embarrassing. She did not want to spoil Isabel's hopes by suggesting that Clarence might be a fair-weather husband. Isabel seemed to have forgotten that marriages had been suggested for both of them, that her sister should have the other brother, Richard. Anne had once imagined a double wedding. Now she was again eclipsed by Isabel.

The next day Anne's uncle, the Archbishop of York, who had joined them in Sandwich, performed the ceremony of blessing Warwick's great warship, the *Trinity*. At this ceremony, the Duke of Clarence shone, being easily the most handsome young man there. He made Warwick look sombre and middle-aged, and even the Archbishop of York was eclipsed. Anne watched her sister gaze at him like a child at the gingerbread men on a

stall. He came down off the gangplank from the *Trinity* as if he
were an angel descending from Heaven on a sunbeam. Small
crystal drops, sewn among the flowers patterning his doublet,
bobbed and twinkled as he moved. On the quayside, he was met
by a man whom he evidently recognised, and whose appearance
at the festivities was far from welcome. Clarence turned from
him after hearing what he had to say, with a face no longer
handsome and shining.

"The Duchess of York," he announced angrily, "my lady
mother, is *here!*"

Anne thought that a note of panic was in the Duke's voice, as
if he had been well and truly cornered. It was inevitable that a
mother should wish to see a son, when he was set upon disobey-
ing her. Anne felt a little sorry for Clarence; the Duchess of York
was a somewhat intimidating lady, and treated as a queen in her
own right.

Clarence himself was both frightened and annoyed that his
mother had followed him all the way to Sandwich. She was beginning to treat him as if he were still in napkins, and to act as if
he were committing blasphemy by daring to criticize Edward.
But there was nothing he could do to avoid an interview with her.

"If you take up arms against your brother the King," the Duchess of York all but shouted at her son, "it is as bad as turning on
your own father! When my husband bred his family, he never
knew one of his sons would rebel against the other—if he had, he'd
have kept from my bed! You insult your father's memory. Edward is the head of the family. He is the King. Do you think my
nephew Warwick's base ingratitude and ambition are worth a
betrayal of your brother? Or is it *your* ambition that incites you
to this folly?"

George cringed from his mother's tongue. Not that his moral
conscience was wounded by her attack, but the mere fact that
his calm, dignified mother should lose patience enough to shout
at him was alarming.

Duchess Cecily had a spot of angry colour in each cheek,
though this was all that betrayed her emotions. She was of a
height with her son Clarence, and her blue eyes speared his own
as if they were wriggling fishes. When he was a child, George

thought his mother as stately and cool as a lily; she was the only person he had never dared to defy. She was still a tall, handsome, straight-backed woman in her middle fifties, and looked younger; George had never seen anyone show her disrespect. He was as scarlet with anger and shame at her castigation as if she had caught him with his fingers in the sweetmeat box and slapped him.

"My lady mother, I don't *want* to take up arms against the King. Arms are out of the question."

"Quarrels like this always end in arms!" snapped his mother, before he could finish speaking.

He gazed huntedly around the room, searching for excuse or escape. His mother walked to the window, the familiar beads at her waist swinging as she walked. George had never seen her without that rosary, the gold beads and cross with the scallop shell of jet hanging from it. That dangling black lump had fascinated all her babies in turn, indeed, he had probably tried to cut his teeth on it himself.

The Duchess rapped suddenly on the window with her knuckles, hard enough to make a diamond in one of her rings mark it. "Look out there," she said.

The windows looked over the harbour. The *Trinity* lay there, her poop high as a tower above the houses. She was still garlanded and decked from her blessing. Embroidered banners of the Trinity and Our Lady hung from her masts. Her deck had been scoured so white it looked floured. She could carry five hundred archers and men-at-arms.

"It is entirely my nephew Warwick's decision whether the biggest ship in the King's fleet does battle for him or against him."

"We only want to persuade him," Clarence's arguments had begun to sound thin even to himself.

"Don't play the innocent with me, my son! You are in your twentieth year now, George, and know the world. Persuasion is a double-edged blade." She had an extraordinary ability to brush aside circumlocution.

"To make him shake off the Woodville influence. It is *they* whom we quarrel with!"

"You cannot *make* the King do anything."

"You favour Edward above the rest of us."

The Duchess made no immediate reply. Whether this was because George had hit upon the truth, or because she thought the jibe too contemptible to answer, he was not sure. It was in fact the truth, but George never had enough perception to realize he had seldom done anything to recommend himself as his mother's favourite son.

"You even favour Richard above me!"

"Nonsense. He may be younger, but his behaviour is more responsible than yours. Thank God, he worries me less than you do—can't you see Dickon needs *less* of my attention? I have not had to chase him over half the kingdom. And if you cannot see that he suffers even more hurt from those you choose to call the King's enemies than you do, then you cannot see beyond the end of your own nose. Don't forget where Richard was brought up—do you think he has made an easy choice? It would be easier for you, yet you persist in this wilful disobedience. It will end in treason, and then I shall not know how to defend you."

Suddenly the Duchess became less of a judge and more of a mother. "George," she said, kissing him on one angry red cheek, "you will not go against me in this?"

He, overcome as he often was by sudden softening emotion, seized this opportunity and put his arms round his mother, promising again that he would never commit treason against his brother.

The Duchess did not have much faith in his protestations but felt unable to do more. She could scarcely put George under lock and key in Sandwich town in the King's name. Cecily, having tried her son, over whom she did have some influence, went to her Neville nephews, over whom she had very little.

Warwick, after receiving her with utmost courtesy, shrugged his shoulders and admitted that there was going to be no change in his plans. Clarence was to be married to Isabel—the Papal dispensation had been obtained. They were going over to Calais in a week or two, where the Archbishop of York would officiate at the ceremony.

"Your money in the Pope's coffers, Richard," scoffed his aunt, "or King Louis' money!"

Warwick cast a rueful glance at his brother the Archbishop. He had no intention of weakening under this female onslaught, but he was not enjoying it. He had been the friend of the Duke of York for so long, and of the Duchess, his youngest aunt; he could not easily shrug off her censure. If her husband the Duke of York had lived, Warwick would have made this formidable woman Queen.

Archbishop George Neville said soothingly, "My dear lady, when we come back from Calais, we fully intend to join King Edward in the north. Then we can set about resolving the matters which are at variance between us."

"In fact," said Cecily, unappeased, "you intend to twist my son's arm. I do not know what means you will employ. Your father Salisbury, who was my brother, your brother Thomas, my husband, my son—all were claimed by civil strife. Twenty thousand men died at Towton to put my son upon his throne. Their lives will have been wasted if you threaten him, and you will be traitors to the realm you have made. I only pray that the end will not be war."

The Earl and the Archbishop both crossed themselves. "There will be no war," said Warwick, and he was perfectly sincere.

"If it should begin again," the Duchess went on relentlessly, "the time will have come for me to retire from the world, and leave what family shall remain to me. They bring me too much sorrow."

3

The Maker of Kings

July 1469 – March 1470

Than sette I from my ryalte
As angell dede from hevyn to helle;
All crystyn kynges be war me—
God amend wikkyd cownsel!

Many a man for me hath be slayn
With bowe and axe and swerde I-drawe;
And that I wite myn own brayn
I-helde nowth my lordys under awe.

God Amend Wicked Counsel
(c. 1464)

"Crimson velvet of Montpellier in Gascony. Two qualities: fourteen and twenty shillings per yard. That's all very well.

"Blue cloth of silver upon satin, twenty-four shillings. Hmm.

"Black velvet upon velvet cloth of gold, a long gown of ten and a half yards—forty shillings per yard! Not to mention the ermine skins, the three and four pence to the tailor, *and* the six and eight pence for a lined satin doublet!"

King Edward looked up from this entry in the accounts and let out a pained whistle.

"I'll find out who supplied that. Forty shillings! No more than thirty-three to the trade, I'm certain, or thirty-five to noble customers. Why should the King pay well above the market price for allowing foreign merchants—not even his subjects—the privilege of his custom?"

Lord Hastings, who was Chamberlain of the royal household, said, "A natural hazard of monarchy, your Grace, which I know you're astute enough to overcome. They should know better than to swindle you."

The two men were sitting on either side of a table drawn up in front of an open window looking out over the inner courtyard of Nottingham castle. In spite of this the room was stuffy, and dust floated in the slanting bars of July sunshine which fell across their work. Outside, there was a great deal of noise from the builders. An ungreased pulley squeaked without intermission against a background of shovelling, as the bricklayers mixed mortar. Blasphemous shouts soared up from the foreman, some so astonishing that the King and Hastings exchanged grins. The King was glad to see his new building progressing. The old royal apartments were cramped and low ceilinged, and the windows were too small. The King, Hastings and several other household officers were sitting like merchants in a counting house, looking over the books, which they did regularly every quarter. Hastings, a man a dozen years older than the King, had recognized in his master the qualities of a successful merchant even in the first years of their friendship, when Edward had been no more than seventeen. These qualities were most useful to a king.

"Hmm." King Edward pursued his point. "Baudekyn of silk thirty-three and four pence a piece—I'll let that pass. Fringe of Venice gold at six shillings the ounce. Could be got cheaper, but not worth quibbling this time. Ostrich feathers ten shillings *each* . . . !" The King groaned, yawned, and stretched his arms above his head until the bones creaked.

"If I told you what Anthony Popagay charged me for a hat with a feather when I was last in his shop . . ." Hastings had to break off in mid-sentence.

The painted leather curtain which hung across the door was thrust aside, and the Duke of Gloucester was hurriedly announced before he burst into the room. Richard was one of the few persons who could burst into the King's presence without reprimand. He had run all the way across the big outer courtyard from the castle main gate, through the inner court and up the stairs. He could run a good distance without panting, but this time he had to catch his breath before speaking.

"You'll excuse the intrusion, your Grace—Lord Hastings. . . ." He laid the letter he was carrying on the table in front of his brother.

"Dick, you very seldom intrude on me; there's only one situation in which I'm not pleased to see you!" King Edward grinned across at his friend Lord Hastings. "What's this?"

"Something I'd wish was anything but what it is. I was at the main gate when it was brought in. Warwick's man. You'd better be forewarned. I've heard the news already. This is from Warwick and his brother the Archbishop. When they were in Calais, they sent this letter out to all the principal towns in the kingdom."

"I'd better read it." The King broke the seals and opened the letter.

"George is married!" Richard blurted out. This was the least part of the bad news he had collected from Warwick's man.

"What!?" As Richard let drop this remark, his brother had discovered the contents of the letter. King Edward let out a sudden roar, like a baited beast.

"Clarence has dared to go this far against me? Trying to make out he's been kept from my council because he's been supplanted by Rivers' family. I'll tell you why he's been kept from my council—it's because he has persistently refused to make useful contribution to it! So he's got himself married to Warwick's daughter, after I forbade it. To spite me, I suppose."

As he unfolded the second part of his unwelcome missive, King Edward realized that the flouting of his commands by Clarence was only a small part of his present trouble—indeed, danger.

"So my mighty lord Warwick *has* been pulling the strings of all these dancing rebel Robins in the north, who've been sent to plague me. Robin Mend All! Amend everything so that King Neville can be crowned!" he raved.

Richard winced. Lord Hastings sat staring, aghast. There were those who thought the King should have realized the truth of this months ago, instead of dismissing much evidence as prejudice.

"Do they think they can lead me by the nose? Does any brother of Clarence imagine Warwick will set him up as King of England in my place? No, I can't believe that. It's too much.

"So my lord of Warwick is calling on my subjects to join him in arms—to march against me, the King! I tell you, his brains have been addled to spleen and pride. His venom against Rivers and the Queen has poisoned his mind. Well, if he wants a fight, I'll give it to him, by God!"

Lord Hastings, when he had read the Earl's proclamation of intent, said, "So they are coming to present their grievances to your Grace in person—for discussion. I've heard of that ploy before. My lord Archbishop of York takes a prominent place, no doubt to show their methods are peaceful—at first. I don't trust George Neville; he fancies himself playing St. Michael in a morality of his own drafting."

"They were at Canterbury last Tuesday, and in London by the end of the week," Richard said, reluctantly, not relishing his role as bearer of ill news. "The City lent them a thousand pounds."

"Did they now?" King Edward's angry shouts had subsided to growls. "I'll find out who subscribed to that loan—down to the last penny, before God, I will! If they're so full of money there must be plenty more they can lend to me." He laughed grimly.

"We must go south to put a stop to all this, before my brother Clarence indulges any further in his play acting, and before Richard Neville thinks he has the ordering of my kingdom."

King Edward looked both angry and rueful, unwilling to admit his dilatoriness. He had been caught, so to speak, with his feet up on the table. Richard noted his determination on instant action with relief, and a feeling that all was somehow now under control.

But it took a few days to raise even a small number of troops. A week had passed before the King left Nottingham to go south. He relied upon his friends the Earls of Pembroke and Devonshire to join him with their army of Welsh archers and west countrymen, so that they might cut off the northern rebels before

Warwick came from London and met up with his mob of unruly Neville supporters.

On the road a tiny band of Pembroke's men met the King. He had seen enough of battles to know at once that these soldiers were beaten and on the run.

"My lord of Pembroke is taken!" a man shouted as soon as they were in earshot. "They took him to Northampton—to the lord Warwick."

"Taken! But how? Where? What's become of Devonshire?"

"Fled to the west country. Your Grace, we do not know what happened, we were parted—our men and my lord Devonshire's. There was some reason—I do not know—we heard our lord had some quarrel. Near Banbury, we were. Your Grace, do not go near Northampton, for my lord Pembroke's head will be taken from him by now, and Sir Richard's, his brother. Highness, we have lost two good lords, for what seems to have been an error."

"So Warwick has sunk to this—taking the lives of Herbert and Stafford to spite me—to show the little boy his uncle can smack his hand and take his toys away. He goes too far. William Herbert was a good friend, too good to lose. God rest his soul, I grieve for him.

"There's only one thing to be done," King Edward said, pulling himself together. "I'll skirt around Northampton and cross the river at Olney ford, and go towards London."

But the news of the defeat of Pembroke and Devonshire meant disaster. Not only had the King lost two of his most effective servants and closest friends, but the few soldiers still with him took fright and during the night fled quietly away, back to their homes. There was nothing left for King Edward to do but ride for London. The only lords of importance left with him were his friend Lord Hastings, and his brother Richard. Neither of them would have left him, even if all three had been destitute and alone on the road.

But the King had forgotten that the manor of Olney in Buckinghamshire belonged to Warwick. The Archbishop of York lay in wait for him, knowing that he would have to cross the river Ouse there. Men in the scarlet livery of Warwick lined either side of the wide ford. Since there were now less than fifty persons with the King, resistance was useless. Richard reined in his horse, staring at them, unable to believe what was happening. The King looked round at his followers, then shrugged and spread his hands in a gesture of helplessness. "No sense in shedding blood," he said, "in case it should be mine."

The Archbishop himself rode forward on his dazzlingly white horse to meet the King. Richard watched this third Neville brother. The Archbishop had not, of course, donned armour to perform this almost military manoeuvre—he knew the King had too much sense to fight his way out of the encounter—but he would probably have looked well in it. He was tall, elegant and when on foot walked with a long-legged, easy stride in his flowing scarlet gowns. Now thirty-four, he had been made Chancellor of England at twenty-five, a bishop two years later, and Archbishop of York at thirty. He was both erudite and astute; some speculated that one day he might become the second English Pope. Glass painters gave the younger, more warlike saints in their windows the same sort of blond, smooth hair on their tonsured heads, the same smooth features. All that was missing, his enemies said, was the nimbus of holiness; Neville had tried hard to remedy this deficiency by acquiring the wide scarlet brim of a Cardinal's hat, but this had gone to his venerable Grace of Canterbury instead. Richard had previously admired his many gifts.

Neville said, "Your Grace, it is fortunate that I am able to meet you here without any misunderstanding or violence. My brother and myself would deeply deplore any brawling between our more unruly servants, while we are in fact the best of friends." He looked at the King's sullen, milling servants and knew the anger of Gloucester and Hastings.

"My lord of York," King Edward said, shortly, "it is clear that I have no choice but to be at your disposal, if I do not wish to suffer the fate of my friends Herbert and Stafford. I would be grateful if you would allow my brother and my friends here to depart, since they intend no brawling."

"Your Grace, if I may accompany you to my brother of Warwick, I am sure that the problems which have arisen between us can be quickly resolved, and we can all begin to work together again on the affairs of this realm." Neville was not in the least abashed. He was the politest of gaolers.

Richard turned his horse away from the scene at Olney ford undecided as to where he should go, or what he should do. He had been dismissed as too young and of no importance by the Archbishop and told that he might go away. The King was being taken to Warwick Castle; there was no question of accompanying him.

Lord Hastings, who had been treated in the same way, thought himself exceedingly fortunate to be Warwick's brother-in-law. He was the only one of King Edward's intimates not censured in the Neville petition. This was partly on account of the family relationship, and partly because Hastings' influence with the King was thought honest, and because he was known to dislike the Queen's family nearly as much as the Nevilles themselves did.

The first face that Richard looked for among the King's dismayed companions was Lord Hastings'. For all his easygoing, womanizing ways, Hastings was a calm, dependable man, who had always shown himself friendly to Richard.

"Your Grace must regard my castle of Ashby as always open to you. Probably the King will be taken to Warwick; we would do well not to be too far away."

"I should go to my brother Clarence," Richard said, "though I doubt if I can influence him."

Hastings laughed. "It would be easier to stop a bolting horse. Go to your mother, the Duchess of York, and see what she can do, though I believe even she is powerless now."

In spite of this advice, Richard felt that it was his duty to speak to Clarence, to try to reason with him, to prevent him exceeding altogether the bounds of family feeling. The brothers met briefly at Coventry, where George was keeping almost royal state in one of the best houses in the town. Richard knew that he was wasting his time from the moment they met.

"If you've come to tell me to lick the boots of brother Ned—*royal* Ned—you can save yourself the trouble and get out!" George said. He had adopted the tone of voice he used for menials who had got on the wrong side of him.

"I don't want you to lick anyone's boots. What do you want out of all this, George? Do you think you'll be better off after holding the King to ransom? You've lived like a prince, the King's heir, ever since you were ten years old. What cause have you got for ingratitude?" Richard adroitly circled round to the other side of the table, putting it between himself and his brother. Where he was concerned George had always been easily roused to violence.

Clarence leaned forward, picked up the nearest object, a heavy book, hurled it at Richard's head and missed. A hundred pounds' worth of fine book crashed on the floor. Richard had ducked instinctively.

"You little creeping louse!" George yelled. "Worming your way in here to preach at me! Get out before I have you thrown out!" He was beside himself with temper, looking round for some other missile which might do Richard an injury. "If you want to know what I'll get out of it," he shouted wildly, "then I may as well tell you—I'll get a kingdom! Edward has abused his power, he has no right to rule—I'll call him a bastard to his face if I see him. Do you think I've enjoyed seeing the crown on his head all these years? Rolling about with his whores—every time he picks a new one, he pays off that bitch of a wife with more money and favours—a titbit for a brother, a husband for a sister. I won't stand it any longer—why, I know I'd make a better job of ruling than he has!"

This final statement was delivered in a shriek, and it shocked Richard into instant action. In an uncontrolled fury, like those of his childhood, he hurled himself on his brother. George was still bigger and stronger than he—unarmed, he never could compete with him. They scuffled undignifiedly, and George kicked his shins; in the end he bore Richard down by launching his superior size and weight on top of him. When George drew his knife Richard, pinned down and struggling, watched the thin steel blade waver in front of his eyes, and was very frightened. He thought for a moment that his brother meant to blind him, or to cut his face to shreds. He shut his eyes and lay very still. The next thing he knew was that George had jumped up and given him an almighty kick in the ribs, which nearly winded him.

When he had managed to scramble to his feet, gasping like a stranded fish, George was savagely attacking the arras, jabbing and ripping with his knife in a childish display of rage and frustration. Richard fled.

The discovery of what really lay in George's mind, revealed in wild indiscretion, left Richard far more troubled than his brother's violent hostility towards himself. He doubted if the King had estimated one tithe of George's discontent and ambitions, or how dangerous they were, or how soon that danger might become an open threat.

At Warwick Castle that August, Anne Neville was paralysed with alarm every time the new resident in her father's household appeared. She realized quickly that King Edward was a prisoner, though he was treated as a guest. He was allowed to walk in the castle gardens which were, of course, walled, and the doors discreetly guarded. Here she unwittingly discovered him one afternoon. Her dog rushed ahead of her into the garden and disappeared round a corner, where a furious barking made her think at first that he had found a cat asleep in the sun. But when she came round the corner herself, she saw with horror that the target was not a cat. It was King Edward. He was sitting on a garden bench—or he had been sitting. Now he had his immensely long legs propped up on it out of the way of Ben. He was snapping his fingers and making mock growling noises at the little dog, sending him into a leaping frenzy of barking.

Anne's voice came out in a squawk as she called, "Ben!!" The dog slunk back, still yapping and growling, and she grabbed his collar, descending in an undignified heap to the ground as she did so. King Edward stood up. This made things infinitely worse, because he was so enormous. He cast a shadow that quite enveloped her. But he was grinning as if he almost enjoyed being caught making silly noises at a little dog by Warwick's daughter.

"Lady Anne," he said amiably, "your father may hold my head in his hands, but I'd be happier if your Ben left me my ankles."

"Oh, but. . . . Oh, your Grace, I beg your pardon. . . . If I'd known you were here. I. . . . Of course, I wouldn't have let him out. He doesn't like strangers. Oh dear, he didn't . . . ?"

"No, he didn't."

In spite of her relief that the King was unpunctured by Ben's teeth, Anne trembled so much she could not immediately get up from the ground. King Edward, seeing that his mere presence was causing her distress, regretted his barbed remark about her father. This one was an innocent, he could see.

"Well," he said, "if Ben hadn't gone for me, I wouldn't have had the pleasure of meeting you. I don't believe I've spoken more than half a dozen words to you before. Come and sit beside me and introduce me to Ben."

From the way she sat gingerly on the edge of the bench leaving a good foot between himself and her skirts, it was obvious that she had been well instructed in his reputation as a seducer. She could not know that he did not have any interest in seducing innocents. She kept glancing nervously around, as if to be found talking to him would land her in trouble; this was probably so. They'd know in any case; in this castle, walls had eyes.

King Edward was as friendly with dogs as he was with people, and he never worried about paws on his hose. As Anne watched him scratch the little dog's ears and charm the growls into ecstatic pants and grins, she thought that for one who was a prisoner and in danger of losing his crown, and had already lost two of his closest friends, the King showed remarkable resilience. He was so big and looked so healthy, it seemed strange to see him cooped up at Warwick, unable to ride out hunting. His good looks and, above all, his bulk, intimidated her. He had a skin a girl might envy, fair and clear, and very little lined. Where his beard began he was fair, and his big chin did not show stubble, but the rest of his thick head of hair was light chestnut brown, the color of some horses.

The conversation was going to be hard going, but he did not seem to mind. "You were born here at Warwick, weren't you?" he said.

"Yes, your Grace." She was astonished that he should know, or remember.

"Where do you like best to be, of all your father's castles?" He restrained himself from adding: And God knows there are enough of them. She looked up at him, then lowered her eyelids, as if merely to look was to invite advances.

"Middleham."

King Edward turned his eyes directly upon her, interested. They were dark grey, with golden flecks swimming about in the colour, and his eyelashes were thick and golden, too. He looked like an amiable lion. She was wary of him, as one might be of a large uncertain animal.

"What is there special about this place Middleham?" he asked. "My brother Richard has always sung its praises since I sent him there. I thought it would either make a man of him or kill him. I'm not over fond of the north." He watched the deliberately remote, pale little face turn a vivid red.

"Yes," was all she said.

Edward wondered if there was any connection between Anne's blush and Richard's unwillingness to say anything at all about Warwick's daughters. Not that there was any point in giving the subject any thought, but he knew that Warwick had wanted Richard for this girl. Damn Warwick and his schemes for marrying his daughters. He now had Clarence dancing to his tune like a street bear. That George was willing to be led into a position of open warfare against his own brother was more wounding than anything Warwick had done. Richard suffered in all this, too; Heaven knew what was in store for him, if the boy managed to live past seventeen. He had always felt fatherly in his responsibility for his youngest brother. He thought of what could so easily have happened at Olney—Richard dead before he was ever fully grown, like their brother Edmund, who had been murdered at Wakefield bridge ten years ago.

Anne saw the King's face change with his thoughts and become harsher and older, as his habitual buoyancy of spirits deserted him. She was afraid, in case she had offended him, perhaps with the inadvertent suggestion that she and Richard had once been friends. She did not want him to think that Richard had been secretly planning the same sort of things as Clarence.

The King, realizing his change of mood might kill this stilted conversation, said, "Prisoners sometimes make poor company,

Lady Anne; you take Ben for his walk. You'll see me again. I
don't know how long I shall be your father's guest, but I can see
it will be for a while yet."

Because she was schooled in good manners, she did not jump
up from the seat at once, though her relief was plain. She hovered a moment or two, then took her leave. He watched her go.
She was a curious little thing—no shape at all, as straight up and
down as two sticks, but the shy gaucheness apart, her movements were quite pleasing, light as a butterfly. Too like a cab-
bage white for his taste, but then he had no fancy for girls of
thirteen. The well developed in tit and bum were easy on the
eye young, but he preferred his women over twenty, or even
over thirty, and the more experienced the better. It was depress-
ing that while he was in Warwick's custody, it was certain that
he was not going to get any women at all. The devilish old hawk
eye knew him well enough to take satisfaction in depriving him
of female company. Warwick had assured him that the Queen
would not be harmed in any way. The most she would suffer was
a blockage in the money supply, which would no doubt increase
her hatred of Warwick to a degree frightening to contemplate.
He preferred to restrict his contemplation of his wife to her bodily charms. Last time he had seen her, she had been recovering
from childbirth and not available. From the first moment he had
met her, she had been perfecting the art of playing him on a
line, like a salmon. He got home frequently enough, but by
Heaven she was clever at holding him off. He usually thought of
Elizabeth with increased desire when she was absent.

He suddenly felt more like a prisoner than ever, and desperately wanted to escape the confines of Warwick Castle. Even to
see over the garden wall seemed an urgent necessity, though all
that lay beyond was the higher, curtain wall. Yet he wanted to
climb it, which was nothing but a foolish, schoolboy idea. He
was the King. Also, he was rather big and heavy for nimble
climbing. Richard could go up a wall or a tree like a little ape.
Poor Dick, he thought, what will become of you; may God and
Our Lady in Heaven protect you, wherever you are.

During the week in which he was at Warwick, two pieces of
news arrived which increased the King's anger against his cap-

tors. Lord Rivers, the Queen's father and Constable of England, the King's chief military officer, together with his son John, were beheaded at Coventry on Warwick's orders. The Earl had his revenge upon the begetter of all the tribe.

As if this were not enough to injure and insult the King, the Queen's mother was arrested—upon prejudiced evidence—and accused of witchcraft. Anne's mother, white, trembling and gullible, whispered that a Thing had been brought to Warwick, and lay within the very walls of the castle.

"The wicked, evil old woman," the Countess whispered. "A man-at-arms, made of lead in the image of my husband, a horrible little puppet, broken in the middle and bound up with wire. She has been seeking the death of my husband! And people have seen others—a little man and a woman tied fast together with a lock of hair—the King's hair," she said meaningly. "These wicked people invoke the Devil," she crossed herself, "to bring about marriages, using these—Things."

She meant, of course, the King's marriage. She had forgotten, however, that the Duchess of Bedford had a will to get her own way—and her family's aggrandisement—quite as strong as the powers of witchcraft, and that her daughter had enough attractions and the King enough weaknesses to need no images to bring about what the Duchess desired.

Her mother's words frightened Anne, in case her father should suddenly fall ill, or waste away, and she was glad when they left Warwick to go north to Middleham, taking the King with them. There, in the Earl's home stronghold, where rescue was impossible, King Edward was allowed more freedom, to go hunting and hawking as if he were not a prisoner, but a guest. From the high walls of the round tower, Anne watched him ride out, in the company of her father and her uncle John, talking to them as if the deaths of his best friends and his father- and brother-in-law did not lie between them. She decided that the King was a clever dissembler, of an amazingly equable temper, and that he was playing a waiting game.

There could be no better place in which to wait. Harvest was beginning. Beyond the heavily shaded pasture of Sunscough Park, where brood mares and foals browsed belly deep in grass, towards the river Cover, lay open fields, whose pattern had begun to change from a smooth sea of gold to trampled stubble and ranks of stooked corn. Earl and Marquess appeared intent upon their sport, but they held a captive lion gambolling at their side.

Warwick had summoned a Parliament to meet at York in the third week of September, for the purpose of forcing ratification of his actions upon it. Did he intend to proclaim Clarence as King? This would make Isabel Queen. Anne could not imagine her sister as Queen; would she be any better than Elizabeth Woodville? An unkind thought for a sister to have. How, Anne wondered, could her father bring all this about without bloodshed, when it had taken so much to bring King Edward to his throne? How much more would be spilt in making King George?

By the end of August, the meeting of Parliament had been postponed. Richard, who had received his summons with everyone else, received the writ of *supersedeas* cancelling it, with relief. That Warwick could think of no better excuse than the untruth that England was threatened with invasion by France and Scotland, was evidence of his own weakness. Since his brother's capture, Richard had busied himself with sending out spies and canvassing support and mostly keeping company with Lord Hastings in the Midlands. The results had been encouraging. It was obvious that Warwick had flown too high, and that he would have to restore the King to power, or face an outbreak of savage war. Riots were occurring all over the country and on the London streets, a sure sign that the imprisonment of the King would not be tolerated for much longer.

At York, Warwick himself met his brother the Archbishop, who had ridden north, with the grim facts of their quandary.

"We have trouble, George, as if there were not enough elsewhere, from a different quarter. As you know, not all our Neville relatives here in the north have been our friends. That old villain Humphrey Neville of Brancepeth is busy up there on the Border, where they live thirty years behind the times, with raising the ghost of Henry of Lancaster. It's only a matter of time before he has the Scots joining him and descending upon us. I've sent out commissions of array, but there's been delay, or downright disregard of them. If I stay here and go against our cousin Humphrey, I shall find myself taking on Scotland on my own." He drummed his fingers on the table, irritable in his admission of failure. "The truth is, I cannot hold the kingdom on my own."

"Richard," said the Archbishop, all practicality and sweet reason. "You need a king—a king whose armies you may be seen to lead as you used to do. Let him out of Middleham and bring him here, where everyone can see him at his own business again. We have pressed ahead too far, too soon, though it galls me to admit it."

"It galls me, too," said his brother grimly. "But you're right. The alternative is bloodshed. I don't want that now, it's to no one's advantage. Better to bend the knee to our King again— quietly, civilly, as if we intended nothing else. He has no choice but to make peace. King Edward IV shall be restored—for the time being!"

The west coast of Wales in winter was as indecipherable as its customs and language. A curtain of mist and drizzle cut off Cardigan town from all the rest of the world, hid the river and drove the people off the quays. The bridge led nowhere. Richard felt equally cut off from events in England, by a hundred miles of impassable mountains. King Edward could be deposed and dead a fortnight before ever he heard of it. This was the worst that might happen; at best there would be tiresome outbreaks of violence. Richard had left London in October on his first independent commission, loaded with new offices at the expense of Warwick, who could not expect to go unpenalized for his misdeeds. This had put the perennial problem of order and government in wild Wales into Richard's hands. In addition, he had been given the highest military office in the realm, the Constableship, which he was now incapable of exercising effectively because of his isolation in Wales. It could only be a matter of time before he was recalled to England. Warwick was not the man even to make a pretence of eating humble pie for long, and Clarence was still drunk upon dreams of a crown.

Christmas passed, without any breaking of the uneasy stalemate between King and Earl. Indeed, King Edward had far exceeded what might have been expected in the way of peacemaking. He had been generous to Northumberland, the least culpable of the Neville brothers; John Neville's son had been given a dukedom and promised the King's eldest daughter in marriage. Richard shrugged to himself when he heard of the dispensing of this bait; it would make little difference. By February he had received enough warnings to alert him into readiness to leave Wales at an hour's notice, should the King have need of him.

The news, when it came, was nastier even than Richard had feared. On the 17th March, St. Patrick's Day, a King's messenger rode a horse to death in reaching the Duke. The King's summons was urgent; Richard gave orders to be ready to travel before he had finished reading the letter. Out of some feuding in Lincolnshire, between the Welles and Dymoke families, a rebellion had arisen against the King himself. A skirmish had been fought at Empingham near Stamford, and the rebels had broken ranks as soon as faced by the King's force and run away. In their flight, they had cast off their livery jackets, hoping to escape unrecognized. Many of them, including their leader, had been wearing the livery of the Duke of Clarence. A man known to be Clarence's servant was found dead, carrying enough written evidence on him to make things unpleasantly clear to the King. His brother was determined upon an attempt to seize his crown, urged on and abetted in his treason by Warwick.

Richard tore the letter into shreds. Soon the whole realm would know the terrible rivalry between his brothers. The King had said that he was well provided with men, and that his army was able to meet whoever challenged it. Nevertheless, Richard's services were needed urgently: he must make for York in all haste to meet his brother. York! That was more than two hundred miles away, across the mountains. Fears for his brother's safety made him drive his men, and himself, harder than he had ever done before in his life. Though the roads—such as they were —mostly followed the river valleys, the going was rough, and the weather worse. The snow on the mountains had not begun to melt. They rode late each night until the dark made it too dangerous, and set out in the morning just before dawn.

By the time they crossed the Border and were travelling north across Cheshire, Richard had heard that the King had arrived at York, and was preparing to march in pursuit of Warwick and Clarence and, if need be, to bring them to battle.

Beyond the flat Cheshire plain, they began to climb the familiar Pennine hills and to experience familiar Pennine weather. The cold rain came down in bucketfuls, and the countryside had not yet stirred even into signs of spring. They could see some distance ahead in this bleak landscape and thus spotted a body of men on the same road, moving towards them. Not enough men for an army, perhaps, but certainly a force of alarming size.

Richard halted. Whoever was moving a force this large was an important lord, and the fact that he was coming southwards meant that he was not going to the aid of the King. Richard suspected his identity before his drenched banners even became visible. When they did—the gold eagle's foot, the blue and white arms with three stag's heads—he knew that he had guessed rightly. Lord Stanley, the greatest lord in Lancashire and Cheshire, was Warwick's brother-in-law. The only explanation of his movements must be that he had decided to join the Earl. He would have to be stopped, though God knew how, when he had ten times the men Richard had.

Richard said to one of his older companions, "Will he stand and fight, and kill us all?"

"From what I know of him, he won't. Not against you, your Grace. Too wary of the trouble it might land him in if your brother the King catches up with him."

Richard, hoping this estimation of Lord Stanley was correct, urged his men onward. With growing dismay, he watched Stanley's reaction to his move. The troops were being ranged up across the road in a truculent manner. The rain blew across the half mile or so between them like a flimsy barrier of collapsed cloud. Stanley must by now have realized who was approaching him. Soon, he sent forward a herald, resplendent but wet, in green. This was a remarkable showing for a mere baron.

Richard, desperate, and ignoring the cautions spoken by his

companions, went forward himself to meet Stanley's man, wondering if the devious lord was watching him undertake foolhardy actions.

He wasted no time in parley with the herald. "Go back to my lord Stanley, and tell him I'll have a word with him, here. Tell him I act on the King's behalf." He wondered whether Stanley would come alone, or if this sharp summons might bring a couple of thousand Stanley retainers thundering down upon himself.

Lord Stanley came. Not alone, it was true, but with only two six-foot-tall men-at-arms accompanying him. As he rode, hunched up in his collar in the rain, he had the aggrieved air of a bird disturbed in its private roost.

If he asks me what I am doing near Manchester . . . Richard thought, tensing himself and trying to stop shivering. He was aware that he must make an unimpressive figure, looking more like a drowned rat than anything else. Lord Stanley either had a more water-resistant cloak than he had, or had been out in the rain for a shorter time.

"I go to my brother the King, my lord. I believe that you do not. Nevertheless, I wish to use this road unmolested. Will you let me pass?"

Lord Stanley's eyes popped. The King's very young brother had spoken to him as if he were, well, anyone. There were ways of talking oneself out of these undesirable encounters. The peremptoriness of this youth was not at all what he liked to deal with.

"I don't know what your Grace intends to do if I will not. . . ." Lord Stanley began blustering. Rain was running from the brim of his hat like small waterfalls.

"My lord, if you do not move your army aside within the count of ten, I shall ride straight through it." Richard held up his hands, ten fingers and thumbs. He clenched first one finger, then another. Lord Stanley stared, aghast. The boy had the nerve of all the devils in Hell.

"I have nothing against your Grace. You cannot intend to . . ."

"My intention is to bring the King's rebels, whoever they are, to heel."

With this parting shot, Richard rode past the spluttering lord, signalling for his men to do the same. The discomfited Stanley glared in rage at being so outfaced, but made no move to oppose the young Duke. A policy of wait and see was best pursued. Warwick and Clarence were marching north, expecting Stanley to join them. But King Edward was this time acting with energy and decision against his enemies, and Lord Stanley had changed his mind about being caught in their company. Judging from the haste in which the young Constable rode to his brother, his total disregard of danger, the proper forms of address and of reasonable explanations, the King was remarkably well served.

4

Lucifer Unwise

April – July 1470

Almighty Jhesu was disobeied,
First by Adam and Eve in paradise,
Thurgh the fals devel to theim conveiede,
And in hevyn by lucifer unwise,
And in erthe bi Iudas in his false guyse.
Have not ye now nede aboute you to loke?
Sith God was deceyvede by wiles croke.
. . . . And be ye ware of the Reconsiled
That hathe deserved to be reviled.

George Ashby,
Active Policy of a Prince (c. 1470)

"A four and a five!" said Isabel triumphantly.

The dice rattled, clicked and flipped out onto the board.

"Four and three." At only eight moves into the game, Anne
was in a position of retrenchment. She slid an ebony man on to
her sister's three-point, and another on to her own nine. While
Isabel cast the next die, Anne leaned sideways to sniff at a vase-
ful of white narcissus. Flowers which meant the end of winter always gave her special pleasure.

"You're dreaming today, Anne," Isabel said, "I shall win." She
piled the coins into a little stack, which collapsed. They were
only allowed to play for halfpennies; Warwick did not permit his
daughters to gamble, and himself never played for high stakes.
The Countess rarely played at all and had never been able to
master the skill of backgammon.

As Anne tumbled the dice in the cup, the door of the room opened, the arras twitched aside and her mother came in, letting through with her a blast of cold air. Anne's throw jerked across the board and rolled to rest against its rim.

"We have just received urgent orders from your father. We must be packed and ready to leave Warwick the instant he reaches here. We are going to Calais." The Countess was dreadfully flustered and could not meet the startled eyes of her elder daughter.

Isabel stood up, awkwardly. "To Calais!" She stared at her mother. "But how can I go to Calais, like this?" This was her first pregnancy, now almost into its eighth month. She had been sitting with it wedged under the edge of the backgammon board. Now that she was upright, it stuck out alarmingly, so that she seemed to have to lean backwards to prevent herself being overweighted and falling on her nose.

"How can I travel in this state?" said Isabel again, shrilly. "Where is my husband? He won't let me go."

"He has no option," her mother returned, rather tartly for her. "The alternative is to give himself up to his brother the King and hope for mercy. You must go where your father wishes."

"Oh-h!" Isabel burst into noisy tears.

"Hush." Her mother enfolded her in her arms and petted her, and made her sit down again.

"If I could," the Countess said helplessly, "I would keep you here. But sometimes women must obey their husbands' wishes, whatever the difficulties involved."

"Why?" Isabel wailed. "What has happened that we are to be chased from England, when my father swore to see Clarence crowned before midsummer?"

"I cannot tell you anything, except that King Edward has somehow gained an advantage. Your father's supporters in Lincolnshire have failed him; his brother John has deserted him.

"Anne, stop sitting there with eyes like saucers. Your father is coming from the north in great haste; he will be here by tomorrow."

Late that night, when Isabel was already in bed, and the Countess, Anne and all the women preparing to retire, the Earl

came home. It was the night of the first of April but blustering
and cold as if March objected to relinquishing its hold. They arrived in a squall of sheeting rain, by a moon that showed by fits
and starts, as clouds raced one on each other's heels across its
face. The great courtyard of the castle was filled with sudden
noise, clattering of hooves on the cobbles, grinding of wheels,
dozens of men shouting all at once. Then above all the din, very
near the door, came Warwick's voice, hard and cutting as the
crack of a lash, ordering his men to dry and rest first the horses,
then themselves, and to be ready to be on the road again at first
light.

Anne managed to catch a glimpse of her father as he came
into the bright light within doors. She had seen him come home
in anger and adversity a good many times recently but never,
never, as grim as this. He came scattering rain drops from the
hem of his cloak, his clothes and high boots all black and water
sodden. On his face, though, the rain drops ran off as from stone.
Because torchlight dappled the rain and the flecks of mud, it
resembled not just stone, but the hard and impervious granite.
He brushed aside his frightened wife and did not even notice
Anne watching him. He could have been blind and deaf, so
inflexibly was he committed to his inner purpose. He was like a
man who had looked on Medusa.

Clarence, who came in behind him, ignored by him as was everyone else, had a face like a proclamation shouted aloud. His
sullen anger and high-strung fear were made entirely public. His
servants and Warwick's kept to separate groups, though they
seemed to be milling about in equal numbers. Because her husband had not heeded her, the Countess seized upon her son-in-
law. Given this opportunity to relate his woes, Clarence began
in the manner of a river in flood.

"To Calais! Tomorrow! My brother is after us! We are in
flight, my lady mother, running like curs, while Edward cracks
the whip!" His voice, normally mellifluous, rose in a tottering oc-
tave like an unsound bell. "My wife will be in danger of her life
—who has thought of that . . . ? I am being taken to France to
be the bootboy who grovels to that hellcat Margaret of Anjou, to
help my father Warwick to ally with her and resurrect that rav-

ing old lunatic King Henry VI! He's remaking a king who has
been as good as dead these nine years, and destroying my inheritance. I'd sooner see my brother wearing his crown with fifty
Woodvilles worshipping it, than have the resuscitated corpse of
Lancaster propped in the throne!"

"Stop!" Warwick's voice cut across Clarence's tirade like the
breaking off of an icicle. "May I remind you, my lord of
Clarence, that your brother has proclaimed you a rebel and
traitor just as he has me, and that you need me to get you out of
England to save your skin. While in my house, before my wife,
control your tongue!"

The Earl had the effect upon Clarence of a tyrannical schoolmaster, though in his youth George had usually been the one to
tyrannize those who taught him. He did not dare to say more.

Anne stared at the trio of faces, her father's more granite cold
than ever, Clarence's unhandsome with rage, her mother's pale
and shivering as a will o' the wisp. She thought at first that
Clarence had gone clean mad, then realized that her father
though in full flight from England, had new plans to unseat King
Edward, and that George of Clarence had no part in them. What
connection these plans could have with Margaret of Anjou, the
deposed Lancastrian Queen, and with France, was completely
bewildering.

A week later, on the town quay at Exeter, Anne sat amid
chaos on an enormous leather coffer containing her mother's
clothes, and wished that she did not have to leave England. The
servants, helped by quay labourers, were going up the gangplank at a trot, chests on shoulders, bundles on heads. There
were only a few hours in which to stow the baggage on the carvel of Exeter her father had commandeered to take his family to
Calais. They had fled from Warwick Castle, travelling night and
day, with the King in pursuit, only four days behind them.

In the shade of a large building which Anne knew was the
customs house, from the royal arms over the door and the coming and going of many merchants and clerks, her father and
Clarence stood talking to the master of the ship that they were
to travel in. A very worried-looking man who was the Mayor of
Exeter had joined them, together with several sea captains who

would make up their fleet. The Mayor must be now have received the King's letters naming her father a traitor and rebel, but he had not dared to keep the Earl out of the city. Being a rebel seemed to make very little difference to the way in which Warwick was welcomed in a sea port, and if it were not for all the frenzied haste and her mother's near panic, it would have seemed like any other time they had taken ship for Calais.

Anne now had full knowledge of her father's plans, and the unrelenting fact that she played a part in them. She was being taken to France to be given to Queen Margaret's son in marriage, so that her father might be reconciled with the House of Lancaster, and King Henry might be restored to his throne. It was too monstrous for her to believe. Her newly intended husband had always been referred to by her father as the Duke of Somerset's bastard! Her father, marrying her to the French Queen's bastard! At first she had watched him closely to see if he had gone suddenly mad. Her father, who had risked his life Heaven knew how many times for the House of York, after more than twenty years of loyalty, would embrace his deadliest enemies and kill his friends. That was what it meant now: the deaths of King Edward and his brother Richard. King Edward, whose mentor from childhood Warwick had been; Richard, who had lived with them as a son, as her brother. Richard was seventeen. She did not want to imagine his death. She could not understand how her father might live within the carcase of his old self, doing as he did. To Anne the whole business seemed so unreal. Her father's fool got up to antics less strange.

There was nothing real beyond Exeter quay, and the sun falling on her face. It felt warm as summer. She supposed that she might get freckles from sitting in it. Not many, just a dusting over her nose like pollen. Until forced to join in the encroaching muddle, she wanted to stay in the sun. It lulled her further into the feeling that all this was happening to someone else.

It was the tenth of April, and the west country wallowed in spring as in a bath of warm, scented water. The town gardens were crowded with flourishing, colourful flowers, the orchards canopied with blossom of apple, pear, plum, medlar and cherry. Under the sagging, frothy branches the citizens had set out their

hives, and the bees were at work everywhere, even straying
down to the harbour. Anne squinted as one skimmed past the
end of her nose. The quay stank of old fish baskets, tar and
pumped-out bilges, with now and then a charnel reek from raw
hides or wool fells. There was a ship flying pennants with the
castle emblem of Castile, loading bales of Devon cloth. A crane
dumped chests of something very heavy in its hold, probably tin
ingots. Great earthen jars of Spanish salad oil stood awaiting
collection by the Exeter grocers, side by side with hogsheads of
wine, like groups of big-bellied friars. Over on the far bank of
the river, repairs to the quayside were going on. The dull thud-
ding of a beetle driving piles dominated all the other hubbub.
Men were working in the water without their hose, their pink
bottoms sticking up in the air. The buildings in the harbour, the
warehouses, were of glowing rust-coloured stone. The colours in
the west country were warm, like the climate. Anne had been
surprised to see fields so green so early in the year; in the north
things never looked really green until the end of May. The pastures near Exeter were a luscious green, like brand new silk velvet, fold upon fold, a draper's dream. The cattle were plump already; no winter-starved beasts here. In the sweeps of
ploughland, in the town fields, the earth was an extraordinary
colour, red as a new crock. The sprouting corn grew like cress on
red-wrinkled cloth.

A whistle shrilled nearby and Anne jumped. She would have
to go on board soon. The ship, a fast low-built carvel, newly
fitted out for the Earl of Warwick's fleet, waited with furled
sails, gulls perching in the rigging or diving for the rubbish the
sailors slung overboard. There was a man up in the crow's nest,
shouting across to one of the other ships. A great many people
all around were shouting. As if from a distance, she heard her
mother calling her name, and she got dazedly to her feet.

The carvel sailed on the outgoing tide at about four o'clock.
Luckily the wind favoured them, a deceptively soft and coaxing
springtime wind. As the ship left the river Exe, darkness was
falling and the sun melted away in yellow lines like liquid butter
into slices of grey cloud. They followed the coast down to Dartmouth, because Warwick refused to leave his ships of war that

were berthed there, for King Edward to appropriate for his own use.

Below deck, the Countess ordered her servants about ineffectually. As most of them had much experience of embarking on ships, and of the stowing of gear into impossibly small spaces so that what was required should not be at the bottom of the pile, things went on as usual without much heed being paid to her. When they had finished, however, it was evident that the ship was too small. The cabin which the Countess and her daughters were to occupy might allow the entry of six persons crammed together like red herrings, but allowed only half of them to sit at one time. Anne knew her mother was terrified that the travelling from Warwick, the jolting about in a lumbering chariot, and the sea voyage, might send Isabel into labour before her time. The Countess's own experience of childbirth had increased her fear. Like she had been herself, Isabel was queasy in pregnancy, prey to all sorts of fears, her small-boned body overtaxed. However, the journey now to Calais was short, and the Countess hoped that if the weather held there was every chance of her daughter being settled on dry land and having a week's lying-in before the child arrived.

The largest and most comfortable space in the cabin was of course given to Isabel. Anne looked at her sister, who was lying back on all the cushions and bolsters they could muster. She was doughy pale, her small, even features marred by puffiness. The mound of her belly seemed enormous in proportion to the rest of her. Surely she wouldn't get any bigger in the next four weeks; she had the look of a bladder ready to go off pop. Anne thought: supposing I look like that with a baby on the way when I am married. How could her father demand that she marry and risk carrying Edward of Lancaster's baby? What would he think when she was bloated with poor crazy King Henry's grandchild until it looked as if she'd need a wheelbarrow to carry the thing? She told herself every day that Queen Margaret would refuse to hear of it. Margaret of Anjou, her father had once said, was as obstinate and proud as the Pope's mule. In the matter of this marriage, Anne could expect no support from her mother, whom she knew to be frightened of Queen Margaret, and who would never speak out against her husband's wishes.

Anne sometimes, not very often, felt sorry for her mother. The great Earl of Warwick, whose father had sired four sons and six daughters, and his grandfather Heaven knew how many of either, had only two little daughters as heirs. Maybe it was because her mother felt useless and ashamed that she *was* so useless. Also, she seemed never able to forget that she was two years older than her husband, and in consequence looked it. That insipid fair colouring was unfortunate, and the very fine hair so pretty in young girls became faded and wispy on ladies of forty.

Isabel looked like her mother, especially now, when she was unwell. Clarence seemed to like her very much, and spent prodigally on jewels and fine clothes for her, so that her adornments almost, but not quite, matched those of his brother's Queen. He did not run after other girls—at least not yet. Anne found her brother-in-law as changeable as the weather, and not easy to know. He took no more notice of her than of her sister's shadow.

Clarence came below deck to see his wife and found her in no state to take much notice of him. She kept dropping into a doze, which was disconcerting. He had begun to look scared and mutinous. He had better keep out of her father's way, Anne thought. Warwick tolerated no mutiny from anyone of either sex, on board ship or on land. If Clarence got in the way of the crew, then royal Duke or not, he could expect to be sent scuttling with an angry blast on a whistle.

Anne, desperate to escape the stifling, lantern-lit cupboard of the cabin, said, "My lady mother, may I go up on deck now? It's so stuffy here."

"Yes—no. Anne, you will be in the way up there. It's too late. I want you here." The Countess was flushed and flustered. Wisps of greying hair escaped from her cap.

"I feel sick." Anne fully meant to sound both pathetic and threatening. "If I could breathe some fresh air. . . ."

Her mother gave way. She did not want people being sick in the cabin just yet. Anne had never been ill on a ship; that she should start to feel squeamish on a night of comparative calm was annoying. Sometimes her mother suspected in Anne a contrariness which needed firmer handling than she felt able to give. It was useless to expect any aid from her father; the Countess dared not trouble her husband with his daughters' problems. She looked distractedly around, hoping to make a little more space in the cabin. "Would your Grace take your sister on deck for a little while. Isabel needs sleep."

Clarence did as his mother-in-law said, with none too good a humour. He went up the steps first, then leaned down to give Anne a hand, but she preferred to keep both hands to herself, using one to hoist herself up and the other to cope with her skirts. She hauled herself out into the fresh salt air with relief. It was a moonlit night, but horn lanterns hung everywhere. The ship's three masts were heavy with sail. Her father was probably up there in the poop, where there were even more lanterns and men. Whatever else had been forgotten, the Earl of Warwick's streamer had been hoisted from the main mast head, the wind tugging it to point the way to France. The bear and ragged staff meant that the Captain of Calais and master of the Channel was at sea again and did not hide the fact, though he had been proclaimed a hunted rebel.

"The shipmen steer by the Seven Stars," Anne said to her brother-in-law, who stood staring over the side to starboard at the land. "My father's men always call them the Little Bear, for good luck—the Bear in the sky will guide his brother on the sea."

"They should fly the royal arms of England, and the black bull of Clarence. I am on this ship." George sounded petulant.

Anne nearly opened her mouth and said, "But you're a passenger, not the commander!" but stopped in time. George was so easily offended; he could cut off his flow of good humour and fun very suddenly. Anne thought that when he was a little boy, he might well have stamped his feet and had tantrums.

Footsteps approached down the deck, and her father joined Clarence at the rail. The master and his mate waited at a respectful distance. Warwick said, "Your Grace, when we leave Dartmouth I intend to sail for Southampton. My ship the *Trinity* lies at anchor in the Hamble river. I am loath to leave that prize for Edward. There are so few ships of over three hundred tons burden in England that I'll not let mine fall into Woodville hands!"

"My lord, is it necessary for us to put in at Dartmouth? It will delay us."

"George, it is necessary for us to have every ship we can lay our hands on. Remember, we are coming back."

Clarence said nothing in reply to this. Anne thought that he was thinking of when they did come back, when Henry VI was King again, and not him, King George, as her father had originally planned.

Warwick turned his eyes upon his younger daughter. "Anne," he said, "bed."

Anne, obedient as a little dog, went below, standing for a moment with her head sticking out of the hatchway. Her father went back down the deck, lightfooted and sure as a sailor on his own ship. He was always relaxed on board ship; even now, a fugitive, he looked confident, like a cat strolling round his territory.

When Anne woke, the ship was moving. It must be next morning, and they were leaving the river Dart on the outgoing tide. She lay quiet, for her mother and sister were not yet stirring. Isabel was snoring slightly, as she had begun to do as her pregnancy advanced. The stuffy cabin was enough to make anyone snore. The place Anne slept in was so small that she had to curl up with her knees almost touching her chin. She lay looking up at the figure of St. Anne with the child Mary, which she had hung there; it went everywhere with her. She needed their help now. Not that on her father's ships she had ever been worried that they might sink. Her father had his own book of navigation, like most captains, which listed all the landmarks, depths and tides of the English, French and Breton coasts. He could have sailed the ship through Channel waters as well as the Exeter master. He had to do that once; he had acted as helmsman from Exmouth to Calais, helping King Edward to escape his enemies.

They heard Mass in her father's cabin. A corner had been made to serve as a chapel. The chaplain himself had to sleep on a mattress in a space suitable for a large dog. Warwick's chaplains had to get used to this. Then a cogboat was lowered and the Earl was rowed away to board one of the other ships. The carvel of Exeter stood off the Isle of Wight while Warwick sailed to the mouth of the Solent, hoping to slip in to collect his great warship the *Trinity*. The next day he came back, and there was one less ship in his company. Everyone had expected to see the painted sails and high poop of the *Trinity*, but it was not there. Anthony Woodville, now Earl Rivers and eager to avenge his father's death at Warwick's hands, had come boldly out of Southampton and driven the Earl's ships away, capturing one of them and all the men in it. Warwick raved of how the upstart Anthony had pirated his best ship, which was not really true, as Woodville had only been doing his duty to King Edward.

On Palm Sunday, they came within sight of Calais. All that remained of the great English conquests in France was a few miles of marsh and sluice more fit for frogs than men, the two fortresses of Guines and Hammes, and this town, built where no sane nation should have built a town, on treacherous sand. The sea was a more expensive enemy to keep at bay than the French. From it, Calais looked impressive. Nearly a mile of high defensive wall stretched between the castle and the Beauchamp Tower, and the wall was studded with gun-holes; each one had shutters painted with the cross of St. George. Behind the wall were the steep tiled roofs of houses, the towers of the two churches and the Woolstaplers' Hall. The church bells' pealing came to them over the sea as close as if they walked in the streets. In front of the wall, dozens of wool merchants' ships were moored at the quay and jetties. Nearer still, on Rysbank, the sandspit that enclosed the harbour, the tower fort bristled with guns. The shutters were open, and the muzzles poked menacingly forth. The Earl of Warwick was proud of the defences of Calais; he had seen that the guns were the newest and best that German or Flemish smiths could forge, and there were nearly two hundred of them, of iron and brass.

When his ships had anchored, Warwick sent men in a boat to warn his Lieutenant, Lord Wenlock, of his arrival. Before they had time to row back, Calais fired its guns. Anne first noticed that the red and white crosses in the walls had disappeared. Then came the crump of firing, the belches of smoke, the fountaining splashes as stone balls plunged into the sea within a hundred yards of the ship on which stood the Captain of Calais himself. The men came back, rowing for dear life, and as they shinned up the rope ladder, they looked frightened. This was because they brought the news that Warwick's Lieutenant had refused to admit him to Calais. The King's proclamation had already arrived there, and Lord Wenlock dared not ignore it, for the town was full of King Edward's men, over whom he had no control.

"Wenlock is in his dotage!" Warwick raged. "When I put in to Calais I'll have his head!"

It did no good. Rysbank tower opened fire, and this time the shots fell alarmingly near to Warwick's ships, and they had to withdraw. Once out of range, he downed anchor again and prepared to wait for Wenlock to change his mind. Below in the cabin, Anne saw her mother's face become more frightened than ever, and Isabel's dissolve into stark terror. The Countess was alarmed enough even to challenge her husband.

"Richard, you see your daughter's condition. What will we do if the baby comes? Surely Wenlock cannot refuse to allow us ashore, at least?"

Warwick turned on his wife a glance of barely concealed contempt, for her meagre understanding of their situation. "Whether Wenlock refuses or not, how can I allow you ashore here? I cannot send hostages into the hands of my enemies. Do you suppose that you would be anything but prisoners? You'd probably be shipped straight back to England."

Anne was astonished that her mother found the spirit to retort. "King Edward," the Countess said, flushed and trembling, "would do your daughter less harm than any more tossing about on this ship!"

To this show of defiance by a usually submissive wife, Warwick made reply by turning his back and striding off to the other end of the ship. Isabel began crying hysterically and said that her father did not care what happened to her and her baby, now he no longer wanted George to be King. But neither she nor Clarence dared say this to his face.

They stood off Calais for several more days. Warwick sent more messages to Lord Wenlock, but the answer was always the same. Listening to the fulminations of both her father and her brother-in-law—for Clarence was indignant that Wenlock dared treat him no better than Warwick—Anne wondered how much longer they intended to wait. It was becoming increasingly uncomfortable on board for the women. Anne disliked going for days without washing adequately, and it was a struggle to extract fresh clothes and linen from the wedged mass of their baggage. Worse were the arrangements for their bodily needs; the sailors used buckets on ropes to sling in the sea. Anne's discomfort increased because her time in the month had arrived. Her mother kept reproving her for snapping.

The chaplain, not for the first time during his service with Warwick, prepared to celebrate Holy Week at sea. The cook put lines over the side and brought up fresh fish, which was their only relief. Anne had watched with distaste when horrible great stockfish had been brought on board at Exeter, dirty linen colour and hard as boards, looking like hides hung up to dry.

Soon the men were able to forget their predicament in action. A band of ships belonging to Thomas Neville, the bastard son of Warwick's uncle Lord Fauconberg, managed to join them. He was a fierce, jaunty little man, who loved nothing better than acting the sea reiver, and was the only person Anne had ever seen treat her father to a conspiratorial wink. He had slipped away from King Edward's fleet, believing that Nevilles should stick together. He announced that a fleet of Burgundian merchant ships was approaching, and what better opportunity for seizing some valuable plunder? They'd make a living on any sea, Fauconberg boasted. Together, Nevilles would show King Edward and Duke Charles that no one, English or Fleming or French, could beat them.

While the Earl and his cousin indulged in their successful piracy, a storm blew up. This was not severe enough to endanger the ships, but it was enough to do what everyone had dreaded since they had left Warwick. Isabel went into labour.

Whenever the ship pitched or rolled, anyone who was not holding on to a fixed part of the cabin was hurled from one side of it to the other. The women pressed round Isabel, trying to keep her squeezed in a more or less stationary position with their own bodies. The baggage was tumbling about, thud-thudding from side to side. Anne shut her eyes and hung on to a wooden post with both arms. Each wallow of the ship banged her body against its squared side. When Isabel let out the first shriek, she opened her eyes. Her sister was being sick, partly into a basin held by the midwife. It was dark in the cabin, the lanterns lurching about and spluttering out, and the shadows opening and shutting like huge jaws. The noise the ship made was terrifying; it creaked and groaned and ground its teeth as if it were about to fall apart.

One of the midwives, feeling about among the bedclothes, said to the Countess, "It's the waters, madam! The child is coming. There's no stopping it now."

Anne saw that her mother was almost speechless, and reaching hastily for another basin. The women turned and shooed the Duke of Clarence out of the cabin. No man could possibly be allowed anywhere near a childbirth. Not that George had been able to do much in the way of holding his wife steady, he too often needed to resort to a basin himself.

"Lady Anne," said the one midwife who was not also being sick, and thus likely to be left in command of the situation. "Will you pop your head out and ask someone to tell the cook to boil water—as much as he has pans for."

"Blessed Mary, help me in my need," wailed Anne's mother. "My lord husband is pillaging while his daughter suffers! *I* will send to Lord Wenlock again." The Countess was beside herself. Anne had never seen her really angry before. "Surely the cowardly old man cannot refuse us in this extremity?"

It's too late, Anne thought, as she moved obediently to the hatchway. The sailors cannot launch a boat in this, and how can we move into harbour—the wind is against us. By the time we'd got Isabel on land, everything would be over. She was very glad to be able to put her head out in the air. She was luckily not being seasick herself, but the smell of other people's vomit was—ugh—enough to ensure that she would be if she stayed below much longer.

Anne sent a scared-looking sailor lurching along the deck to the cook. Outside, the wind was still blowing a gale, but the rain had stopped. Huge clouds were bowling through the sky, toppling over each other in a race to reach England.

She forced herself back in to the cabin. She never knew how long Isabel's labour lasted. No one had so much as glanced at the hour glass, which had smashed in the storm anyway.

"Push him out, my lady!" roared the midwife encouragingly. Anne understood why it was called labour. She dug for towels and sheets in the baggage and passed them to where they were most needed. Ever afterwards, Anne would shiver at the sound of ripping linen.

The baby was born dead.

"It's a boy," someone said hopelessly.

The woman stood holding it, her arms bloody to the elbow. The baby was all red and shiny. Anne's stomach threatened at last to escape her, though the ship had become steady, unnoticed. The women washed the baby, and the Countess wrapped it in the Chrisom cloth. It was a perfect child, not too big or too little. Fair duckdown gleamed on the applesized head. It should have been alive.

Isabel was still pouring blood. They kept stuffing dry towels between her legs. There was a hideous pile of sodden sheets and towels growing on the floor, dark, like liver. The cabin stank so foully it had become unendurable. Anne turned about and without a word struggled up the steps and out of the hatchway. No one noticed her going. Once on deck, she leant over the rail and was sick. She trembled and cringed, heaved and hiccupped, tears spurting from her eyes, though she was not aware of actually crying. The picture of Isabel, pretty, fastidious, Isabel, with her knees up and straddling and all that stuff splurging out, screaming and, between screams, vomiting into her own hair, had been like something that only happened in Hell. Anne had seen her own dogs, and a mare, give birth, but that had been easy in comparison. The bitch had seen to most of the clearing up herself. Animals made very little noise, too. Anne was not the first to be brutally enlightened. Plenty of girls of thirteen had babies.

A sound of noisy masculine weeping managed to distract her out of her own nightmare. Sniffing and wiping her nose on her sleeve—her handkerchief had got lost—she saw her brother-in-

law Clarence sitting on a coil of wet rope, his head in his hands,
bawling like little boy lost. Someone had told him already. Anne
was almost surprised that he cared so much. Men liked to have a
son for the first baby. He kept moaning that he wanted to die.
Then as if acting on a sudden impulse, he leapt up and flung
himself down the hatchway. In a minute he emerged, clutching
the little chest of baby clothes, which had been ready for the
dressing of his son. This he proceeded to hurl into the sea. For
one horrified moment Anne thought he was going to throw himself after it, but he merely sagged against the rail, hanging over
it as desperately as she had done herself. Maybe he had intended to throw the dead child itself into the sea. She did not
like to watch him; handsome people looked worse suffering their
indignities, somehow, than ugly ones. Instead, she watched the
chest lurch away, filling gradually with water until it sank. It
was very early morning. Isabel's labour must have started the
previous afternoon. All the sea and sky were palest grey and
chill, milky and blurred as if draped with damp cheese cloth. The
church bells of Calais were jangling out over the sea. It was
Easter Day.

The little garments had not sunk. They floated away in a long
line. A tiny shirt, the arms extended, buoyant on a bubble of air,
looked as if occupied by a headless, legless mite. Anne shud-
dered. Yards and yards of swaddling bands danced along the
waves, longer than a grand streamer. Three dozen napkins went
more sluggishly. Minute socks were scattered like petals in a
pond. Bibs and bonnets, trailing ribbons, went the same way.
Everything went the same way. Clarence would soon see his
firstborn son cast into the sea like its unworn clothes.

The storm had died. In the calm, her father and half-uncle
came back, crowing like cockerels in triumph, their ships loaded
to the waterline with booty. Fauconberg bounced onto his nephew's ship only to have his mood of self-congratulation shattered by the news. Warwick's wife, half dead with seasickness
and exhaustion could scarcely bring herself to speak to them.
Lord Wenlock sent a boat out from Calais with a cask of wine.
What use was wine now? It wouldn't help Isabel. Besides, they
had plenty on board. But Warwick did not send the gift back.

The baby was sewn up in canvas and buried in the sea. Odd, Anne thought, the Duke of Clarence's son lying at the bottom near Calais for ever and ever. Her first nephew. She supposed there would be others. Isabel would have to go through all that again. Warwick watched his grandson disappear, his face expressionless. Only a few months before, he had planned to make that child a new Prince of Wales. Now he was intent upon remaking the original Prince, Edward of Lancaster. Clarence, who never did anything by halves, was refusing to speak to Warwick. He didn't say much to anyone else, either. He was a picture of sulking misery.

Anne's mother spent all her time with Isabel, who did nothing but cry. A still-birth could mean months of wretchedness and tears. It would be no surprise if childbed fever set in, and if that happened, Isabel would swiftly follow her baby into death. The Earl, his youngest daughter noticed, kept away as much as he could from the women's cabin, on the excuse of inspecting the ships he had taken as prizes. Anne had never before felt so unwanted, yet she was now more important to her father than Isabel.

It was not long before King Edward caught up with them. Ships flying the cockle shell pennants of Lord Rivers were sighted, then others with a white lion on a red ground; the energetic Lord Howard had put to sea in all haste. "There goes a fine sea captain!" said Fauconberg regretfully. This, from him, was an accolade, and it proved not to be bestowed without cause. Howard flushed the Earl of Warwick out of his anchorage beside Calais, and chased him down the coast of France. As the pursuit grew hot, Warwick decided that he must rely upon his old friendship with King Louis, seek the aid of France and do his haggling with Queen Margaret on French soil. On May Day his harried fleet put in to the Seine estuary and the Earl at last landed his family at Honfleur.

Anne would have been grateful to land in the dominions of the Turk. Her legs felt as if made of soap. Isabel was too ill to walk yet. Even Clarence's long, elegant legs had to feel their way onto land. The citizens of Honfleur were suspicious at first of the English Earl and his ships of war, but when Warwick had some of his Burgundian loot brought ashore, and set up a sort of market stall to dispose of it for as many livres as he could bargain, they became more cheerful.

Once on shore, Warwick behaved as if he had received no setback. He sent messages to King Louis asking for a personal interview, as from one monarch to another. He sat in Honfleur while King Louis' envoys tried to persuade him that it was dangerous to do so. The Count of St. Pol's territory lay too near for comfort; he was a friend of the Duke of Burgundy, and therefore likely to be hostile. He was also Elizabeth Woodville's uncle. King Louis' anxiety over the Burgundian ships Warwick had seized was conveyed. King Louis insisted that they should be moved from Honfleur and moored somewhere more discreetly off the Cotentin, instead of being flaunted in waters so near Burgundy itself. Duke Charles' temper would only be inflamed by this; he was already threatening to invade France. It might be judicious for the Earl to retire to the Channel Islands, out of reach of both France and Burgundy.

Warwick had intended to cause a disturbance in the realm of France. He preferred to act the bold adventurer rather than the skulking fugitive. He would do nothing until he had talked with King Louis face to face. He planned to send his wife and daughters up the Seine to some abbey, St. Wandrille or Jumièges, while he travelled to meet the King wherever was convenient, but he changed his mind at Louis' urgent request and arranged instead that they go deeper into Normandy, to Bayeux or Caen. King Louis, allowing Warwick the victory in the first manoeuvre, agreed to a meeting.

By the end of May the Earl was ready to make the journey to the castle of Amboise in the valley of the river Loire. He would take with him his son-in-law Clarence, as much as anything to stifle the growing discontent by including him in the plans, and his brother-in-law John de Vere, Earl of Oxford, who had managed to escape from England by a different route a short while after Warwick himself.

Before he set out for Amboise, Warwick sent for Anne. It was an interview about which he had been uneasy for some time, and when she stood in front of him, he was struck both by her pathetically immature looks and the adult reserve on her face. It did nothing to make his task more pleasant. He had the honesty to resist adopting a tone of jovial reassurance, so came straight to the point.

"Anne, my plans have gone better than I expected. I am going to Amboise to talk with King Louis. After that he will summon Queen Margaret and plead my cause with her. When some satisfactory agreement has been reached, I shall come back to Normandy and prepare to return to England. You shall go to Amboise. I want you to be ready, Anne, to assume the dignity of Princess of Wales."

Anne's eyes, grey like his own, transparent and clear, but not, he thought, at this moment innocent, stared at him. Now the news she so dreaded had been finally delivered, she felt cold, but not able to say anything. She nodded.

Warwick continued, glad to meet at least silent compliance. "The Prince, whatever may have been said regarding his antecedents, is a well-educated youth, of some ability. It may be necessary in future for him to take on the direction of government before his father's death, that is, if King Henry's incapacity continues. You may be Queen of England, little daughter, sooner than you think."

The eyes looking at him widened at that. The childish bony chest jerked as if on a soundless indrawn breath. The expression was unmistakable, panic-stricken terror. It had a most unpleasant effect on Warwick. He felt like an executioner. Poor little frightened mouse, he thought involuntarily. However, he pushed on, to overcome the distressing sight of his daughter's face.

"Any daughter of mine could have expected a husband of no less rank than Duke. The highest rank of all is not so very different. It will be a proud day for a Neville. You must know this."

Anne still said nothing. Her mouth was too dry. In any case, there was little to be gained by saying anything. Nothing made her father more angry than complaint or argument. He was being gentle enough, but he would not be deflected from his purpose. On the table in front of him were his money calculations, little piles of counters in neat rows, a sheet of notes. How much from the sale of the Burgundian ships, how much in loans from King Louis, how much from Lancastrian supporters in England. He had it allotted to the last farthing and sou. She was worth nothing except to her father's ambition and Neville pride. For this he had her life for sale.

"Non! Non! Non!"

King Louis IX of France winced. Not only was it wearisome to witness once again Margaret of Anjou's obstinacy enduring into its fourth week, but she hammered her words at him threefold, as if invoking the invincible Trinity. But King Louis was a patient man, working towards his own ends.

"Madame, *ma cousine*," the King of France pointed out to the deposed Queen of England, "this will not do. You will throw away a Heaven-sent gift of aid. Monseigneur de Warwick offers men, ships, money. . . ." He ticked off each item on his stubby, peasant's fingers. "And above all, he offers himself. The people of England like him even better than King Edward. You need a man, madame," he said brutally, "to head your army, not a boy or a woman." He nearly added—and not a moon wit like your husband King Henry, either. If this woman had subtlety to temper her force of will she would be the match of a man, which was as near as he would get to admiring her toughness, but her obstinacy, like all foolishness, exasperated him.

Queen Margaret gave no one else the opportunity to answer. Her clear, imperious voice had a resonance which Louis felt sure she cultivated; it could cut across men's voices with ease. "You ask me to welcome Warwick like a long-lost brother? He is the reason why I, the Queen of England, am living on charity at St. Mihiel-en-Barrois—or here at Amboise at your expense, Majesty. . . ." Margaret often gave back as good as she got. "Why my husband, the rightful, anointed King of England"—she did not ram home the fact that Henry VI had also been anointed King of France, as she was quite capable of doing—"is a prisoner in the Tower of London, while that Yorkist stallion Edward subverts the allegiance of his true subjects. Warwick is the reason why my son, the heir of England, has lived nine years in exile and forgets his father and the realm that is his inheritance. Warwick has called me a bitch, a French bitch—a whore—and my son a bastard! My son, the grandson of Harry the Fifth and of your kinswoman, Louis! Your Majesty asks me to forgive him this? I tell you, it is impossible. The wounds he has inflicted on me will bleed till the Day of Judgement!"

"And I tell you, madame, to put the gifts of God to your own advantage." King Louis' expressive voice was distinctly curt. "I suggest that you make God's instrument, Monseigneur de Warwick, the means of restoring King Henry and yourself to the throne. That will no doubt help to staunch your wounds. You have friends who would give their lives to achieve this, but not all of them together can do what the mere name of Warwick can do. I have not asked you to love him, nothing to soil your honour."

"Your Majesty presses me too hard. I cannot and will not see him. I have no more to say. Nothing." That was clearly that. She asked his permission to withdraw, but she went as proudly as an empress.

Louis turned to fondle the greyhound that sniffed familiarly at his hose. "Many rain drops wear away even granite," he observed, apparently to the dog. "She will talk to him. Soon we shall see the Queen of England and my friend Monseigneur de Warwick truly married! Then he will win England." He did not voice his true thought: win it for me, for France, and bring us to the first fruitful alliance for centuries.

Instead, he said, "Why, of course my dear cousin Henry of Lancaster will be restored. He has been anointed in France with the sacred coronation oil of St. Remy—God will undoubtedly fight for him!" He crossed himself piously, then winked and let out a great hoot of laughter. His dog jumped up happily to lick his nose. The only response to this outburst of mirth was a few polite smirks from the exiles. The English often thought King Louis' jokes were in bad taste.

King Louis, as he was accustomed to do, continued to spin his web, to bind together the protagonists of his schemes. Warwick, waiting at Vendôme, began to find his son-in-law Clarence unendurably quarrelsome, and suggested that he should go back to Normandy and make himself useful in readying their expedition to England, for at a conference with Queen Margaret, he could only be a nuisance. To Warwick's surprise, George of Clarence did as suggested and went off in a huff to Valonges, where they agreed to meet later.

No one remembered a very tiny fly helplessly enmeshed upon the edge of King Louis' web. On the few occasions when he thought about his little daughter, Warwick projected her image into the future. He saw her as Princess of Wales, then crowned Queen; his grandson would be King of England. To the child he had watched grow, who had claimed more of his affection than he would admit, he scarcely gave thought. He was not a man to dwell in the past; it fell away from him like a discarded cloak.

King Louis, as he invariably did, succeeded in what he had planned. In the hot, high summer days of July, he set out with Queen Margaret, by barge down the river Loire, to her father's ducal town of Angers. Louis, on tenterhooks, sweated to keep her to her word, reading rebellion in her face every hour of the day when the Earl of Warwick was to come to the castle of Angers.

The meeting took place in an inner private room. Warwick went straight down on his knees on the bare, tiled floor. Louis disliked this, but in the circumstances would have done the same himself. It gave Margaret satisfaction, and thus might work to their advantage.

Margaret, her whole being rigid with proud distaste, turned towards Warwick as if pivoting on unbearably rusty hinges. She directed her gaze at some point above his head, and one might think she saw snakes rising from it.

"You, my lord . . . you . . ." She could not bring herself to actually utter his name. King Louis put his hand on the image of the Virgin at his neck, for reassurance.

"I do not need, my lord, to remind you of the wrongs you have done me. You are here to beg—to beg my forgiveness—for the unforgivable. What have you to say?"

"Madame, *la Reine*, I am here to ask your pardon for the wrongs I have done you. But I ask you to consider this also. In the first days of our quarrel, I also suffered wrongs. My family suffered. I care for my family, madame, as you do for yours. I took action against my enemies. No more than any man might who has suffered wrong. I have come to ask forgiveness, and to offer it in return."

King Louis saw Margaret's pride flare. Warwick was bolder than he had expected. One did not reprove this woman for her past conduct. Yet she would have to concede that some truth was spoken. Warwick's speech was coolly reasoned. Louis inwardly applauded; he could have done no better himself.

"You are a bold man, Monseigneur de Warwick." Margaret sounded as if she addressed Lucifer himself. "Where does Edward of York stand in all this? You will betray him?"

"Once I risked all for Edward. He rewarded me with a thumb to the nose, and my brother of Northumberland with a magpie's nest. I admit, if he had treated us well, I should still be at his side. There you have my honest confession, madame. But the breach is irreparable. I come to you repenting my desertion of my true King. In return for your pardon, I offer my loyalty. In return for just treatment, which I never had from Edward, I offer my service to Lancaster for as long as that shall be given me. I offer you my daughter for your son, so that our heirs may rule England. These are not soft, dissembling words, madame. I give you the truth as I see it."

"You cannot have a more honest proposition, *ma chère cousine*," said King Louis, hopefully.

Margaret had her last fling. "My son shall never get heirs on Neville stock! Your loyalty stinks of sewers! Judas knocks at my door. Edward of York is for sale. How do I know Henry of Lancaster may not be hawked for a higher price in future?"

Warwick did not reply. He knelt on, arms at sides, unmoving, expressionless. He had delivered his terms. He waited for Margaret to void herself of her venom and give him a direct answer. Whether it was the encroaching dusk, or increasing strain, furrowed lines showed moment by moment deeper in his cheeks. He eats a bitter fruit, King Louis thought—and Heaven defend him from cramp!

Margaret let her enemy kneel, while she bit her lips and frowned. "If I, whom you have made a pauper, find your thirty pieces of silver, what pledge have I that your wares are sound?"

"The word of the Most Christian King, of his Majesty King Louis of France, madame," said Louis with the utmost gravity. "My word, upon the most sacred relics in France." Then coaxingly, as if to a dog, "Marguerite, your answer?"

More minutes dragged by. The room was almost dark. Warwick's face grew more deathly. His blood beat in his ears. Was the French bitch going to keep him on his knees until he fainted? King Louis wanted to scratch; remaining seated for too long irritated his piles.

"Very well," said the proudest woman in Europe. The darkness seemed to lighten, the air to cool. "I will work with you, Monseigneur. But I repeat, my son shall not marry your daughter. There is no honour nor profit to us in such a match. Forget it. My pardon in return for loyal service. Restore King Henry VI and you will be justly rewarded. But let this be understood. Any betrayal, and I will hunt you, Monseigneur de Warwick, to the death.

"Now, your homage. Then I will leave you to the company of France."

King Louis watched while Margaret, unable to keep her hatred from her face, let Warwick put his hands between hers and swear his fealty. Then she left them, regal, head held high, as if she had made no concession at all.

Warwick was still on his knees. King Louis hastened to help him up, all brotherly solicitude and triumph. "Ah, my friend, my friend, we are as one!" He was grinning until his odd, curling upper lip seemed to stretch from ear to ear. "Give me two more days, *mon ami,* and *La Reine Marguerite* will agree to the marriage of her son with your daughter!"

The Web

July — September 1470

Reioice, ye realmes of England and of Fraunce,
A braunche that sprang oute of the floure-de-lys,
Blode of Seint Edward and Seint Lowys,
God hath this day sent in governaunce.

John Lydgate,
Roundel on Coronation of Henry VI (1429)

The abbey cloister smelled of cool shade under Caen stone
arches, hot sun on new-mown grass, and the farmyard on the
other side of the wall. Anne was allowed to walk within the
guests' precincts, but not on any account to stray beyond them,
or into the monks' quarters. She supposed also that now that she
had become such an important person, there was some danger of
being snatched away, by the agents of King Edward, or Duke
Charles of Burgundy, or the Count of St. Pol, or anyone else who
might profit from possessing her.

Today the bees had swarmed on the abbey bell, so that it
could not be rung for Sext, and a monk had to climb up a ladder
to the bell turret and bring them down. Even the brother hoeing
weeds from rows of turnips stopped his stirring of the dusty soil
to watch, and the one who was scything the lawns put off half
his task until the afternoon. The monk who looked after the bees
came out wearing a straw hat with a veil, gloves on his hands
and his sleeves tied tight with string so the bees could not fly up
them. Teetering on top of the ladder, he had calmly swept the

swarm, hanging like a heaving bladder on the bell clapper, into a basket. When he put the bees into an empty skep, he looked grumpy, for he hated late July swarms; all the honey had been taken from the old hive before the bees came out, and they might not last the winter in their new home.

After the hour of midday prayer, the monks resumed their tasks of hoeing, scything, hedge clipping, and gathering the fruit from the cherry trees. Anne hoped that some might reach the guest table. Wasps buzzed over the maggoty fruit which had fallen on the ground. A cock flew up from the farmyard to perch on the wall. He craned his neck about, surveying his kingdom and eyeing Anne, his glorious red comb and wattles all a-wobble, the sun making his russet feathers multi-hued as a pheasant's. Like Chanticleer in the tale, Anne thought. Chanticleer let out a lordly crow, presented his magnificently feathered rear, emptied his bowels down the wall and flapped off. After the monks had been called to Vespers and returned, and the chiming of cow and goat bells told her that the animals were being driven to the byre for milking, Anne was summoned by her mother. This might mean one of several things. The Countess was always indignant when Anne was not immediately to hand, firmly believing that young girls should not be left to their own devices. She might be expected to amuse Isabel, who was now trailing about indoors with a white, feeble look on her, too listless to play at board games. Anne and Isabel had long ago discovered that they had no special interest in each other's company. Anne had at times been a solitary little girl, as far as this was possible within the teeming, often changing population of her father's household.

Her mother was twittering more than usual. Anne suspected the cause of this immediately; it was inevitable.

"Anne," the Countess said, "word has come from your father. His—negotiations have been successful. You have been betrothed already, by a proxy, to the Prince. We are to go at once to Amboise, as guests of King Louis and Queen Charlotte, to meet the . . ." she swallowed, and avoided her daughter's eyes, "Queen Margaret, and the—er—Prince." She paused, overcome by her own nervousness at this prospect, seeking refuge in irrelevancies.

Queen Margaret had always been to York and Neville alike, a bogey, a witch in the wood to frighten children with.

"We are nearly into August. It is a long hot journey in this summer weather. Isabel is to stay here in Normandy; the Duke of Clarence is coming back with your father to join her. She will go home to England as soon as it is safe to do so." Anne saw her mother's eyes become tearful; even she, the timid wife would have preferred to risk going back to England with her husband.

"How long will it be . . . ?" Anne said, in a little voice, like the rustle of leaves.

Her mother's red-rimmed eyes had a vague, unhappy look. "You mean before your—marriage? Who am I to know that? It depends entirely upon the success of your father's enterprise in England. Queen Margaret will not hear of it until her husband— King Henry—is secure on his throne again. And, of course, a dispensation has to be obtained from Rome. Your uncle the Archbishop of York may be able to see to that."

So it was not to be at once. Anne's fear receded a little. Supposing her father failed to win England? That might mean no marriage, but it might also mean years of exile and poverty, even if he did not die in the attempt. She knew that she did not want her father to fail, but she did not want him to destroy King Edward, either. She still hoped that Queen Margaret would change her mind, and that the Earl would have to look elsewhere for his daughter's husband.

King Louis sent envoys to escort Warwick's wife and daughter southwards. Anne had plenty of opportunity on the journey to look about her at the realm of France. She always liked to see the nature of the places through which she travelled, unless she was in a chariot and the weather very bad so that the leather curtains had to be closed. France looked quite different from England, though the fields and orchards of Normandy were in some ways so similar. The castles they passed were strange shapes, with high conical turrets, and all were armed with strong defences. There were so many despoiled houses and villages, in ruins for years, and fields that grew such luxuriant weeds that they must be good land wasted. The great war with England had been over for twenty years, but since then France had been torn

apart by civil strife. Her father said that it was only in the last
few years since King Louis had begun to rule that things had improved. The countryside seemed peaceful enough, but their
party was guarded by a far greater number of soldiers than
would have been usual in England. There were less people than
at home, and even where the land looked most prosperous, the
poor looked poorer, poorer even than the people near the borders of England and Scotland. France was so big; they had to
travel such a long way, and that was not even halfway to the
real south. It was hot, though some of the time they passed
through the shade of great forests and sandy heaths thick with
pines.

When they were nearing Amboise they saw yet more soldiers
on the road. Though King Louis would ride anywhere in his
realm almost unattended, and often ate his meals in the huts of
poor peasants, and would speak to anyone who interested him,
he could not endure being spied upon in his own dwelling place.
Most of all he hated the pilfering of game from his hunting forests. Amboise, Anne was told, had the finest hunting forest in all
France. The place itself was no more than a village beside the
river Loire. The vineyards were good there, sloping in tenderly
cared-for rows down to the wide, placid river. On the south side
of the Loire, rising out of a rocky cliff, was the castle, white-
walled like a battlement of sugar. A fine stone bridge had been
built for the convenience of the King, where a statue of Our
Lady watched over travellers, and swans floated beneath the
arches, while fish plopped in the water, making spreading circles
of ripples all over the river.

King Louis himself came out from the castle and some distance along the road to greet his guests, which was done with
more ceremony than he usually afforded women, as he wished
to demonstrate that he honoured his friend the Earl of Warwick's family.

In front of the King marched the hundred archers of his Scots
guard, as flamboyant a troop of soldiers as could be seen anywhere. The sons of all the noble families in Scotland had done
service with the Kings of France for generations. Instead of just
livery colours with badges, such as King Edward's men wore, the

Scots guard had jackets of red, white and green stripes, embroidered all over with gold, a picture of St. Michael putting Lucifer to the sword on their chests, and their helmets had nodding plumes of red, white and green, upright, like a cock's comb. The Captain who marched in front was grander than the others and covered in fluttering gold spangles. How they must have hated the welcome given to Warwick and his family, for he had been no friend to the Scots.

Anne had to come forward to kiss the French King's hand. She was too shy to raise her eyes to look at him while doing this but afterwards caught a glimpse of his profile, and was astonished that a man's nose could stick out quite so far.

Margaret of Anjou did not appear, though she had been a guest of the King at Amboise since leaving Angers after her meeting with Warwick. This was a deliberate slight and was not meant to pass unnoticed.

Queen Charlotte, Louis' wife, into whose care Anne and her mother were delivered, was thirty years old, fair and bovine, and running disastrously to fat. She looked shiny-nosed from the heat as if she had just come from the bakehouse. She folded Anne in a motherly embrace, which was kindly meant, if a little damp and sweaty. Her apartments, to which the guests were borne off, seemed remarkable for numbers of chattering women and an almost complete absence of men; King Louis had no interest in the day-to-day company of his wife.

The first thing Anne noticed about the castle of Amboise was the smell of dog. There seemed to be a strong general animal odour but dog predominated. Anne had been brought up in places where dogs of all sizes lived with the humans, but they had been trained not to mess indoors. This French castle reeked of years of dog over-population and lax habits; Anne decided to walk warily, especially when she went barefoot to bed.

That evening Anne and her mother were invited by Queen Charlotte to inspect the Dauphin. He was one month old and not thriving. His mother became alarmed every time he wailed or puked, which was often. He was a pitiably ugly baby, stick-limbed, bladder-headed and slobbery. One was expected to pay him compliments. About a score of nurses fussed over him, try-

ing to get him to take the breast, but he was a bad feeder and
brought back everything from one or the other. The Queen
of France changed her messy little Dauphin herself, which
disgusted the Countess and amazed Anne. She did not expect a
Queen to sit in her own nursery, placidly unwinding yards of
soaked swaddling bands; imagine King Edward's beautiful wife
doing such a thing!

Queen Charlotte looked up from the malodorous bundle, and
said sweetly, over her son's thin bawling, "I hope you will be
happy here with us, my lady Warwick; you must be so anxious
for your husband. If there is anything at all that worries you,
and we may remedy, you must tell my lord the King or myself at
once. We will do all we can for you and your daughter." Then
she said, "Of course, you are aware that we do have other guests
at Amboise." She paused. "Madame *Marguerite la Reine*," she
said flatly, "is indisposed."

Anne could see that Charlotte disapproved of Margaret of Anjou's lack of courtesy. It was also clear that she disapproved of
the business which had brought her ill-sorted and unwilling
guests together at her court, for she looked at Anne and said,
"*Ah, ma pauvre petite,* while you are here, child, you shall be
treated as my own daughter."

Though the Queen could not openly voice her disapproval,
many people at the French court were willing to do so. Marriages were, of course, to be arranged according to the best
profit, but there were limits beyond which it was shameful to go,
and where one could incur the displeasure of God and all Christian people. Anne's own intended marriage was, she realized,
frowned upon by almost everyone except King Louis and her
own father. Perhaps, she thought, in disillusion, everyone else
was eager to disapprove because those two were the sole
beneficiaries. . . . She felt like tainted goods put on the market
by dishonest hucksters.

Queen Charlotte and her two sisters, Bona and Marie, did
their best to entertain. Bona was the one Anne's father had intended to marry to King Edward, the scheme whose failure had
begun all their troubles. Her stodgy looks would not have found
favour. Besides the Dauphin Charles, Charlotte had two daugh-

ters: Anne, who was nine and quick as a lizard, and Jeanne, three years younger. Little Jeanne was deformed. She had one leg much shorter than the other, a hump back, and one eye which turned alarmingly outwards, as if she were continually squinting over her shoulder. The other eye was soft and brown, with the longest lashes Anne had ever seen. One caught glimpses of beggars in the street with horrible deformities, but Anne had never seen such things at close quarters, especially in a child. She tried not to show that she was frightened and revolted. Jeanne's face seemed prematurely old and wizened like a little ape, such as fashionable ladies kept on a chain or carried in their sleeves. She had the eager-to-please manner that should have belonged to a pretty little girl, but her prattle only caused people to shudder and turn away. What made matters worse was that, like her sister, she was quick and forward for her age and already understood her disadvantage. She took to Anne at once, hobbling towards her, offering a huge peach, pink and gold and furry-skinned, without a blemish. But when Anne cut its flesh away from the stone with a small knife, there was a nasty fat grub wriggling inside. She could not eat it, and felt herself dangerously near to tears. Supposing, when she was married, she should have a baby misshapen like this child; it was hard to know which was worse, this ugliness, or the incomprehension of an idiot. Women had children like these, and sometimes they did not die, but remained an everlasting reproach for their parents' sins. It would be just the result expected from the dishonourable marriage planned for her.

On her second day at Amboise a great deal occurred, none of which helped to increase Anne's estimation of herself. After dinner, she happened to be walking along a corridor when she looked out of the window. It faced onto a small courtyard, paved with white stones, which seemed to throb with heat. An elderly hound was walking slowly round the outer wall, where a narrow rim of shade still lingered. All was quiet; she could hear the shuffle of its leathery old paws, and the click of its toenails. It headed into a shady archway and flopped, blocking the passageway to humans.

On the other side of the yard, a kennel man was examining the foot of another hound. He was squatting like a frog, the dog wedged between his thighs, the top of its head held back against his chest; one hand grasped its jaws together, the other probed the big squashy pads. The fingers found what they wanted, a thorn or splinter, which had caused the dog distress. The man gave a satisfied grunt, released the animal, which struggled to its feet, looked round in amazement, gave his hands many lavish licks and bounded off.

As the man got stiffly to his feet, he noticed for the first time the girl leaning far out of the window. He had been unaware of an audience. He was a shortish man of peculiar shape, thick-set in the shoulders, long in the arm, and inadequate in the legs, which were short, spindly and very bandy. He walked across the burning white paving stones, his shadow bobbing grotesquely in front, his wooden beads knocking against the hunting knife at his belt, the sun dazzling down on his wide brimmed hat, which was as big as a meat dish. With that bow-legged gait, he looked like some of the grooms at home, Anne thought with a pang, then saw his walnut dark skin, the black and pewter hair and dog-brown eyes, and decided that he was not an Englishman. His manners were quite unlike a servant's, too. He rolled right up to Anne's window and stood with arms akimbo, staring straight into her face. It was not an insolent stare, merely one of intense, candid curiosity. The deep-set, treacle-coloured eyes were the sharpest she had ever seen; in the first moment she was sure he had noted and appraised every hair of her head. The black eyebrows lifted, the long mouth curled itself into a smile, revealing a few discoloured teeth, and he politely took off his hat. Anne, acutely discomfited by his scrutiny, felt as if the heat from the stones had risen to her face, and was about to withdraw herself hastily when the man spoke quickly and amiably.

"My lord of Warwick's little one is comfortable at Amboise?" he asked, in French.

Too astonished for speech, Anne stood gaping at this ugly man. No servant would speak to her like that or have known who she was. Unprepossessing as his looks might be, his clothes were worse. He wore a jacket of rough cottage-spun grey wool, on which the white hairs of the hound had left a thick fur. It was bunched in carelessly at the middle by a huntsman's belt. A plain linen shirt showed at the neck very white and worn from many boilings. He was hairy all the way up to where his chin was shaven, which showed the strong shadow of the swarthy, and now his head was uncovered, she saw that he was bald, except for a fringe all round. His hose were coarse black cloth, baggy at the knees. His boots, sagging at the ankles, unfashionable in the blunt toes, cobbled like a peasant's, were rubbed greasy with wear. All three garments appeared to be splashed with fresh bird droppings. At these close quarters, Anne was fairly sure that there was dog shit on his boot soles, which was scarcely surprising in this castle.

As they stood there, staring at each other, a fly brushed the man's nose, making him raise a hand to scratch it. A hand thick-fingered, ringless, the dog's lick not yet dry on its back—but the nose! Anne felt the blush flood back into her face, as unbelieving realization of whom she stared at so rudely dawned on her. The nose did it—a truly remarkable nose, hugely long, hooked over and drooping at the end, where black hairs sprouted from the nostrils. . . . She had been told that the King of France dressed like a peasant and was always surrounded by swarming dogs. If she had taken more notice of his face the day before, this embarrassing encounter would not have happened. There he stood, the Most Christian King of France, Louis XI, King of Kings, who held her future, and her father's, in his dog-slobbered hands. King Louis had been described to her as unkingly in his behaviour, but she had not expected anyone as odd as this. King Edward had casual manners, but he would have looked gorgeous even if disguised as a peasant, an unmistakable king. Anne's heart pounded with fright and annoyance at seeming so foolish. She could not curtsy to Louis, because to do so would remove her entirely from his sight below the window sill. For once her voice sounded nervous and strange, speaking French. "Majesty, forgive my rudeness. . . ." Then, in delayed answer to his question. "Yes, her Grace Queen Charlotte had been so kind. . . ."

King Louis grunted dismissively. The fly came by again, determined to land on the massive promontory of his nose. "Pouff!" went the King, blowing it off course. Then he scratched his bald-

ing head. Anne thought he looked like a bailiff buying wethers at
a fair.

"You like dogs, my little mouse? And hawks?" he asked.

Anne nodded; there was nothing else she could do and, in any
case, it was the truth.

"*Viens*," King Louis said.

A little alarmed, Anne went along the corridor and out
through the small door at its end. The King was coming towards
her on his bandy legs, his hat on again.

"We'll go to the kennels. My hounds at Amboise are the best
in Christendom." He would send a man to the ends of the earth
for a hound. "Have you seen a spotted cat, that rides on a horse's
rump and can run down the fastest deer? Or birds, all scarlet
and green, from the lands of Prester John?"

Anne shook her head dumbly and followed him. King Louis
was curiously irresistible. He talked non-stop, his eyebrows wag-
gling, his bright eyes darting, his broad hands gesticulating.
Anne did not need to say much, because he left her no time to
answer questions, or to ask them. She was glad that her French
was fluent, but even she lost the thread when the King's words
tumbled over one another. She could not remember half of what
he talked about; there were a great many sharp comments on
events and other people, mostly French nobles, but he did not
say an unkind word to her, and he had nothing but good things
to say about her father.

After they had gone only a little way, King Louis opened a
door in a wall and peered through. What he saw seemed to give
him satisfaction, for he grinned and stepped through, beckoning
Anne to follow him. The door led into a garden, laid out with
gravel walks, low hedges, roses and fruit trees. In the garden
were several women in a group and, a little distance from them,
two or three men. At the sound of the closing door, they all
looked round and, at the sight of King Louis, made the proper
obeisances. The King marched straight up to the group of
women. They had been chattering, but now fell silent.

"Madame," King Louis said, "I have here Monseigneur de
Warwick's daughter. I should like you to greet her, now that she
has been at Amboise two days."

One of the group turned to face the King. She was plainly dressed, without jewels, but Anne knew instantly whom she confronted, and became very frightened, sliding into a wobbly kneed curtsy, from which she did not immediately rise.

Margaret of Anjou, once Queen of England, stared down at the girl she had never seen, and who had been imposed upon her son, against her wishes. It had been easier to ignore the betrothal before the girl was forced in person on her attention. She did not at once acknowledge Anne. Instead, she met the sharp, sardonic eyes of her Valois cousin, who in his way had just delivered his rebuke to her. "Your Majesty has me at a disadvantage. If I had been informed that you desired a meeting with me, Louis, I would have been more ready to receive you."

Louis, who had intended to catch her unawares, grinned again, and said amiably, "But I am delighted to find you here, Marguerite—and my lord Prince. . . . *Mon cher Edouard,*" he yelled, as if on the other side of a hunting field, "*Viens ici!*" He looked at Margaret. "It is he who must receive his betrothed, *ma chère Reine,* sooner, I think rather than later!"

As Margaret had not yet deigned to notice Anne, one of her women, knowing the situation, bent and whispered not unkindly, "Get up, child." When she had done so, Anne saw that Queen Margaret was staring at her. She had never seen the Queen before or if she had done so had been too young to know of it, and was quite ready, on account of rumour, to find her dressed in men's clothes, or something equally outrageous and formidable. But this woman was entirely feminine, neither tall nor strapping. Indeed, if it were not for her arrogant manner, she would have been beautiful. She had one of those faces in which the bones look just as handsome even when age has tightened the skin over them. That skin was fair, with only the lightest of lines and a tautness under the jawline, to show that she was forty. Her mouth was very red and her underlip very full, like her father's and brother's, and as ready as theirs to show moodiness. Even with that Medusa's glare in them, her eyes were strikingly beautiful, huge and hazel-brown, with lashes that could have fluttered like a courtesan's, if Margaret had ever chosen to use them in this way, which she had not.

Her son, Edward of Lancaster, Prince of Wales, had something of her looks and much of her manner. Though she was so
frightened of them both, Anne was surprised to find the Prince,
whose paternity she had always been taught was in doubt, a
princely and good-looking young man. He was well mannered
enough to bow to Anne and to kiss her hand. King Louis performed the introduction; the Prince's mother was standing
proudly by as if it did not concern her.

The Prince was dressed for hunting, in a green short coat,
which showed off his long legs, also in skin-tight green. He was
not one of those gangling, half-grown-out-of-their-sleeves six-
teen-year-olds. His height was between middling and tall, his
build very slim, and he stood straight and poised, as if he were
ready to leap and run like a deer. His hair was straight, brown
and glossy like a bay horse's coat, trimmed neatly a fraction
below his ears, and his skin was beautifully clear and deeply
tanned, pink cheeked with health; against it the whites of his ha-
zel eyes looked very bright. His teeth were white also, and his lips
very red, like his mother's. In fact, though Anne did not know it,
he most resembled his grandfather, Henry V of England, having
the same high cheekbones, long jaw and jutting chin with a deep
cleft in it; this was a source of huge satisfaction to him, as his
grandfather was his idol. King Louis, to whom the victor of
Agincourt had been a lifelong bogey, would have preferred that
he favoured his French progenitors, though his mother's father
René of Anjou did not inspire idolatry. His great grandfather
Charles VI of France had been mad, and was best forgotten,
which was something Louis himself had tried all his life to do.
The Prince was his father's son, not the Duke of Somerset's,
Louis was certain, though he often wondered what circum-
stances had enabled Henry VI to perform such a miracle.

"I am taking Lady Anne to see my animals," Louis announced.
"My lord Prince, you will join us? Madame?"

Clearly Margaret disapproved most violently, but was in no
position to defy her cousin. The King of France had a way of
giving his commands in casual phrases, while expecting them to
be carried out to the letter.

"Very well," she said, and turned her eyes away from Louis' grin of triumph. She had still not addressed a word to Anne.

The Prince was willing enough to obey, because he was full of curiosity at meeting his future wife, though he still looked a little apprehensively at his mother, knowing her disapproval. She had instilled into him that he was marrying only to save his inheritance, and that Warwick's daughter was an undesirable match.

"Madame—Lady Anne, Monseigneur de Warwick's daughter. Lady Anne, this is my dearest cousin, who is rightful Queen of England, and who will be your mother." King Louis was forcing Margaret to acknowledge Anne.

Margaret of Anjou extended her hand, and Anne curtsyed again, making the gesture of kissing it. A motherly embrace was too much to expect. Anne felt that her fears about the Queen had been entirely justified. The silent hostility was even more hateful to receive than she had imagined. No one in her whole life had dared to treat her as an upstart or an inferior, yet this was clearly how Margaret proposed to treat her.

On this occasion, however, King Louis had his way, and escorted the boy and girl off to view the animals, though they were fully as interested in viewing each other. He made an unlikely chaperon.

Amboise was a very large castle, almost a village in itself, and it held more animals than humans. Careless though he might be of his own appearance, the King's kennels and mews were beautifully ordered. Anne had been in ones more smelly on days less hot. Because she liked dogs and hawks, her interest was captured, and her alarm at her companions lessened. The greater number of the animals were kept in cages; Anne saw many furry small things, some of which looked like monkeys, some more like cats. Other cages seemed to contain only mounds of hay and straw, but the King pointed out that some creatures slept during the day, and were hiding in their beds. Goats and sheep of different markings and different shapes of horns wandered freely, followed by pretty kids and lambs. Big cages built along a sunny wall were full of birds, all sizes and colours, who had built their nests in branches. By the time they had got this far, they had been joined by several dogs, one a big white greyhound the

King addressed fondly as Paris; Hélène, he said, was occupied with her puppies, which he was sure was the best litter in France.

The King showed off a camel with special pride. This had two humps, and long, yellowish wool. It stood in its stable chewing the cud, which it spat out malevolently in their direction. It smelt extremely rank. Anne supposed it was for riding—after all, Saracens rode camels—and wondered if King Louis had tried to ride it. He would look even odder perched up there, squeezed between the humps. As they left it, they nearly fell over a porcupine, who was trundling about quite freely. He was called Sebastien, because of his quills.

They visited the King's spotted hunting cats last. The cats lay on their sides in their cages lazily. They had sleek fur and long legs, and small neat ears close to their heads. They slept in the sun, twitching their long whiskers.

The Prince said, "These are beautiful; they are the best animals here. I should like to take a pair back to England with me."

King Louis raised his eyebrows; he was jealous of his hunting animals. "Hm," he said. "If you are a good boy, I might be willing to send you some. I should have to ask the Duke of Milan for another pair to take their place; they are valuable to me. And what would you do with them in England?" Louis had a low opinion of England, and of the hunting offered there. He snapped his fingers suddenly. "If I bring them to England when I come to visit you and your father—and my lord Warwick, of course—you must let me have six couples of the best lymers—the big hounds with long ears—in England. You'll see he keeps his bargain, won't you, Lady Anne?"

Anne nodded shyly, thinking that the King showed amazing optimism. A King of France visiting England was an unheard of thing, especially as King Henry was called King of England and France. The people would probably boo, or worse.

The Prince, his mind still on spotted cats, said, "I'll hunt the deer in the forest of Windsor, with a cat sitting behind my saddle, with a red leash and a collar with my silver swan badge on it. The cats jump on the back of the deer, hang on with their claws, and break its back, tear its throat. It saves one having to dismount to do it oneself." Then, "My lord father may have one, too, if he is not too old now for hunting."

Henry VI was only two years older than King Louis, who let out a guffaw, and dug the Prince familiarly in the ribs. "Hunting," he laughed, "is the only pleasure left to us old men!" To Anne, he said, "Will you have a spotted cat to sit behind your saddle, little mouse? Be careful, big cats eat little mice!"

Anne, who liked to follow the hunt, did not much like the idea of the deer being jumped on. The Prince sounded as if he liked bloody kills. She found this distasteful. The cats' claws were like a hawk's talons; she watched them kneading in and out, and heard a purring nearly as deep as a growl. She thought the creatures beautiful but not to be trusted. The Prince was attractive enough to surprise her agreeably, but she shrank from signs of cruelty in people.

As they walked back into the living quarters of the castle, a big green popinjay flew out and landed plump on the crown of the King's hat, where it sat swaying and cocking its head on one side. He seemed quite accustomed to its behaviour. It spoke in a human voice, interspersed with fits of laughter uncannily like King Louis' own. *"Le Duc Charles est un pedero merdeux!"* it squawked, and descended from the royal hat to the King's shoulder. He appeared delighted and, grinning away to himself, began feeding the bird sunflower seeds, which it cracked in its wicked-looking beak. Anne was so astonished at what it had said that she blushed and did not look at the Prince, who was laughing his head off.

"Mignonette," the King called the bird, unsuitably, "talk for father Louis." It repeated its offensive remarks about the private inclinations of the Duke of Burgundy, added "God save Picardy", a few whistles and hoots, "Long live Louis", and when he nodded approvingly, it went straight into the *Pater Noster*. Anne stared with fascination; its beak and the King's nose were close, and rather alike.

When he had finished laughing, the Prince said, "Majesty, when I am truly Prince of England, I will make war on the Duke of Burgundy with you. He is not good at fighting battles; we will beat him and make him our vassal!"

Nothing could have pleased King Louis better. "He is *my* vassal already," he said dryly. Then, to make the Prince feel that he had suggested an English–French war alliance out of his own intelligence, when in reality, he, Louis, had worked towards this end ever since Warwick set foot on his shores, he said, "My Prince, you are a true English fighting cock! You bring my lord Warwick and plenty of Goddams over to Calais, and we will set fire to Duke Charles' tail with his own flint and steel!"

After the Feast of the Assumption, King Louis left Amboise to go to Normandy. He was worried because the Duke of Burgundy was sending his ships to raid French ports, and had trapped the Earl of Warwick's fleet in the harbours at Harfleur and La Hougue, causing a delay which might lessen the chances of the Earl's success in England. During the time that the King was away, Margaret of Anjou kept the Prince from any meeting with Anne and, in her husband's absence, Queen Charlotte had no authority over her guest. Anne's mother, although humiliated, was relieved, for it meant that she did not have to endure the frightening company of Margaret.

A letter came from Isabel in Valonges, saying that she now felt a little stronger, and that her father could not leave France because of the Burgundians. She also said something about Clarence which worried her mother. Isabel had seen letters sent to him by his own mother in England, and by his sister Margaret in Burgundy. Both pleaded with George to desert the Earl of Warwick and to return to his brother King Edward. Both were exceedingly forceful women, and Isabel had realized they had more influence over her husband than anyone else. The Duchess of York told her son plainly that he had disgraced his family and his honour, but that there was still time for him to make some amends for it; if he did not, she would cease to regard him as her son. Isabel complained that George thought more affectionately of his sister the Duchess of Burgundy than he did of her. One could not imagine what he would do when his wife's father made war on his beloved sister's husband. While conceding that the loss of Clarence would be a blow, for he owned huge estates and could muster many soldiers, the Countess thought that any desertion by him would be a disaster for Isabel. It was bad enough seeing one of her daughters torn between enemy factions.

On the ninth of September, a lucky chance enabled the Earl of Warwick to leave France. A gale scattered the Burgundian blockade on the Cotentin, and the Earl sailed his fleet out on the following calm, side by side with an escort of French ships commanded by the Admiral of France. They made a rare sight, if only because the leopards of England and the lilies of France displayed together in friendship on the Channel had not been seen in the memory of man. With Warwick went Jasper Tudor and the Earl of Oxford. They all knew the risks but believed enough in success to be optimistic. Though they would never forget past enmity, Warwick was a man to follow.

Anne knew that the news of her father's departure had made her mother very frightened indeed, though whether this was because of fears for his safety, or the prospect of being left without his protection, she was not sure. She wondered what would happen to them, left to wait in a strange land, if disaster should befall the expedition. She felt that if her father were to die, King Louis would lose all interest in them; he was quite likely to sell them back to King Edward if it would profit him.

The Prince was full of plans for war, fretting that he had been left behind while his uncle Gaspard and the Earl of Warwick went into action. What would he do for the rest of his life if they failed?

The World Upside Down

July — October 1470

> Sum tyme I rodde in clothe of gold so red,
> Thorow-oute ynglond in many a town;
> Alas, I dare nowth schewe now my hede—
> Thys world ys turnyd clene uppe so down!
>
> *God Amend Wicked Counsel* (c. 1464)

"Poggio the Florentine told a story about a donkey!"

"The girl who couldn't make out why her husband hadn't got one as big as a donkey's!"

Snatches of noisy conversation floated across from where Thomas Grey, Elizabeth Woodville's son, was lounging against the gallery of the tennis court, surrounded by an admiring group of cronies. Their talk was often bawdy. Grey was in his shirtsleeves, for he had been playing, and his hose were of particoloured silk, blue and green, like a peacock. Richard found his screeching suggestive laughter offensive. Grey's younger brother Dick stood as usual in his shadow. Of these two nasty youths, Tom was the nastier, if only because of his seniority. He was near Richard's own age but had the advantages of being both a head taller, and as beautiful as one might expect a son of his mother to be. His long, floppy hair was the exact shade of hers, but when you looked closely, his eyelashes were almost white, like a ferret's. His light eyes ran speculatively over every woman that passed.

"Gloucester, will you give me a game?"

"Not now. I'm on my way elsewhere."

Tom Grey grinned unpleasantly, as if he had known it was not worth asking such a dull fellow.

"Hey," he said more familiarly, "I've a riddle for you. What is it: the more one seeks it, the further one is from it?"

Richard shook his head, preparing to move away.

"*Le fond d'un con!*" Grey and the others all collapsed in coarse laughter.

Richard felt himself grow red in the face, which was just what Grey had wanted. This was partly, however, because of his furious desire to throttle the Queen's insolent son, or to tip him head first over the gallery onto the tiled court below.

Down there, the King was playing with Anthony Woodville, the new Lord Rivers. King Edward would have been an outstanding player if he had given more time and effort to the game. He leapt about the court with every sign of enjoying himself without a care. As he said, "It serves no purpose, to march up and down, chewing my fingernails."

The Earl of Warwick was expected to invade the kingdom at any time to drive the King from his throne—and the Queen too. At a time when the realm was on the verge of civil war again, all the Queen's son could think of was scoring off the King's brother, and tales of Poggio the Florentine and a donkey's member.

Bitterly, Richard compared himself with his brother Clarence. George had known whose side he was on. He had chosen exile in France rather than endure Grey and his minions, the umpteen uncles, aunts and hangers on. No, Richard called himself to heel, George had not chosen exile, he had been given no choice, having made himself Warwick's puppet. One brother the tool of a traitor and himself a Woodville lover, Richard thought. He could not wait to get away from Westminster in the service and company of the King. At least he would then not have to see or hear these Woodville parasites, whom his own painfully given loyalty to his brother was helping to keep fat.

Not that his own allegiance was of much interest to anyone except himself. He was too young. If only he were a year or two older; if he had a household of his own, an income sufficient to live by, retainers upon whom he could call, all the things which

George had possessed from childhood by right. But he was the youngest son. It would not have entered his head to question the King's plans for his provision in the future, or his brother's generosity; it was simply that he needed now to play a man's part, as the second royal Duke in the kingdom, and found himself ill-equipped to do so.

When King Edward came bounding up from the tennis court, laughing and victorious, Richard smiled too, for he could not remain gloomy in his brother's presence. He felt guilty at his own discontent.

The King patted his belly with some satisfaction. "I shall have no need of new harness," he said with a grin, "if Anthony keeps me running as fast as he has done today!" King Edward had, at twenty-eight, more than the beginnings of a paunch. "What I'd give to be seventeen again!"

"Give me some of your years, and I'd be more than happy," Richard said.

Something of his previous state of mind must have shown in his voice, because the King glanced at him shrewdly and said, "You'll feel your years soon enough without any I could give you. I've had enough bad news for one morning. The north is in a turmoil and ready to flare up like a bonfire at any moment. I plan to go to York, to shake my mailed fist at them." He clenched his hand, and admired his large muscles bulging under his sleeve. "I wouldn't be surprised if the lord of the north heads for home."

Indeed, it would be no surprise if Warwick were to land in Yorkshire, where his own following were strongest.

In the last days of July, the King left to go north. It was the third time Richard had travelled the north road that summer. Waltham Holy Cross, Ware, Royston, Huntingdon, Wansford Bridge, Stamford, Grantham, Newark, Doncaster, York. . . . It was a good road, the surface hard and gravelly, with a steep camber on either side which drained off water. Once he had seen men repairing a hole on one of the long straight stretches near Huntingdon, and the road had been made of rusty-looking compacted gravel, a man's height in thickness. Those foundations were very old, he had been told; the Roman army had made the

road at a time so long ago he could not calculate, and it was still
so iron hard the men could not get a pickaxe into it. They were
doing daywork for the parish, shovelling gravel into the hole and
hoping for the best. Richard wished that every time he had to
march soldiers, they might use a road as good, and he was going
to do a great deal of marching soldiers.

Road-weary as he was, Richard felt glad to see the pale stone
walls of York gilded by the evening sun, the weather-vanes on the
many churches glinting, all of it laid out like a gingerbread city
on a green cloth for his delectation. He felt as he always did in
the north, as if he had come home to somewhere he had left only
a day or two before, though he had no special proprietary rights
in the place—for here Warwick's kingdom began. He never felt
so much a Neville as here; he could scarcely believe that he and
his brother had come to subdue the north, to spill their own
Neville blood.

As it turned out, they did not have to spill any blood. There
were only a few hundred rebels, led by Henry, Lord Fitzhugh of
Ravensworth, Warwick's brother-in-law. When Lord Fitzhugh
heard that King Edward in person had marched as far as Ripon
and was after him, he fled northwards to Scotland. Most of the
rebels were members of his family, many of them women. How
some wives and mothers seemed to enjoy packing their menfolk
off to fight. Richard hoped that when he had a wife she would
not send him off so gleefully to face death. A wife! There was
not much prospect of his marrying with the kingdom in such a
turbulent state. His prospects were uncertain and he was still
largely financially dependent upon his brother the King.

At Ripon, Richard was appointed to head the commission to
try the rebels. By the same warrant, he was given an office that a
few years before would not even have entered his head to dream
of holding. King Edward made him Warden of the West
Marches against Scotland. This was Warwick's office, one the Earl
had held since he himself was seventeen. Richard knew that in
the present circumstance he would meet with hostility where he
had once looked for friendship. The people of the north did not
take kindly to new faces, were mostly Warwick's supporters, and
had an instinctive dislike of "young pups." Richard was very

sure that he would have a hard row to hoe. After all, he had spent only four years of his life here in the north, even if during that time he had never thought of himself as anything but a native. He was a Neville; this was the best way to go to the people. He felt too young to carry the enormous burden ahead, of winning acceptance in the north, without a family to back him, for all his Neville relatives would see him as Warwick's enemy. This made him as miserable as he knew his cousin John Neville to be. John had been deprived not only of his Earldom of Northumberland in order to reinstate Henry Percy, but had been ousted from his office of Warden of the East Marches. The Marquisate of Montagu was poor compensation. Yet he had struggled with his family loyalty and still supported King Edward. But Edward in a cynical mood had said, "He will go to his brother Warwick in the end. I will not wait to be betrayed by another of them. I want a man who owes his position in the north to me and is not a Neville."

But Richard's new office in the north was a burden he was given no chance to assume. News came that the Earl of Warwick's fleet was assembled at La Hougue, though unable to come out, past the Duke of Burgundy's ships; it was only a matter, however, of how long they could hold him there. King Edward alerted the Kentish ports, but still made no move south. Richard was among those who urged him to do so, but he said that he preferred to wait for definite news that Warwick had crossed the Channel, and to discover in which part of the kingdom he intended to land.

At York, King Edward had the toothache. This made him even more disinclined to set out southwards. Richard had never seen his brother so devastatingly sorry for himself, one side of his face like rising dough, wincing at every step and thoroughly unsociable. For days he put off the inevitable pincers, praying the pain might go away. He wrapped a toothpick in a scrap of linen saturated with oil of cloves, which would be sure to draw out the mischievous worm in his tooth, and dabbed away. The pain lessened, then redoubled; King Edward capitulated and sent for his surgeon.

He was still nursing his damaged face when a messenger

pounded into York to tell him that the Earl of Warwick had landed in Devon on Holy Rood Day in Harvest, and had been welcomed in Exeter like a returning hero. With him were the Duke of Clarence—everyone looked the other way when informing the King of his brother's doings—Jasper Tudor, and the Earl of Oxford.

By the Feast of St. Matthew, King Edward was ready to leave York. He sent word to his lords to ready their men, and to John Neville to bring in his soldiers from Pontefract. The next day they moved to Doncaster, where they rested a night or two at the house of Carmelites, waiting for John Neville to catch up with them. Warwick was marching towards his Warwickshire estates, and the town of Coventry, where he was certain of support. This time there might be a battle—win or lose all.

On the second night at Doncaster, Richard was woken at some hour of his deepest, dead sleep by a tremendous shouting. He hated being woken suddenly, and the shouting seemed directed in his ears with all the volume of a giant's yell in a vaulted building. He mumbled crossly and rolled reluctantly over, but before he had time to lever himself up on his elbow to confront his tormentor, someone had stripped the bedclothes off his shoulders and begun to shake him. Anger and alarm drove sleep away quicker than any other remedy, and he jumped awake, shouting back, in a slurred, stupid fashion.

"That's enough! Am I a sleeping scullion for you to show the toe of your boot? What does this Devil's din mean?"

His squire had too urgent a message to be discouraged by angry protests. "Your Grace, he's on the Doncaster road already —armed men—marching at night—coming to take us! We'll be murdered in our own beds!" The candlelight distorted the man's face into that of a grimacing puppet.

"Who? How can he be on the Doncaster road; he's a hundred miles away—or do you think he's grown wings like Lucifer?"

Richard thought only of Warwick. It was not possible for him to be near Doncaster when he had been south of Coventry the day before. They had woken him on some Tom fool alarm.

"We have one of Montagu's captains here," said his squire, urgently. "He got away while the going was good. Will your Grace see him at once?"

"Montagu!" Richard went cold. Surely John Neville could not be marching for Doncaster with any evil intent. There must be some mistake. John was probably pushing on at night to catch up with them, as the King had asked. "Bring the man in," he said.

John Neville's man found the Duke sitting on the edge of his bed, yawning and rubbing his eyes with his fists, a small, thin boy with a mop of tousled, curly hair. Not another lordling wet behind the ears, he groaned inwardly; I'm wasting my time. Why not let 'em all be swept into the Neville net. But birds kept out of the net did live to pay rewards. The Duke looked sleepy, creases from the pillow down one side of his face. But he looked expectantly at the man, demanding instant information, without wasting words.

"Your Grace, I have been with my lord Montagu's men at Pontefract." He had Neville's griffin badge on his sleeve. "He is marching to join his brother the Earl of Warwick. He briefed us yesterday, saying we were now Warwick's men and King Henry's! That was the first we knew of it; he'd always sworn we were King Edward's men. It seems he won't take arms against his blood brother, and if he joined with you, he could see a battle coming—once a Neville, always a Neville."

Richard cut in on him in a curt way that was startling, coming from one who looked as if he should be still at his grammar books.

"The King will make a decision on this. If you are telling the truth, you will be thanked as appropriate. If not, well, bearers of false news are treated as thieves where I give orders."

Neville's captain felt he had underestimated both the boy's age and his authority.

"Come with me. You can give your news to the King yourself." This was an order.

Because he did speak the truth, the captain had no real cause to be apprehensive, except that he might be caught and murdered before these lords got themselves on the move. He was a hard nut of a soldier, but his heart beat faster as he thought of speaking to the King. He followed the Duke along the bare corridors of the Carmelite friary. The Duke's head was on a level with his chin, and the boy was all wrapped up in a long gown of a very expensive fur, long-haired stuff that made him look like a little squirrel scurrying along.

King Edward had been roused in the same abrupt way as Richard. Because he had not been drinking the night before, or enjoying a woman, he was wide-awake, fresh-faced, and not in the least out of temper. He did not believe in worried frowns until he was sure he had cause for them. Like his young brother, he was swaddled in a ransom's worth of fur, but roughly twice as much of it was needed to cover him. Everything about King Edward was very big, from his face to his feet, stuck carelessly into red slippers. The man wondered fleetingly and irreverently if the organ the King was well known to make frequent use of was in proportion to the rest of him.

"Tell me exactly what you know of this supposed treachery," the King said. He sounded very straightforward and level-headed, not in the least haughty or unapproachable, as a king might well be to a captain of archers. When the man had finished, the King sat down on a chair, pulling his fur gown round his bare knees.

"I believe," he said, consideringly, "that you are giving a truthful account of the situation as you see it. However, there may be some misunderstanding. John Neville, my lord Montagu, has always sworn that he would never go against me. He is an honest man." He turned to look at his brother. "What do you think, Richard?"

The young Duke was looking very unhappy, as if he knew the answer, but that it was a wrench to speak it. Looking at his feet, he said, "John Neville is honest. Too honest to pretend that his own conscience will let him march with us against his brother."

The King looked at him searchingly for a moment, his big, handsome face revealing both affection and respect. The boy did not see the look, for he still had his eyes fixed on his feet, and might have just been made to swallow verjuice.

The King got to his feet, taking his decision quickly. "See that my lords Hastings, Rivers and Say are woken. We must confer on what is best to be done."

Other men from Neville's force arrived in the next hour, and each one confirmed the bad news. Everyone seemed in favour of immediate flight from Doncaster southwards, as the imperative was to escape before Montagu could catch up with them.

Pandemonium began. Richard pelted back down the corridors to his own rooms, clutching the door jamb as he skidded round it with one slipper falling off. Three squires came running at his yell. One of them pulled on his hose, while another dragged his shirt over his head, and began frantically to tie the two together with points; the third fetched his boots, shoved them onto him, and then rummaged in his baggage for the warmest, most weatherproof and safest garment that he possessed. Luckily it could be found in time—a jacket of brigandines made of double layers of velvet and cloth, with metal plates sewn between. This he pulled on straight over his shirt, and was out of the door before anyone could do up the fastenings for him. The squires were left to collect whatever they might remember to grab—knives, a tinder box, a razor for the Duke, who only needed to shave every other day; they forgot the soap.

Outside, the horses were being saddled, swerving about skittishly because they had been brought from their stable in the middle of the night into an atmosphere of haste and excitement, and into the dazzle of flaring lights. King Edward was already mounted. Richard heard his voice shouting, "Where's my brother?" and someone put the reins into his hand. He hurled himself aboard, and the animal leapt halfway across the yard, barging everyone else. Above the crash of its hooves, and his own curse, he heard a yelling laugh from the King, who had recognized this thunderbolt which had come in answer to his call.

By the end of the following day, they had left Montagu far behind, and reached Newark. King Edward hesitated there considering going to Nottingham and trying to rally men. But all the news brought in was so bad—wherever Warwick went, he was raising troops with ease, and meeting no opposition—that the King decided he would not risk becoming Warwick's prisoner again, and that the only course of action open to him was flight, not just from the immediate danger, but from England.

Rivers suggested that they should ride at once to the port of Lynn, where he had much influence. Richard knew that Anthony Woodville held the town in his purse and controlled its elections, and for once did not grudge the Queen's brother his patronage, if it helped them to escape safely overseas. Burgundy was the only possible refuge, King Edward hoping that his brother-in-law the Duke's quarrels with the King of France and with Warwick would at least ensure that he would not be turned away.

So the next day they rode south-east into Lincolnshire, and the following morning took the causewayed fen road which led along the shores of the Wash, and was the most direct route to Lynn. Richard, who had travelled in many desolate places, had seen few to equal the dreadful fenland. On either side was flatness, nothing to the south but endless waterlogged fen, nothing to the north but saltings and a distant grey ocean. The road drove straight on before them, dividing the miles of emptiness, the rain dancing frenziedly in the puddles and on the scummy fen dykes, the cloud glimmering like daytime moonlight on sheets of water. The passing of so many horsemen disturbed the marsh birds, who rose in flocks into the sky, but their squawking was blown away by the wind, as were the voices of the travellers. The wind was strong enough to blow the clothes off your back, and cold enough to freeze the bones of the dead in their graves in the churchyards of the fen parishes. That wind must be able to blow uninterrupted across the sea from the lands of ice and snow, and it gathered ferocity as it came. Even King Edward turned blue in the face, and the skin on his lips shrivelled and would have dried if it had not also been raining. Richard felt like a fishbone hung out to bleach in the wind.

If the ride along the fen road was miserable, the crossing of the outfall of the river Nene was a nightmare. While the ferrymen's service was adequate for the usual traffic, it was a long and difficult job for them to cope with the great number of men and horses suddenly demanding a crossing. There were only a few small boats, and only a limited number of crossings could be made on one tide. The weather grew worse. The waters of the wide river mouth could be as dangerous as the open sea during storms. One boatload was caught in a fierce squall, and flipped over as quickly as an egg in a pan. Only two passengers were rescued, but the boat was saved. Richard, who had begun his life beside the river Nene on its more kindly reaches, and had several times escaped drowning in it, did not want this fate to catch up with him now. He watched his brother the King being ferried across with more fear than he felt himself on climbing into the boat. But they both landed safe, sodden and daubed with fishscales, on the other side. The priests said Mass that Sunday morning in a lean-to smelling of tar.

By the evening they had managed to reach West Lynn, where the ferry over to the town was easier than the one at Long Sutton, as the river was much narrower and enough boats were available to carry everyone. The Mayor of Lynn, forewarned by servants of Lord Rivers, came out to welcome his unwelcome visitors. It was already ten o'clock, and everyone in the town was going to bed. The torches lit up a king who looked what he was, a fugitive. Mayor Westhorpe put the town under a curfew and a watch on the gates. He did not know if the Earl of Warwick was going to chase King Edward to Lynn. He reckoned that he had about two days in which to see the King's party on their way to Burgundy. He also hoped that if and when Lord Rivers returned with the royal brother-in-law, the town of Lynn would gather its rewards.

Early on Tuesday morning, Richard walked up the gangplank from the Common Staithe of Lynn onto a ship bound for Middleburg in Zeeland. He had just left his brother the King, who had embarked upon a separate ship. Edward had enveloped him in an enormous hug, nearly lifting him off his feet, kissed him several times and said that he would have preferred that they sailed together, but that it was more prudent not to, and that their mother would never forgive him if they were to drown together. Richard was not only terrified of drowning, after his experiences in crossing the Nene, but feared even more that Edward's ship might be lost, and he himself be left to fight their cause alone. Without Edward, he thought, there would be no cause to fight. He could not envisage being the only male

member of his family left. This made him think with some resentment of George, who was probably by now enjoying himself
in luxury on his own property.

King Edward had settled himself on board the Lynn merchant
ship as if he did that kind of thing every day of his life. Richard's
last sight of him was of his enormous length lying back comfort-
ably among canvas-covered bales of cloth, as if lounging in a soft
bed, his feet propped up and his arms behind his head, a cheerful grin on his face. The crew had cast him admiring glances for
his coolness already.

Richard stood at the side of the ship and watched the water
creep up the weed-hung timbers of the Staithe. When it was
near the top of the green tide mark, they would sail. High tide
was at eight o'clock. He was hungry; he had eaten his breakfast
at five. However, he dreaded the result if he were to start eating
now. He had not been on a sea-going ship since he had been
packed off into exile at the age of seven to the same destination.
Then, his brother had not been King. Ten years later, crown and
kingdom were lost, and life itself was uncertain. Before, Richard
would have fought anyone who had suggested that such events
were possible. Now he had to admit his brother's fallibility. He
thought that the King had been ill-served.

The master had made it quite clear that the Duke of Gloucester and his servants were surplus and unwanted cargo, and
that the safe arrival of his grain and cloth in Zeeland in time for
carriage to the November Barms Mart was his priority. The
goods were the property of a merchant of Norwich, and a jurat
of Lynn, who would not want to be mixed up in the affairs of
dukes. Not that the master would have minded so much had the
Duke been going overseas in the ordinary course of events,
though of course he would never have gone on such a humble
ship, in such discomfort, but this was a one-way passage, without
much hope of collecting the fare. The rings the boy had taken off
his hands, and collected from his companions, would fetch a
good enough price in Middleburg, but, he thought gloomily, it
would not compensate for all these lordly landlubbers cluttering
up his ship, who'd probably all be sick as dogs before they'd left
the mouth of the Ouse.

When Richard saw the gap between the side of the ship and the Staithe widen suddenly, he knew that they had weighed anchor and were beginning to swing out into mid-stream. King Edward's ship went first. It took some time for them to sail out of the Ouse into the open sea. The North Sea was a limitless grey waste. The sailors said the wind was good and the sea fair, but to Richard it looked hideously rough, the waves like banks and ditches. He was sure it must be the coldest place on earth— he had thought that of the shores of the Wash, on the fen road, but the open sea was worse. Also, it moved. He did not like to think too much about it moving, or to watch it too fixedly.

He looked back towards England, and suddenly remembered that the day was Tuesday, and that it must be the second day of October. It was his birthday, and he had not thought of it till now. He was eighteen. This fact seemed to have very little significance. Three months ago it had been something to look forward to.

When he could not see the land any more, he fished a set of beads out of his purse and began to pray, as he had not had time earlier, for his brother's safety, and his own.

William Wayneflete, Bishop of Winchester and lifelong friend of King Henry VI, hurried across the lawns of the Tower gardens and through dark corridors towards the apartments where his King—who had not been King for nine years—was living out the last day of his life as a prisoner. Wayneflete was extremely agitated. Another day, he thought, and the wild Kentish rebels would have stormed the Tower, and then, well, the kingdom would have fallen in ruins. He glanced at his companions, the Mayor of London, Richard Lee, grocer, and a gaggle of harassed-looking aldermen worrying about the money they were losing in the atmosphere of uncertainty and near panic. They had been alarmed at the news which reached London two days previously that King Edward had fled from Doncaster, trying to escape from England. The prospect of a realm without a king was dreadful to contemplate. The Kentish men looting the Dutch-owned breweries in Southwark, and battering London Bridge itself showed how easily mob violence could break out.

King Henry was better than no king, and the City dignitaries hastened to restore to him the kingdom over which he had reigned for forty years.

Wayneflete sighed when he thought of the burden he was about to place again upon the inadequate shoulders of Henry of Lancaster. Firmly as he believed in Henry's right to rule, the Bishop was too experienced a politician to pretend that the Lancastrian King had ever possessed much capacity for the task. Too often he had tried to steer the ship of state clear of the shoals on which Henry had landed himself. The trouble was, Henry had such implicit faith in his non-existent abilities; King from his cradle, he believed that if he pursued a moral life, he could be guilty of no wrong. His piety and moral purity were, of course, an example to all Christendom. When he was only twenty-four Pope Eugenius had awarded him the Golden Rose for his signal services to Holy Church. But Wayneflete knew, better than most, that in his youth Henry had been both autocratic and unnecessarily sententious; as a churchman and a minister of state, the Bishop had often been torn between respect and irritation. He had seen Henry in his sickness become pathetic and rudderless, and fervently hoped that the present news would not bring on further attacks.

Now, with the realm near riot, the best that might be hoped for was that the old reverence the people had always had for Henry would prevail. The Earl of Warwick was on his way from Coventry to London. This fact, supposedly reassuring, only increased the Bishop's agitation. For twenty years Warwick had been one of the most outspoken leaders of the opposition to King Henry's policies, and Wayneflete was aware that, as Henry's Chancellor, he had been too prominent an instrument of them. The world had turned so suddenly topsy turvy. At least Warwick was bringing with him someone dependable in Jasper Tudor— the King had great trust in his half-brother—though many of the other Lancastrian lords were still in exile or, the Bishop thought regretfully, in their graves.

Wayneflete had visited Henry many times during his five years' imprisonment. His rooms in the Tower were better than most noble prisoners might occupy. Henry had a private oratory laid out with jewelled crosses, reliquaries, and a large painting of St. Edmund the Martyr, which a less generous enemy than King Edward would not have allowed him to retain for his use. He still had many books brought in by friends; some were even gifts from Edward himself. He was allowed visitors, for Edward realized that any political plots woven round him would probably be abortive due to his lack of interest or comprehension. His guard and servants had been chosen for their discretion and humanity. Edward of York was the least vindictive of men, and if Henry were careless of his domestic arrangements, shabbily clothed and did not bother to shave every day, that was in own choice.

The Bishop found Henry at his one modest meal of the day. In front of the King was propped a picture of the Five Wounds of Christ, which he always set before him at meals, to remind himself of God's sacrifice while he indulged his human needs. His servant was reading a passage which the Bishop recognized as from *The Abbey of the Holy Ghost*. As he fell silent, Wayneflete knelt at King Henry's feet and kissed his hand. The lap in front of him was full of crumbs.

"My very dear lord, your Grace, I have the greatest news that I might bring you." He chose the right words instinctively. "God has, out of his bounteous mercy, in the course of his natural justice, restored you, my liege lord, to your rightful inheritance. Edward of York has abandoned his stolen kingdom and fled from England."

"Mm-m?" King Henry's eyes swivelled from Wayneflete, elderly and creaking on his knees, to the Mayor and back without immediate signs of understanding. His eyes were large and brown, and doggily enquiring; lately they seemed to have a purplish bloom in them, as in those of the aged or poor-sighted. He continued chewing, thoughtfully. Wayneflete thought that he might be kneeling too close and tried to edge back, but his seventy-year-old knees were not equal to it. He watched a sliver of onion drop from Henry's lap onto one of his shoes. He knew that since all pressure of affairs had been removed from him, Henry had done everything slowly. The long-sighted eyes gradually focused with recognition upon the Bishop, and upon the City notables, standing at a respectful distance.

"Mm-m?" King Henry said again. "My dear Bishop, William, I am glad as always to see you. I trust you are in better health than I am. What brings you here?"

Wayneflete swallowed and repeated his news. Most men would have been overcome by powerful emotion, but Henry seemed to accept his deliverance as an expected, destined event, awaited with faith all the years of his deposition. Then, the thought process overtaking him, his brow puckered, the grey eyebrows contracted, and the prim mouth and long, blurred likeness of his famous father's aggressive chin began to quiver.

"Edward of March," he said querulously, using Edward's youthful title, "is sure to come back."

Wayneflete felt a twinge of exasperation that Henry should so typically look on the gloomy side. Henry, though still utterly sure, as he always had been, that God would one day restore him, had become more vague and slow, due to his secluded life and lack of exercise. He was always complaining of sluggish bowels; the costiveness had afflicted his mind also. Yet, poor soul, for one who had suffered so much, it was a wonder he had kept any wits at all. The hardships of his fugitive years had aged him. At forty-nine he looked nearer sixty, and behaved at times as if he were older than Wayneflete himself. But since he had been in the Tower, free of his wife, who in the Bishop's opinion had been the greatest disaster ever to befall him, unmolested and communing with God, he had not once retreated into that cataleptic state which most men regarded as madness. The sickness of the mind took many strange forms, Wayneflete thought. His conversations with Henry during the imprisonment had been entirely sensible, and the King's memory on theological matters was remarkably good, indeed, he could dispute with scholars of the Church on their own ground. He was able to live a life like a monk, according to a Rule, and he did not really wish to be disturbed in it. He said that he endured his imprisonment and loss of his earthly kingdom by looking forward to the heavenly one in store for him. This return to the cares of an earthly King would take away from him his pleasurable days of contemplation.

Henry, though a devout practitioner of Christian charity, had never shown himself very aware of the feelings of others. But this time he perceived the Bishop's acute discomfort and raised the old man up off his knees. The next surprise was that Henry knelt down himself, folded his hands, closed his eyes and murmured a prayer of thanksgiving. Then he asked the Bishop for his blessing. This moved Wayneflete to tears. These glimpses of simple humility and trust were the bonds that bound the King's personal servants and friends to him, and disarmed his enemies even when most infuriated by him.

Bishop Wayneflete, the Mayor and his entourage, escorted King Henry, the contents of his chapel, and several boxes of books, to more stately apartments in the Tower. The rooms most suitable, spacious, light, richly fitted out and overlooking gardens, were in fact most unsuitably furnished—for a queen's lying-in. Elizabeth Woodville had decided to bear King Edward's fourth child at the Tower, in characteristic opulence. She had fled precipitately to the safety of Westminster Sanctuary, leaving a considerable impedimenta of floral bed hangings, gilded basins and ewers, cradles quilted with silk and, most embarrassing of all, a birthing chair. King Henry did not seem to notice anything incongruous about this; probably he did not know what it was.

The most imperative, and difficult, task was to see that King Henry was dressed as a king should be dressed. He could not possibly wear anything of King Edward's, for he would be swamped and look ridiculous. Though he was a tallish man, Henry's peculiarly angular and slightly gawky body was a tailor's nightmare. During his imprisonment this bony frame had become encumbered by a pot belly, and only a wizard of the shears could make him appear to wear his garments, however rich, regally. Meanwhile, the barber removed three days' stubble from Henry's chin, trimmed the wispy eyebrows, clipped the straggling grey hair, even snipped the ageing, neglected tufts from the royal nose and ears.

Instead of showing trepidation at the prospect of meeting his old arch-enemy, the Earl of Warwick, King Henry seemed to accept the Neville *volte-face* as only right and just. The day after his liberation, he insisted on celebrating the feast of St. Francis of Assisi, the saint who had lived without worldly goods, even while he was being loaded with his royal possessions once more.

Then, on Friday, the first of the Neville tribe arrived to pay him homage; the Archbishop of York rode into London from his manor of the Moor in Hertfordshire, accompanied by an archiepiscopal army bristling with very unecclesiastical arms, and took over the Tower from a somewhat relieved Mayor.

George Neville remained his clever, civilized and urbanely reasonable self. He came before King Henry as if he had never given his allegiance elsewhere, and when the King murmured a passage from Jeremiah: "Turn, o you backsliding children, saith the Lord . . .", the Archbishop smiled his attractive, white-toothed smile, and said he would take that very text for his speech when addressing King Henry's soon to be summoned Parliament.

On Saturday afternoon, at about three o'clock, London burst into a roar of welcome for Warwick. The sight of all those barbarous-spoken northerners in their smart red livery, and the familiar ragged staff was actually reassuring, a sign that order was going to be restored by a popular man.

Warwick knew, immediately upon seeing King Henry, that a form of regency was going to be necessary from the start. The sooner the Prince came back from France the better, so that the task of prising him away from the grip of his mother and making a ruler of him could begin. Now that the barbers and tailors had got to work on him, Henry VI was much improved—older, of course, and maddeningly slow, but still recognizably Henry of Lancaster. He was mercifully not a madman, but his capacity for government was even less than before.

It was necessary that the people should be given an opportunity to see their King restored, loyally escorted by the Earl of Warwick, the new Lieutenant of the Realm. New lodgings for the King, away from the Tower, were thought advisable, and the palace of the Bishop of London close by St. Paul's was selected. Later that afternoon, a royal procession proceeded through the City and along Cheapside. This did not have the effect intended.

On horseback, Henry now seemed so uncertain, for one who had been an energetic huntsman. The October sunlight of late afternoon unfortunately shone into his eyes, making him squint and blink more than others about him, as if he had been brought

too suddenly out of prison gloom. In spite of the efforts to make
him presentable as a king, he had an unwashed greyish look, a
mildewed lankness about his sparse hair. Even the robe he wore,
made up hastily in the last two days, and of superfine quality
blue velvet, lined throughout with cloth of gold, seemed to catch
the light the wrong way on its nap, producing a moulting appearance, as if the King were still wearing the same blue velvet
gown as on his last public appearance nine years before. The tailors had not been adequate to their task. When Henry took off
his hat, his bald head was alarmingly pallid, veined with blue,
with the same fragile domed look of a baby's, the skull bones visible. The older Londoners were sympathetic, even welcoming,
but the younger, especially the women, made disparaging remarks about moth-eaten kings and poor old man, remembering
the Phoebus-like appearance of King Edward on show to his
people.

The contrast of this docile figure with Edward of York was apparent to no one more than to George of Clarence. George rode
in his appointed place in this parody of a procession—beside, and
a fraction behind, Warwick—with a sullen, disdainful expression
spoiling his good looks, as if he would have liked to dissociate
himself from the whole pitiable spectacle. It was he who should
have ridden in royal state through London; he, George, who
could have been Warwick's king, not this doddering old lunatic. The street on either side swarmed with scarlet jackets and
the ragged staff. God knew where his own men were, he could
see scarcely any of them. Spasmodic shouts of "Warwick! Warwick!" came from the crowd. He seethed with resentment
against Warwick's flaunted power, against the devilish old King
of France, against Edward and that bitch Elizabeth Woodville
for having caused all their misfortunes, against his brother Richard for having done the honourable thing and not disgraced his
family, and against King Henry, who had already reproved him
for using a mild oath, and for wearing a beribboned codpiece,
which the silly old fool had considered indecent—anyone would
think he had been walking about with it undone! In a week's
time, he would be twenty-one. He had achieved nothing.

George had made up his mind. If Edward came back, he

would leave this pack of mummers and display as much brotherly love as he could muster. He would, no doubt, be forgiven. It
would be a galling episode, but worth a little grovelling. However, that lay in the future. At present his mind was occupied
with the problem of avoiding a meeting with his mother. He
dreaded being summoned to her and dreaded even more her
seeking him out. When he was a child, he had been able to
hoodwink most of the female servants and relatives, but not his
mother. Even from the distance of Baynards Castle, he imagined
her being able to read what went on in his mind.

As he expected, on the very first evening, his mother sought
him out. It was after a banquet given by the Neville brothers in
King Henry's name. George returned to his lodgings in the
Bishop of Salisbury's house—it was another resentment against
Edward that he had not been given a London house of his own—
fuddled and ill-tempered.

The Duchess went straight in to the attack. "I hope you are
satisfied with the havoc you have wrought, George. This is the
bitterest day of my life."

"It's not my fault that King Henry is wearing his crown again.
I never wanted that."

"I know what *you* wanted. There is nothing for you in this
wicked new regime, this puppet kingdom."

"I am slighted by all of them. They ignore me; they break
their appointments with me. Tudor and Oxford would have my
blood. My father-in-law won't protect me." George said this pet-
ulantly, wine had brought out all the self-pity in him.

His mother gave him a long look, devoid of sympathy. She had
known this son's weakness since early childhood. Yet she could
not bring herself to abandon him. He had many enemies. "Write
to your brother the King; ask his forgiveness."

"I have to grovel, do I?"

"You must make what reparation is just. You have wronged
him."

"If he were to come back now, he wouldn't last long."

"It may be a little while before the time is ripe."

"Will he forgive me?"

"Your eldest brother has a generous nature. You don't know how lucky you are in him."

"I'll see."

"And I'll speak to you again, George."

Oh, I have no doubt of that, he groaned inwardly, his head pulsing, his mouth sour. He wanted his bed, and to be rid of his mother. But he knew that, in the end, he would do as she had asked.

A day out from the port of Lynn, it seemed to Richard that God might well intend that he should die by drowning. He had found out that the only way in which he was going to avoid succumbing to abject seasickness was by remaining on deck in the fresh air. This meant becoming paralysed with cold, so that his fingers no longer had any awareness of what they clutched. He had also discovered that sailors spent a large part of their time soaked to the skin, without showing the signs of suffering so evident in himself and his companions. A natural fastidiousness within himself made him determined to endure all the rigours of the sea weather, rather than join the wretched, vomiting group which huddled in the foul, cramped shelter below deck.

Just when he thought he was more cold, wet and hopeless than he had ever been in his life, they came in sight of land. Not that he could have made out the darker grey blur of the coastline of Zeeland on a uniformly grey horizon, but the sailor up in the crow's nest had better eyes on the sea than he had.

No sooner had they come in sight of land than an alarm went up. Ships had been spotted, had evidently seen them, and had changed course to bear purposefully down upon them. They were the ships of the Easterlings, the Hanse trading towns, who were waging outright war against King Edward for his hostile action in turning them out of England. For once Richard regretted that he was on an English ship, flying the English standard; it would have been safer to travel on a Dutch ship. The Hansards were ferocious and merciless pirates, out only to capture or destroy. The prisoners they took were never heard of again, unless ransomed from their grim gaols in Danzig, or Lubeck. No one in England was likely to ransom Edward or himself. Maybe it would be better to stand and fight. The defeated would be thrown overboard. Richard wanted to be buried in consecrated ground.

The worst part of it was his own helplessness; he had been trained only for fighting on land. The Hanse ships were accoutred as ships of war, though they carried big cargoes, and the vessel from Lynn was scarcely armed. They did not have grapples for closing with the enemy, or troops of crossbowmen or guns mounted on the decks. They were entirely at the mercy of the skill of the Norfolk sailors and their captain. It was not the first time they had been chased by the Hansards.

It seemed that whatever orders the captain gave, whatever effort the crew made, the gap between King Edward's little, fleeing ships and the wolfish pursuers narrowed. Once they were caught, and surrounded, they would be disabled by cannon fire, arrows and crossbow bolts, grappled and boarded, looted and murdered. The Hanse ships gained on them, nearer and nearer, and it seemed to Richard that nothing could save them.

Yet, as if God heard their prayers and saw their plight, a miracle happened. They ran suddenly into a bank of sea fog, dense as wool and wet as rain. The captain decided, in extremity, to slacken all sail and lie up for a while as still and quiet as they could, in the hope of losing their pursuers.

Richard could not tell how long they lay there silently in the fog. He could neither hear nor see the other ships. Darkness fell —total darkness. They showed no lights. The Hansards did not attack.

When at last dawn came, the fog had cleared. There was no sign of the enemy. But half their own small fleet were missing; King Edward's ship was missing. Somehow he must have become separated from them in the fog or the night, and had sailed on while they stood still.

The captain said that now they had shaken off their pursuers, they could head in to the island of Walcheren as planned. Planned! They had not planned that they should lose the rightful King of England on the sea, or to the revengeful Hansards!

7

The Seventh Sacrament

October — December 1470

Filles a marier ne vous mariez ja
Se bien ne vous scavez quel mary vous prendra
Car sa jalous; a jamez ne vous ne luy
A cueur joye n'avez et pour ce penses y.

Song (15th century)

"*La vendange!*" Queen Charlotte reined in her horse and pointed towards the fields sloping down to the Loire. In the vineyards of the north bank, from Amboise to Tours and Angers, west to the sea and east to the mountains, a swarm of human ants was busy harvesting the grapes. "It is late in this district always," Charlotte went on. "This year is good, not a great year perhaps, but we have been lucky, the sun has shone for us. The grapes are very ripe, *ma petite*, you shall see, taste. We will visit the pickers, then go to see the treading!" She seemed as excited as a child.

Anne thought it was strange that a queen should care so much about what was, after all, only agriculture, and happened every year. At home Anne had seen business-like ladies about their estates take a wheat ear between their fingers, rustle it, and sniff knowledgeably, but they did not get as excited about the harvest in the way these French people did about their grapes. The day before, news had been brought to the castle that the grapes were ready, not a day too soon or too late. Every year it happened; King Louis was the first to hear that it was time for the vintage.

He watched over the wines he called his drops of gold with far more benevolence than he did his children. Anne found that everyone shared in his reverence for the grape harvest. Even Margaret of Anjou seemed to mellow at this time; the vintage must bring back memories of her childhood, when she lived at Saumur and Angers, so famous for wines.

Charlotte led her party up into the vineyards, keeping Anne close to her side. The peasants who laboured up and down between the rows of vines, their clumsy boots kicking up dust from the crumbly soil, seemed not unduly disturbed by the royal onlookers; bald sweating heads and neat white coifs appeared as straw hats were doffed, grins split brown faces, mauve and sticky about the chins. Rough grimy hands extended offering bunches of grapes. Anne found her lap full of them, leaking juice onto her gown. She put a handful into her mouth, and the juice was sweet as sugar syrup; a trickle of it overflowed and dribbled down her chin, and she used her sleeve quickly to mop it up. Looking round at others in the royal party, she saw that they were all stuffing grapes into their mouths with much greater abandon than she had, heedless of squirting and drooling juice; some spat out pips and skins, others were happy to swallow the lot. She decided to copy them, and crammed her mouth with over-ripe and squishy fruit. How much more the pickers deserved to refresh themselves with grapes. They worked quickly and hard to get the work done within a day or two, bending to cut the bunches from the vines with knives, filling hand baskets, which the women carried on their heads to the end of a row of vines, where donkeys with panniers stood patiently, waiting until they had a full load. The grapes filled the pannier baskets, piling up until the little animals seemed to sag under the weight. "*Hue! Martin!*" was the yell from every direction.

"Why do all the asses have the same name?" Anne asked, puzzled.

"Everyone in Touraine calls their donkey Martin," Queen Charlotte told her. "It is because the holy St. Martin of Tours one day let his donkey eat the spring shoots on the vines—he was riding in the vineyard and too busy praying to pay attention— and all the vines his donkey ate gave twice as many grapes when the vintage came. So the men of Touraine began to prune their vines every spring. You can see how good the yield is."

There were ox-carts also, two huge wooden tubs set on wheels to carry the grapes back to the winery. When they had ridden around the vineyards, and as many grapes as it was possible to eat had been eaten, they all followed the donkeys and ox-carts back to the castle, slowly, dustily, and with laughter. The oxen never quickened their stride, even when prodded with goads.

In the castle winery, the loads of grapes were being tipped out into troughs for treading. Everyone was treading, singing and laughing a great deal, sounding drunk already. Anne wondered what grape pips and stalks felt like between your toes, scratchy and squelchy at the same time? She hoped the peasants scrubbed their feet—most peasants' feet didn't bear thinking about. They gave her wine to drink, white with a yellow glow, like buttercup reflections, which made her feel silly very quickly. Queen Charlotte and her ladies were giggling at the treaders.

This year the final treading of the vintage took place on the feast of St. Denis, making an additional cause for celebration. It was a festival King Louis always kept with splendour, sitting at a banquet under the banner of the oriflamme, clad in rich robes and quite unlike the usual workaday and cobbled king.

Anne found her thoughts straying from the martyred saint, decapitated by the pagans, to England, wondering whether her father had taken many lives in his effort to win back King Henry's throne, or if indeed he had succeeded in his task. A few garbled stories had arrived in France, some saying King Edward was dead, some that the Earl of Warwick was dead, but mostly that King Edward had been killed, and that his head and his brother Gloucester's had been seen grinning on spikes on London Bridge.

This last appalled Anne; it was nearly as bad as hearing that her father's head was occupying the same place. She had never before given much thought to what she would feel if someone she knew well were to die by beheading. She was not old enough to remember the bad days of war in England, and had been sheltered by the absolute power of her father. The thought of Richard's life being destroyed, when he was only seventeen, and of his head being pecked at by kites on London Bridge, made her cry. She tried to remember what Richard looked like, but could only visualize certain things about him, rather than what he looked like from top to toe. She began to wish fervently that she had been married to Richard years ago, when it was first suggested. He was not as good looking as the Prince, of course, but just now she would have infinitely preferred him. She longed for the familiar, for known faces. She knew that King Louis was pressing for a dispensation for her marriage, but the Papal legate seemed to be making no progress in the matter because of the complications of consanguinity. No doubt it would be expedited, once definite news came from her father.

She did not have long to wait. On October 13th, the day on which the Prince was seventeen, the feast of the English royal St. Edward the Confessor, a letter arrived from the Earl of Warwick. Someone told Anne what her father had said. "The whole kingdom is now placed under the obedience of the King my sovereign lord, and the usurper, Edward, driven out of it." The usurper Edward and his brother had fled, taking ship from the port of Lynn, presumably for Burgundy, though no news had been heard of their arrival there yet.

King Louis, brandishing his letter from Warwick, summoned Margaret of Anjou, and Anne's mother, immediately.

"Madame," he said, "Monseigneur de Warwick has won England for you more quickly than I had hoped, with no blood spilt. Did I not tell you that my friend M. de Warwick could achieve things other men could not?"

"The wheel of Fortune turns very swiftly," said Queen Margaret. "I think we must wait to see if it will turn again, and throw M. de Warwick down to damnation, where he undoubtedly belongs. I hope for the sake of my poor husband the King, and for my son, that he will not be punished by God just yet."

"Humph," said Louis. "Madame, I hope to see you return to England by Epiphany at the latest, and to have attended to my lord Prince's marriage before then."

"When I am sure that it is safe for my son to do so, I will go back, not before. As for the marriage, that is scarcely my concern, as you forced me to agree to it."

To show his delight and confidence in Warwick's achievement, King Louis ordered three days of public rejoicing in France. He himself went off on a pilgrimage to Our Lady of Celles in Poitou, which he had vowed to do in thanksgiving if his plans and Warwick's succeeded. When he came back, he told Anne's mother that he had urgently requested the Bishop of Bayeux to procure the dispensation for Anne's marriage, and had backed his request with a large sum of money borrowed from a cloth merchant of Tours. Louis had begun to dwell upon how expensive it was to maintain Queen Margaret and her son, her fellow exiles, and Warwick's wife and daughter. He estimated that this had already cost him nearly 3000 livres, and he thought they would probably be staying more than another month. The sooner Margaret took herself and her son back to England, the sooner Warwick might see his way to helping Louis attack the Duke of Burgundy.

The King now began to plan this war with enthusiasm. In mid-November, at a meeting at Tours, it was declared that the Duke of Burgundy had, by his treason and aggression against his sovereign lord, forfeited his title and lands, which might be duly seized. The Prince of Wales signed an agreement with King Louis, promising to assist in waging war, and, when he returned to England, to persuade his father to openly declare the nation at war with Burgundy. By this time, they knew that Duke Charles had allowed King Edward to stay in Zeeland, and had provided him with some money, but had not yet received him at the Burgundian court. Louis wanted to attack as soon as possible and deprive Edward of a safe refuge. Ambassadors were to be sent to England with suggested plans for a campaign, for Louis was sure Warwick would give him the help he wanted. And if the ambassadors sent a good report of affairs in England, Queen Margaret would take her son home.

Before the Bishop of Bayeux left on this embassy, the dispensation for the union of Anne and the Prince arrived. The first reports from the French ambassadors in England confirmed that Warwick was firmly in charge of the kingdom. There was now no impediment to the marriage.

Anne was married to Edward of Lancaster in the castle chapel at Amboise on a grey day in early December. It was an event which made little impression on the world. Everyone seemed impatient to get it over. Indeed the day itself was so dreary and unmemorable that Anne could scarcely remember afterwards which end of the week it was. Some things, however, she did remember.

On her wedding day she woke out of fitful sleep and found her heart beating at a wild running pace, and nothing she did to try to calm herself would slow it down. She found that the women who washed and dressed her looked at her archly, in a way she did not like at all. It was like silent sniggering, as if they said behind their hands: you don't know what we know, but you soon will! They were squeezing her into a gown of palest blue silk, with a very deep neckline, which showed up her neck like a chicken's wish bone. It slithered over her head and snaked down her as if it were frost lined. The sleeves had to be sewn up on her, and were so tight she could bend her arms only a little. The cuffs covered all but the very tips of her fingers. Her hair hung down her back, as a bride's should. They had to keep smoothing it, because the cold made it fly about and crackle. Round her neck they hung a swan jewel, in white enamel, gold and rubies— the Prince's device. King Louis' dogs wore collars around their necks bearing his badges.

King Louis, as usual at this time of year, rode out early to hunt the deer. When he came back, his nose reddened with cold and a blob of mud still on one eyebrow, he took the place of a father and gave away Anne to a husband she did not want. When the Grand Vicar of Bayeux joined her hand with that of the Prince, she thought they would be able to feel the racing of her heart. Little birds felt like that, when picked up in human hands. Once long ago she had cried because a bird had died in her hand, its heart beating itself out in fright. All the young Prince felt was a small childish hand as cold and unresisting as a dab in a net. Anne promised to love and obey her husband, in French, so faintly that her voice could scarcely be heard. Margaret of Anjou fretted in impatience and anger. King Louis would not have been surprised if she had broken in on the ceremony and tried to stop it, even at that last moment. But she did not. The candles smelt, as if they were not made of best quality wax, and guttered so, the chapel must be full of draughts.

After it was all over, a banquet was held in honour of the Prince of Wales and his new wife. Anne could not eat. The tenderest meat was like sawdust. The golden wines of Touraine had lost their glow of summer sunshine. King Louis thought of the new alliance with England, previously so unimaginable, and was content with his policy. Now that his aim was accomplished, he was not disposed to be deliberately unkind. He was aware that Anne was neither stupid nor spiritless, for all that she sat there like a mouse crouching under a chair. In order to lighten the atmosphere at the banquet, he had commanded his players to enact the story of *Le Maître Pathelin*, which at any rate made him roll about with laughter, and should give all the guests similar enjoyment, even if the married couple did have their minds on other things.

Anne watched the players with as little comprehension as she would have shadows jumping about on a wall. When the one who was supposed to be a shepherd began bleating like a sheep, she gave up altogether and shut her eyes.

Unfortunately, her husband noticed her sitting there with her eyes shut. He was beginning to feel very apprehensive about what was to come afterwards. He would have felt more confident if he were sure that his bride was shy out of mere modesty and inexperience. But this girl did not want to go to bed with him, he was certain. This fact was a blow to his considerable pride and vanity, and made him resentful. In spite of his mother's contempt for Anne, and her insistence that if events went wrong in England he would be saddled with a wife of no usefulness to him, he would have liked to feel that he had made a conquest. His mother had wanted the marriage to remain unconsummated until they were safely back in England and she could judge for herself how secure Warwick's victory was, but King Louis had insisted, because he would not allow his friend the Earl to be undersold in his absence. Old Louis would be there, behind the bed curtains, to make certain the bride did not get up a virgin; he was a thorough and practical man. This contributed much to the Prince's apprehension. To make matters worse, Pierre Robin, his physician—or rather his grandfather King René's physician—hovered over him, inspecting everything he ate, as if he had an old man's digestion. Ever since he had been very ill with measles when he was fourteen, his mother had set Robin to watch him, as if he were still ailing, which he was not.

King Louis escorted the couple to their bed chamber like a sardonic guardian angel from the realms of darkness. He was distressingly good humoured, and cracked jokes which embarrassed the Prince and made Anne blush. She had not previously disliked the King, even though she had realized he took no account of the feelings of women. He was very matter of fact, however, and it would have been much worse if he had been personally salacious. He supervised everything as he might have a mating of valuable hounds. A lot of other people were indulging in licentious talk and behaviour because they were very drunk, but this always happened at weddings. Anne did not make the effort to hear what they said, except when it was so loud and rude as to make her blush. She felt as if her skin was shrinking. She found the idea of getting into bed naked with a young man so strange; she knew what he would do, but had no notion of what it would be like. Edward was looking sulky, and this frightened her. They could not even comfort each other in their separate plights.

Queen Charlotte's sisters put Anne to bed, giggling, while the King looked on dispassionately. The girl in that white shift affair had about as much shape as a choirboy; he thought that, unlike the Duke of Burgundy, the Prince of England's taste did not run in that direction. He was concerned only that the Prince should perform his duties adequately, not with the boy's disappointments. Whether or not the girl became pregnant was immaterial; there was plenty of time for that when they got back to England.

The Prince, who had been instructed exactly in what he should do by the gentlemen in his mother's retinue, thought that they had forgotten to tell him one thing, and that was how to get things started when the bride sharing your pillow looked about ten years old and was staring frozenly up at the tester as if you did not exist. His only experience had been with one or two clean and compliant whores selected by his mother, and who had not left him to initiate the operation. Everything had been so easy and pleasurable. He stared down at Anne, whose brownish hair trickled all over the place, making it difficult to lie beside her without tugging on it. Her soft, little girl's lips were firmly closed.

"Are you comfortable now?" he asked in a stilted way; he meant, are you ready? He wanted to see her lips move.

"Yes, your Grace." This had the effect he wanted, her teeth were neat and even, but the words sounded chilling.

"I am your husband. My name is Edouard."

She said, "Yes," again, and her shy grey eyes slipped him a glance before resuming their stare at nothing.

He wondered if he should kiss her. When he did so, her lack of response made him clumsy, and he missed the place he was aiming for, and skated off her cheek towards her ear, and got a mouthful of long hairs. Anne turned her face slightly away from the feel of his saliva. He smelled of wine recently drunk, though otherwise he was perfectly wholesome, scrubbed and scented as much as she had been. The tiny movement revealing her involuntary distaste turned his uncertainty into hostility, and made him hurry into the action he had hoped would happen at their mutual wish. Even then, not forgetting to be considerate, Edward remembered to take the weight of his athletic young body on both arms, instead of squeezing the girl's breath out. But he found the business more awkward than on the previous occasions because he was not too sure of where to go, for lack of helpful guidance, and in any case he had not realized how narrow was the margin of error. She was small, *virgo intacta*, and unco-operative. This made him rougher than he had intended. He felt her go rigid as a board, but she made no sound. What made things worse was that just when he thought himself home and beginning to be in command of the situation, King Louis outside the bed curtains burst into raucous coughing. This had the effect of creating an unfortunate hiatus, which only increased the Prince's feelings of damaged pride, and led him to seek a hasty end.

Anne was left sore, and sick. It had hurt a great deal. No one had ever touched her roughly before. She desperately wanted to get up and wash. Prince Edward was lying on his stomach with his face squashed against the pillow, and his muscly legs were still against her own. She did not like to edge away from him, for she sensed that he was neither pleased nor satisfied. Tears scalded her eyes and fell off her face with, to her, almost audible plops, onto the pillow.

Then Edward spoke, his words muffled by plump down pillow and bolster. "Did you like it?" he asked, half curiously, half resentfully, as if he had hoped she might say yes, but thought that she would not. She was taken aback. She could not say—no, I hate you, for that would not be entirely true. It had been horrible, but imagine how much worse it could have been if he were old, ugly, or smelly. His skin felt not unpleasant, smooth, and very warm.

"I don't know," she said, stupidly, then could not help letting out a snuffle. That was a mistake, because it told him that she was crying. He turned his back with a flouncing movement and moved away in the bed with exaggerated care. She was left feeling that the performance had been a dismal failure, and that this was her fault.

King Louis stuck his head in between the bed curtains. *"Eh bien, mes enfants?"* he enquired. At any other time his extraordinary and unpretty profile peering through curtains would have been funny. Anne went red with shame. The Prince's efforts had bunched up her shift round the top half of her body, and she huddled under the sheet, holding it under her chin. King Louis showed no embarrassment at all. "Well?" he said.

The Prince, his sullen, handsome face the same raspberry colour as Anne's, nodded. The King grunted approvingly and withdrew his head. Anne cowered, thinking that he might ask her to reveal the evidence. But they heard the long toes of his shoes flap away across the floor. After he had gone, they both retreated into opposite corners of the enormous bed and pretended to sleep.

In the morning there was no time for even the beginning of a conversation. The women came to dress Anne, to peer at the bot-

tom sheet which had to be sent by special messenger to King
Louis, while the Prince's grinning servants whisked him away.
When she saw her mother later, it was only to be told that after
the first night, she would not be sharing a bed with the Prince;
Queen Margaret insisted upon this. The Countess seemed both
doleful and evasive, as if she felt herself to blame for having a
daughter who had proved so unsatisfactory. Anne felt so relieved
that she did not care what anyone thought. Secretly, she had
made a mark on the calendar in her Book of Hours, on a certain
day two weeks previous to her wedding. She now counted off
four weeks from her mark, and made another, in red. She then
began to count the days to safety or disaster in a little table of
neat spots, five in a row. She marked one in carefully every day,
and each time she kneeled down afterwards with her beads and
prayed desperately for deliverance.

A day or two after the marriage, Queen Margaret, her son,
Anne and her mother set out for Paris, on the first stage of their
long journey to England. Paris, the greatest city in all France
was not inviting either to the eye or to the nose in the winter
season. In the flat plain, the long range of walls could be seen
from far away; the towers and turrets might have looked fair on
a blue-skied, sunny day, but against a sky of lead they might
have belonged to any unremarkable city in the world. Closer at
hand, the walls could be seen to be of light grey stone, old and
unclean, the marks of ancient rains making long greenish brown
streaks down to the ground, like the outflows, of garderobes. The
town fields were mostly under plough, herringbones of water
lying in the furrows, the pastures soggy and unoccupied. Rows
of colossal dung heaps steamed and fumed along the roadside
and under the walls.

The Prince was holding forth about how he would lay siege to
Paris, which was something he did every time he came to a new
city. This did not seem very tactful, when he was about to be
greeted by its citizens.

"When Fabius Maximus took Capua, he laid waste to all the
growing corn in the countryside, and then withdrew until the
fields were sown again and the Campanians had used all their
stored grain, then laid a siege and starved them out. Of course,

with a big city like this, which receives all the goods of the world along the Seine, it would be important to blockade the river. And no one should begin this sort of campaign in France too late in the year—the rains can come in September. My grandfather King Harry found that out. He was King, but he had to live off green apples and walnuts, like everybody else." The Prince knew and treasured every legend of the Agincourt campaign.

"Your father was crowned King of France here," his mother said, pointing to the great towers of Notre Dame. "It did him no good. While King Louis lives, the English will make no more wars on France. I hope that the old enmity will soon be forgotten, though it will not be easy. The English are so obstinate and prejudiced."

The part of Paris the Queen pointed out was built on a long island, behind a high wall, the cathedral one end and the old royal palace the other. In front of the walls were gravel walks beside the Seine, and worn out, dog-scratched patches of grass which might in spring be lawns, and a row of willow trees, bare and spiky like up-ended besoms.

Just before they crossed the first arm of the Seine, there was a tableau of Our Lady, and St. Anne welcomed the daughter of René, King of Sicily and Jerusalem, the Prince of England her son—and his wife—to the *Île de la Cité*. On the bridge itself, a group of young men pressed forward rather frighteningly and yelled, "Go home, English!" which seemed unjust, as the Prince was three-quarters French, and the only English person was Anne herself. The Prince became red and angry, and it was explained to him that they were students from the University, and always rude or causing trouble.

King Louis had given orders that the house in which he usually stayed in Paris, the Maison des Tournelles, should be prepared for his guests. The house was comfortable enough, for the King, who could make do with the meanest hut, also appreciated comforts, but it held the dampness of age, and was enclosed by high walls. Anne could see from the windows the city wall itself, and an enormous, very high bastion like a castle keep, which loomed and cast its shadow wherever she looked.

Her surroundings conspired to make her even more miserable, and she caught a cold, which spoilt any enjoyment she might have got out of the Christmas season. Life in the entourage of Queen Margaret was more frightening than when they had been at King Louis' court, and Anne trod very warily. The first time she was called to attend upon the Queen was the worst. Even handing a garment or a jewel to another lady made her feel all thumbs, and then she dropped the Queen's rosary and the string broke and the beads rolled all over the floor, and one of the Pater Nosters went under a chest.

Margaret looked at the beads, then at her, and shrugged. *"Pas d'importe,"* she said, without venom, or even interest.

When they had finished grovelling about and retrieved all fifteen, Anne stood there shaking so hard that she imagined the floorboards squeaked under her. She felt as if she would be sick with fright, and tears clouded her sight and her nose felt hot and swollen, and that everyone must notice. Some of them did, but not in any way to reprimand.

"You will not be eaten here, your Highness," one of them said afterwards. This was the Provençal one, Lady Vaux, whom Anne knew to be Queen Margaret's dearest friend. Katherine Vaux had come to England with her when they were both sixteen.

"Do not be afraid of her Grace the Queen. You must understand that things have not been easy for her. She came to England when she was almost as young as you, and she found no kindness there. The English always hate people or things that they do not know or understand. Madame still feels that your father is her enemy; twenty-five bitter years cannot be wiped out in one day. But don't despair, things will be better later on, when affairs in England have been settled. You will get to know your husband better, too. Stand up straight and look the Queen in the face; if you shake and shiver in front of her, she will be annoyed."

But Anne remained uncomforted. She was desperately homesick for England. Nowhere seemed so far away now as Middleham Castle, remote and as unimaginably distant as the Indies. She even began to miss Isabel a little. At least a sister was a sister, and part of familiar life. When they had been younger, they had quarrelled often, but done many things together. On the Eve of St. Agnes in January, once, she and Isabel had made dumb cakes in the nursery. If their mother had known, there would have been trouble, for Isabel who was five years older and should have known better, and for the servants as well as themselves, because their mother was afraid of country heathen customs. Anne had dreamed of no one at all that night, and Isabel had said this was because she had broken her silence while eating her cake with a fit of giggling and choking. Isabel swore that she had dreamed of someone tall, fair and handsome —the possibility of marriage with Clarence had been tacit even then. Anne could tell that she had made it up, and had probably slept as they both usually did, without dreaming. Isabel had said then that she was surprised Anne did not dream of her cousin Richard; she spent enough time making eyes at him. Anne had been furious, because she did not like her innermost feelings exposed by her sister's silly teasing. The memory was hurtful now.

Before they had left Paris for Rouen, her husband the Prince had demanded to visit one of the famous sights of the city, the gallows at Montfaucon, on which a hundred men could be hanged at once, and was never untenanted by their dangling bodies. He had even asked Anne if she wanted to go with him, but she had hastily declined. Her cousin Gloucester would not have done such things for pleasure, or been so stupid as to think she might want to also.

8

The Exiles

January – March 1471

Blessid be god in trinite,
Fadir & son & holygoste,
Which kepith his servauntes in adversite,
& wold not suffre theyme to be loste.
As thou art lord of mightes moste,
Save the kyng & his ryalte,
And illumyn hym with the holy goste,
His relme to set in perfyt charite.

The Battle of Northampton (c. 1460)

Richard stood in the *Craene Plaetse* by the *Pont de la Grue*, or in the *Place de la Grue* by the *Craene Brugghe*. He made himself learn every new name of a place or a thing in both French and Flemish. Bruges was a city of three languages—in order to do business with the merchants of a score of different nations, he had to string together sentences of bad Latin, which he found almost as difficult as Flemish.

He looked up at the town crane. It stood idle because the day was a Sunday and the feast of St. Sebastian; the treadwheel that worked the lifting gear was empty. All along the tall arm of the crane, outlined against the sky, stood little cranes—the birds—carved and gilded, and perched in a neat row, the biggest one surmounting the pulley at the top. Snow was heaped on their gold backs and piled in little crests on top of their heads, like ermine cloaks and hats.

King Edward had just ordered a gown lined and collared with vast quantities of ermine and a hat to match, all at the expense of their host in Bruges, Louis of Gruuthuse, Lord of Holland. They lived in the Gruuthuse palace, ate the excellent Gruuthuse dinners, and used the Gruuthuse credit with every merchant. Their own, after all, was non-existent. A king without a kingdom, without much prospect of regaining it, and largely without the support of his brother-in-law the Duke of Burgundy, in whose lands he was exiled. A pension of 500 shillings a month, and one interview granted—Edward had to travel a hundred miles to Aire in Artois to receive the honour—scarcely amounted to a brotherly welcome.

Because he had cold feet and cobbled boots, Richard moved away from the crane and onto the bridge. He was lucky enough to have a fur-lined coat on his back—thanks to Louis of Gruuthuse. He looked like a young man of a moderately prosperous merchant family and so went almost unnoticed in the streets. In Bruges only the dazzling and sumptuously arrayed merchant princes in the styles of many countries attracted attention. King Edward was stared at a good deal in the street, but that was more on account of his height and looks than any distinction of garb to show that he was the disinherited King of England. Surely some of the richest men in the world, proclaiming their status in their appearance, lived in Bruges. Richard had already, in the company of Edward, dined with several of them. There had been precious little gained by this apart from the meals. Duke Charles had so far forbidden his subjects to openly support Edward. Tommaso Portinari, the Florentine agent, had been favourably disposed but, as a member of Charles' ducal council, had scarcely been in a position to act upon his own judgement.

Richard's own assets made him about as rich as a pedlar, but perhaps more hopeful of an upturn in fortune. In the house of Gruuthuse, they lived like princes, but went out into the street without so much as the price of their next meal. At Duke Charles' court at Aire, he and Edward had been decked in the pick of Gruuthuse's jewels, and spent enough on their gowns to keep a hundred Englishmen in Burgundy for a month, for at Duke Charles' court one had to put appearances before every-

thing. Now, no one knew of the holes in his shirt or mended out-
door boots, except his fellow exiles, who were in even worse
straits.

He had arrived in Zeeland last October owning nothing but
the clothes he stood up in, a razor and a comb. When he had ridden to meet Edward at The Hague he had been obliged to borrow £3 2/3d (he only remembered the exact sum because it was
the first of his many debts) from the bailiff of the town of Veere
in order to purchase a horse and achieve the journey without
starvation. Mercifully, the news that Edward was safely in the
north of Holland had reached him soon after their landing,
though for the first few days he had not known whether his
brother were alive or dead. If it had not been for the friendly
hospitality of Gruuthuse, they both might have ended in a debt-
ors' prison in Holland.

He cleared a space with his gloved hand on the parapet of the
bridge so that he might lean on it. The snow had a crust on it
like a pie. There were long scoop marks where children had
grabbed handfuls for snowballs. They were pelting each other
now. He himself remembered snowballing, without even bothering to wear gloves. He looked down at the frozen Reye, where
skaters of all ages sped along as if they were being called by the
worke clocke bell to their daily tasks, instead of being at feast-
day pleasures. Children tiny enough to need a baby-walking
frame on land were towed along at the skirts of older ones.
Those without skates slid about and ruined their shoes on the
ice.

The Guild procession of St. Sebastian was over, and the
onlookers dispersed about the streets, for dinner or skating.
Bruges was a city of processions, no feast day was complete
without one.

On the steps leading down to the ice, booths had been set up,
selling hot ale and skates. Richard fished the last coin from his
purse. The sight of all the people of Bruges enjoying themselves
invited him to join them. He was alone, having wandered away
from the procession, telling his servant to go home, and had
nothing more to do until tomorrow. Doing nothing out here was
better than doing nothing indoors. He had missed dinner at the

Gruuthuse huis, but one could be well fed there at any time of day. He had skated on ponds and rivers since childhood, and knew he could get about on the ice, if not with the accomplished ease of these Flemish people. He did not want to think about the times when the castle moat at Middleham had frozen and he had fooled about with the other boys. England, in the raw, fierce north country winter . . . Warwick's castle . . . the faces of friends who were now enemies.

He put on the bone skates and started off in an easterly direction towards the next bridge. He was circling about, trying his skill before setting off, when a woman swooped across his path making him check and waver. She turned neatly and came back.

"*Pardon mijnheer!*"

He smiled politely, shook his head, and began to move, when he realized that he had seen her before. Her face lit with recognition also.

"*Goeden dach mijnheer!*" Then "*Ah! Inghelsche!*" she exclaimed, and halted gracefully at his side. He came to a less elegant standstill.

"I am Vrouwe van den Watere, of the bookseller's shop in the cloisters," she said in accented French, which he was at least able to understand. "You remember, *mijnheer?* A few days ago Seigneur Gruuthuse was showing the English king the products of my workshop. . . ." She began to move slowly, because she could see no sense in standing about on the ice. They skated along in unison.

"Yes, madame," he said, "I do remember. He told us you were not only the owner of the shop but that some of the work was your own. Are there other women in Bruges as accomplished?"

"Bruges is full of accomplished women," she smiled again. "My husband when he died left me a well-established business. I was a pupil of M. van Vrelant. I have been lucky."

She looked lucky. There was something about the calm, competent manner of her progress over the ice, and her smiling face, which proclaimed good fortune and a happy acceptance of God's providence. She was wearing a gown of fine black wool cloth, pulled in by a wide red belt, the shirt folded back to show a red lining, and with fur at the wrists and high neck. He was not sure

of her age; she was not old, but he did not think less than
twenty-five. It was somehow a relief to meet someone whom he
could recognize in this crowd of Brugeois hurrying past on
skates, and who seemed happy to pass the time of day with him.
She had evidently been equally happy to skate with only her servant for company. She greeted several people as they went
along.

When they reached the Pont St. Jean, there was a stall with a
woman making wafers. The smell of sizzling batter cooking between the hot irons mingled with spicy steam from mugs of hot
ale also on sale. The frosty cold and liveliness of the skaters
made certain the stalls did good trade. Richard was acutely
aware that he had missed his dinner.

"It smells good," Vrouwe van den Watere said, and smiled.
Her nose and cheeks were becomingly pink. "I will eat."

With a sinking feeling Richard knew he was going to appear
ill-mannered and allow a lady to buy her own food and drink.
There was no point in pretending to hunt in his purse. It was
empty and would remain so until he got back to the Gruuthuse
huis.

"I have no money," he said, and knew he was as red in the
face as the woman cooking wafers.

She looked at him, and smiled again. "But I have," she said.
"We will eat."

She took coins from her purse and spoke to the vendors in
Flemish. The hot wafers were eaten as they dropped from the
irons the woman took out of the red coals. Richard took off his
gloves, stuffed them in his belt and warmed his hands on the
round belly of an earthenware mug of ale. There was cinnamon
bark floating in it, and a clove. When the red hot iron had been
thrust into the ale to heat it, it had hissed and steamed as if
alive. The foot of the mug was indented like the edge of a pastry, indents which bore the marks of the potter's fingers for ever.

She ate up her wafers with quick appreciation, and drank her
ale in sensible draughts, not in coy sips, as some women would.
"*Goede!*" she said at almost every bite, and smiled often.

Richard could have wolfed two dozen wafers without taking
the edge off his appetite.

"Will you dine with me at home, *mijnheer?* It is late, and I am hungry!"

He nearly swallowed the clove and had to spit it out before saying yes. At home he would have wondered, in his rank and position, whether he should accept the invitation of ladies to dine. Here things were different. He was nobody, and this woman was used to dining her business clients and colleagues without expecting any comment upon her actions. She was so naturally friendly, perhaps she realized the English exiles were in no position to issue invitations themselves. Besides the offer of dinner was a stroke of luck. She was no more than ministering to a hungry Englishman.

They skated back along the canals, moving fast now. When the canal went under the Waterhalle, they had to come up and walk along the Wolle Straete and go down again at the Zoutdyck.

Vrouwe van den Watere lived in a good house facing the Dyver.

"The house of the lord Gruuthuse is only a few minutes' walk from here. You will not have far to go. My servants and apprentices are on holiday today and have been to Mass and now are out amusing themselves. Perhaps you would like to see my workshop—it is better to do so while it is empty. I can show you more of the work we do."

"I should like to do that, madame."

"But more, you would like to eat!" she smiled widely again. She had one dimpled cheek. He always liked dimples; they seemed to make smiles contain more genuine amusement.

"Yes," he said and had to laugh. She laughed with him and he began to feel much more at ease. The room in which they were to eat surprised him. It was furnished and hung with goods of a quality he would not expect to exceed in his own house—if he had one—indeed it was better than his own rooms at Westminster. He might see more opulence at Eltham or at Warwick Castle but would also feel more draughts and discomforts. And it was so clean. Floorboards of clean light wood, a cupboard on which handsome plate was set out and some single, unusual ornaments—a Turkish carpet in front of the cupboard, a vase of white pottery with a deisgn in bronze and blue, holding a single peacock feather, and a big platter of the same ware. A string of prayer beads hung on the wall, made of very delicately carved boxwood. The most unusual feature was that where there should have been a fireplace, there was a stove, a box-like thing with a glowing window, made of green patterned tiles. The warmth from it reached every corner of the room, even on a day of sharp January frost.

The dinner served in the house lived up to its surroundings, being a combination of delicacies and solid Flemish food. It was amazing how much of it they managed to eat between them. She kept urging him to have more, and he needed little encouragement.

"You are generous, madame."

"Madame! No more madames. My name is Thonine. I do not have too much madameing among my friends."

He smiled. The beer was very good, cool and clean and sharp, quite different to English brews.

"What do you call eels—*anguilles?*" He asked over a dish of which he had eaten more than half. It was the best cooked version of a favourite dish.

"*Een paling.* Eat more!"

As they ate, she asked him questions. His name, for the first time. He hedged round this a little.

"*Richard van—?*" she looked inquiring, dipped a succulent piece of chicken in the salt.

"Richard Gloucester." He wondered if she would realize now, and whether it would spoil the directness of her manner.

"Is there not a Duke of Gloster in the English party—is he not the English King's brother? Is this the same name? Do you serve him?"

"Yes, I serve him." This let him off the hook. "The name is a town in England."

"Ah! I see. Eat some more. We have plenty here."

He did as she said.

"Is my house as good as the English have in London?"

"Better. You understand comfort in Bruges. The English like

to show off gold and silver, but they do not bother about draughts and bugs."

"Bugs! I hope there are none in this house! Or fleas—I wage war on bugs and fleas. You are obviously a gentleman of good family, do the nobility in England go about scratching?"

"Often. Even in the King's palace, where I live sometimes, I've had, well . . . they keep coming back. We don't have stoves in England—I like this one."

"It came from Cologne; my husband brought it back. My friends admire it. Do you serve the King?"

"Yes."

"What is he like, tell me. I've seen him—such a big, tall man. Is he really such a seducer of women?"

"Sometimes."

She laughed uproariously at this. "I will have to meet him. Perhaps I could sell him a book!"

"He has no money to buy books."

"You are all, how do you say it—*d'une complexion?*"

"In the same boat."

"Hm. Fortune will change."

After they had eaten and the meal had been cleared away, she took him to see the workshop. This lay behind the main dwelling part of the house, with the apprentices' living quarters over it. The place was very clean again, and tidy, remarkably free of paint stains. It smelt of size, paint and glue. It was colder there, because the fire was not lit.

"We write books, paint initial letters, borders, pictures. One of us is a bookbinder. Some workshops separate these tasks, but I have found it more satisfactory to do everything under one roof."

Laid out upon the tables in boxes and jars were the pens, brushes, bone smoothers for parchment, and several glasses for magnifying the finest work. Parchment folios of books in progress stood on wooden stands at the scribes' desks.

Richard said, "I have always wondered how the writers can make their letters so even and perfect for page after page. After we ordinary people are taught to write and make our letters from the horn book by our schoolmasters, we all end writing hands of all shapes and sizes. Even the clerks cannot write a book hand."

"It is mostly a matter of practice—perhaps even the least of the skills. I'll teach you how to write a fine Roman hand in the latest fashion—how to hold the pen, and form the letters. It is easy."

"Show me some of your own work."

She led him over to one of the desks. On it were a row of little jars, several peacocks' feathers, glowing with the colours of a kingfisher or a beetle's back, and a row of mussel and whelk shells, pearly within, ash grey or ribbed buff without. She had been painting the shells onto the border of the page of the book, and they were so lifelike as to appear to be mirrored images. He was almost ashamed to be startled by the evidence of her competence as an artist. He had never met a woman so gifted before.

"When I have finished the shells, I will start upon a border of the peacock feathers. I am looking forward to that. I always try to make the colours shimmer as they might on the bird, but it is never quite. . . . There is oil in the feathers, you see—it cannot look quite the same in paint. But it is a test of skill."

"The shells are beautiful," he said wonderingly. "I should like to see you at work on them."

"Another day, you shall. Now I do not have my colours set up. Besides . . ." for some reason she did not finish what she was saying.

He bent over the painting she had been doing, to peer more closely at the detail. Some of it was so fine, he was sure she must use a brush with only a single hair. He was holding the sides of the stand on which the unfinished painting rested, when she touched his left wrist, sliding her forefinger and thumb round it, as if about to measure it up for reproduction on the page. Then she did the same to the right.

"You have wrists of different sizes," she said, as if she made a great discovery.

He felt as if it were he who was making the discovery. "Yes, I have."

She was standing close, and he looked intently at her face, as if they had only that moment met. She had brown eyes, which was unexpected, because her skin was clearly meant to go with blonde hair, though the hair was hidden away under folds of white linen.

"Why?" she asked with simple logic.

"I was trained for fighting. When I was young I was not tall or sturdy enough. . . . But I survived and seemed to grow to it. One arm stronger than the other."

"What a mystery you are!"

"No, surely not a mystery?"

"But you are. There is a great deal I do not yet understand. There must be more to you than I can see."

She paused, then leaned forward—she did not have to lean far—and kissed him softly on the lips. "I am inquisitive," she said. "I want to know more."

The delightful shock of her sudden and amazing action made him feel as if he had been turned upside down and righted again the same moment.

"Why?" It was his turn to say. His breathing had become very slow, preparatory to becoming very fast indeed.

She laughed. Then she laid the smooth palms of her hands on either side of his face, holding him, after her laughter, suddenly grave. "Why should you say why, as if you did not expect such attentions? Interesting men are always mysteries—that is why it is good, trying to seek the solution. I would like to begin now!"

It was a beginning which led on to other things with remarkable speed.

As downstairs in the room where they had dined, there was a tiled stove in the bedroom, which when fed with more wood gave out a marvellous warmth. It was true, what was said in London, about the Flemish vrouwes. . . . She was the colour of the inside of one of the shells, and her mouth as warm as the stove. He had never realized his own capacity for pleasure before, until he tried to match it to this woman, who was no raw girl. King Edward couldn't do better than this.

When, after a long time, it was possible to make conversation, she said, "How old are you?"

He told her.

"So young? I'd have thought you were of age. You look older than eighteen."

"I'm still a minor in the charge of my brother the King," he said, laughing, then realized he had given himself away. He scarcely ever referred to his brother by name alone, and it had slipped out. She would have known sooner or later.

Her soft brown eyes—velvety like the fur on some dark bees—opened wide and stared at him, or as much of him as she could see—their eyelashes brushed together.

"*Den hertoge van Gloster!* You misled me before." She could hardly get up and kneel before him and kiss his hand, she was in a position of disadvantage. So, for that matter, was he.

"No, I did not wish to mislead you." The closeness of her lips made him kiss them again. They were velvety, too, rose pink.

"You were like yourself," he said, against her cheek. "If I had told you I were—how do you say—*den broder van Coninc van Ingelant*—you would have behaved as someone not quite yourself."

"And now I have acted as myself, I cannot put on a mask as if I were at the carnival."

"No!" he said triumphantly.

"So that is why you are so masterful," she said at protracted length. "You are a duke!"

"I doubt it—it's because you invite me!" They both rolled about together, laughing.

Vrouwe Thonine van den Watere sent one of her servants to accompany her lover back to the Gruuthuse huis. Richard went with the man as if he had walked out through the curtains of a dream. He remembered now all the questions he might have asked Thonine van den Watere. He knew nothing of her dead husband, or whether she had children. That made him begin to worry about his own child, little Katherine, who was now nearly a year old, and fostered with her mother's family. He could do nothing for his daughter. He would have liked to see her. But he inhabited a different world now, as if the previous one had never existed.

For more than a week, he went often to the house upon the Dyver. It was inevitable that his nightly absences from the

Gruuthuse huis should be noticed. The entire party of English exiles knew that he was involved in an affair, but his own efforts at discretion kept them from knowing with whom. King Edward did not probe much, although he grinned a lot at his brother and looked almost proud of him. This was nearly as bad as years ago, when Edward had taken a fatherly concern in his virginity, or rather in the desirability of his losing it by the time he was fifteen. Edward had always made his affairs casually public and could not understand Richard's unwillingness to reveal anything at all.

Once or twice, Richard was able to go to the workshop to watch Vrouwe van den Watere at her painting. Her total absorption in her work and her harmonious relations with the craftsmen—and women—that she employed, impressed him deeply. She was as good as, and better than, the men. He felt he was not going to encounter anything quite like this again. God knew what he might be likely to encounter; he had schooled himself not to envisage the future, not able to see anything in it for himself. He occasionally wondered what he would do if Charles of Burgundy turned them out—go to the Italian States perhaps, where the Dukes were always wanting foreign mercenaries. This was so sufficiently unreal a situation as to be not worth the thought.

At the beginning of February King Edward sent Richard to see their sister at Lille. The Duchess Margaret had letters from Clarence, and from their mother. King Edward wrote letters to his prodigal brother which were models of patience and assurances of forgiveness, which their sister would send to England together with her own pleas.

Richard found his sister at Lille much the same as when he had seen her in early January. That was, surrounded by an elaborate court, gorgeously dressed, loaded with jewels, but with no sign of Duke Charles, or that he even visited her from one month's end to the next. As adults, Richard and Margaret scarcely knew each other.

When Margaret had left England two and a half years ago she had been twenty-two, a mature bride, self-willed and handsome, and fond of the admiration of men. She and Clarence had been

very close since childhood. Richard sometimes thought she was
the only person George cared for. If anyone were able to persuade him to return to his natural family allegiance, it was Margaret.

When Richard got back from Lille, King Edward called his
followers together, and told them that their chickens were coming home to roost and the loans so assiduously applied for had
begun to materialize. The biggest triumph was the agreement
with the Hanse merchants. In return for a restoration of all their
privileges in England, they would supply 14 ships and 1500 soldiers, good troops, hand gunners among them. The money Duke
Charles had promised had arrived. The bonds for several other
loans had at last been signed and sealed.

"There is no sense in any more delay now," King Edward said.
"We have enough—well, the minimum—but if we delay we will
lose any advantage we have. I have heard from England that
Warwick's position is precarious and Henry of Lancaster is incapable of governing. Margaret of Anjou and her son have not yet
left France. While they delay, Warwick's troubles will only multiply. If I can strike while they are so weakened, then we have a
chance. A chance so slender I shudder to think of it. But the
time has come for us to act, not to think.

"My lords, I want you to suffer no misapprehensions. Any one
of three outcomes is about equally weighted, as I see it. Item
one: We may succeed in England and overcome our enemies.
Item two: We may, as you are well aware, die in the attempt.
Item three, which comforts me not at all: We may be driven
back to Burgundy with our tails between our legs. If this were to
happen, my noble brother-in-law Duke Charles would eventually
turn us out to beg our bread round Europe." Richard took his eyes
from his brother's sober, utterly resolute face, to glance round at
his companions. He saw that both Lord Hastings and Lord Rivers
were hanging upon the King's words as much as he was himself.
Will Hastings was a fine man, the best of all King Edward's close
friends. Rivers too, Richard had to concede, had not faltered in
loyalty; for the first time he felt some liking for the Queen's eldest brother. Anthony Woodville was a strange companion for

their adventure yet he was proving himself steadfast and re-sourceful. He was the best of the Woodville bunch.

"So there you have it," the King said to them. "I am deter-mined to go back. I give you a fortnight in which to prepare. Then I suggest we commend ourselves to God, and Saint George —and we'd better make a long list of those saints who will pro-tect us because we may never again need their favours as much as we do now.

"Other than this, you know what we need—money, ships, men, weapons, good Flemish horses—don't waste space on supplies other than arms—in England we live off the land. I rely on each of you to scrape together whatever you can beg, borrow or steal in the name of my long-lost credit, even down to the last horse-shoe nail and the flight feathers for our arrows.

"I'm no Icarus, flying foolish too near the sun. I'm Edward of March again and, by all the saints, I'm more determined to have my life and my crown than even I was before Towton, before all my battles. I have the best New Year gift a man could—news of the birth of my son Edward. November the second, the feast of All Souls, and it was a month before I knew of it. Now I have a son, a Prince, to fight for. By God, if by his Grace I cross the sea safely, we shall see another Towton this Palm Sunday!"

As he said it, tempting fortune in all his smiling confidence, towering above them all, Richard believed every word. We can-not fail, he thought, because my brother *will* not allow failure. He could have hugged and kissed his brother with a child's en-thusiasm. Instead, King Edward embraced them one by one, An-thony Woodville, Lord Hastings, the many other knights who were dependent on him for their lives, and finally he stood with his arm round the shoulders of his brother Richard, who looked as usual beside him a little absurd, a boy.

"In this adventure," King Edward said, "my brother Richard is a limb of myself. We live and die with each other."

It was the best thing Richard had ever heard Edward say to him, and it made him deeply happy, until he left the house and went out into the town to begin the inevitable haggling with sundry merchants upon his brother's behalf. Then he thought of Thonine and became troubled. He had met a woman in Bruges who had actually wanted him, and he was fascinated by her. It was the forthrightness without boldness, the allure without artifice. He wanted to make love to her endlessly, to talk to her until words ran out, to watch her unknown pattern of life revealed to him. Now he could not even spare the time to go to see her during the day, to watch her make shells and feathers out of parchment and colours. He had only a fortnight of days and an equal number of short nights, maybe less. He determined to make the most of them. It would be hard, telling her that there was so little time. It was hard for himself, but he was becoming used to the cruel indifference of fortune.

He left the Gruuthuse huis in the winter dark each night with his mind buzzing with calculations of sheaves of arrows, and helmet sizes and the doubly incomprehensible languages of Flemish and German hand gunners. At the house upon the Dyver, he never once had a petulant welcome. Thonine accepted whatever hour he managed to arrive, without comment, fed him, talked to him of everything except ships and arms and Flemish caution and hard bargaining, and opened her body to him with a freedom and generosity he had never before encountered. She freed him from the sense he had of guilt that he should be committing the sin of fornication knowing he would desert the woman so soon. No one in Bruges bothered much about this sin.

One night she said, close against his ear, letting curls of his hair fall between her lips, playing with them with her tongue, "In two weeks' time we have the carnival in Bruges, at Shrovetide. Will you be here then?"

She was not a person one dreamed of feeding with false hopes. "No," he said, and began to smooth flat strands of flaxen hair down over her full, beautiful breasts.

"A pity," she said with gentle regret. "Everyone, great lords and citizens and beggars go masked in the street, unknown to each other. You and I would have met as equals in the world."

"But we are equals here, and we don't wear masks."

Later, when she was holding him like a child and he was on the verge of sleep, regret overtook him again. If only, he thought —though his life had taught him not to use this wishful phrase— he had met her when he first came to Burgundy, instead of on the feast of St. Sebastian in January. He felt that to be with her for a while would be a journey of discovery not only for himself and herself, but a window opening upon the world of women, not just of their bodies, but their souls, their mysterious minds. Yet he was left with a scant fortnight of snatched, desperate and overwhelming desire and not even time for pondering on the enjoyment. His body yelled aloud its needs at night, to be enclosed within hers, both cause and effect of her pleasure, but during the daytime he scarcely gave it a second thought. To him life seemed often a whirlwind hurrying towards the grave, a series of passing images. It was as if one were running along a long corridor, lined with windows, some of which opened as one passed. He could never have time for staring out through open windows, however tantalizing the view. Sometimes he was afraid that he might pass a window and see through it the truth of God and Christ His Son and all the angels and be hustled on, denied his vision by the demands of his place in life. Only the contemplative could gaze on visions at his leisure.

When the last night came, he did not say that it was, but he knew that Thonine knew as well as he did.

"When you are in England and a rich man again, will you remember Bruges?"

"If I forget Bruges, I will never forget some things which happened to me there. I will persuade all the rich men in England to order books from Vrouwe van den Watere at the house upon the Dyver."

She laughed. "I shall be overworked." Then, "I shall pray for you. I should like you to come back to Bruges, but I will pray that you stay safely at home."

"I shall need plenty of prayers. Our chances of victory, defeat or death are all equal."

"Yet you are willing to risk your life to make your brother King of England again?"

"Yes."

"He means everything to you, your brother, I can see. Too much for your own good."

He pulled away from her a little. It was the first thing she had

said which did not please him. "If you knew my brother the
King, you would understand."

"I understand more from knowing you. I shall also pray that
after you and your brother succeed in this adventure, the path of
your life will not be as rough as I fear it might—you see, I said I
know you a little."

"Then it will only be running true to previous form," he said
sharply, uneasily aware that she thought she comprehended
something he did not.

She sighed. "Perhaps."

A few days later, Richard went on board a ship tossing in the
harbour of the port of Vlissingen. He was back where he had
first landed, on the island of Walcheren, in whose harbours a
fleet of ships—thirty-six of them—was assembled to take King Edward back to England. March had scarcely left February behind.
The bitter wind bounced and bowled over the curdled waters of
the North Sea and made his clothes feel as flimsy as the cloth
round a cheese, though he wore a lambskin coat with the fleece
inwards.

The wind blew coldly and implacably against them, and for
nine days it did not change. They could not go back on shore, for
the ships were anchored too far out. Nine days seemed such a
long time to be wasted in such a horrible predicament. He wondered what Bruges had been like at carnival time, having heard so
many stories of what happened during this sort of revel. In England Shrovetide was rather more sober; running with pancakes
scarcely compared with the drunken orgy of *mardi gras*. Perhaps
Thonine had taken a new lover. He was not sure of how she
would be when he was not there, or even of how she had been
before. She did not speak of any previous affairs. Not that it
made any difference; he would never see her again, and he was
in no position to give much thought to women now.

It had taken several days to stow aboard all the equipment,
horses and men. Richard had on his ship 297 archers and men-at-
arms and hand gunners besides the crew and two boys, all more
or less piled on top of one another like whitebait in a net. When
he went below, there were wagons with boxes and bundles and

baskets stuffed under, round and over them, barrels of arrow staves piled high—once he found himself eye to eye with chickens poking their necks out of a basket coop perched up on top of harness and armour and tubs of pickled fish belonging to the Hanse men. The men were stowed in hammocks with their feet in each other's ears, and the stink was worse than the lion pit at the Tower. Worst of all, the 300 odd persons on the ship spoke between them at least half a dozen different languages, and tended to be quarrelsome.

Any crossing of the North Sea in late February was certain to be miserable, but nine days of monotonous heaving and rolling on the sea without getting anywhere at all did no good to the morale of the invading force, or the condition of its stomachs and bowels. Richard found himself no better a sailor than before, and shivered on deck within easy reach of the side, praying desperately that each successive dawn might bring a change of wind, listening to retching and grousing and groaning in various Dutch and German tongues. It went on from Sunday to Sunday, and they did not know whether Margaret of Anjou had been able to reach England from France and to build up a powerful resistance to their own little invasion force. Their only hope was that the Lancastrians suffered the same adverse weather, and were equally powerless to move.

Le Temps Perdu

March 1471

Also scripture saith, "woo be to that Regyon
Where ys a kyng unwyse or Innocent."
Moreovyr it ys Right a gret abusion,
A womman of a land to be a Regent—
Qwene Margrete I mene, that ever hath ment
To governe all Engeland with myght and poure,
And to destroye the Ryght lyne was her entent,
Wherfore sche hath a fal, to her gret languor.

A Political Retrospect (c. 1462)

On the night of the second Sunday in Lent there was a frost. It made ice on the ship's deck, and the sailors cut their hands on the rigging. When Richard came up at dawn, he found that they were not tossing about as much as they had during the last nine days, but he was warned that it was like glass underfoot and as easy to go overboard as winking an eye.

The captain said, "Wind's changed. Due east. Should make way in half an hour, if your Grace is agreeable."

Agreeable! The last person capable of making the decision to sail or not was himself, or for that matter his brother the King.

"Master Lister, when you think fit."

The captain nodded. "Got to move fast," he said. "Take our chance."

On all the ships anchored near, men were at the same tasks, shouting and clambering in the frost-stiff rigging. The bare masts blossomed with sails, and the noise of wind in the canvas grew louder; it groaned and roared like lions with bellyache, flapping and straining. The anchor chains came up with a rattle, and King Edward's fleet sailed for England.

The crossing was swift and easy, with the east wind chasing them, and by Tuesday evening they stood off the coast of Norfolk. It was a deceptively clear evening. The sinking sun danced on a sea sparkling like mackerel scales. The little fishing town on the cliffs looked only a stone's throw distant, the boats drawn up against the jetty at the cliff foot. The captain said it was Cromer. The great lord hereabouts was John Mowbray, Duke of Norfolk, King Edward's kinsman.

A boat was lowered from King Edward's ship, and a party went ashore. It was dark when they came back, and they rowed to where King Edward waited for news, then to Rivers' ship and then to Richard's. Richard leaned over the side to shout down to them. Their boat was heaving and pitching under the tall wall of his ship, the sailors using rope fenders, lanterns swinging light across the grim faces of the landing party.

Sir Gilbert Debenham, who was a local man himself, and had been recognized on shore, said the Duke of Norfolk was in London, in custody; Lord Howard was in sanctuary at Colchester, and the county in the hands of the enemy. The Earl of Oxford and his two brothers had a firm grip on the east of England—it was alive with their men. To land here would mean certain disaster. The King had given orders to sail north and to try the Yorkshire coast, in the hope that Percy of Northumberland would be open to negotiations.

This meant things were about as bad as they could be. The captain of Richard's ship, who was a Norfolk man, did not like the change of plan, and obeyed his orders to an accompaniment of protesting grunts, much hawking and spitting and glowering. The wind was freshening all the time from the east and the ship bucked like a wild colt. Richard, who clung to the side trying to stop himself shivering in case the crew thought he was afraid— which he was—hoped they knew their seamanship and were going to obey orders. If they did not, he was beginning to feel too ill to exert his authority over them in his ignorance of the sea.

Across the mouth of the Wash, the seas became rougher, and by the time the battered, straggling fleet was battling through the night up the coast of Lincolnshire, they had become monstrous. Richard, clutching the Agnus Dei which hung round his neck, huddled on deck and shut his eyes. If he were going to drown, he did not want to see the waves coming. Some of them were sluicing down over his head as it was. Most of the lanterns had gone out. He dreaded what must be going on below, but there was no point in looking, there was nothing he could do to help the suffering men and horses. The storm went on and on. Someone yelled at him that one of their ships had sunk, capsized and been swallowed by the sea. It had been full of horses, and a score of grooms and crew.

Land, when it came in sight in the murky afternoon, proved that they had by God's guidance kept on course. There were far worse places than the long flat beach of Holderness to run aground. With the wind still whistling out of the east they would be driven ashore. The captain prayed fervently to Our Lady that the bottom would not be torn out of his ship, nor lives be lost.

The getting ashore from a grounded vessel was a hazardous operation. Boats were useless, but luckily as the tide ran out the water was shallow enough for wading. Richard thought it his duty to go down over the side first. His fingers were so numb it was difficult to grasp the rope ladder, and at the end of it he found his shortness yet again a disadvantage and the sea came up to his neck and he had to swim. In the end he got ashore on foot and he heard a few feeble cheers as he knelt on the pebbly beach, others struggling up beside him. They probably thought he was praying, but the simple truth was that his knees had given way, before prayers for his deliverance entered his head. But now he was back in England he could not die of the effects of seasickness and icy water. There was too much to be done.

He did what he had to do all through the evening and into the dark of night. It meant going back into the sea half a dozen times, every hand being needed to help men and horses ashore. The horses, poor beasts, were lowered from the ship into the sea,

splashing wildly, out of control of the men who tried to hang on
to their halters. Everyone, including Richard, was kicked more
than once; someone broke an arm.

At the end, when they thought that everything was ashore,
some of the German hand gunners came jabbering to Richard in
their own language and someone had to translate for him into
French. "*Les saucissons!*" they yelled—and it seemed their tubs
of sausages had been left on board. If they were willing to risk
the sea again to save their sausages, Richard told them to get on
with it. Most of the cheeses had been saved, and not much the
worse for it, the salt beef had not suffered either, but the bread
and biscuits had turned to soup. Every man ate what he could
lay his hands on.

Once again Richard found himself driven onto inhospitable
shores without knowing what had become of his brother. King
Edward's ships might have gone aground elsewhere along the
Holderness shore, or been driven into the Humber river. If Richard had allowed himself to imagine that it had been lost, he
would not have wanted to endure the night. But endure it he
had to, crouching behind an almost useless windbreak of barrels,
trying to make his sea-sodden brain decide what was best to do.

"Madam, you will hinder your own cause if you do not return
to England immediately. I have been here a week already. My
lord of Warwick must be waiting at Dover now to receive us. I
beg you to reconsider."

Sir John Langstrother's hornlike and bristly eyebrows had set
into a position expressing all his anxiety, bottled-up exasperation
and perplexed deference to his Queen's wishes. His complexion,
weathered by a lifetime of service with the Knights Hospitallers
of St. John in the sunny islands of Cyprus and Rhodes, was the
colour and texture of well-used cowhide; sweat had begun to
film it like oil. He could neither understand, nor condone Margaret of Anjou's refusal to budge from France, when her presence was so urgently needed in England.

"My lord Prior, you have heard what the Bishop of Bayeux
has had to say about affairs in England. I cannot be certain yet
of my son's safety." Always the same answer; Margaret's will in

matters regarding her son was adamantine. She sat in the small room of the narrow house in Honfleur like a lioness guarding the mouth of her lair. But she, who had been so fierce, was now afraid. Now the moment for action had come, she could not bear to take her precious son to an England uneasy in the hands of Warwick. Mistrust and fear had robbed her of her will.

Langstrother, driven by fears of Warwick's reaction to his failure to move the Queen, continued his efforts. He owed this much to the Earl, who had more or less forced the usurper Edward to accept his election as Grand Prior of his Order in England.

"But madam, the mere presence of the Prince in England will rally our supporters and make our victory more certain. We must employ all our resources against the usurper Edward; he has only the one chance to invade England. He will risk all, and we must summon *all* our power to destroy him." Langstrother had long experience of land and sea warfare in the east, and had expected the Queen, who had played the soldier often enough, to have more grasp of strategy.

"Yes, yes, of course you are right. We'll allow just a few more days, until we have more news of Edward of March."

A few more days! Sir John Langstrother eased his collar, which had begun to stick to his neck. Even now, Warwick would be glaring out from the cliffs of Dover, seeing no ships in the Channel bearing the Prince and his mother, and wondering if he dared to be absent from London for another day.

The Queen's procrastination brought about nothing but violent disagreement with her son. Now that he was in his eighteenth year, the Prince did not accept meekly the rule of a woman. He loved his mother, but this did not stop him from arguing, or her from obstinately holding to her own views.

"Madame, *maman*, our ships are waiting in harbour. We will be protected on the sea. . . ."

"England is the dangerous place. And the weather is bad."

"Am I to be kept from danger all my life? Do you expect *La Manche* to be a millpond in February? You treat me as if I were a child!"

"I treat you as something precious, the heir of England. Your father is still living. You are not King yet, neither will you be Regent until you are of age."

"I am seventeen! Old enough to fight. . . ."

"Never! As long as my voice is heard, you will not fight in battles. You are in the same position as a king. Never risk your life fighting, it would be doing your subjects a disservice."

"But a king who is afraid to lead his own men in the field is always thought a weakling. *You* should know that, madame!"

"There is a great deal of difference between sharing the rigours of the field with your army and risking your life in the mêlée. By all means to the first, but. . . ."

"But my grandfather King Harry fought! So did King Louis at Montlhéry—and I've spoken to men in our service who saw Edward of March fight when he was much younger than I am, and meet no match!"

"Edward of March was an overgrown giant at fourteen, and a bloodthirsty young villain, too. Edouard, these are no arguments. I have not lived hunted and penniless for years to keep you from our enemies only to see you lose everything now through your own folly."

"If I agree to skulk at the back in the battle, will you order our ships to sail now?" the Prince said, deliberately, knowing it rude to bargain with his mother like a huckster.

"*Non, non, non . . . non . . . !*" The language of their intimacy was always French, and seemed to lend volume and velocity to their speech. The Queen was becoming strident. She was beginning for the first time to doubt her command of her son, and of her own situation.

"You keep me from my wife!" He hurled this irrelevant accusation at her.

"If you had a wife more suitable for you in family, I would willingly bless your union. But you have no desire for her, I know that. You use this to bait me. Edouard, I only try to make you do what is wisest."

"We *must* go to England!"

"So we will, when I say so."

The Queen did not say so, and the wrangling went on for a fortnight. The strain of being at odds with her son told on her more than any of her previous troubles. Anne, when obliged to wait upon her, noticed that her skin looked as if it had the winter megrims, with taut dry lines round the eyes and colourless, as if shrouded in cobwebs. Her hair, which for a woman of forty had been a pretty auburn fair colour, was streaking rapidly with grey.

The Prince, unable to get his way, retaliated by seeking the company of Sir John Langstrother, and making plans for the eventuality of his return to England. He was fretting like a high mettled horse to be at war. After he had beaten Edward of March in battle, he would lead an army against the Duke of Burgundy, and with King Louis as ally, would conquer the arrogant Duke and divide his possessions for the benefit of both England and France. After that, a crusade—maybe he would be able to make his ageing grandfather René of Anjou truly King of Jerusalem. Langstrother, regretfully knowing anything but a defensive campaign against the Turks to be the perennial dream of Christendom, smiled. To the Prince he was a fascinating figure, with his monkish Prior's habit and burly military bearing. He had a Greek servant, who wore gold earrings and looked as if he had come off a Venice galley with an ape on his shoulder. The Prince dreamed of adventure beyond the sea; he had known little but penurious exile in France. Sir John was impressed by his enthusiasm for what lay ahead; the handsome, eager young man's return to England would be the best thing that had ever happened to his father. Little good had happened to poor King Henry. Edward of March had outgrown his early promise, for which some had welcomed him to the throne. The Prince would have the same advantage of youth and vitality. That he had been born on the feast of St. Edward the Confessor perhaps made him special; in him lay the hope of England's succession.

In order to further flout his mother, the Prince kept trying to be seen in the company of his wife. The last thing Anne wanted to do was anger the Queen, so she hid in her rooms as much as possible. Not that she did not want to talk to her husband, but she became so tongue-tied in public when he approached her. Several times when they were walking from Mass, he tried to position himself at her side.

"Sir John Langstrother says that if we don't embark by the feast of the Annunciation, he will pack up and go back to England alone. I am *needed* in England. My father is not good at fighting. Have you ever talked to Edward of March?"

"Yes."

"Did he try to—well—touch you?"

"No!"

"I thought he did that to every woman. What's he like? I can't remember him, except that he's very tall."

To this Anne had no adequate answer. "He's very tall."

"I am told he has never lost a battle. I want to make sure he loses his next one. I wish I could kill him myself, in hand-to-hand combat. All three York brothers must die, or we will have achieved nothing."

"But. . . ."

"Clarence is not with them? Well, I think he will be soon. I could see he was chafing against your father's rule. I'd sooner not have him as an ally, he causes trouble wherever he goes. What about the other one, Gloucester?"

To Anne's relief there was no opportunity to pursue this subject, because the Queen bore down on her son and led him away. Anne had no wish to talk about her cousin, Richard of Gloucester. He was part of those things which had faded from her life as if they had never been. Probably he was in much the same predicament as herself, waiting in the cold winter weather to cross the sea to England.

Shrovetide passed, and the feast of St. David. St. Patrick's Day came, and St. Cuthbert of Durham. Sir John Langstrother packed his baggage. Then, on the eve of the feast of the Annunciation, when the seas were heavy enough to send up sheets of spray level with the roof tops, a battered and drenched vessel put into Honfleur from England. They had weathered the storms. So had Edward of March, calling himself King. He had landed in England—in the north—and had been there a week already.

The last information on Edward's movements had been that he was held back in the roads off Vlissingen by gales and could not sail. Now, with her enemy already marching to meet Warwick in battle, Queen Margaret at last gave the order to embark.

The ships' captains looked at the sea in the harbour and the sky over the Channel with pessimism. They obeyed orders and made ready, and in the morning saw their passengers come aboard under a lowering sky and in winds so strong they were nearly blown off the gangplank. The ships could not struggle out of the harbour mouth. Fortune, scowling from the storm, would not let them leave France.

10

Warwick est Mort

March — April 1471

Or a-il bien son temps perdu
Et son argent qui plus lui touche,
Car Warwic est mort et vaincu:
Ha! que Loys est fine mouche!

Entre nous, Franchoix,
Jettez pleurs et larmes:
Warwic vostre choix
Est vaincu par armes.

Burgundian Popular Ballad
(1471)

Richard Neville, Earl of Warwick, the King's Lieutenant of the Realm, stood grinding his teeth, before the closed door of the chapel in the Bishop of London's palace. The hour was eight in the morning, and King Henry was at his devotions. At such times he kept at bay his secular advisers by the simple means of bolting the door. It was the only time he showed determination.

Warwick prowled up and down like a grey, loping wolf. He was too tired with travelling and frustration and anxiety to bare his teeth in a wolfish grin. He merely cursed profanely and inwardly, knowing that nothing of importance, such as the news he carried, mattered to his sovereign. One might as well ask a monk of a secluded order to rule a kingdom. Warwick could have gone to his own house after the journey from Dover, bathed and breakfasted and refreshed himself before bothering to come to the King.

After about half an hour's interminable wait, the door opened and priests swarmed out, bearing all the paraphernalia of Mass, and wafting clouds of incense up Warwick's nose. When he finally got inside, King Henry was evidently nearer to Heaven than to earth.

"What can I do for you, my lord?" the King asked mildly, his attention elsewhere.

The reply—"Clearly, nothing!"—nearly burst out of Warwick. The King had spoken as if to a humble petitioner who had managed to waylay him.

Warwick, if he had been less grey-faced and tired, would have gone red with spleen. Instead he controlled himself and said, "Your Grace, I have been on the road from Dover all night! I waited there for several days. Her Grace the Queen has not yet left France."

"Dear me," Henry murmured. "I should be very glad to see my dear wife the Queen. I hope this delay is only temporary."

"So do I!" Warwick could not keep this in.

"Why should this be so?"

Because your precious wife is reluctant to give you or me any assistance in keeping control of this realm, was the answer immediately springing to mind. Warwick said instead, "Edward of March is making ready a fleet in Zeeland. When—it is no longer a question of if—he invades this realm, we should meet him in a position of strength, that is, your Grace united with the Queen and the Prince and his wife my daughter."

"I shall scarcely know my son, now he is a grown man," King Henry said, sighing.

Considering that the Prince had gone into exile when he was ten and that even when he was born Henry had declared that he must be the son of the Holy Ghost, it probably was true to say that Henry knew little of his son.

To Warwick's intense annoyance, King Henry picked up his book of devotions and began to move towards the door. It was his infuriating way of indicating that the interview was at an end. Never any curt, terminating words, merely a withdrawal into some other world. Each time brought Warwick nearer to apoplexy.

Dinner later that morning with his son-in-law Clarence did nothing to improve Warwick's temper. The behaviour of George when he did appear at Warwick's table had begun to follow a predictable pattern. He would be surly until he had taken enough wine to loosen his tongue, as if he resented his father-in-law's hospitality. Then he would swerve like a careering horse between truculence and gaiety, depending upon whether Isabel was present or not. This led with more wine to colossal indiscretion in increasing volume and if the wine level was sufficient, back to surliness again.

This time, contrary to expectation, George began to ask questions.

"When are the Queen and the Prince likely to leave France?"

"When the lord God, who orders the elements, allows."

"What is the King doing?"

"Nothing!"

George carefully bunched his fingers, leaving the first two extended. His fist cast a shadow on the wall like a rabbit's head, and when George moved his fingers, its ears waggled dejectedly. "That is King Henry," he said, "a shadow on the wall." Then, as he made the nose twitch absurdly, he giggled.

"You sail very close to the wind sometimes, my son," Warwick said viciously. George was at the amusingly provocative stage, and Warwick found this unamusing.

"But we are not shadows," he said sourly. "If your brother sets foot on English soil, we will have to make a stand. No terms. You had better make yourself ready to go to your estates in the west and collect every man you can muster."

"My lord father," George said smiling, "I am ready to set out tomorrow if need be."

It was as well that Warwick did not know just how many balls Clarence was juggling with, and had been for months. He had known that from the beginning Warwick had gone out of his depth, and he saw no reason to go under with his father-in-law. He even thought that it might be just possible to bring Warwick and Edward to terms. The idea of acting as a family mediator, who had never wanted a quarrel in the first place, appealed to him. The ground was prepared, all he had to do was wait for Edward to come back to England.

Warwick, left staring into an inhospitable future, was nearer to drowning than even Clarence guessed. A terrible sense of the futility of his actions began to enclose him like a case of lead, like a coffin. He had never been a man who had gone back on his words lightly, yet now he had broken the promises given to the man who had done most for him, King Louis of France. Not that he had done so willingly, but the opinions of Englishmen, and their Parliament, was that they would never ally with France to make war on Burgundy. That war had already begun. Warwick's promise of aid for Louis, of conquest, were impossible to keep. This, and dread of what Louis might do when he realized it, the absence of Queen and Prince, the uselessness of King Henry, the hostility of those who were supposed to be his new allies and obviously imminent defection of Clarence, brought him to a state near despair.

The desolation of the dunes and marsh lands of Holderness, still dotted with lakes after winter flooding, was nearly equal to the fens round the Wash. Richard had somehow exerted some semblance of authority over his frozen, frightened, salt-water-sodden three hundred and got them on the move in a southerly direction. He endeavoured not to give away the fact that he had not the faintest idea where he was going, whether King Edward was alive or drowned, or whether the miserable land would sooner or later produce an ambush. He merely set them in the direction of Ravenspur, the place where Edward had intended to go ashore, and clenched his chattering teeth, pretending that the King would be certain to meet him there. If his brother was not there, well, the chances were that he might die in the Humber marshes, and that would be that. He vowed that if God did allow him to survive this and any successive dangers, he would never forget to give thanks.

He had not ridden his shivering, salt-sticky horse more than a few miles when a sizable body of men became visible, clustered around a few fishermen's huts behind the sea banks. He halted his men and rode forward alone—it would avoid any instant fighting. If they were Henry Percy of Northumberland's men there might be a chance of a parley. His relief at the sight of the familiar murrey and blue jackets, darkened with sea-water, of his own party nearly undid him, and he fell out of the saddle into his brother's arms, clutching him wordlessly while they both shivered like reeds in the March wind.

"Thank God," King Edward said, "you had the sense to head in this direction. Thank God you're safe, Dickon. I don't want to be finished before I've begun." As they retreated into the shelter of one of the huts, he said, "We must wait for Anthony, and trust that his judgment is the same as yours."

Later in the morning, Anthony Woodville caught up with them. He had been driven ashore a little further north than Richard, in the same plight, and had followed the track south almost by instinct. That between them they had only lost half a dozen men through drowning was a miracle of God.

Together they decided that they must move on, as boldly as possible, towards York. It was damnably dangerous, but at least there was a chance of winning over Percy, whose rule extended over all east Yorkshire. Yet as they marched, there was no sign of Percy, and every sign of a hostile country.

"What will you do?" Isabel of Clarence's voice held a shrill note, and her husband did not respond well to nagging. She was frightened.

"I've not made up my mind—yet!"

"But, *when* . . . ?"

"When I'm ready. When the time is right." Clarence turned his back on his wife and pulled the bedclothes up to his ears. She could just see his hair sticking out. She laid her hand on his back, feeling the smooth skin. She prodded his shoulder blade.

"How will you know that it is not too late?"

"Leave me alone!"

Isabel gave a little yelp, as if he had kicked her, and began to sniff.

George of Clarence rolled over to face her, exasperated, thick of head from the evening's wine and wanting his sleep. On the whole he quarrelled less with his wife than with other people, and now even he did not want to begin wrangling. He wanted to sleep.

"Isabel," he said angrily, "I've told you already, we must wait. When I've heard that Edward has landed safely in England—all we know is that he was seen off the coast of Norfolk and sailing towards the Humber—and when I've heard who has supported him and who hasn't. When I know whether the Queen and the Prince have left France. When I know what Pembroke, Somerset and Devonshire are likely to do if they have not."

"Then you will desert my father and . . ."

"Isabel, we've said all these things before, several times. I thought you agreed with my plans. If I stay with your father, bring in every man I can, and we manage to destroy Edward, where shall we stand then? Your father will be left among the wolves. And I? Well, I'd be the first piece of prey they'd seize on, and I don't want to be eaten. Do you want me to be sent to the block by the Lancaster Queen and her party? You've seen how I've been treated by Pembroke, by Oxford, by Exeter and the others, they're only waiting their chance to get rid of me.

"Not that I'm going to put my head into a different noose by joining my brother before I know if he has any chance of success. So I wait. Henry Vernon will let me know how things are going in the north . . . it won't be long to wait. And now I'm going to sleep."

Isabel lay still, crying quietly. The Bishop of Bath's palace at Wells, where they were staying, was so silent at night. In the day it was quiet and secluded in its gardens, where primroses grew and thrushes sang and banged snails against stones. The thought of the helpless snails made her cry even more, thinking of her own plight. The promise of her much desired marriage to King Edward's heir had been in no way fulfilled. She was now in the position of the wife of a traitor and rebel, whichever side prevailed. George meant to betray her father. He seemed to think it was possible that King Edward and Warwick might yet come to some motley patching up of their quarrel. Isabel thought this would be very unlikely; she feared things had gone too far. When she had seen her father in London, he had been grim and remote, and she scarcely spoke to him. One thing was clear, he despised and disapproved of George, and she had wanted a husband of whom she could be proud, in whose splendour she could bask, and feel cherished, and safe. She had none of these things, and though Clarence was handsome, twenty-one, a prince, and sometimes a lively companion, she felt that he was more of a stranger now than when they had been planning the excitement of their forbidden marriage.

Also, he was no longer Edward's heir. There was now a baby Prince, though locked away in Westminster sanctuary. George's long sleeping form in the bed beside her was infinitely mysterious, but it had become a mystery without pleasure or excitement. To those who were far away from her, like her mother and her sister Anne, she gave very little thought.

Clarence did not leave Wells until a week later. During this time, he busied himself with much letter writing, the despatch and receiving of messengers—or spies. Isabel watched him, absorbed and apparently happy in his intrigues, and felt herself helpless. On the feast of the Annunciation, a curt message had come from her father, asking that Clarence should join him at Coventry, and saying, as they knew already, that Edward was approaching Nottingham.

That day, George announced that he was going to meet his brother. He seemed excited, as if he looked forward to his abasement and forgiveness. There would not be too much abasement.

"I shall weigh the balance," he said, "Edward cannot do without me. He has got as far as Nottingham unscathed, which means some of my friends have lost their wagers. Henry Percy of Northumberland, and Lord Stanley, and the Earl of Shrewsbury have all, well, stood still. Prudent men.

"I'll meet Edward somewhere south of Coventry. Then I can try to bring about some sort of terms with Warwick. Isabel, I won't forget he is my father-in-law."

Isabel, her eyes round and pitiful—which he did not notice—said, "Will there be fighting?"

"I hope not," her husband said optimistically, as if by his actions he might direct the outcome one way or another.

King Edward also hoped that there would not be fighting—at least not yet. York had provided a very uncomfortable experience; he and fifteen others had spent one night in the city trying to convince the city council that he intended only to claim his father's dukedom of York. He knew they were not convinced; they were hard men who were not going to be made fools of. He had come out of York alive, and knew himself lucky, and that his luck was by then worn very thin.

After that, King Edward's fortune changed. Henry Percy of Northumberland made no move against him, and, as Julius Caesar said, who is not against me is with me. Better than Percy was the reluctance of Warwick's brother Montagu to challenge him. With less than five miles between them, as Edward marched towards his father's castle of Sandal, Montagu waited at Pontefract with an army, which he did not use.

Richard tried to send word to John Neville, to find out if he would join them, but received no reply. Neville would not desert his brother Warwick, but neither would he try to destroy King Edward. Yet by his inaction he partly betrayed his brother.

After this, when he had come safely through both Nottingham and Leicester, and messages had begun to arrive from Clarence, King Edward knew that he could now seek out Warwick and challenge him.

Richard's horse was fidgety with waiting, as he was himself. It chewed on the jingling bit, then tried to nose at Lord Hastings' mount, and its hooves made little sucking sounds in the mud as it shifted uneasily. Richard flexed cold fingers in wet gloves and was thankful that the rain in which they had set out from Warwick town had now stopped. The wind lifted the hair on his neck, drying it. He, King Edward, Hastings and Rivers, all sat waiting in a little silent group. Behind them, their army waited also, drawn up as if in battle order. Their banners, which were beginning to look worn and rain stained, flapped damply over their heads. No need now to dissemble and wave Lancastrian ostrich-feather badges about, the sun-in-splendour gleaming in the bright watery light.

King Edward, who had been sitting half turned in his saddle

into the wind, his head on one side, listening, said suddenly, "I can hear them."

When he had said it, Richard could also hear, a faint murmur, a whispered grumble of sound, like the beat of thousands of feet and hooves on the ground.

"How many men does Clarence have?" said Lord Hastings casually.

King Edward shrugged. "Four thousand? More than is healthy for us."

"I hope," Anthony Woodville said, "this is not another trick."

"No, I'm certain enough." King Edward shrugged again. "If it is, we have more men." He paused and grinned, without humour. "I hope."

Richard kept quiet, his eyes moving between his brother and the ground ahead, where the great width of the Fosse Way crossed the Banbury road. Clarence was coming up from Banbury with his army. The crossroads was wide, an expanse of mud and strewn gravel and verges poached up by traffic.

Soon the approaching army was in sight. At its head, as Warwick had asked, was the black bull banner of Clarence. George had made every effort to raise all the men he could. There were nearly as many of them as the King had. King Edward reached out and touched Richard's arm. "We two go first," he said.

They rode forward in silence. The others followed them, about a dozen in all. As soon as they did so, they saw Clarence copy them, coming forward himself, followed by a number exactly the same as the King's. They met right in the middle of the Fosse Way, just the three brothers. Suddenly, everything was seen to be well; there was no trick.

George looked that day like his name saint, apparently having forgotten that a hair shirt and bare feet might have been more appropriate. Richard noticed with some envy that his brother was shiningly clean, his hair especially; it blew around his head like a nimbus. George was smiling as if all his resentment and sullenness had left him, never to return.

King Edward, quick to gauge his brother's mood, grasped George's hand and leaned over to kiss his cheek. "You are the most welcome sight I've seen in England," he said. "I've not felt myself to be home again until this moment."

Close together and smiling at each other, the resemblance between King Edward and his brother Clarence was at its strongest. Edward was bigger and heavier and less angelically fair, but the greatest difference was that he looked a man, while George still had a boyish air, which was of course part of his charm. He might have been the youngest of the three brothers, especially now when Richard was scruffy, weather-stained and very tired, thin and insignificant looking.

Richard tried hard to bring to his face an expression of radiant delight to match that of his brothers. He found this difficult. He was genuinely glad that George had decided to join them, but he was mistrustful of George's reasons. Not that King Edward had any illusions on this score either, but Richard was less able to dissemble by sharing in this show of brotherly love for the benefit of the onlookers.

Nevertheless, George made things easier by greeting Richard with more enthusiasm than had been usual during their previous life together. He had forgotten what an agreeable companion George could be—sometimes. After the performance between George and the King, Richard managed a fairly creditable show of hand squeezing, kissing and amiable chat. Yet in even George's friendliest grin lurked a tinge of mockery, as if he knew Richard's feelings and laughed up his sleeve at his younger brother's inability to entirely disguise them. This was the old George whom, when he wore that particular expression, Richard had so often wanted to punch right between the eyes.

When the reunion was complete, and George had spoken a few words to the King's army in his best manner, still all gracious smiles, they marched back to Warwick town. King Edward still wanted to bring the Earl out of Coventry to give battle, now that he had an army almost doubled in size since his last challenge, and was more confident of victory. George had begun to talk of terms, of a reconciliation with Warwick as joyous as between himself and the King. He asked if he might send messages to Coventry, to persuade the Earl. In some amazement at this ill-judged assessment of the situation, King Edward said, "If he surrenders and comes out of Coventry town, he shall have his life. More than that is impossible, surely you realize that, George? God knows, I cannot send him to the block, but. . . . Do you think that he will accept? He's a man of what—forty-two? Could he face the Tower for the rest of his life? George, he is in too far now, I think we'll find he prefers the trial of battle."

Richard, with a sinking heart, knew that what the King said was true. George was deluding himself by his desire to shine as a clever peacemaker. Indeed, he was inordinately stupid if he thought that Warwick would perjure himself with every party to whom he had given his word, and with himself.

They gave Warwick a day. His answer was chillingly brief. No surrender.

On Friday, King Edward advanced once more upon Coventry, again challenging Warwick to come out and fight. That he did not was almost a relief, because by this time Montagu, Exeter and Oxford had all arrived to join the Earl. That night, back in Warwick, King Edward said, "Tomorrow we march for London, as fast as we can move. Warwick can only lose by refusing to fight now, and I can gain much by taking London. It will put Henry of Lancaster in my hands, and enable my friends there to join me. The Archbishop of York will have no choice but to surrender—I can't see George Neville fleeing in the night to join his brother's army. In London even Mayor Stockton is a good friend of mine."

Richard, knowing the situation of his own troops who had scavenged the countryside between Warwick and Coventry to the last loaf during their five days' toing and froing, was relieved to head for London. He was also, though he only admitted it to himself, relieved that the fighting had been postponed for a little. The idea of battle, to destroy Warwick and Montagu, distressed him even now, when he knew that sooner or later it must occur.

On Saturday evening they came to Daventry and in the morning, because it was Palm Sunday and King Edward always commemorated his great victory at Towton on this day, they all went to the church of the Holy Cross for Mass. The King led the procession round the church himself, a sheaf of willow palms in his hand, and all the people of Daventry turned out to gaze at him. It was a sunny morning, the birds singing and busy building nests in the eaves of the church. There were more green buds on hedges and trees here than in the bleak north. These signs of spring seemed a good omen.

Richard and Clarence followed their brother into the dim, chill interior of the church, and when the King came to the rood screen before the chancel he knelt, as he should, to honour the Cross while the anthem Ave was sung three times. Richard and George knelt behind him, side by side, as if they were little boys again. While they were murmuring their prayers and just as the chanting ended, there was a sudden, clearly audible little click. It came from just above their heads in front. George nudged Richard's arm, and he looked up. Fixed to a pillar in front of them was a small box of painted wood with doors, containing an image of a saint. The doors hung apart, swinging slightly, as if they had just opened. Inside was a little painted alabaster of St. Anne. The odd thing was that the box doors had been closed because all images had to be hidden as a sign of mourning during Lent. It seemed that some other people had begun to notice what had happened and, even as they watched, the doors swung gently to again, hiding St. Anne from the curious stares.

Everyone began talking, regardless of the fact that they were in the middle of divine service. Word of a miraculous revealing of St. Anne buzzed about the church.

George whispered in Richard's ear, "It must have been the kneeling of all these mighty armoured knees, and the weight of the royal person—setting up a wobbling in the pillar that made the door open. What a piece of luck—we can go on our way blessed by a miracle! Blessed be God," he finished, aloud.

Richard, who had always found his brother alarmingly irreverent, ignored this frivolity and stared at the little crudely painted wooden doors. When King Edward had been in exile, he had made a vow to St. Anne—of course, George could not know this—that if she would help him in his time of trouble, he would always make offering to her, wherever he found her image set up. Maybe this was her way of reminding him. On the other hand, George might possibly be right. Richard did not put trust in miracles unless he was sure that they were truly so. This one, well, he was not sure, and it had to be George who put doubt in his mind. King Edward said nothing, but gave thanks to God and St. Anne, and allowed the talk and rumour to rush upon its way out of the church, around the town and into the ears of his army. Such a prognostication of good fortune would hearten them, convince them that God would take their part. So they marched later that day to Northampton in good spirits, and the church of Daventry was enriched by the King's doubled offering in gratitude for the favours shown by St. Anne.

From that time everything happened as King Edward had hoped. Northampton was friendly to him, and he marched down Watling Street at good speed without any hindrance. By Wednesday night, when he lodged at the Abbey of St. Albans, news began to come to him that London was ready to capitulate. The Archbishop of York had no intention of trying to hold out until his brothers arrived, and sent a message to King Edward to that effect. London dropped into Edward's lap like a ripe and bursting plum.

The next day the aldermen of the City of London and the Recorder—the Mayor had retired to bed at the end of February, pleading sickness in order to avoid any political involvement—sent the guards at Aldersgate off duty to dinner and opened up the gates themselves to their returning King. This time the people had the heartening sight of the three York brothers united at last. They rode straight to St. Paul's, to make a thank-offering at the Rood at the north door, as was customary, then they turned to the Bishop of London's palace.

At the gate to meet them was the Archbishop of York. George Neville was as magnificent as ever but somewhat pale; even he was not clever enough to wriggle out of this situation.

He said, for once without his dazzling smile, "I am your Grace's humble servant from this day forward."

"My lord, it is unbecoming to a pillar of Holy Church to utter untruths. I have already received your submission. I will not stand here and bandy words with you—that can be done later—I've work to do. You know where you will spend tonight, and a while to come—the Tower. You had better make yourself ready. I have quite a little bevy of bishops to send along there with you. Your brother Warwick will be deprived of your co-operation.

"Now, you can do me the service of taking me to Henry of Lancaster, whom I must relieve of his burden once more and take into custody."

Neville had no arguments that he dared put forward. He tried to find Clarence in the grimly determined-looking throng of lords around the King, but George Plantagenet had uncharacteristically removed himself from the forefront.

Richard followed his brother as of habit, and together with Rivers and Hastings they were escorted by Neville to King Henry. Richard had not set eyes on Henry of Lancaster for nearly a year, and wondered if the return to the royal dignity had changed him.

Henry was sitting in the Bishop of London's chamber of presence, with his shoes off, warming his feet alarmingly close to the fire. He was settled into his big chair like a grandfather, reading a book held at arm's length. A pile of more books was on the floor beside him, reaching as high as his knees. Arranged on a cupboard near to the hearth were his various devotional objects, from which he had never been separated.

King Edward and his friends halted at the door, in an acutely embarrassing silence. Richard began to feel himself inwardly squirm. Henry of Lancaster continued his reading, while the Archbishop of York coughed and nerved himself to address the King he had helped to unmake, had patched together, and now knocked down once more.

"Your Grace. King Edward is here." For once George Neville could find no words of suitable artistry for this moment.

Henry did not immediately look up and appeared to read on to the end of the sentence. Then he closed the book with a snap, almost irritably, and laid it down on the top of the pile. He looked up, and saw clearly the faces of the men who had come to usurp his kingdom and imprison his body for the second time. Young Neville, the clever one, with whom he had been having some interesting discussions, was approaching, looking not so young, and ready to deliver a Judas kiss. Today, Thursday, was the day Our Lord was betrayed. Henry shut his eyes and sighed deeply. When he opened them, Edward of York was standing over him like Goliath, and looking like a schoolboy who had been chastised for a sin he would not admit to himself. It was an awkward moment. Edward continued to stand, as if to deny that he was in the presence of seated royalty. Richard averted his eyes, unable to bring himself to watch.

It was Henry who made the first move, which to some onlookers seemed the gesture of the simple-minded, but in fact did retrieve a few shreds of dignity for himself and his captor. He got up from the chair, and though he was getting on for six feet tall, he appeared like a withered leaf beside Edward of York, ready to blow away. He did not remove his hat, clinging to his royal estate, but he held out his hand. Edward held out his hand, too, and clasped it.

Henry said, in his thin, rather emasculated voice, "My cousin of York, you have returned to England, I must welcome you. It appears that I must give myself into your safe keeping."

Richard wanted desperately to turn from this disguising and blunder out, but he was prevented by the fact that Hastings was just behind him, looking over his head.

King Edward, who had long ago forgotten how to blush, was fiercely red in the face. He looked still like a boy, who had extended an arm to a blind beggar in face of the derision of his friends.

Addressing Henry as if he still acknowledged him as Duke of Lancaster, he said stiffly, "Your Grace's person will not be molested in any way while in my care."

"Yes, yes, I accept your word," Henry replied mildly, and everyone sighed gently, as if a long and involved task had just been completed.

King Edward turned to go as quickly as he could, to leave the collecting into armed custody of Henry and the ecclesiastics. As Richard followed him thankfully out of the Bishop of London's house, his skin felt as if spiders had crawled over it. Even now, one could not call Henry half-witted; he was simply not adequately witted to cope with the world. Edward had managed to preserve some dignity in his actions, but it was damnably difficult to recognize it.

Richard tried to put it out of his mind as he rode on through London and out to Westminster, to another scene he found distasteful, though many others found it touching. At the Abbey the Cardinal Archbishop of Canterbury was waiting, triumphant, to receive his nephews by marriage at St. Edward's shrine and to set the crown once more upon the rightful King.

Then they walked through the Abbey precincts and into the sanctuary. King Edward's reunion with his Queen was unaffectedly joyous, but Richard wished himself absent from it, as he always did from ceremonies in which Elizabeth Woodville shone. He knew himself to be churlish this time, and when inspecting the new baby Prince, tried his hardest to smile and to show some warmth towards his sister-in-law. He did better than his brother Clarence who, judging from the expression on his face, was eating very sour grapes indeed. The baby looked much the same as all others—he was now nearly six months old and less frog-like than the very tiny ones. He had a little lardy face, which probably meant he was fair like his mother, though his hair was hidden under a frilly bonnet. King Edward was beaming, baby in one arm, his Queen in the other. Richard watched as his brother's arm tightened upon her waist, edging upwards towards her breast. From the look upon the King's face, it would not be long before another royal infant was on the way. The three small girls were skipping up and down, defying all efforts to make them demurely look on at the return of their father. King Edward scooped up the two littlest ones, Mary and Cecily, and Elizabeth, who was five and tall, clutched one of his legs and shrieked with glee. Edward adored children, allowed them to swarm over him like puppies, would even endure wet laps and sudden pukings unruffled. Richard forgot about the Queen, standing there in her pride, and watched his brother, until little Elizabeth seized his hand and led him off, chattering a long and garbled tale of their stay in the sanctuary. He infinitely preferred her company to that of her mother. Elizabeth Woodville was undeserving of such delightful children. Yet Richard was glad that the King now had an heir; the boy was undoubtedly an advantage to their cause, even if his mother were not.

That night they all were rowed down river to Baynards Castle, an enormous, noisily celebrating family group, more in accord than they had ever been before, or probably ever would be again. Clarence had drunk about a pint of Rhenish wine to begin with, and thrown off his pique. He sat in the barge and grinned at his brother Richard like a young Bacchus and mimicked various persons they had met that day; Archbishop Neville, certain aldermen of London, even poor Henry of Lancaster. It was impossible not to laugh, because George was a clever mimic.

Their mother greeted them as they stepped ashore from the quay within the castle walls, and their sisters swelled the numbers. The Duchess of York was smiling, in her relief at the reconciliation of her two elder sons. Richard realized that his mother was still beautiful. She kissed him and held him close. Although she did not wear perfume, she was faintly sweet smelling, like incense.

"Dear Richard," she said, "you have been as loyal as any brother, any King, could deserve. It has been hard for you. God will reward you."

"The hardest part is to come."

"I will pray for your safety, for the safety of all three of you, my sons. Now you are all three together, you will overcome your enemies."

Soon they left their mother's house. Richard's first concern that night was to secure himself some sleep, because in the morning, the sad Good Friday morning, the mustering of the King's army would begin, to make ready for the march to meet Warwick.

The day of lamentation had come, in more ways than one. Warwick sat opposite his brother John in a room in the Abbey of St. Albans, and chewed his pen. He had been writing letters—fruitlessly—it was too late now; if his followers were not with him, then they never would be. It was Good Friday and at an hour when all the brothers slept, after their day of mourning; that quiet, blank, waiting day, The Eve of Easter, was almost upon them.

Warwick looked at his brother. Montagu was thirty-eight, and in this light looked fifty-eight. To tell the truth, he looked on the verge of the grave. He had gone more bald recently.

"Will you fight?" John said, as if he'd asked the price of eggs at market.

"Yes."

"This is the end."

"What do you mean?"

"You're finished. Look at you. . . ."

Warwick had not looked in a mirror recently. "What if we win?" he said.

"Then the wolves are waiting for us."

"Edward may be destroyed."

"For what? Once, Edward was your white hope. And I thought at one time you'd an affection for young Richard. It's a wonder that boy hasn't wrecked himself over this business. So we must destroy them?"

"Before they destroy us."

"Richard, we've done that ourselves. You know it."

"If you weren't a grown man, John, I'd clout you for that."

"Do it then!"

"Get out!" Warwick scarcely raised his voice. His brother left him, when it would have helped for John just to stay there, all night, not speaking. Or perhaps it would not help. Nothing could, now.

Warwick broke his pen, threw it aside and took up another. He had it in mind to write a last letter to the King of France. It would be a last letter, too, if he put his real feelings onto paper. On 4 April—a week ago—King Louis, realizing that the promised help from England was not coming, had signed a three-month truce with the Duke of Burgundy, a preliminary to a treaty of peace. Warwick, who had been unable to keep his promise of aid, had been cut out of Louis' plans as ruthlessly as dead wood out of a tree. For the first time he could see why men feared Louis of France so much. Warwick had received previously only good fellowship, charm and co-operation from Louis, now he had seen the other side of the coin. Louis was a man to whom other men—or women for that matter—meant nothing at all; he cared only for France, God and Our Lady, and dogs, in that order. It was sometimes said that men who, like Louis, played lunatic practical jokes, were always strange, cold fish.

Warwick's anger that Louis should so casually cast him aside like a pair of old shoes was unrestrainable. He began to write, his pen very nearly making knife slices in the paper, the words branding it. Nothing less than a harangue against the treacherous Louis, violent accusations of perjury, poured out of Warwick's brain, things which never could be said to the face of any king without instant arrest, enough to endanger life. He might as well have sent Louis a keg of gunpowder and a touch wire with instructions to him to blow his head off. When Warwick had finished writing, he folded and sealed the letter with equal savagery and immediately jumped up, called for one of his messengers, and sent the man off in the middle of the night to France.

When he sat down again, rage and bitterness vented a little, he felt empty, hollow as a drum. He had cut off his escape route to France; King Louis was scarcely likely to welcome him after receiving that page of invective. Worse, Warwick began to doubt the justice of what he had said. Louis' reasons were clear enough; he was in a desperate situation in Picardy, with Duke Charles besieging Amiens, and treachery among his own followers, and he had heard that Edward had sailed to England. The aid from England had not come as promised, and Louis had acted in his own best interests. Warwick remembered his promise; it was the last letter he had sent to Louis, the words he had written on it himself—"Sir, I promise you that all which is written above will be held to and accomplished in every detail, and so I have promised the ambassadors; and I will see you very shortly, if God pleases, for that is my whole desire. . . ."

God had not pleased, and nothing had been accomplished. It was himself who was perjured, not King Louis, and it was only the last in a chain of broken words: to Edward who had been king and thus obscurely to Edward's father and to his own father, who had been allies; to Margaret of Anjou, a word sworn on a piece of the True Cross at Angers, to subdue England to his will, and he had failed. They said those who broke their oath upon the Cross of St. Laud would meet death within the year.

He reviewed the situation, without hope, or attempt to work out a remedy. Edward had taken London and imprisoned King Henry once more. His own brother the Archbishop had capitu-

lated. Somerset and Devonshire had ridden off into the west just
when they were most needed. The Queen had not reached England. Oxford and Exeter were with him, but only waiting their
chance to destroy him, when he had served their purpose. His
brother John was still with him, but even this gave him no comfort; John's despair was obvious, and himself the cause. He sat
on into the night, while the candles grew icicles of wax, petrified
in the cold, as he was. His thoughts wandered only briefly towards his wife and daughter Isabel, but of little Anne he could
not bear to think, for he had left her among the wolves, with no
way of escape.

He thought of nothing but the simple fact that he must stand
and fight. Beyond that he could imagine nothing.

King Edward's army moved slowly up the hill out of Barnet
town like a great funeral procession through the night. But instead of a blaze of wax tapers and candles and the chanting of
priests, there was the dark, no moon, with only an occasional
shuttered lantern winking out, and the low grumble and clank of
an army on the march, trying to keep silent. Mounted scouts had
been sent ahead, cloth tied over their horses' hooves. They reported that Warwick was no further off than the top of the hill,
his army drawn up across the fork of the roads leading off to St.
Albans and Hatfield. It was a strong position, protected by hedge-
rows, and he had the advantage in numbers and was also well
supplied with guns.

Even on a moonless night like this it was surprising to Richard
how much one could see in the dark, when one's eyes got used to
it. On either side of his horse's silvery dappled neck were the
dull gleams of the rounded crowns of helmets, the white blur of
soldiers' upturned faces. The blades of halberds carried high
glinted like a waving steel forest.

Richard led the vanguard of the army, and in the morning
would be expected to lead the attack. That King Edward had
entrusted him with this most important section of the army was
both an unimaginable honour and a colossal responsibility. His
feelings swung between elation, fear, and a creeping desolation.
His mind, in the few uncrowded moments allowed it, kept think-

ing of those other times, when the legends of his own boyhood were made, when Edward, Warwick and Montagu had been together, marching on their enemies at dead of night, sometimes along this same road. He remembered the telling of the tales, when they came back.

The strong strides of his horse carried him step by step nearer to the end of it all, when either Edward and himself, or Warwick and his brother Montagu, would be finished for ever. He could not let himself weaken, that would invite death. Whenever there was a minute's lull in the orders and questions and problems, visions of weapons of fiendish design loomed twice life-size in his mind.

There were good men around him; his brother the King had seen that he was well advised. Nevertheless the final decisions lay with Richard himself, and any foolishness or error on his part would hamstring the efforts of even the best officers. He had never fought a pitched battle in his life. All that Warwick had taught him he would not forget, but he was without experience. This he was about to acquire the hard way.

Richard knew what he had to do. Somehow, he had to manoeuvre the vanguard of about 3,000 off the road to the right, spreading them out across the heath into lines, so that they would meet Warwick's left in the morning. The men moved with surprising ease. The archers were no trouble, being used to stealing across country under cover of night. The horses were the noisiest; the uncut stallions of the knights could always be relied upon to squeal and lash out at the wrong moment.

It turned out that Warwick's army was so near that it would be dangerous to walk forward out of the front line, in case one walked straight into theirs. It was possible to hear the murmur of voices, though nothing could be seen. In the middle of the night, when all was quiet and the men were trying to get what sleep they could, Richard found himself straining his ears to catch the voices, insanely listening for Warwick's, as if Warwick would be wandering about in the dark in a part of his army commanded by someone else.

Richard had learned that the captain he was to encounter was his sister Anne's discarded husband, the Duke of Exeter. Years of exile and enmity had probably made the embittered Duke even more foul-tempered than he had been before; he would give no quarter to any Yorkist.

All night cannon were banging away and shot whistling overhead, but it all fell beyond Richard's lines. Most of it seemed to be coming from the left, from the centre of Warwick's army. After midnight, Richard dozed off, sitting with his friends on wooden cases of weapons.

He started awake and was on his feet at the sound of footsteps. An uncanny sight met his eyes. The glow of a lantern partly open hung by itself among what looked like new-sheared fleeces. As it bobbed along like Jack o' Lantern, the hazy light brightened and the dark shape of a man formed up behind it, suddenly close enough for Richard to see the grease spots on his jacket. It was cold, and his breath puffed out, mingling with a swirling smoky whiteness. Fog. Richard stared around. The folds of his woollen cloak were covered with a silvery fur like mildew and the polished steel of his armour with a dull bloom of moisture. Fog floated across his face like clammy cobwebs.

"Lord Jesus!" he said under his breath. "How are we to fight a battle in fog?" Then aloud, "When did this come down?"

"Not half an hour ago, your Grace."

"What is the time now?"

"Nearly three o'clock by the sand glass, your Grace."

Richard's heart leapt up, and lodged in his gullet. "Then it's time!" he said. "At four o'clock we must be in order and ready to attack."

His voice sounded to himself like a croak. A cannon blast made him jump out of his skin. He had become as tense as a crossbow cranked up to its limits. His ears felt strange, as if he were underwater, and he could hear his heart knocking in them. He tried swallowing, but his mouth was too dry. He was perished with cold, yet sweating.

As his captains roused their slumped and comatose men, muffled voices came from all around. It was still dark, and bodies materialized almost from under Richard's feet, and were swallowed again by the fog. No one could see more than an arm's length in any direction. Soon Richard would have to lead his men in search of the enemy. It would make no odds, he thought grimly, if they were to blindfold him, twirl him round and shove him off to find Exeter's army, like a child playing Hoodman Blind. Because they were all on high ground, the fog might clear as daylight progressed. It was the most that might be hoped for.

Richard knew that he would not see his brother the King again that morning; there was no chance for toing and froing. The plan had been made clear last night. The attack was to be made at very first light, whether Warwick showed signs of moving or not. King Edward always had believed in being the first to attack.

When the signal was given, the trumpets blared through the fog like horns of brass. Richard began to walk forward, out in front with the men-at-arms, the archers at either end of the line. The knights of his own household were close around him; Lord Say at his left elbow was growling imprecations to keep his temper up. They seemed to be creeping forward like caterpillars, feeling their way, expecting any moment to meet the bristling staves and drawn bows of Exeter's front line. But it was horribly silent ahead. Guns were firing over to the left, but no arrows were being loosed at them.

Richard's feet and knees told him what his eyes did not; the ground was sloping away quite steeply in front of him. As he went carefully downhill, the grass grew squishy underfoot and he slid once or twice. He knew suddenly with terrifying certainty that he was leading the army down into marshy ground, and that Exeter was nowhere in front of them. The fog thickened like stirred milk, the lower they went. Richard was as lost as a blind man and on the verge of a disastrous error of judgement. He stopped walking and laid his hand on Lord Say's arm.

"We are marching in the wrong direction," he heard his voice saying. "We'd better wheel round so that we face towards the left. That's where the gunfire was coming from. We've overshot the end of Exeter's army."

The words came out as if placed in his mouth by the merciful agency of God. The instinctive decision was as right as possible under the circumstances. Soon they were moving uphill again, and as they went the slope became greasy with mud as their steel-clouted shoes cut up the grass. Noises of fighting came from further over to the left. An arrow whizzed past Richard's helmet, another glanced harmlessly off Lord Say's shoulder. Then the arrow shower began in earnest and, as the ground began to even out, they burst upon the enemy in the fog. Richard had no time to remember his terror of a few moments before, when he was hurled into hand-to-hand fighting. The enemy were yelling their heads off, surging and milling forwards and sideways.

Richard realized that he had made a flank attack by chance and thrown Exeter's men into confusion. There was confusion among his own men, too, still scrabbling to get up the slippery slope, scarcely knowing in which direction to advance. All the ways of fighting, of handling weapons, the techniques of killing, had escaped Richard's conscious memory. His men formed an armoured wall around him, while Lord Say bawled through his vizor slit, "We must keep our ground up here, your Grace. If they force us back down there, we're dead men!"

Then he might have been alone, fighting Exeter's entire three thousand by himself, except that he could only see in the fog the ones in front, with their weapons flailing at him from all directions. It took all his effort to keep his feet squarely on the ground, to fend off blows and to deliver as many as possible himself—hard. Above all, not to move backwards, when Exeter's men rallied and began to press forward. He was glad now to have older, experienced men around him; they fought with dogged persistence, sparing of their energy, unlike the young hotheads whose yelling charges among the enemy made them blown and panting just when their strength was most needed. Richard tried to follow the example of Lord Say, who stood solid as a rooted tree and parried everything which came at him, wasting no breath on yelling.

Soon the enemy began to heave and surge and press forward relentlessly and it became more and more difficult to stop edging back. Both sides made a solid wall of noise which was growing worse, though he did not realize that it was partly his own panting breath within his helmet. He had no idea of how many men he had killed or wounded; if they fell under the blows of his axe, they disappeared under the feet of all the rest, their screams lost in the din. He could see that the blade of his weapon was red, and feel that the leather palms of his gauntlets were wet, though that might as well have been from sweat as from blood running down its handle.

Gradually, he was forced back a couple of yards nearer to disaster, to the slippery downhill slope which would lead to wholesale slaughter. Then he went down for the first time. A man tried to trip him with a halberd stave and his feet slid from under him —the ground felt as if covered with tallow—and he fell, the halberd blade plunging down on top of him. He got his knees up, curled like a hedgehog instinctively trying to protect himself from injury in the place everyone dreaded it most, and several men trod on him, seemingly all at once, and then strong arms hauled him up as if he weighed nothing. A defensive circle formed about him. Lord Say, seeing him whole, yelled, "We need more men! Send to the King—your Grace, we need reinforcements—they're weighing on us like lead!"

"Not yet!" Richard yelled back, shaking his head from side to side like an obstinate mule. Falling, being trodden on, the panic feeling that if more feet descended he would suffocate, had made him shake all over. The only remedy was to hurl himself at the enemy again. He must hold out—he could not take his brother's men.

He saw Lord Say crash down, his helmet crushed into his skull by the blow of a mace. His own squire John Milwater was no longer with them; those who disappeared could only be in one place, underfoot. Before he could do more, a whacking blow coming from the side sent him off his feet like a spinning top. This time the panic of being down among trampling feet lasted longer; a terrible weight across his back pinned him down, and he thought someone had broken him in two. That was his chief disadvantage in fighting on foot; he was small and light, easy to knock down, in spite of being strong and agile. He was pulled up again by sturdy arms, and someone yelled to tell him the weight on his back had been one of his own squires, who had thrown himself down to take the jabbing weapons in his own body; he was dead.

Richard began to feel that he could not hold out much longer.

He could not tell where he was treading, only a confusion of lumps and humps, armoured hardness, and worse, yielding softness and an appalling sliding in slushiness. He could hear nothing but a deafening roar like mighty oceans; his lungs laboured like overworked pumps, and air seared them as if he were a fire eater at a fair. He could see very little because sweat ran from him like water and the saltiness prickled and blurred his eyes. Briefly he felt a burning pain in his left arm, a sensation of gouged flesh, but soon forgot it. The fog still cut him off from the rest of the battle. He could not know if his brother the King did well or badly, whether he was alive or dead, whether all the rest were routed and he were fighting on uselessly, alone.

He wedged one foot against the breastplate of a dead man lying behind him and fought on. If Exeter's men did not give soon, he thought he would be killed where he stood; he and the men around him were fighting themselves to a standstill of exhaustion.

Suddenly, a sound penetrated the noise in his head and helmet, coming urgently from in front of him, again and again. It was the rallying call of trumpets, trying to strengthen a weakening side. Exeter was no longer driving forward in attack.

Richard's men-at-arms found themselves able to push forward, step by step, faster and faster, until they were almost running, and the enemy wildly in retreat. Richard stumbled forward over a litter of bodies and limbs; in places he had to climb over the heaps, regardless of which were living or dead. The high pitched yells and screaming of a rout told him he had won a victory. It was only just in time.

The fog seemed to have thinned out a little. Richard suddenly in the confusion found himself tripping over something roundish and hard, which could only be a severed head, still wearing its helmet. He was unwittingly embracing an archer in a jacket of the unmistakable parti-colour, the King's murrey and blue. The embrace became genuine; a greasy, gory arm laid on his bore a smeared and tarnished golden sun. Then there were more of them all about him, archers and men-at-arms and knights, all yelling in triumph. The glorious moment came when King Edward strode out of the thinning mist like a giant of olden time.

As the brothers met, their breastplates banged together tinnily and Richard found himself half crushed in the hug of an enormous, very bloody-fronted bear. There was no sense in forcing hoarse-voiced greetings, it was enough to find each other alive, to know that victory was certain. Then Clarence stumbled on them, too, and all three hugged each other, enmities forgotten in the heat of the triumph, still not knowing what had happened to bring it about, but giving thanks to God for it.

The mist was clearing, and they could see the fleeing figures of victors and pursued. Richard got his feet tangled up again, this time in one of Exeter's banners. He had put his mailed toe through the carefully embroidered flames of his brother-in-law's fiery cresset and, judging by the heaps of bodies nearby, the cresset had burnt itself out. The ground was a red mush into which feet sank, mud made not with rain but the blood of men.

They had got just beyond the fork of the roads leading northwards when some of King Edward's men who had been in the forefront of the pursuit came running back to meet them. Warwick had been killed, before he could get to the tethered horses, none of the other lords with him. They were sure of their news—dead as a stone, they said.

They found Warwick as they had been told—stone dead. When the men-at-arms he had led to help his brother Montagu had been put to flight by the irresistible advance of King Edward, Warwick had made for where the horses were tethered. Before he got there, a group of the King's archers, who could run faster than he could, had cut him down and killed him with the indifferent efficiency they might a sheep.

They were trying to pull the rings off Warwick's fingers and had collected the loot—his dagger with a jewelled hilt, his gilt spurs, his sword belt, also jewelled—and were beginning to unbuckle his armour of fine Italian work when a barked order from King Edward brought them to heel.

Richard, his bruised, aching body moving now like a sleep-walker's knelt down and turned the Earl on his back, intending to remove his helmet, then stopped. The archers had killed him by the quickest method: tripped him, clubbed him and laid him on his back like a beetle, then opened his vizor and used knives. Richard saw the result.

King Edward, standng over his kneeling brother, saw also. He took Richard by the shoulders and all but lifted him bodily to his feet.

"Leave it," he said, almost roughly. "There's nothing to be done."

Richard was dumb. Perversely, he knelt down again and felt for the Earl's hand. The men had not had time to remove Warwick's signet ring. Richard slid the massive lump of gold off the sinewy, rather knobbly jointed third finger. There was still a trace of warmth left. Richard tried to mouth a prayer, but no words came. He made the sign of the cross instead. He stood up just as King Edward was about to haul him to his feet again. The ring lay in his hand, a big, heavy, man's ring. On the roundel in front was a motto Warwick had used. *Seulement Un.* One only.

King Edward looked at his brother. "There will never be another," he said. "May God have mercy upon him."

At this moment, Clarence joined them. "What . . . ?" he began. Then, "I did not wish this on him. My wife's father. . . ."

King Edward restrained himself from reply. Whatever Clarence had wished for, he had tried to obtain, and hang the consequences. He seemed unable to relate cause and effect.

The King said instead, "George, you've done well today. You have good men in the west country. There would have been no battle today without you." This might be interpreted in two ways, though the King smiled and laid a hand on his brother's arm. Then he said, "Richard, without you, I'd have been lost."

That was the greatest tribute of all. Yet Richard was too battered in mind and body to sense the victory, or to feel elation. He was thankful that God had preserved his life, but that was as far as he could think. Someone had killed Warwick by sticking a knife through his eye into his head, and God had watched.

There were other inert figures in red jackets with ragged staves on them, lying around. Some of the Earl's men had been trying to escape with him. One of them was still alive—just. His limbs twitched a little, like something a hawk had caught and dropped on the ground preparatory to eating.

Richard, when he should have been at the King's disposal and
ready to begin clearing up operations after the battle, for some
reason turned his back on his brothers and went over to take a
look. He turned the wounded man enough to see his face. It was
a very young man, little older than himself. The eyes were open.
The face had very little blood on it and was immediately recognizable. Richard, fresh from his brother's magnificent accolade,
was overtaken by a monstrous pain, as if he shared the other's
suffering. Recognition between them was instant. Of all the
corpses and near corpses Richard might have stumbled on—even
Warwick—this one he could bear least of all.

The face of his friend John Parr looked up at him in amazed
disbelief, trying to speak, and to clear the agony. During the
years Richard had been with Warwick, this boy had been his
friend. He was the younger son of a poor branch of a north
country family, most of which had taken the part of King Edward. John, lucky to be in Warwick's household, had stayed
there after his apprenticeship as one of the Earl's squires. He
had taught Richard all that he knew of the north country moor-
land ways, of talking to the people, of living off the land, the
names of birds and trees, all of which John had been born to,
and Richard had not. They had fought each other, and given
each other more bruises than ever might be counted. John would
not fight again. He was going to die, within a matter of minutes.
Because there was nothing else to be done, and they were beyond
speech, Richard held his hand. There were no priests near.

After that the finding of Warwick's brother John, Marquess
Montagu, not far off and butchered in even uglier fashion,
seemed inevitable. He must have tried to defend Warwick, in
the instinct of brothers. Under his armour, John Neville was
wearing two devices of gold, one a ragged staff, as was natural,
but the other the sun-in-splendour, as if he had intended to proclaim to those who might find him that his heart had been torn
equally into two. He had not wished to live.

It was then, as if from a very long distance, Richard noticed
that blood was dripping from the fingers of his left hand, spot-
ting the ground. It took a few moments to realize that he still

wore a gauntlet, and that the blood making its way through was coming out of himself. He took no notice.

King Edward, however, who had sharp eyes, did notice. "You're hurt, Dick," he said. "Get yourself to my surgeon— now!!"

The boy John Parr was dead. Richard moved away, obedient to his brother's orders.

Easter Day. The bells of Barnet church proclaimed it, and went on ringing, not for the victory of Christ over the grave, but for the victory of the King over his enemies.

That night Richard lay in his own bed in the palace of West-minster and could not sleep. The events and horrors of the past day repeated themselves in an endless pattern in his mind like the jangle of bells. He did not want to see or to hear, or to know, but he saw and heard, over and over.

He had knelt in St. Paul's that evening with his brothers and given thanks to God for his life, their lives, and for the victory, which was as cold within him as the naked dead left on the field at Barnet. He had gone back to the palace, eaten a little, soaked his hammered flesh in hot water and felt no better. His left arm was more painful than he would admit. Someone had managed to make a cut in it as neatly as if they were using a carving knife; it had gaped like a split loaf. Only a flesh wound—not very deep but hellish long. The worst part had been having to look at what was going on in the surgeon's tent. He had stood like a rock while shreds of padding from the jacket worn under armour were removed from his wound with tweezers, and been band-aged up until his arm would not fit into any sleeve. It was as if he were unable to shake himself free of the fog of the morning. He was so exhausted, he could not sleep. It was too much effort to toss and turn, so he lay still. Quite suddenly, without warning, tears burst out of him as if out of a smashed water crock. Some men were taken like that a while after they had endured the sur-geon's knife without a whimper. He turned on his face and stuffed the sheet against his mouth like a child and wept until there were no more tears left in him to weep.

11

Checkmate

April — May 1471

This world I see, is but a chery fayre,
All thyngis passith and so moste I algate.
This day I satt full royally in a chayre.
Tyll sotyll deth knokkid at my gate
And unavised he said to me, "Checkmate!"
Loo, how sodynly he maketh a devorce
And wormes to fede here he hath layde my corse.

This World I see is but a Chery Fayre
(15th century)

Easter Sunday was almost over. There were no bells to greet
Queen Margaret at Weymouth. She had been so ill that she
could not walk ashore unaided. Twenty-one days they had been
held up at Honfleur; twenty-one precious days run out like sand
from a shattered hour-glass. The gale which had blown the
Queen's ship into Weymouth Bay had driven some of the others
God knew where. Anne did not know whether her mother was
drowned, shipwrecked, or ashore in another harbour. No one at
Weymouth had news of her father less than a week old. She had
not believed that a worse situation than her family's plight of the
previous Easter could arise. This time her sister Isabel was the
only one of them to be safe.

While Queen Margaret uncharacteristically took to her bed,
the Prince threw himself into his longed-for role of military commander. He sat down with Sir John Langstrother, Lord Wenlock

and Dr. Morton, to spend half the night dictating letters to all the lords who might be expected to raise men and rally to Lancaster. With luck, Warwick would be already on his way from Coventry, uncle Gaspard Tudor from Wales; Somerset and Devonshire had probably made an army of west countrymen a certainty. What chance would the meagre forces of the York brothers stand against all this?

The next morning they left Weymouth and travelled north as far as the Abbey of Cerne. This was on the recommendation of Dr. Morton, who had many friends there. Queen Margaret, still suffering the effects of *mal de mer,* was in bed again before daylight had gone. Anne had nothing to do but keep out of the way. She felt strangely ill at ease in the tranquillity of a west country spring evening. All was so quiet, except for the many domestic noises of a great Benedictine house. The Abbey buildings lay among the smooth green hills like sheep in a fold. Anne thought, staring at those hills, that they had a very strange shepherd. On the side of the down was an enormous shape, a giant's figure outlined in white on the green, nearly as big as the hill itself. He was brandishing a club. He was displaying a great deal else, like the sort of drawing one found on the walls of guard rooms in castles, and was not supposed to see. He was a menacing giant. Anne stared at him in fascination and dislike. She felt unhappy and unsafe. The world beyond the Dorset hills was a dangerous place, full of the noises of anger, quarrelling and fighting—and killing. In this state of mind, even the sound of horses on the road alerted her to alarm. These horses were tired, flagging in pace, but still urged on by their riders. They came in sight on the downhill road, below the feet of the white giant, and broke into the half-hearted canter of the nearly exhausted at their journey's end. Anne watched them draw rein in front of the Abbey guest house. She was close enough to see the faces of the riders. Among them was no one she recognized. They brought bad news. Their faces were grim, not those of men sent to welcome home their Queen and Prince.

The Prince himself ran out to greet them before they could even dismount. The leading horseman climbed stiffly down from the saddle and knelt to kiss the Prince's hand. He was a big, dark, handsome man, not young, but not yet greying. He got up from his knees, and he and the Prince embraced like long-lost brothers. Anne, tensed and watchful, hesitated to go forward herself. The servants who had come wore badges, some of a gold portcullis, and some a dolphin. This must be Edmund Beaufort, Duke of Somerset, who had been so long in exile from England that she had never seen him. One of the old Lancaster supporters who had never compromised, who had lost his father and his elder brother in the cause. With him were his younger brother, John, and the Earl of Devonshire. Somerset moved with the Prince towards the house door, his grim face unrelaxed.

Anne followed them into the house. Beaufort and Devonshire, and one or two others, followed the Prince straight to his mother's room. Queen Margaret was in bed. She lay propped up by pillows, her face hollow-cheeked and green tinged. With her head uncovered and her hair in two long braids she looked smaller than when up and about, shrunken almost.

"My lord Duke! Edmund, John, my lord of Devonshire, you are an even more welcome sight than the shores of England! I am sorry to greet you in such a feeble state, but you know how the sea punishes me for embarking on it. At last—some news!"

They all three knelt and kissed her hands fervently.

"I wish," said Somerset, "I had news which would give you more cause to welcome me, madame. It grieves me to see you so unwell. If it were possible, I'd leave this until you had recovered, but it cannot wait.

"Madame, Edward of March met Warwick in battle at Barnet heath, near St. Albans, yesterday morning." He was looking down at the shrouded figure of the Queen, under the blankets and silk counterpane, avoiding her eyes. His voice was harsh with restraint of the emotion he felt at breaking this news to her, and the need to show that he estimated that it might have been worse.

Anne stared at him, at the other still figures.

"March had the victory," Beaufort said. "Warwick is dead. Montagu, Exeter, too. Oxford escaped."

Warwick is dead. Anne heard the words and recognized their

meaning, but they had no immediate effect on her. She heard Queen Margaret cry out into the terrible silence.

"Lord Jesus—why have you done this to me!?" She turned on her side and beat her fists against the pillow. "Why, why, why. . . . I've been lured back to this devil's land only to be told this! He has failed. All words, words! He was a false traitor from the beginning. Why didn't he wait for us?"

"He was killed in the rout, Montagu trying to save him. Wait? Madame, he waited too long, that is why he is dead."

The Queen's women were round her bed, trying to comfort her. Anne did not move.

"Pack my baggage!" Margaret shrieked. "We'll go back to Weymouth tonight and be in France again by Wednesday. Anywhere is safer than this treacherous land!"

"But Madame—please, not so hasty. Think, Warwick gave battle on his own account. He lost. But *we* are the main army, which he did not even call upon. If he had waited for us to come up from Devon, March would have been beaten. The battle was bloody—they have lost many men. But we are fresh. All the west country will join us, already they flock to my lord Devonshire. Pembroke will join us soon, from Wales. I believe we are *stronger* now. Those who would not fight for Warwick will lay down their lives for us—for you, the King, the Prince. Lucifer is better dead!"

Better dead. My father's dead, Anne thought.

"Madame, *maman!* Edmund is right! Surely we can fight now on our own account, without a traitor in our midst, like Jonah. We have so many good, experienced, faithful men. We are so determined. God and the saints will fight for us. Men will follow *me, maman!*"

"No! The risk is too great."

"Risk!" The Prince's voice rose in anger. "Always risk! Does Edward of March worry about risk? He only won this battle because he did not meet us. He risked far more than we shall. He had a brother near my age; he has to take his chance with the rest."

"March's brother is of no account!" his mother snarled. "You are heir to the crown. Your blood is precious."

"Heir! Yes, I am, and I want my inheritance, *maman,* I want my crown! I want to be Prince of Wales in more than name—not to be a pauper princeling for the rest of my life!"

The Queen burst into hysterical weeping. "Out, all of you! Leave me, leave me. . . ."

They all surged out in confusion, except for the women grouped around the bed. Anne was left standing alone, like a stone exposed by the tide. She was not quite sure of where she was, or that anyone had left. She felt dizzy and cold. No one had noticed her, not even her husband. No one had thought to give her the news at first hand. Probably no one among Somerset's party knew what she looked like. She did not know how long she stood there, intruding upon the Queen's rage and misery. Lady Katherine Vaux and Petronille and Marie were trying to soothe Margaret, telling her that she had overcome many worse defeats than this—the death of a man who was, after all, her enemy.

"He was a coward—I always knew it," Margaret railed. "Look what he's left on my hands—a useless girl with no inheritance and tainted blood. Why did I ever, ever allow it—my son would have made a great marriage. Now all is spoilt, and I allowed it. Ah, Katherine, it is all my fault, my cowardice. If I had come to England sooner, we would have beaten March before ever he gained a foothold. *Ah, le temps perdu!* All my fault, and my son begins to hate me for it. . . ." She was distraught, breaking into fresh sobs, which would have been heartrending to hear if Anne's heart were in any condition to be reached. It felt as if it had dropped out and disappeared under the floor. She stumbled out.

A useless girl with no inheritance. She fled out of doors without any purpose in mind. It was growing dark. Useless, with tainted blood—she, a Neville! Now the Queen will persecute me, she thought. She will want to get rid of me—where will it end? I believe if they win, she will have me poisoned, to leave her son free.

An hour later, when it was completely dark, Sir John Langstrother's Greek servant found her, while on his way to tell his master's grooms to be ready to leave in the morning. He trod on the hem of her gown before he noticed her. He thought at first that he had found a servant girl, in the middle of an English monastery, and couldn't believe his luck; then, in some alarm, recognized the Prince's wife. What she was doing out there alone in the dark he had no idea, and the last thing he wanted to do was to be caught in her company. He was a very beautiful young Rhodian, and the English were very suspicious, aggressive people, who treated him as if he were a filthy, barbarian Turk. He realized at once what she was doing, for her sobs had not yet abated, and were beyond her control.

"Madame Princess," he said in English, translating carefully in his head from his own language. "I am most sorry to disturb you. But, please, will you go into the house. It is not right that you are in the dark. What for do you weep?"

He could not follow her reply. But he had remembered who she was. The Earl of Warwick who had been killed in a battle, which seemed to please some people—she was his daughter. The poor little thing had been left to cry, with no family near her, nobody to take any notice of her at all. He had lost his own father, taken as a slave by the Turks, so he understood.

"Please," he said again, "will your Highness go indoors?"

"Will you do something for me?"

He stood like a nervous horse, wondering what she would say.

"Ask the Grand Prior if he will tell me a little more of what happened, when he has heard himself. I don't know—how my father died."

"But these lords, should they have told you this? No one has told you? It is worse not to know. Why do you not ask them?"

"Ask them?"

"Yes. Go to them. You are the Princess."

She found the Beaufort brothers, Devonshire, Wenlock and Langstrother deep in conference with the Prince. A meeting of men, the Queen excluded. The Prince's face glowed like a lamp with excitement, though the hour was late and the others were haggard with long travelling. Yet they warmed to him, watching him closely, kindled by his enthusiasm.

"Keep as far west as we can."

"To the Severn Valley. Then we can be certain of meeting Pembroke as soon as he comes out of Wales."

"Edward of March will have further to go to catch up with us. Is he in London?"

Anne waited for them to stop talking and notice her. Then she said, "My lords, since you have neglected to tell me, I should like to know how my father died." She was surprised at herself, sounding so haughty.

They all gaped at her, then Somerset rose to his feet. The Prince had the grace to go very red. Somerset bowed gravely and courteously to her.

"Forgive me," he said, "for an unforgivable omission. I did not know your Highness."

Anne did not see why Beaufort should apologize when he was the least to blame. Her own husband—meaningless title—had ignored her, and his mother had taunted her.

"The man who brought me the news of Barnet field is not with us. I can only tell you what he told me."

They brought up a chair for her, and she sat opposite her husband, who would not look at her. She steeled herself to hear something horrible, heroic, dramatic. When Somerset had finished she found that she had been moved only to a dreary desolation. They had expected her to weep. She did not. Her father had died so prosaically. Somerset knew that this was often the way of battles. The Prince was disappointed.

Warwick had been beaten and tried to save himself for another day. This was not cowardly, but sensible under the circumstances. No one expected generals to fall on their swords like Romans in these days. He had bad luck, and had been killed by men who did not even know which lord he was. The only heroic act had been Montagu's, who could have escaped, but stayed to defend his brother, and died.

"My father always did say his brother John was his right arm," Anne said, so coolly, that they looked at her strangely.

The Prince sent for Lady Vaux and asked her to go with Anne and put her to bed. It was not until afterwards that Anne realized that he had not meant to hurt her deliberately, but had been so entranced by the thought of his coming life as a man and a soldier that he had thought of nothing else at all.

In the morning, Anne asked if she might buy candles to light for her father and her uncle John. She was the only person in the Queen's retinue to do so.

After that night at Cerne, Anne scarcely saw her husband. Queen Margaret, for once overruled by the men of her party, had given up her determination to return to France, as if she knew that a battle to get her son to leave now would be lost. From this time, they were an army on the march, and the Prince was in his element. Katherine Vaux, Petronille and Marie said it would be tedious, and hard, and hardest of all on the women. Anne was bundled along like a piece of baggage, unpacked one night and done up again in the morning.

From Cerne they went to Exeter, a city always loyal to Lancaster, and above all to Courtenay, the heir to the old Earldom of Devonshire, which had been given by King Edward to an upstart favourite. Heartening numbers of troops were coming in, though they were paid largely in promises and were expensive to the towns through which they passed.

At Wells, the Bishop's palace was ransacked and his prison smashed open and prisoners let out, while Queen Margaret and her son stood and watched. It was the first time Anne had seen deliberate destruction and looting as an act of revenge. Bishop Stillington, who was King Edward's Chancellor, was absent. His plate was carried out of his house, spilling and clattering out of baskets, with whoops from the looters. A man came out with a chamber pot on his head for a mitre and carrying a crozier. The Prince was doubled over; Anne had never seen him so happy, so bursting with life. The Queen and her son laughed in harmony for the first time in weeks. The hinges on the doors and the latches from the windows were forced off, for the iron to be forged into weapons for the army. The soldiers even stole the daisies from the Bishop's lawns, to wear on their jackets and hats as favours—marguerites—for the Queen.

When they got to Bath, they heard that Edward of March was at Cirencester. He had re-mustered his men after Barnet and moved them towards the west with greater speed than had been expected. This meant that he was about thirty-five miles away from them, but only twenty from the first bridge over the Severn, at Gloucester.

Somerset said, "Each day that we avoid him is to our advantage. Pembroke is determined to have his Welshmen at Monmouth by Saturday night. If we can cross the Severn at Gloucester on Friday, we can meet him less than a day's march westward. Also, Lord Stanley has promised to bring in the men of Lancashire and Cheshire to us on the Welsh border. Then we will have an army which will outnumber Edward of March's two to one. We'll finish the House of York for ever."

"How can we prevent him from advancing too near us?" asked the Prince eagerly. He seemed to think he could extract everything but the Sybilline prophecies from Somerset.

"We can't," Somerset said grimly. "We can only hope, pray to God and St. George to preserve us, and march until we drop."

"We need guns," Queen Margaret said in her incisive way. She had to all appearances regained her authority over her commanders and her son. "We need every man, every groat we can pick up; each bowstave makes us stronger. I propose that we go from here to Bristol. It is the second city in the south, and the merchants are almost as rich as those in London. Yes, yes, I know, it may lose us half a day in time to get there, but the support we will gain will more than compensate us."

"Hmm. Edward has a reputation for getting more miles out of his men's feet in less time than seems humanly possible. I don't like the idea of even an hour's delay in making for Gloucester. Bristol is not a loyal city in any special way, though I see no reason why it should be hostile. But as you say, madame, we need guns, men and money. Bristol it shall be."

Anne, trailing somewhere behind Queen Margaret and the Prince, saw them received at the High Cross in Bristol by a wary Mayor. He was a large man, solid with the wealth of his city, intent upon offering expedient aid, and bidding a quick farewell to the Lancastrian Queen. Her armies had an evil reputation, and he had heard of what had happened at Wells. The city was on holiday because it was May Day. People were dancing in the streets, just as they were in every other town in England.

Every May Day, wherever he had been staying at the time, Warwick had feasted the whole district at his own expense and given all his people a holiday, including the children from their lessons. Now there was no one to order what went on in the castles of Middleham and Warwick, no one to pay for such festivities. King Edward would make an act of attainder against her father; all his possessions would be forfeit. New constables would be put in charge of the castles, and everything in them would belong to someone else.

Anne realized that now she had nothing which she could call her own, except for her clothing, and the few things she had in her meagre baggage. Everything she really cared for, her dogs, her horses, her books, her favourite wall hangings, the picture of St. Anne and the Holy Family with Warwick and his wife kneeling, very small, at the bottom—all these would be used or abused by strangers. She had by now heard that her mother had survived the stormy voyage from France and landed at Portsmouth. When the Countess had heard of her husband's death, she had at once fled into sanctuary at Beaulieu Abbey, where the Church would protect her from whatever revenge she imagined King Edward would inflict upon her. The Countess clearly did not wish to involve herself any further with Queen Margaret in case this should make things worse for her. Anne wished that she were safe at Beaulieu, too.

The next morning, they heard for the first time just how near King Edward's army was to them.

"Katherine, prepare yourself for a long, long day," Anne heard Queen Margaret say to Lady Vaux. "We must follow the river Severn and we must reach Gloucester before the usurper Edward catches up with us. We must march night and day. I shall keep this army moving until it can go no further. We must delay Edward by making a feint in his direction. I have sent mounted men-at-arms east from here on to the Malmesbury road. He should come forward to meet them, thinking we are prepared to do battle. But I shall press on northwards so fast that I will leave him behind." I, she said, as if she were in sole command of the army. She was alive, alert; women, Anne thought, are capable of so much.

"Who wins this race," the Queen said, "wins England, and with God's help, it shall be I."

The canvas walls of the tent bulged and slacked with each breath of the night wind. Up on the hill, where King Edward's army was encamped, the wind was cold, though the previous day had been hot. The flap of the tent was open, drawn aside. Outside was dead of night, with clear stars and a moon. Inside was warm in comparison, and sheltered, and much darker, the seductive dark which makes sleep so irresistible. Sleep had long ago ceased to be seductive and become an iron-armed mistress, a necessity which had to be fought, as St. Anthony of Egypt had fought his fleshly temptations in the desert. Every night for the last two months, as midnight approached, Richard had fought with sleep and won a short-lived victory, as long as he kept on his feet and ignored the loving arms of the nearest chair, the smiles of a cushioned seat. Worse was the effort to get up again after sleep's attentions, when the dawn in the sky was still only a greenish leavening and there was still a full hour of torch gloom to go before even greylight. He had seen one season out and the next in like this. At least now they did not wake to the sound of sheeting rain, and go forth in rusty breastplate in seas of mud and perishing cold. His boots were now dry inside, though still on him as he fell asleep.

A figure filled the tent doorway, bent almost double to enter; men with torches brought light behind it. King Edward, stooping and ducking slightly as he had to in most tents, walked across the matting on the floor, kicked a piece of armour against another with a loud clatter, and bent over his sleeping brother. He beckoned up a man carrying a torch. "Shine it in the Duke's face," he said.

The clattering noise of metal had made no impression; Richard was too far gone in sleep. He was lying fully clothed in the oddest position for a sleeper, sprawled on his front, his arms and legs untidily awry. He looked like a swimmer without water. He was lying on top of something angular and lumpy—a canvas bag with some articles of equipment inside it. In normal times no one could have slept for more than five minutes in such discomfort. Richard had been there the best part of three hours. The King shook his arm vigorously and obtained no response. Thinking as he did so—you cruel bastard of a brother—he lifted Rich-

ard bodily up into a sitting position and shook him hard. He
came awake at once, and sat blinking in the light of the torches
like an owl disturbed.

King Edward said grimly, "We are sitting here on Sodbury
Hill for no reason. We've chased after a shadow. We should
have headed north for Gloucester immediately from Malmesbury. Those men over here are just a ploy to delay us. The main
part of their army has reached Berkeley already.

"Listen, Dick, we have got to move as we've never moved in
our lives before. If we can go fast enough, then I think we will
trap them before they gain an advantage. I've already sent a
messenger riding to Gloucester. I want Beauchamp the governor
to shut the gates on them, to keep them from the bridge. The
bridge is their only hope. If they can't use it, what alternative is
there but Tewkesbury, where there is no bridge, only a ferry? By
God, if Beauchamp is as loyal as I think he is, we shall have
them like eels in a trap!

"Richard, I gave you charge of the vanguard of my army at
Barnet and was repaid a hundredfold. You have the van now,
and in the battle, which I believe will be at Tewkesbury. You
march first. I trust you to make the pace for the rest of us. You've
a chance to learn how to move an army fast in difficult country.
The hills here go up and down like a dog's hind leg. The ones
who can't stand it will be left to take their chance. When the sun
is up, if it's as hot as yesterday, give them a ten-minute break
every couple of hours, maybe a little longer at midday—though
where their meal is coming from, I don't know; we've next to no
provisions left.

"Don't force the pace—it's more important to keep going
steadily all the time. The road north from here leading along the
ridge of the hills should bring us to within five miles of Tewkesbury by evening. There will be no question of the French Queen
trying to cross the Severn—the ferry would take too long—they
know I would catch them at it.

"The road we take will be hard and hilly, but we'll be dryer
underfoot than they will down in the valley.

"Dick, I'll see you during the day—I'll be riding about, seeing
how things are going—but much of it is in your hands. God go

with you." With that the King kissed Richard's sleepy, unwashed face and strode out of the tent.

Richard looked at the hour-glass. It stood at three o'clock. He went through the multitude of tasks that had to be done when an army broke camp at double speed, his mind sharpened and his body tensed, as if sleep had never existed.

Dawn came to the Cotswold Hills, as they moved off. The smell of crushed downland grass and dung and soldiers was all around them. The mist was thin, like steam rising, so that they appeared to walk on clouds, like the heavenly host. Nothing heavenly about this host though; it had not shaved, or washed, since Malmesbury or before, and it grumbled and swore at the enforced haste. Sheep grazing across the track scattered in mindless alarm. A soldier who had laid an overnight snare had got a coney; he might as well have left it, he would have no time to make a stew before it was time to fight. He had Richard's own boar badge sewn on his sleeve, clean and white, and there were the marks of darker cloth where some other badge had been unpicked for the sake of discretion. Richard knew that he was one of Warwick's men, and had said nothing.

The day stretched ahead of them, something between thirty and forty miles to cover—how many hours? Maybe as much as fourteen. The terrain they covered was a rise and fall of hills, open country and sheep runs. The men marched now with a swing; it was early, and as fair a May morning as one might imagine, but by midday they would feel the heat of the sun.

The road from Berkeley to Gloucester was very dark, passing deep through beech woods, which shut out the moon. It was one o'clock in the morning. The carriage in which Anne travelled with the Queen and her other women had stuck in mud. The Queen put her head out through the curtains and shrieked for help. Around them an army on the march at night was a weird, frightening sight. The many pitch flares lit the gargoyle faces of tired soldiers making of them a procession to Calvary, or to Hell. The march was only just beginning.

When at last the city of Gloucester came in sight, it was mid-morning, and the army groaned as with one voice at what it saw.

The south gate of the city was closed. Armed men lined the walls. They had mounted guns to cover the road which led round beside the Severn to the bridge.

The Queen was struggling to control her hysteria as she sent messengers galloping with threats to Sir Richard Beauchamp, the governor. If the gates were not opened, the city would be fired on with guns, stormed, put to the sword and looted to the bare ground.

The sense of panic was contagious. Anne, who had been numbed ever since leaving Cerne, felt real fear of war for the first time, of blows, blood and rape; women were so completely helpless. Before, she had not much cared who won this race to the Severn. God knew what would happen to her if Edward became King again, though anything seemed better than being the unwanted wife of King Henry's heir. Now her feelings began to take colour from Queen Margaret's, and she felt the desperate need to escape, to cross the bridge which was barred to them, to be saved from the wrath of Edward.

It took less than five minutes to realize that Gloucester was a hopeless proposition. There was no possibility of storming a way through, it was too strong a garrison town. There was no time—a siege might take weeks, they had only hours. The Prince, so happy and confident that he would win the race to the west and meet his uncle Tudor, seemed unable to believe the hostility of the city.

"But we have many friends here," he said. "Send to Sir Richard Beauchamp and tell him we will destroy Gloucester if he does not allow us to pass."

Messages were useless. Beauchamp knew that he was safe. King Edward was on his way. The French Queen did not have time to start banging away with guns. She would have to move on; there was not time even to rest, when her army needed it as desperately as she needed to keep them moving.

By mid-morning, everyone in King Edward's army had stopped talking. It was too hot, and the flies were too bothersome and the hills too steep and the feet too sore for chatter with one's companions to be anything but a waste of breath. On the left hand, far below where they toiled along the hills, lay a sunlit expanse of the Severn Valley, the river like a great silver eel among the pastures, and beyond, the heat-hazed mountains of Wales. May Day had brought in a premature burst of high summer. Where a few weeks ago they might have slid about like ninepins in greasy mud, now the sheep country had dried like a housewife's sheets in the wind and the trackway dissolved in a fine, floury dust which powdered all the grass verges grey and in which the sharp Cotswold stones rose to the surface in heaps. Stones kept sticking in the horses' feet and laming them. The dust felt like lye soap gathering on hot faces; it seemed able even to pass through cloth. Yet perhaps the sun being in the ascendant was a good omen; he shone in greater splendour than any of King Edward's banners, following them in the sky. The trackway avoided villages and towns, and it was difficult to tell what sort of progress they were making.

Scouts were sent ahead to search for water. News of a spring or well would be more encouraging than even a sight of Queen Margaret's army and the knowledge that their quarry could not escape. But there was nothing, no spring, no stream, not even a farm pond. The army did not carry enough water, and all the beer had gone. Only the grass was succulent, and the horses snatched at it feverishly, until green slobber spread along the reins of their bridles. Once they rode through a cloud of blue butterflies, which had been settled, drinking from the downland flowers.

Someone brought Richard wine in a flask. It was warm and made his mouth taste rusty and his lips smart as if on fire. He touched his face and looked at the other men and realized that the sun had burnt him. It had got the backs of his hands as well, judging from their itching. His left arm hurt; it was healing, but bandaged and painful in the heat. He saw a man sitting in the grass, his shoes off, whimpering over his feet; his hose had disintegrated at toe and heel and his blisters had burst and begun to bleed. By the end of the day he'd either be crippled or left to lie by the road. It was possible for a man to die from feet wounds gained on forced marches.

At midday there was not even a cloud shadow in the sky. But

there was water, a small river, lying at the bottom of a valley so narrow and steep-sided that it might have been made by some giant ditch digger. It might be water, but it was also a fiend-made obstacle. The vanguard of the army had the advantage here of being able to fill their flasks and water their horses before it had been stirred up by hundreds of feet and hooves. Richard's own horse sucked the water up for minutes without raising his head, then took a breath, lifting his nose and blowing and shaking water and grass slobber all over everyone standing near. They were the lucky ones. Before half of the others had crossed, the stream had turned into mud, which even the horses did no more than futilely snuffle at.

The drop down into the hollow and the haul up out of it caused as much trouble as the churned-up stream bed. Even with extra draught animals hitched to the heavier carts, some guns and weighty items had to be carried across by teams of men before the wheeled vehicles could be heaved out of the mud and up the slope on the other side. To get the whole army across seemed to take an intolerable length of time, during every minute of which the enemy would be gaining on them.

King Edward came and stood beside his brother as they rested their horses, to watch the struggle, alternately cursing and yelling encouragement. Edward's particular brand of badinage with his men was something Richard envied. Not that he was ever ill at ease with his own men, but he lacked the ebullience of Edward, and a gift for vulgarly humorous repartee. The soldiers loved it, storing up the memory of his often unkingly words for telling to their grandchildren. Today, the King was in lively wit, as if he challenged the enemies of heat and thirst and an impossible country to beat down his spirits.

Clarence joined them. He was supposed to be assisting the King with the middleward of the army. At last, Richard noticed, George had stopped looking clean and shining, and was as sweaty and dust-smothered as the rest of them, and being rather fairer than the King and himself, he was even more sunburnt and freckled.

"Well," he said to Richard, half jibing, half grinning. "Do I live up to your example of the worthy soldier, brother? I scarcely recognize myself!"

Richard shrugged. It was too hot to rise to George's bait. He tried to run his fingers through his hair, but it was impossibly tousled, and harsh with dust and dirt.

"I do believe he's enjoying himself," George said. He was watching the King joke with Lord Hastings, his expression part curiosity, part mockery and part grudging admiration. "I'm not!"

"Nor am I, and I don't need you to tell me so."

"Bad tempered pup!"

"Where are we, do you know?" Richard asked, in an effort to stop the all too familiar sparring with George. His brother knew the Cotswolds; he did not.

"North-east of Stroud, if this is the river Frome. About fifteen miles more of high Cotswold, God help us."

Even King Edward's good humour and energy were worn down during the afternoon, as the hills became steeper and the going rougher. The men moaned of the brutality of the stones underfoot. One could see further than ever, half England seemed spread out below. The enemy could be seen, too. Richard stared with narrowed eyes at the distant columns, mostly recognizable only by the wink and sparkle of metal catching the sun—it was too far to distinguish colours, or even the difference between horse and foot—down on the flattest part of the green plain, before the lines were swallowed by woods.

He felt little curiosity about his enemies. Most of them he knew only by repute. He could not care if Somerset and the other Lancastrian lords were marching to damnation, though when it had been Warwick he had gone against, every step had turned a knife in his breast. Their own army was visible all the time, winding along the ridge of the hills, so slowly that it must appear not to move at all. God, their march was like a race of snails.

Each hour became a day, each minute an hour. The horse Richard was riding got a sore under the saddle girth; it was the third horse he had used that day. One had been lamed on the stones, another tired out. The fourth was sweating, though it had not been ridden.

When Richard began to see his men stagger upon their feet
with weariness, one of his scouts came back to say that the village of Cheltenham was only a mile or so ahead, and that the
tower of the Abbey at Tewkesbury could be seen in the distance.
Soon they reached the top of a great hill, scarred with stone
quarries, which swept steeply down to the plain. Beyond, the
sun glowed more gently now, upon the Malvern Hills. Richard
could see Tewkesbury. It looked like the Promised Land, mile
after beautiful green mile. We've done it, he thought, we have
outmarched them. The breeze began to dry the sweat in his hair.
He began to say a *Pater Noster* to himself. Then he turned as the
King rode up to his side. They smiled at each other.

"What time is it?" Edward asked casually.

Richard looked up at the sun and ran his hand over his smeary
face. "Getting on for five o'clock." His hands were filthy, caked
with dirt and his horse's sweat and his own; the nails were black.

King Edward grinned hugely—to laugh was a little too much
effort. He let the reins drop slack on the lathered, drooping neck
of his horse and raised both arms above his head, the fists
clenched in triumph. "By the mercy of God," he said, "we have
won the race!"

Somerset said hoarsely, "The last trump wouldn't move this
army another step." The men were lying down on the road, beside the road, in the fields, propped against walls, slumped with
heads on knees or prone on the ground like dead men. "We must
lay up here for the night, madame. It is a miracle we have got so
far. If we must fight tomorrow, then we fight and make an end
of it."

Queen Margaret nodded, sitting slumped on her horse in a
hopeless attitude. She had ridden all the way from Gloucester at
the head of her army to encourage them. Now there was nothing
more she could do.

"Why should we fail?" the Prince said angrily, and looked at
Somerset for reassurance.

"We are probably stronger in numbers than the usurper Edward. He must be as tired as we are; he has been moving even

faster. Why should we not win? The odds are not against us, madame, far from it."

That night Anne lay in bed with her fingers in her ears, trying to shut out the unceasing noises outside. The army lay encamped almost up to the walls of the house. Shouts, clumping feet and grinding cart wheels, and once a ringing clatter like a pile of pewter basins being dropped, as someone spilled quantities of armour on the ground. Sleep was impossible, though she was so tired that all her limbs and her head ached.

When the noises began to lessen a little, and it had been very dark for a long while, the Prince came to her room. When she had got over the initial instinct to scream at seeing a man in her room and controlled her fright, she said nervously, "Highness, what are you doing . . . ? The Queen. . . ."

"My mother cannot see me," he whispered fiercely. "I *am* your husband."

He walked very quietly across the floor, starting when the boards creaked. "I'm man enough to fight tomorrow. No one can deny a man the right to his wife when he's going to fight the next day."

Anne's heart sank. Yet it was perfectly reasonable that he should want to.

He shed some of his clothes and climbed in beside her. The creak and squeak and rustle of the bed frame sounded loud enough to be the entire house falling about their ears. Anne expected the Queen to burst in the door and haul her son out by the scruff of his neck. But no one came.

"Am I a match for Edward of March, if I meet him hand to hand?" her husband asked.

Anne suddenly visualized Edward in armour. The Prince was not small, but no, he was no match.

"He's enormous," she said.

"But he's a dozen years older than I am, and probably fat."

Anne doubted if Edward after months of exile and campaigning was anything but formidably strong and fit.

"Clarence is more your build," said Anne, then stopped, appalled at herself. Her sister's husband! The Prince wanted to kill; it was that, or be killed. She lay as if frozen, unable to say more.

"You are afraid again," the Prince whispered. "Why? Are you afraid of me?"

"No-o." Not afraid of him exactly, just now of everyone, everything, especially this one thing.

After he had finished, he put his face against her shoulder and lay very still. She did not think that he slept. She had an uneasy feeling that she ought to put her arms round him, or make some other wifely gesture, because he had wanted her. Affection? Love? She felt neither, nothing at all, in fact, except bruised discomfort again. She could neither lift her arms nor put a hand on him; she did not have the will left to make these signs.

When he felt sleep about to swallow him, the Prince jerked himself awake. It would be disaster to go to sleep while illicitly in his wife's bed; he was very tired and might well sleep until everyone thought he had disappeared and run away into the night because he was afraid of the battle. He climbed out of his side of the bed, half hoping for a farewell embrace, if nothing else. But Anne pretended to be asleep, more out of shyness than any wish to let him go without saying goodbye.

In the morning, when it seemed to be night still, Lady Katherine came to rouse Anne. They would have to move from the manor house immediately. The enemy army had broken camp at dawn and were approaching in battle order. Gloucester led.

"You see how Edward of March puts trust in his young brother, even if he is the little Yorkist runt," the Prince said to his mother. Anne was shocked to hear him say this about Richard. It was not true; she could not recollect him as so little, or weedy.

"We have the advantage in position," the Prince went on. "It's good. Any attack they make will be slow—there are dykes, water meadows, narrow sunken lanes between them and us, and quickset hedges so thick they'll need to hew a way through."

Anne watched him. He had a beautiful suit of armour, Italian work, with gilt borders inlaid with swans, and fleurs-de-lis and ostrich feathers, and so shiny that when he looked down he must see his face in his knees. It must have been specially made for him, perhaps as an extravagant present from his grandfather King René, and as René of Anjou lived perpetually on credit,

King Louis had no doubt paid for it, or would be doing so. Gold tassels and hawk bells hung from the reins of his horse, and from its trappings of blue and white silk, glinting, bobbing and jingling with every movement. Behind him were the banners, St. Edward the Confessor, the silver swan, King Henry's antelope, the three foxtails of Lancaster, the Trinity, and the Five Wounds of Christ.

The Prince was smiling, drunk on his excitement. When he turned his head and saw Anne, he waved his hand. She did not think quickly enough to return his greeting. Somerset rode up, red-faced and scowling—his men were still tired, and difficult to handle. The Prince wheeled his white horse to join him and rode away.

The Queen hustled her women out of the way of the armies, taking with her Dr. Morton and one or two other priests and servants, and went to wait nearer the ferry over the river Severn. On the other side of the river, all the way into Wales, lay a territory empty of hope. Jasper Tudor had not come in time. Wales was a refuge from the unthinkable.

The movement of the armies had scared the birds from the fields and hedges; flocks of them passed twittering overhead. A fox slunk across the road, leaving his earth for somewhere safer.

The noise of gunfire began quite suddenly and very loudly. Even at a distance, the din was terrifying. Edward of March must have far more guns than they did, and all going off at once, louder than the loudest thunder. Anne held on with both hands to the side of the carriage in which she sat, and tried to stop herself jumping at every crash. Smoke rose up in the sky from where the fighting was, and what looked like more flocks of birds, but were flights of arrows.

The Queen had demanded that messages should be brought to her of every swing in the fighting. Anne crouched at her side—the hems of their gowns were touching on the floor—and listened. Mounted men raced up, and then galloped back again towards the battle.

Gloucester had attacked first. He had most of the guns, and he had archers brought right up front, just behind them. He was giving Somerset a terrible pasting, letting fly with everything at once, while his men struggled forward through water, mud and overgrown hedges.

Somerset, baited like a bull, had stood so much and no more. Having the advantage of a downhill run and more open ground, he led a furious charge.

But Edward of March, quick as thought and bold as a lion, led his men across the scummy dykes and smashed through the hedges, faster than one would have thought possible, striding like a giant at their head, few people daring to tackle him man to man. Gloucester attacked, too, as if he knew what his brother would do before it was begun, then Hastings joined them, not hesitating a moment.

Somerset was routed! His charge was more difficult than he'd thought, and it ran into Edward in the wrong place. No one had brought up the rest of their army to help him against a flank attack. The three in command of the middleward, the Prince, Langstrother and Wenlock, had appeared paralysed by Edward's boldness. Devonshire with the rearguard was still waiting for orders.

The Yorkist army came on like a battering ram. It drove into the standing divisions of the Prince and Devonshire without check. Somerset's flight had unnerved them. They were being driven back towards Tewkesbury town, running like sheep in every direction. It was defeat, rout, all hope lost.

Queen Margaret sat staring-eyed, her mouth twitching.

"*Mon fils*," she croaked, "I must have news of him. Find him for me!"

"Madame, we must escape—the ferry! We'll be across before they can catch us if we go now." Dr. Morton, in no mind to be captured, was the first to take control of the situation.

"Not until I have news of my son!" Margaret moaned in wild unreason.

"Madame! Now!" Morton was a determined man.

"No. My son!"

"Dear madame, Margot," Lady Katherine Vaux said in French, on her knees, holding the Queen's hand. "Save yourself. You cannot help him by staying here. God willing, he will have escaped. He will come to you."

Margaret did not answer her. *"Edouard. Mon fils. . . ."* she said again.

Morton, taking matters into his own hands, leapt onto his horse with amazing agility, shouted at the drivers of the Queen's carriage to whip up their horses and to follow him to the Severn ferry.

So, against her will, the Queen was carted away. Morton and her women bundled her aboard the boat. Anne clambered in after them, moving as if in a dream. A nightmare, rather, for the first fugitives could be seen in the meadows, running towards the river. But the pursuers ran faster—screaming and yelling could be heard.

Queen Margaret looked as if she would throw herself over the side of the boat. Lady Vaux held her by the arm, and Dr. Morton took the liberty of grasping a handful of her skirts. The ferryman rowed as hard as he could; seeing the murder being done in the Tewkesbury meadows, he preferred to be on the other side.

Somehow, they managed to get the Queen ashore, and to the shelter of the only house of substance nearby. A family called Payne lived there, whom Morton persuaded to give them shelter. He had tried to persuade Margaret to move on, to take the road towards Wales. But she sat clutching the arms of her chair, as if they would have to prise her out of it, her eyes starting out of her head, staring into empty air.

"Mon fils—Edouard. . . ." she said yet again, faintly.

"Merciful Mary Queen of Heaven!" Morton groaned. "We do not know what has happened to him. Bear up, madame, until we *do* have news."

They waited at Payne's house all the rest of the day and into the night. No one went to bed. Anne curled herself in a seat by the window and stared out of it, hour by hour. She tried to decide what news it was for which she was waiting, what news she wanted. Not to hear of the Prince's death. Not to hear anything. After a while she became quite numb, without thought. As the sun began to sink a maid came out of the house and took in the sheets which were drying in the adjoining meadow. She shook them to get rid of the cherry petals which had blown in from the orchard. Once or twice the sound of galloping horses came close and then faded away. No one from King Edward's army came to search the house. It seemed his victory was too complete for pursuits to be of immediate importance.

The hours of darkness were the longest. The rooms were lit up with candles all the time, as if a vigil were being kept. Before it was over, someone came to the house. Anne heard Lady Katherine Vaux give a little cry.

"*Mon Dieu!* Monsieur, how did you find us?"

A Frenchman said, "A peasant, in the village. My horse swam over the river. . . ." His voice broke, and he groaned.

"You are hurt?"

"No—yes. I have dealt with it."

"Monsieur Robin, the Queen is distracted. Have you news?"

It was Pierre Robin, the Prince's physician. The mere fact of his having sought them out, and his being wounded, and alone, struck a chill.

"*Ah—non!*" Lady Katherine had seen his face clearly for the first time. It told all there was to tell.

"Let me go to madame first. . . ." she said.

The French doctor began to sob unashamedly.

"How was it?" Lady Katherine whispered. "In the battle? Or capture? Oh, not the beheading. . . ."

"The battle."

"You are certain?"

"I saw." Dr. Robin could say no more. His distress was painful to hear. Anne knew, without any more being said. The Prince had been killed. Lady Katherine came to her, put her arms round her, and saw her quite dry-eyed.

"I must go to madame," Lady Katherine said.

"Yes."

She went away with M. Robin to the Queen's rooms. They were gone a long time. Anne expected to hear the shrieks of Margaret's grief tear apart the walls. But there was nothing.

Dr. Morton came back when daylight flooded the room and found Anne still alone, and an appalling smell of candles burnt down to their ends. Soon after she had realized that her husband was dead, the thought struck her that in the morning, when he had ridden away to the battle, she had not bothered to wave her hand to him. She had not provided any passionate farewells the night before either. But the only thing she could think of was not how he died, or what was going to happen to herself, but that she had not troubled to wave goodbye to him.

Dr. Morton said, "Your Highness, the carriages are ready; we must set out immediately. It is necessary that you come with us. You do not perhaps quite understand your position. Edward of March will make every effort to seek you out. He has of course by now imprisoned our unfortunate sovereign lord King Henry again in the Tower. He will wish to make certain—quite certain— that no heir of Lancaster remains out of his hands. Your husband the Prince—may God have mercy on him—is dead. If by some miraculous chance you are found to be carrying his child, you are more important than you may ever have dreamed possible, to Edward as much as to our party." He did not say this ungently, but the fact was brutal enough in itself. He saw no sign of emotion, or even understanding, in the girl's face.

He went on, "If such an event proves the case, the Queen will do all in her power to get you safely to France. Now we must be ready to take the raod to Wales. We are fugitives now, and the wildest places are the safest. God go with us."

12

Death and Destruction

May 1471

And now sche ne rought, so that sche myght attayne,
Though all Engeland were brought to confusyon;
Sche and her wykked affynite certayne
Entende uttyrly to destroye thys regioun;
For with theym ys but Deth & destruccion,
Robberye & vengeaunce with all Rygour.
Therefore all that holde of that oppynioun,
God sende hem a schort ende with mech langour.

A Political Retrospect (c. 1462)

"Open these doors!"

King Edward grasped the iron handles of the doors of Tewkesbury Abbey church in his gauntleted fists and shook the massive oak structure. He got no answer, except for the thumping, rattling and creaking of the huge bolts on the inside.

"This place is no sanctuary!" he bawled. He knew that the king rats among his enemies were holed up inside.

A crowd of his soldiers began to charge the doors, attacking the locks and hinges with leaden mauls. The hinges gave first, crunching and tearing out of the wood. The doors toppled inwards with a great booming crash.

Men burst through, half carrying the King with them, and rushed down the nave and aisles, whooping and brandishing their swords.

King Edward looked a satanic figure in the church. The fallen door behind him let the midday sun into the dim interior. He was hung about with weapons of several kinds, most of which he had made use of. His lower half was mud plastered, his chest and arms gory, and he was marked round the middle by the green waterweed from the dyke. Under the raised vizor he was red with sunburn, exertion and anger. When the Abbot himself approached, clearly aware of his own resemblance to St. Thomas Becket, shielded by a monstrance held in shaking hands, the King's face became a shade redder. Before the Body of Christ, he was shamed. He roared at his brawling men to leave the place at once, but it was too late. One of them had skewered an archer in the Prince of Lancaster's livery against a pillar. Blood ran down it like dog's piddle down a post.

This sight met Richard as he caught up with his brother. He had to walk over the broken-down door, his mailed shoes making hollow thumps. He looked up at the King, who was standing facing the nervous Abbot, angry and sheepish and shocked out of the heat of the chase. God's house had been defiled by a killing in His presence.

"My lord Abbot," King Edward said, "this is an unpardonable act. I shall endeavour to make what restitution I can. But as you well know, this place has no rights of sanctuary. I give you my word that these men will not be molested until they have been brought to trial for bearing arms against the rightful King." He paused, and went back to the door, slid his stained sword out of its retaining ring at his belt, and threw it outside. An axe and a mace went after it.

"Leave your weapons. The church cannot harbour traitors even if it should prevent murder. Moreover, the church cannot prevent the course of the King's justice, except in the legal sanctuaries."

Somerset charged out from behind a tomb, like a bull into the ring. "There is no king here!" he roared. His words echoed thunderously in the church. "There is no justice! I am King Henry's loyal subject!"

"Of that I'm not in doubt," Edward said, unperturbed by this show of defiance. "You took a while to show yourself, Edmund Beaufort. Who else is in here? Come out. I'm an easy man—those of you who deserve them shall have pardons. How many of you are there? Where is your so-called Prince? Is he in here?"

He walked, unarmed, round the tomb from which Beaufort had emerged. On the other side of it was Sir John Langstrother, squatting on the floor like a mangy old bear, weeping and moaning that he had failed in his duty to look after the young Prince. Blood dripped off the fingers of one hand; he had not even tried to bind up his wound.

"My lord Prior," King Edward said, "where is the Prince?"

Langstrother's reply was so incoherent that it told Edward only that they thought the Prince was dead.

"Where's Wenlock?"

Another roar came from Somerset. "That gibbering treacherous old fool! He's dead, and I hope he's roasting in Purgatory. I made sure what brains there were in his skull were spattered all over the cow parsley in the meadow. He hindered the Grand Prior here—and gave me no help. If he had, your brains would be where his are!"

"My brains are in good order. Help the Grand Prior up, and leave this place. If you cause another affray in here, you will be as guilty as I."

Somerset, though disposed to rant and rail against his fate, knew when he was cornered, and allowed himself to be escorted out with the others.

Two of Clarence's men came in carrying a body, its arms and legs swinging to and fro. They dumped it on the floor of the nave. "Edward calling himself Prince, your Grace." There would be no need to go searching for him.

King Edward went over to look. Richard followed him. The body appeared to be uninjured. The armour was little bloodied and scarcely dirtied at all, as they were, by hard fighting over mucky ground.

Richard looked down at the face of the Prince of Lancaster; he had been handsome. Someone shifted the body sideways. The Prince had been killed by a blow on the head—perhaps by the pick on the back of an axe. He must have scarcely had time for any fighting before being put to flight and cut down. No chance to try his strength in battle—even death came unrecognized from the rear.

Clarence himself strode in. King Edward turned towards him. "Did your men do this?"

"Some mine, some yours, some Tom, Dick and Harry's. They caught him and tipped him off his horse and clouted his head before you could blink. I couldn't have called them off if I'd wanted to. Should I have wanted to?"

"No matter, one way or the other. George, you're whole yourself?"

"Yes. Is he wounded again?" He indicated Richard.

"No. We'll leave the Abbot to deal with this. George, it's time we saw more of what's happening outside."

The King was not one to gloat over his triumphs, though the Prince's death was perhaps the biggest single piece of good fortune which had ever come his way. The Prince had been very young. He looked at the lifeless form on the paving stones, then at his brother Richard, who was staring down somewhat glassy-eyed, as if he had seen too many corpses.

"Richard," the King said, "come with me." It was better not to dwell on these events.

"Let him lie here two days," he said to the Abbot. "Then see to his burial."

Richard went out with his brother into the sunshine. He did not want to dwell on the dead Prince, either. Somerset had been right, only chance and their enemies' bungling had prevented the same fate befalling Edward and himself. For the second time they had won a great victory, and this one must surely mark the end of their troubles.

"How many of them will go to the block?"

"Only as many as it would be dangerous to allow to live. You've seen Somerset's attitude for yourself—there's only one way to ensure that we are not plagued by this and that rebellion for the rest of our lives. Those who have shown themselves to be utterly set against me and my House cannot expect mercy from me. I've been poked in the eye too many times by men I've pardoned and trusted to work to our mutual advantage.

"Henry of Lancaster's son—if that's what he was—is dead.

Henry is in the Tower. That removes the causes of rebellions. Remove the recalcitrants who live only to gain revenge, and we should be able to live in peace. Richard, I've seen enough of war in the last dozen years to last me till the day I die. And I fully intend to die in my bed, God willing.

"I saw you after Barnet, Dick, and saw you sicken—*and* I know why. Well, you go and take a look at the work being done in the meadows here, and you'll know why you've got to sit down on Monday morning and condemn perhaps a score of men for treason. You are my Constable, and you know the forms, and you know the reasons for the verdict.

"I'll draw up a list of those who must be condemned. After that the only remaining problem will be Henry of Lancaster, and that's one on which I shall have to take a decision." For the moment he said no more; there were too many immediate matters demanding his attention.

On Monday morning, Richard entered the courthouse in Tewkesbury town, the Constable's mace borne before him, and the Earl Marshal the Duke of Norfolk following him. The whole procedure of the trial was over in a remarkably short time, the charges of treason rattled out like an alphabet lesson, and the prisoners refusing to plead, knowing the uselessness of words.

Richard watched the fifteen men whose lives he was to proclaim extinguished. Perhaps they were the last who would die for the miserable, expired cause of Henry of Lancaster, which had claimed thousands. The prisoners for the most part held themselves with the utmost dignity. Richard wondered, if he had been in their place, whether he would have acquitted himself as well—would his other companions? He looked at the other chief officer of the tribunal. John Mowbray of Norfolk was an odious fellow, stupid and bumptious. His face was unprepossessing, with an inadequate chin and an Adam's apple which moved up and down as if he had a tennis ball stuck in there, even when he was silent. He was twenty-five and looked younger, being light-haired, light-eyed, pink and pimply, like a youth. The ancient customs of the governance of England allowed many fools to hold high military and judicial office.

Mowbray in turn watched his Constable with curiosity and

some circumspection. The Duke of Gloucester stared into space, unblinking and expressionless as an image. The thin, straight-mouthed face might have been whittled from wood and stained with walnut juice. Even at eighteen, his skin had begun to line; the fine creases were paler, where he had screwed up his eyes against the sun. The remains of a huge bruise was dwindling patchily on one cheekbone. The hand resting clench-fisted upon the table was tanned darker still, another bruise discolouring on it, and a scab peeling off white. Nails pared down level with the skin of his fingertips, one of them blackened, which would later fall off. The white edge of a bandage showed at his left wrist. He had been knocked about in the fighting a good deal more than Mowbray himself.

The prisoners were marched straight out of the courthouse to the scaffold in the market place, where all fifteen of them were beheaded. Somerset was the first, defiant and brave and scornful, unchanged when faced by death. Prior Langstrother went like a martyr to the fire. The axe fell with a heavy thunk! more than a score of times—even a good executioner did not make a clean chop every time. It was, compared to previous aftermaths of bat-tles, a moderate lopping of heads.

The Constable of England walked from the bloody scene hard-ened of feeling, to an extent which surprised himself. There was room in his mind only for relief that he had not met the same fate.

> "In a May morning on Malvern Hills
> A strange thing befell me, a fairy vision methought
> I was weary of wandering and went me to rest
> Under a broad bank beside a stream. . . ."

Dr. Morton broke off from his reading aloud, holding the book open on his knees.

"Tomorrow we must cross the Malvern Hills," he said. "Then Wales will be in sight." He was trying to keep the women—in particular the Queen—from brooding on their plight and falling sick and taking to their beds. It was not an easy task.

They huddled in a tiny room in the most broken-down, ill-ruled monastery that Anne had ever seen. They had been there

three days and should have moved on, but the Queen seemed
unfit to travel. Little Malvern Priory did not own a guest house,
because it very seldom received guests other than those who
could be lodged in the stable. The room offered to the Queen,
who was once again no queen, was the only one whose roof did
not leak. The place was hidden deep in the thick woodlands of
Malvern Chase, and one of those tiny, unprofitable houses which
the mother Priory of Worcester would sooner forget. Of the half
dozen brothers seen, furtively goggling at these disturbing visitors, two were too old to do any work. Their chief worldly occupation seemed to be the keeping of pigs, to judge from the per-
vasive smell and the gruntings heard under the window. The
pigs were the most prosperous inhabitants, fat and lumbering
freely about the place.

"Master Langland dreamed his dream when sleeping on a hill-
side near here," Dr. Morton said. Anne, who wanted to sleep,
could not remember if Piers the Plowman had been a swineherd
also. It seemed unlikely that a swineherd should write poetry.
The one here, lurking under the window with his pigs, was an
idiot. Anne had seen him peering in, and he had been picking his
nose and rolling his eyes and chattering to himself.

Dr. Morton would have made a good schoolmaster, with his
acid tongue and sharp, transfixing eye. He had a bony, watchful
face. But at least he was a man, energetic and managing. If their
safety had been left in the hands of Queen Margaret, she would
not have moved from the battlefield at Tewkesbury, waiting like
a broken-winged bird for the hunter to pick her up. Not that
Anne could imagine King Edward being a vengeful person, or
likely to put women in the Tower in irons, but the Queen had always been a terrible enemy.

Anne wondered why she had been dumbfounded by Morton's
words to her as they left Payne's house. Thankfully, she had
lived through the tense time after Christmas, when she had
counted off the days on the calendar, and by the time they had
left France, she had known herself to be safe. Now she would
have to go through the whole thing again. She did not want to
be pregnant; the sufferings of her sister had frightened her too
much, and she did not want to bring into the world a homeless

fugitive or a prisoner from birth. She did not know if the Queen had heard of her son's escapade on the night before he died. Lady Katherine knew, and if the Prince had lived she might have been expected not to mention it. But his death made it so much more important.

If Queen Margaret knew, she did not care. Now that her son was dead, she cared for nothing, not even life itself.

That night Anne lay on her lumpy straw pallet tormented by fleas, listening to the wind rushing in the great trees. That the forest here had been her father's property—or rather her mother's —was not a source of comfort. People who died as her father had, fighting against the King, forfeited their property. A rustling and scraping in the roof kept her staring in fright into the dark malodorous recesses above, as if some nasty little black demon might creep out. She told herself it must be rats. Their feet seemed armour-plated.

In the morning, before they could leave, a group of armed horsemen came to Little Malvern. Anne realized with sinking heart that the men must have come from King Edward. Someone on the road must have betrayed them. She watched a square, swarthy man clump across the yard in double-soled boots, taking no notice of the pig dung. He caught up an inoffensive scratching hen, and casually wrung its neck. "Here's our dinner, Ellis!" he bellowed. "What a sty, eh! I'll wager this place hasn't been visited in twenty years. The Bishop of Worcester had better bring a dung fork if he decides to come here!"

Ellis, who seemed to be a servant, retreated hastily from a barn, which he had been searching, pursued by an angry sow.

"I want a piss," said his master, and used a wall.

It would be only a matter of minutes before they found what they were looking for. They spoke like north countrymen, though not from the places in which Anne had lived. She ducked away from the glassless window, but not before she had been seen. The swarthy man came quickly in through the door, leaving the others to guard it.

"We-ell," he said slowly, standing four-square with his thumbs stuck in his belt, staring at Anne. "What's this?" He began to grin. He was a man in the prime of life, not ill-favoured, just hor-

ribly swarthy. "Ellis!" he roared. "In here! We won't be journeying any further, thanks be to God. I don't think these swineherd
brothers keep a whore—at least not dressed like this one!"

Anne shrank onto a bench on the far side of the room.

"And which one have we here? Not the old she-tiger—much
too young and tender. Hmm, too young, but could be tender—
I've a good mind to find out. . . ." He advanced on Anne, grinning, red mouth and dark-shadowed jaw.

"Aren't I going to get a feel? I've ridden all the way from
Tewkesbury on the King's business. . . ." He made a grab and
caught Anne up in one vice-like arm, squashing her face against
his own, which was as bristly as one of the hogs. His chest was
unyielding; he had metal plates sewn into his jacket.

Anne screamed until she thought her lungs would split, while
he tried to stop her struggling, and to get his hand into the folds
of her skirt. Just when he had nearly reached his goal, she managed to bite his other hand hard, and Dr. Morton came in.

"I presume that King Edward—for I shall be obliged to call
him so—has sent you to escort us into custody, not to rape the ladies in our party."

The coolly contemptuous tones cut through the swarthy man's
heavy breathing, as he released Anne, pushing her from him,
swearing foully. "Bitch! Screech owl—she's put her teeth in me!"

"Leave her," Morton snapped. "She is the Prince's widow!"

"Warwick's daughter? Well, well, well, I must have just missed
a great privilege! Widow of the French bastard, eh. And who
the devil are you?"

"John Morton, prebendary of Lincoln, Doctor of Law, and
Keeper of the Privy Seal to King Henry. Who am I speaking to—
apart from his being a most remarkable blasphemer?"

"Sir William Stanley, knight, of Ridley in Cheshire, brother to
Lord Stanley—sent by King Edward to arrest the French Queen
so-called, and her party, to answer charges of treason."

"Knight? Hmm. Of course I have not been in England for
some years. A rising family, if I remember."

"I hope so!" Stanley laughed loudly. He was a cool customer,
too, behaving as if he had not been caught by a cleric while
groping under the skirts of the Prince's widow.

Anne, trembling on the bench with her knees clamped together while they introduced themselves, knew with absolute certainty that she was going to be sick. She hurled herself at the window, and was just in time, only botching the job slightly.

Morton viewed the scene with distaste. He called loudly, "Lady Vaux! You're needed here!"

He turned to Stanley. "I would hesitate to take such a peerless example of knighthood into the presence of her Grace the Queen. . . ."

"Watch your tongue!"

"She is a sick woman, a broken woman, you understand, after her son's death. I suggest that you give us a short time to make ourselves ready, and we will come quietly with you. There is no need for you to do more than guard us."

"You're sharp, reverend sir, at ordering my task for me. I'll see the French Queen. I am commissioned to receive her surrender."

Morton shrugged. "Very well," he said. "If it gives you satisfaction. But I do not intend to leave you alone with another defenceless woman."

They went out as Lady Vaux came in. She took one look at Anne—she had heard the screams.

"*Mon Dieu!* Child, what has been happening here? Who is that man? Did he. . . ." She, seeing the practical need, gave Anne her own handkerchief to wipe her mouth and blow her nose.

Anne threw herself sobbing into the lap of the only woman who had so much as treated her as a human being in the last months. Frightened though she had been by the muscular confines of Stanley's arms and the stifling descent of his mouth, her anger at being mishandled against her will was greater.

"If all this King Edward's knights behave like pigs, then we are better dead," Lady Katherine said. "Us poor widows will have to stay together, never let ourselves be alone with these men. Ah, *ma petite*, I must go to the Queen now, I dare not leave her, I am frightened of what she may do. Come with me, and we will all take care of each other. My poor madame Margot will soon be as much a widow as we are!"

"But you cannot behead someone who has been a king, even if

that were not his right. King Henry has been anointed—in France, too."

"These Yorkists can do anything, anything."

"But King Edward has never harmed women—everyone knows that."

"Hmm. We shall see. He is as much of a rapist as this pigman he has sent here."

Sir William had not proved himself to be a rapist, but he was brash, arrogant, and crude in his methods. He found it necessary to belabour the wretched figure of the Queen—and she was wretched beyond comprehension—with a catalogue of her misdeeds. If he had one grain of pity in him, he would have left King Edward's triumph unendorsed. But he was full only of insolence and spite. He stood in front of the cavernous-eyed, sick creature with his arms akimbo and his broad chest puffed out, the livery collar of King Edward's household gleaming round his shoulders. He was in fact a man of more rank and influence than his boorish manner indicated.

"Tell my lord of March," Margaret whispered, uncaring under his vituperation, "that I am at his commandment." She could not even bear to speak the name, Edward.

Dr. Morton, who was not a man much swayed by emotion, was for once speechless with anger, but there was nothing he could have done to stop Sir William Stanley, short of a gag in the mouth. Lady Katherine Vaux suffered more perhaps than the others, for she loved Margaret more.

"And a pity *your* mighty father didn't stay where his allegiance properly belonged," he ranted on, glaring at Anne, and sucking his hand. "Instead of the widow of a bastard and daughter of a traitor, you might have had a husband who'd teach you manners. If my wife put her teeth in me, I'd have the skin off her bum!"

Anne, recovered sufficiently from his assault to get her temper up, heard herself shriek back in the daring voice of someone much braver than herself, "It's a wonder King Edward trusted you to come here—even I know that Lord Stanley was one of those who helped put King Henry back on his throne, and yet who never came to my father's aid, or to ours!"

Sir William, instead of clouting her, as he well might, put back his square head on his thick neck and roared with laughter.

"You make a good daughter for this woman after all, little she-cat, for all you look so tight-arsed and meek. I'm not accountable for my brother Tom's trickery, thanks be to God!

"Now, the lot of you, get ready to leave this place. King Edward will be at Worcester by now, and travelling north after that. He wants you right under his nose, and safe under guard. And if you want to know why—well, if that randy bastard son of yours, madam Frenchwoman, has put his yard up her as many times as he wanted, then we may well have a little problem on our hands."

Lady Katherine, all five feet of her, faced up to the leering and truculent Stanley and spat venomously in his face. She screamed a phrase in Provençal, which no one could translate, but all recognized as obscene abuse.

Stanley to show he did not take women seriously and was not easily provoked by them, wiped his face and shrugged off this also.

"Lady," he said, "you can teach me to curse in your barbarous tongue—it'll relieve the tedium of our journey."

Hateful and callous as he had shown himself to be, Sir William probably passed for a wit in male company. He enjoyed ordering the prisoners about, and when they were ready to leave, declared that he would eat his dinner first. He did so sitting in front of them demolishing the fowl he had filched from the brothers of the priory, and which his resourceful servant had roasted. The others had nothing to eat until they came to Worcester that night.

When the prisoners had been brought to King Edward at Coventry, the King was by no means so eager as Sir William Stanley had been to seek an interview with the defeated Margaret of Anjou. He loathed angry scenes—political or amorous—with women. Tears in his presence gave him an overmastering desire to escape. Even the knowledge of his father's death at Wakefield, the horrible charade of the crowning with paper, Margaret's venomous taunts, did not lessen his awareness that the tears in this broken woman would fill an ocean. Somehow, he could not work himself up to vengeance. He saw her as briefly as possible, because he felt unable to avoid it altogether, and went about grim-faced and silent for the rest of the day.

Richard, spared any meeting with the French Queen, saw her brought in by Sir William Stanley's escort, and wished for long afterwards that he had not. There was no reason why the sight of her should prick his conscience. When he had been a child of seven, he had been frightened out of his wits by his mother's face after she had learned of Wakefield and the death of his father; it had haunted his nightmares for years. Margaret of Anjou's face had as much power to disturb him, even now, when he was an adult, and well schooled in war and suffering. He could not shake off the sight of her; she had looked so small, slender and womanly, a travel-crumpled middle-aged woman, dressed like any citizen's wife. Her enormous eyes stared at nothing, and floated in sockets of stained skin like sooty dead wicks in saucers of oil.

His own mother possessed some quality which had enabled her to survive suffering—even her many bereavements had left her herself, strengthened by her unshakable faith in Christ. But Margaret of Anjou's self had died with her son.

He told himself that she had sent hundreds to their deaths, made as many widows and bereaved mothers. She had tried to prove herself the equal of men, and in her time had shown herself fiercer and harder than they. So why should he soften towards her, when she would gladly have seen him die? She would answer for her sins at the Day of Judgement, but then so would he. He was a year older than her son had been, and into that year had been crammed ten years' experience, so that he thought of the dead Prince as a boy. He was Constable of England, it was his duty to condemn men to death and to see them die, but Margaret of Anjou's face troubled him more than either of these things. He pitied her more than his youth and situation were capable of acknowledging.

Perhaps because of this, he felt more deeply a wish to help Anne Neville, who was doubly bereaved, entirely blameless, and without any protection. Of course there was no reason why he, a single man with no claims on her, should do anything. Her sister Isabel was George's wife; they were the ones who should do something for her, not himself. The trouble was, George was so full of resentment and hostility towards him, chiefly because a position of trust with the King had been the result of his loyalty. How George could expect the same due for himself was staggering, after his treachery. But George always did want to have his bread and eat it at the same time.

Richard wondered if he somehow might manage to see Anne, before they left Coventry, when he would be drawn once again into the maelstrom of raising another army to deal with the turmoil arisen in the north after Warwick's death. But Margaret of Anjou's female companions had been taken away with her.

That night he asked the King if he might see Anne.

"See her? Of course. I've lodged them in the town." Edward began to grin infuriatingly. "Don't burn your fingers," he said.

"Why should I? It may surprise you to know I don't intend anything. She hasn't anyone to turn to."

"Well, don't expect her to turn to you. Dickon, she's had a bad time. I've seen her, and she's not the same girl as a year ago, in more ways than one. You'll have to play a waiting game."

It was typical of Edward to imagine that he intended to play any game at all. How could it be conceivable that Anne should wish to remain with her mother-in-law? Of course, she had been forced into the marriage, she had been among enemies all the time. Her own family, Christ, did he not know it, was his own. She was four weeks short of her fifteenth birthday, yet she had been married to the Prince of Lancaster since just before Christmas. He was deeply angered by the possibility that the Prince's heir might even now be growing inside her, an anger at her enforced plight which he had not yet recognized as jealousy. The Prince had been so damnably handsome—any girl might grieve for such a handsome husband—but the chances were that he had been an arrogant young beast. He'd been a nasty child—Richard was sure he could remember an incident from childhood, a clash with the Prince, in which he had come off worse—the boy had been bigger than he was even then.

When he found Anne at last, it was clear that one of the other women prisoners did not intend to leave her alone with him. I am her cousin, he thought. But this was one of Margaret's women, who had been in France for years; she knew nothing of himself or his brothers.

"Gloucester!" Lady Katherine Vaux turned her back on him. "The young butcher!" she said clearly, in French. He understood, and resented it. Wouldn't their precious Prince have had his share of the butchery, if they had won? And he even younger. "He is probably a rapist pig, like his brother, like all these Yorkists," Lady Katherine added. "Such a little pig!"

The only thing he could do was ignore her. He felt the colour heat his face like a hot iron.

Anne looked upset. "Did you see my father?" she asked him, as if this were the one question she had been waiting to put.

That was the last thing he wanted to talk about.

"Yes," he said shortly.

She lapsed into silence. He could think of nothing to break it. Though she looked much the same as she had when he had last seen her, a little older perhaps, more peaked and strained; he felt as if he confronted a total stranger. He had better get out, before he said anything which would make her manner even more distant.

"If you need anything. . . ." Stupid phrase, her needs were quite beyond anything he could provide. "I mean, if you. . . . I am as close to the King as anyone."

"What does the King intend to do with me?"

"I don't know. Send you to Isabel. . . ."

"Yes, I suppose so."

"When the King has more time. . . . You have nothing to fear from him. There's more trouble in the north. We haven't seen the end of all this yet."

"No." She knew as well as he did why—the Neville affinity were wild as mad men at the deaths of Warwick and Montagu. He decided upon retreat. She was so indifferent to anything he could suggest.

"You will remember—if there's anything. Send word to *my* mother—it would be best—through Isabel. Meanwhile, we'll send someone to *your* mother. . . ."

"Yes," she said, still in that small, indifferent voice.

The Mayor of London, John Stockton, appeared to be in robust health. He had got up from his bed, to which he had retired on hearing that King Edward was about to sail for England, in order that he would not have to muster opposition to the House of York in London. The news of the victory at Barnet had proved of more benefit than doctors, and Stockton had arisen to defend his city against the last belligerent Nevilles, the two bastard brothers of Fauconberg. Now he came forward to kneel to the victorious King Edward. Instead, the King dismounted, embraced the loyal Mayor and wrung him by the hand.

"My lord Mayor, you must be rewarded for your trouble. You and your aldermen, and my lords Essex, Rivers and Dudley here, are the heroes of London. Each one of you is a present-day Horatius!"

For five days, the City of London had kept Fauconberg's mob at bay and had at last beaten them off into unwilling retreat. The south gate of London Bridge had been burnt to the ground.

"You deserve no less than a knighthood!" King Edward said, and there in Islington fields, he knighted Mayor Stockton, the Recorder, and eleven of the aldermen, to the sound of cheers from the citizens who had assembled to greet him.

The King said, "Now that London is ready to receive us, my brother of Gloucester shall lead our triumphal procession into the City. My brother is the youngest of all my captains; he has borne as heavy a burden throughout the past months as I have myself. It is my wish to honour him. My good friend Lord Hastings deserves equal honours, my lord Rivers, my brother of Clarence also. . . . Let us do as the heroes of Rome did, and show ourselves as victors to the people!"

The people that day saw not only the victors but the defeated, the women, all that were left of King Edward's enemies, not enchained in the manner of the ancients but riding in an ordinary carriage. A few ugly yells were directed at Margaret of Anjou, but she did not seem to hear. Anne Neville, who shared her public humiliation, thought that since her capture she had been like a wooden doll, opening her mouth only to answer questions as if someone pulled strings, and that seldom. Anne herself endured the pitiless curiosity and ready insults of the Londoners by shutting herself behind her face as if it were a protective mask. She saw the carriage they rode in drive over the petals and flowers of the white roses with which King Edward and his brothers had been pelted by the crowd. She hated these people, who only a few months before had shouted for Warwick. Her father had been forgotten, as if his bright star had never blazed. It was bad enough to be treated as the spoils of war, but unlike Queen Margaret she had at least been spared imprisonment in the Tower.

When all the triumphal hullabaloo was over, King Edward called a meeting of his most trusted councillors at the palace of Westminster. Before the others arrived, the King led his brother Richard out into the gardens, so that they were alone together. It was late afternoon, but the sun was still high—the day had been appropriately glorious. The gardens were in good order, as the flowers and the gardeners could afford to ignore the changes of regime at Westminster. The King walked Richard round in a large, aimless circle without speaking, in the manner of one trying to calm a nervous horse. Richard wondered briefly what was coming, and then thought that he had a good idea of it.

The peacocks screeched intolerably at each other, strutting along the top of the low wall by the Thames. King Edward bent down and picked up a stone, slinging it into the midst of them. Peacocks and peahens flapped off to hold their meeting in another part of the gardens, squawking like demons.

"Infernal creatures! They've driven people in this palace mad for years. I'd happily wring their necks," King Edward said. Richard thought no reply was necessary.

"I've made my decision," King Edward said abruptly. He did not mean on the desirability of banishing peacocks from Westminster. Richard looked at him expectantly and felt uneasy. The subject around which his brother was hedging was unpleasant.

"It will have to be done. The sooner the better. Tonight. Henry of Lancaster is not yet fifty. Another ten years in the Tower? Another ten years of disturbance and revolt on his behalf? Tudor of Pembroke is still at large, so is Oxford.

"You must understand, Richard, that I am determined never to suffer humiliation and exile again. Never. I am *very* determined. I am telling you this before I broach the subject with the others because you are my Constable, and my brother. It will be your duty to see that my orders are carried out. It is not a pretty task, and I would not have laid it upon you if it were not necessary. It's not a decision I have taken lightly."

"Yes," Richard said. Edward was going to take him indoors, and give him orders to see that Henry of Lancaster was quickly and quietly sent out of this world. In the Tower, tonight. Richard had thought that this would happen, that he would be made accessary to the murder of this peculiarly helpless victim. But was it any more murder than the sentencing of fifteen others to die on the scaffold after Tewkesbury? They had borne arms treasonably against King Edward and had expected their fate if they lost. Henry was guilty of a treasonable existence—still refusing to deny his own right to be King. Yet whatever his right, and he had none, he had been anointed.

Richard did not open his mouth to argue with his brother, to suggest that the deed might be postponed, that the Tower was an impregnable prison, that now they were so strong nothing could unseat them. He was aware that any such arguments evaded the issue. If Henry of Lancaster lived, King Edward would never be certain of reigning unchallenged. Richard could not argue for this. He had to keep his mouth shut, although he could not keep his hands clean. It was neither the first nor the last time that he had dirtied them in the King's service. For his brother, he might imperil his immortal soul.

They went indoors. The others had assembled. Hastings, Rivers, Essex, Howard and the rest unanimously accepted King Edward's decision. They, like his brother, were his obedient servants.

At ten o'clock that night, Richard went by barge upon the ebb tide to the Tower, together with more than a dozen of the lords who had supported the decision made by the King. It was still light enough to see the empty mouths of the bombards and cannon set up on the wharves from Baynards Castle to the Tower, and the barricade of huge wine barrels filled with ballast that were Lord Dudley's defences against the Fauconbergs. Tomorrow Richard was to go to Sandwich to receive the Nevilles' surrender.

Lord Dudley, Constable of the Tower, met them at the water gate. He had been with King Edward earlier and knew the reason for their presence. He told them that Margaret of Anjou had been brought to the Tower to be lodged for the night, and that Henry of Lancaster had been told of her arrival. He had asked to see her, and Lord Dudley had seen no reason to refuse his request. Henry had been so distressed by this interview with his wife, that Lord Dudley feared he might be about to fall into imbecility again. Margaret's temper was well known, and she had probably turned it upon her husband, the cause of all their troubles.

Richard cut him short. "My lord, we have the King's signed warrant here. We must be certain that his orders are carried out."

Dudley sent for one of the headsmen, and they all walked across to the gateway leading to the Inner Ward, opposite the water gate. At the door of the Wakefield Tower, in which Henry lived, they halted. Lord Dudley went up first, with the headsman and a couple of warders who were on duty. Richard followed them, his heart pumping within him, and feeling sick. It was an effort of will to stop himself turning round and fleeing into the night and not stopping until he was on the road to Sandwich. He forced himself to climb the stairs. At the top he was sweating and shaking as if he were an invalid, and it had only been a short flight. As he reached the door, Lord Dudley came out.

"It's done," he said curtly.

Richard went in. The room was empty.

"In the oratory."

Henry of Lancaster lay awkwardly on his side in front of the little altar, his head resting on a shallow stone step. He looked untidy, and very still.

Richard, his heart pounding, knelt and turned the body over gently, as if he handled a sick man. The skin on the back of

Henry's head had been slightly broken. There was an ooze of blood in the hair.

"Why here!?" Richard was furious, and sickened. In front of the altar! Dear Jesus Christ, who has known everything since the world began, this man had been anointed with the holy oils of both England and France, on his head and his useless, unmanly hands, and on the thin, chicken-carcass chest, and the back where even clothed, the shoulder blades protruded like stunted wings. Oh God, and he, Richard, Duke of Gloucester and Constable of England, had given the order to kill him. He had been a king for forty years. Richard could have sobbed out loud. He wanted to kneel at the altar, to make excuses to God for his action. But he could not. They had defiled the place by doing it here.

"Move him into the other room," he said, in a voice which made the headsman jump nervously and Lord Dudley turn pale and shuffle uneasily.

Richard left the Tower as quickly as he could, on the excuse of having to report to the King; Lord Dudley must make the necessary arrangements. The hideous brevity of what had taken place was overwhelming. Richard had to be on the road within a few hours—scarcely time for sleep. He was glad of this, of the chance which would allow him to escape into immediate action.

Ivory Pawn

June — July 1471

O Lorde what is
This worldes blisse,
That chaungeth as the mone?
My somer's day
In lusty May
Is derked before the none.

The Nutbrown Maid
(15th century)

Anne Neville, a widow who had been Princess of Wales, was home again in her father's London house, the Erber. The only difference now was that her father was dead, and her brother-in-law Clarence had moved in as if he owned it already. Her sister Isabel had taken their mother's place. Anne had a room and a bed that she had used many times before, since childhood, yet the house seemed quite strange, like just one more of the many places she had passed through during the last year, in England or France. Sometimes she was not sure which way to turn when she went out of the door, though the corridors were familiar. She even found some of her own clothes in a chest but they no longer fitted her. She had come to the Erber on entering London the first night, given by the King into the care of her sister.

Isabel came to her room on the second night, with her blonde hair hanging down like a curtain of silkworm floss. The brocaded stuff of her bedgown was so stiff with gold thread, it bent like sheets of lead rather than hung in folds. The lining was fur from neck to hem. Isabel was nearly twenty now and a very grand lady, the first Duchess in the realm. She still had rather thin little wrists, which went red in cold weather.

"Anne," she said, full of the sisterly concern she had never previously felt moved to show. "I saw you at supper—you're not eating. Are you sure you are quite well? I know you've had a miserable time, but . . . Please tell me, I want to help you. Are you sickening for something?"

"I don't think so. Nobody starved me, or had the plague to infect me. I'll be better later on, Isabel. I feel so tired, that's all."

"I thought maybe in a week or two, we could ride to Bisham, to offer for our father."

Warwick and his brother had been buried at Bisham Abbey, on the Thames near Marlow. He had wanted to lie at Warwick, in the Beauchamp Chapel.

"I don't want to." Anne sat down on the edge of her bed.

"You used to be like this—well, when you were going to have your monthly courses—is that it?"

"I don't know."

"You don't . . . ? There's no possibility . . . ?"

"If you mean, am I going to have a baby—the Prince's baby—I don't know. I'm not sure yet. Four weeks ago—there was no chance. He was kept away from me. But . . ."

"When did . . . ?"

"The night before he fought."

"Oh, Anne." Isabel put her gold-crusted, furry arms round her sister, "and he was killed. Did you hate him very much? You didn't love him, did you?"

"Neither."

"My pet, you've suffered. But we'll soon know, in another week or two."

"Yes."

"I felt bad, too, for a long time after the baby. It's better now. But I'm frightened of having another."

Anne felt unable to sympathize. When Isabel had gone, Anne looked in the mirror at herself. Maybe she was thinner in the face than she should be. She would be fifteen in exactly three

weeks, but looked as much of a waif now as she had at twelve.
She might have a more womanly shape, but she was sure Isabel
had been better endowed with curves at the same age. The sea
voyage, the weeks of travelling and living in cramped conditions,
the irregular and sometimes inadequate meals, the disturbed
sleep, had brought her out in spots, dulled her eyes and made
her hair lank. All she wanted to do was sleep. Isabel kept asking
if she wanted anything. She could think of nothing at all. She
said the prayers for the vigil of the Ascension, then got into bed
and lay flat out and felt her stomach. It fell in, like a sheet with a
puddle in the middle, and her hip bones stuck up sharply. Even
if it was there, it would not begin to swell for weeks. She curled
on her side, hid her face in her arm, and escaped into sleep.

Isabel reported their conversation to her husband, on Whit
Sunday when he got back from Kent where he had gone to attend upon the King at Canterbury and Sandwich to deal with
the Fauconberg rebels.

"Have you spoken to her?"

"Yes. I'm afraid we may have to wait a little before we can be
certain."

"You're sure?"

"She told me outright."

"Hm. Don't let her out of your sight."

George stretched his long legs out and raised his arms over his
head. "Intolerable grovellers in Kent. Fauconberg was left in the
lurch. Two good pieces of news—he has a pardon, and the Archbishop of York is to be let out of the Tower."

"My uncle freed? So soon?"

"Edward is in generous mood. More good news—I am still
Lieutenant of Ireland, God be praised. Would you like to go to
Dublin soon, Isabel?"

"No. I don't want to go on the sea again."

"Would you refuse to come with me?"

"No-o. Only a bad wife would do that."

"Oxford is going back to France."

"Mm. He hates us."

"He is not the only one. Pembroke will dig himself into Wales
for as long as he can hold out, and then follow Oxford.

"When we were in Kent, my brother Gloucester asked me how your sister did. Richard is a dark horse, and I can't be certain, but I think he's after Anne."

"I know nothing of Richard, but I always thought that she hankered after him a little, though she never told me as much. Anne is so secretive sometimes. She is behaving now as if I were a stranger to her."

"My brother will soon be nineteen; he wants to marry. Well, he'll have to look elsewhere. We have plenty of reasons to keep him away from Anne."

Several of these reasons, George of Clarence did not intend to discuss with his wife. The death of his father-in-law Warwick had put into his hands possibilities of wealth and power which previously he could not have dreamed of. The Neville lands alone were a juicy windfall, but only to whet his appetite for the great Beauchamp and Despenser inheritance. This was the inherited property of Warwick's Countess, who was at present still cowering in fright in the sanctuary at Beaulieu Abbey. George fervently hoped that she would stay there, even end her days there, fugitive from King Edward, whom she had no real reason to fear. It would make his plan to divest his mother-in-law of her lands, in favour of Isabel, so much easier.

George poured himself more Rhenish. He would have another morning with his secretary, William Molyneux, calculating the income which Warwick's lands had produced. It was an enjoyable occupation. Beyond this, he could look forward to retaining friendship with his cousin, the Archbishop of York, even to seeing him restored somewhat to favour. If any Neville were to come out of this trouble unscathed, it would be Warwick's youngest brother. The problem of his sister-in-law Anne would resolve itself in the due course of nature, at least to a stage at which some action would be possible.

By St. Barnabas' Day, her birthday, Anne began to feel alarm seep into her apathy. The battle at Tewkesbury had been fought on Saturday, May 4th; it was now June 11th. Five and a half weeks had passed. After her wedding, the waiting had been bad enough, but now she found herself lost in a nightmare from which there might be no awakening. What would King Edward

do when he found out that the line of Lancaster had not ended
with the deaths of King Henry and the Prince? If there was a
baby, and it was a boy, then it would be doomed before it had
time to live. What would Clarence do? He was certain to be the
first to know, and Isabel had been fishing for information to give
to him.

Anne had decided long before that her brother-in-law was un-
trustworthy; now he had become menacing. His interest in her
own condition, and the fact that she had been taken to his
house, could only mean that his reconciliation with his brother
the King was hiding a desire to go on plotting. For this reason,
he wanted to have custody of any child that Anne might bear,
for he could have no better weapon in his hands to use against
his brother. Anne tried desperately to think what she could do.
There was nothing. She could not appeal to King Edward, for he
would probably imprison her in the Tower; for the same reason
she could not approach the Duchess of York, who would act in
her son's interests. To appeal to Gloucester, who had seemed to
want to help her, would only lead to the same end. Richard
would not save the archangel Gabriel from drowning if it were
against the King's interests. Her own mother was helpless in
sanctuary and would be just as helpless out of it. Her uncle the
Archbishop of York would be too grateful to King Edward for
his freedom to do anything to thwart him. All her father's friends
who had survived were in the same position. The Lancastrians,
who would have been only too eager to help, were scattered and,
in any case, their help would consist of spiriting her away to
France, only to abandon her when the child was delivered. Besides, she was not quite certain that there was a child. Isabel
said that you had to miss twice before you could be sure.

George of Clarence quickly found that the net he had cast so
carefully to catch a fortune was fouled up by his brother Richard. This had already become evident by the beginning of July,
when they had both taken an oath of loyalty to the King's little
son, at his investiture with the title of Prince of Wales.

Richard had been given Warwick's home territory in Yorkshire, the lordship of Middleham. He had surrendered his Welsh
offices and was preparing to go north to take up his duties as

Warden of the West Marches, and to deal with the threat of a Scots raid. It was clear that Richard wanted to step into Warwick's shoes in the north. In addition, Richard had received Warwick's office of Great Chamberlain of England, and he was already Constable and Admiral. George, who should have thought himself lucky still to be Lieutenant of Ireland, was jealous. He had wanted the Great Chamberlainship for himself, and resented not only the loss of the income from the office, but the fact that his brother the King had loaded Richard with responsibilities unusually heavy for one so young. George could not stomach the truth, that Edward thought Richard more able than himself. If he had known of the request which Richard had made to the King before leaving for the north, his resentment and anger would have known no bounds.

"I can't understand your eagerness to go among those barbarians, Dick. The Scots are an evil race, but those people on my side of the Border are near Scots themselves, and even worse!" King Edward said this cheerfully, for he was glad to have someone who wanted to take on the unruly north. "You'll have a rough ride, you know. Aside from all the old Lancastrians, the villains and cattle thieves, you'll find some hard men in high places in the towns. They won't take kindly to royal infants being thrust upon them!"

Richard grinned up at him. "They'll have to take what they find. Do I look such an infant? I feel as if I'd seen a hundred years in your service already."

The King looked him up and down for a minute and ceased to tease. "No," he said, "you don't—far from it, and the fact is a great relief to me. Being in my service has put more years on you than I'd care to see, but in this case it's an advantage. You'll soon learn hard bargaining and straight talking in the north. Meanwhile, you can cut your teeth on Fauconberg. He's a tricky, loudmouthed nasty little man, and I doubt if he'll keep his pardon and safe conduct till Christmas."

"He may be useful. One pardoned Neville is more to our advantage in the north than all the dead ones." Richard opened the casement to let out a huge bumble bee which was trapped. As it lumbered away, too heavy for its wings, the sun-warmed air brought in the scent of lavender and sewers together, and a deafening screech from a peacock. He shut the window hastily.

"His trouble," King Edward said, meaning the peacock, "is too many wives." This gave Richard the chance he had been waiting for.

"I want one," he said.

"What! A little peahen!" King Edward roared with laughter.

"No."

"You're trying to tell me you want my permission to take a wife?"

"Yes."

"Well, it's to be expected. Though you've done well enough without one. You've got a little daughter, haven't you? And there were some mysterious assignations in Bruges. You were missing from the Gruuthuse table most evenings towards the end. . . ."

Richard was becoming red in the face.

"I want your permission to marry Warwick's daughter."

"What?!" One could not say that King Edward let out a bellow of rage, but it was scarcely a shout of pleasure. "You wait until the very last moment, before you disappear into the wilds of the north for months, to ask me this, when I have no time to think about the answer. On the face of it, I don't like the idea. You'd be more use to me if you made a foreign marriage. Why, of all the wealthy young women in this realm do you want the widow of my enemy, the daughter of the man we have destroyed? Do you know if she's carrying? Or hadn't it occurred to you that it might be an inconvenience that your prospective wife may be going to produce an heir to the House of Lancaster? By all the saints, Richard, I thought you had grown up ahead of your fellows, but now I'm not so sure!"

"There are advantages," Richard said stiffly. He had expected a reaction of this kind.

"Then you had better tell me what they are, because I can't see any!"

"The Neville lands in the north. And you said I'd be having a rough time up there—if I were married to Warwick's daughter the people might take to me more kindly. You've never lived there; the feeling for Warwick—and for Montagu—was very strong."

"Hm. You may have something there." The King paused and swatted at a fly, diverting his irritation. "But not much. For God's sake, Richard, you're half a Neville yourself—you don't *need* the girl. As for the lands, well, with Warwick's wife refusing to come out of sanctuary, and the girl safely in a nunnery, you have no need to worry about being unprovided for. You can have—within reason—whatever of Warwick's lands you care to ask me for. And you'd better not forget George in all this. I'm not having you stirring him up and making trouble for me to deal with."

"I wouldn't dream of encroaching on George's rights."

"Hm. Your ideas of George's rights—and mine for that matter —are very different from his."

By now, King Edward had begun to recognize a mulish streak in Richard, which he did not often see.

"Richard, leave it with me," he said reasonably. "I won't give you the answer no, now. But I can't give you my unconditional approval either. Leave it until you come back to London, then we can discuss it again. I doubt if I shall like it any better, but I shall have had time to think about those advantages you seem so tempted by. And we will know one way or another if the girl is carrying. If she is, then I have a lot more thinking to do."

"May I have an answer by Martinmas?"

"Of course. If you're back by Martinmas. Dick, you're going to be up and down the north road on my business so often you'll have a sore arse."

"It's had too much practice for that," Richard said with feeling, and smiled, glad that he had not had his request turned down flat, and that he had not seriously displeased his brother.

As he rode out of London on the north road the following day in the garrulous and not very trustworthy company of Fauconberg, Richard weighed once again the advantages to be gained by marriage to Anne Neville. He was fully decided now to settle and make his life in the north. He felt at home there, and it would put a couple of hundred miles between himself and the Woodville tribe. He knew that as he grew older, he would become even less able to tolerate their arrogance and greed. It would be safer to avoid quarrels by being absent from court most of the year. If he were to take Warwick's place as good lord to the north, Warwick's daughter would be the best wife he could choose. Also, she was entirely the sort of girl he would like for a wife. She was very pleasing both in personality and appearance, and not a stranger. If, as the King would rather, he made a useful foreign marriage, he might be saddled for life with a shrew or a lump of dough, who would only drive him to adultery and make his life in the north twice as difficult. The more he thought about Anne, the more determined he became to have her. He remembered all the absurd occasions from childhood when she had come to his notice, and his thoughts made him smile to himself. Perhaps these shared things would make it easier to become a successful husband.

With the coming of the month of July, the thing Anne dreaded and Clarence waited to hear, seemed confirmed. The weather had become exceptionally humid, and London sweltered. Behind the walls of the Erber, in the rose gardens, it was more tolerable, but smells came over the walls and troubled the inside of the house in places previously clean. Instead of wholesome bees, there were blowflies among the roses. While Clarence was busy, Isabel led a very quiet life and watched her sister. Anne had now missed twice. This fact was reported to Clarence, who said, "This must not go beyond our two selves. Not even her maids must know, yet.

"I am hoping to be able to persuade my omnipotent brother that Ireland needs me. We may depart for Dublin, taking your sister with us before the child is due, so her condition may be hidden. Once in Ireland the child can be kept secret until I think fit."

"What if it's a girl?" said Isabel, looking round-eyed at him, amazed at his daring.

"Lose it in the Irish bogs!" George said flippantly. Then more sensibly, "There is no lack of convents of nuns either here or in Dublin."

"But my sister may not wish to enter a convent."

"You'll have to weigh your sister's wishes against your inheritance, Isabel. My brother Richard wants to marry her. He asked the King's permission on the day before he left to go north. It's as much in your interests as it is in mine to keep her from him. The King doesn't like the idea, and I believe he may take my part—he doesn't want to break the spell of brotherly love!" George began to crow and cackle with outrageous laughter.

Later, Clarence talked to Anne herself and succeeded, as he intended, in frightening her almost out of her life, so that she might be prevented from crying for help from other quarters.

"We think it best, Anne," Clarence said, in an unusually avuncular role, "that you remain with us now, for your own safety. The King suspects your condition. I have done my best to persuade him against it, but he seems determined to have you safely housed in the Tower until he knows what your confinement has brought forth. I am beginning to fear he may even go so far as to send men to raid my house and carry you off. He has only held off so far because we are now reconciled and he wishes to show me friendship. Thus, you realize how important it is that confirmation of his suspicions regarding you shall be kept from him, and from anyone else who might inform him."

Anne stared at him with eyes he thought like a frightened rabbit's, and which he avoided. Pleased with the effect of the first part of his speech, Geroge drained his cup of wine to help him over the second part.

"The Tower," he said. "You know what happened to Henry of Lancaster in the Tower. My brother the King, I'm willing to admit, is not a bloodthirsty butcher, but he knows how to act for his own safety. Do you think a grandson of Lancaster has more chance of life than the grandfather? There are plenty of ways— that might not be construed as murder."

Immediately, Anne saw herself being pushed downstairs at the Tower—"Tripped over the step, your Grace!"—or frightened by the lions, or fed evil herbs in her food, so that she might miscarry, and rid the King of his trouble. Clarence was right; he would not need to wait for the child to be delivered. There began in her the wish to defend the helpless unborn creature everyone fought over. It was her child, within her, no matter if the father were unloved and unmourned.

When Isabel wanted to be entertained in the evening and asked her sister to play chess, Anne played so badly that it was as easy to take the men from her as apples off a tree. Anne watched her last pawn, a pathetic little knob of ivory, whipped away by her sister, and could bear no more.

"I'm not worth a pin to you!" she said, her voice unsteady with anger and misery. "No more than the least one of these pieces. What shall I do? Dear Lord Jesus, what shall I do?" And before Isabel could get a word out, Anne had snatched up the chessboard and scattered the red winning men all over her sister. Then she dissolved into tears.

Isabel had experienced before a similar display of impotent rage from Anne. It made her feel nervous, because she did not know what to reply. Usually she felt superior to Anne, but now her meek little sister had thrown the chessmen at her head. She picked a rook out of her lap and said, "You've a little devil of temper always hiding in you, Anne." Isabel sounded injured, but Anne was crying so noisily, she did not seem to hear. Isabel handed her an extra handkerchief in silence.

Then she said, "George won't harm you, Anne. We want to do what is best for all of us."

"Harm me! No, I don't expect he will, I'm too useful at the moment—or what's inside me is! He wants a little heir of Lancaster to use against his brother the King. He's not finished plotting, has he, Isabel? If you love him, as you say, you'd better try to stop him, before you both end in bad trouble!"

Isabel, amazed that her younger sister had read her husband's intent more clearly than she had, began to be a little afraid. George's plans, aways so attractive, like bright rainbows, might prove as evanescent.

Anne, weeping no less because she knew she had taken childish measures against her sister, suddenly found the answer to her own wails of helplessness. There was only one way—to escape from the Erber and Clarence's custody, to escape from the King and all his relatives and friends, and disappear into London.

The silkwoman came to the Erber every week to collect orders for fine sewing and such items as trimmings for gowns. Sometimes she came more often, when the Duke or Duchess had special requirements. Mistress Ellen Langwith had no cause to love the Duke of Clarence. Her brother had been a man-at-arms killed in the Lancastrian Earl of Oxford's service, but business was business. She was the best silkwoman in London, who in her time had made shirts for the King.

In the silkwoman lay the only chance that Anne could see of salvation. If she could find some means of persuading Mistress Langwith to take her from the Erber disguised as a servant. . . . It must be done without revealing her identity—no one would dare to meddle on her behalf if they knew who she was. . . . She supposed that Mistress Langwith might give her employment. Sewing was the only accomplishment that she could offer to the world that might provide a means of support. She would have to support herself somehow. Beyond that, she supposed nothing.

Either Anne was cleverer and more plausible than she could have imagined herself to be, or she looked so little like a person who was the Duchess of Clarence's sister that the silkwoman was easy to hoodwink. She swallowed Anne's halting explanation of herself as the young widow of one of Warwick's retainers, persecuted by the Duke of Clarence for one pitiful scrap of land, and agreed to take her out of the Erber disguised as a servant. There were about two hundred of Clarence's dependants about the place; Anne presumed that Mistress Langwith knew of the presence of her real self in the house, and that it was only by luck that she had not been recognized. It was amazing how easy it seemed to be to shed one's rank with one's rich garments.

When the day of the silkwoman's next visit came, Anne walked out of the gates of the Erber in the servant's clothes which had been brought in for her, without attracting even a second glance. The most difficult part had been the evasion of her sister and those set to watch her inside, not the escape itself.

Anne had given no thought to how they would reach their destination—the silkwoman's house and shop somewhere off Friday Street, near St. Paul's. They went on foot. Anne had never

walked through the streets of London before. It was as frightening as any of her previous experiences on land or sea. Yet Mistress Langwith went briskly along, her pattens clattering impor-
tantly over cobbles, broken paving and lumpy dirt, as if she
owned the city. When doing business in great households, she
had seemed such a gentlewoman, low-voiced and self-effacing.
Now her voice, when addressing carters who got in her way, or
pedlars nudging for her custom, was loud and sharp with a wit
Anne only half understood.

The people in the street all behaved as if they owned it, barging roughly along, not caring who was shoved aside. The shop-
keepers' impudence, in popping out of their doorways to all but
drag inside the unwary, Anne had heard of, but she had never
expected to feel them clutch at her own elbow. She hated to be
touched and importuned in this way. The raucous bustle of London assaulted her eyes, ears and nose. Your eyes had to dart constantly hither and thither in case people were about to run into
you, or you were going to step in something disgusting—though
this was difficult to avoid—or even to put your foot in a hole and
trip up.

Though the day was hot and the City sun-drenched, it was impossible to get a glimpse of the blue sky, because the houses so
overhung the streets, and the sweltering stinking air was sealed
as if by a lid. In the faces of many of the hurrying people lay an
anxiety beyond the ordinary hot and botheredness of those at
work on a summer day. Mistress Langwith pursed up her lips
and shrugged; there was plague about, she said, and getting
worse every day. Anne wondered if when they got to the sewing
shop, she would be able to wash as frequently as she was used to
do; she hated being hot, and she was getting hotter at every
step. There was always plague to be frightened of in London in
summer, and it seemed more frightening out here in the streets
than when one was living behind the walls of a great house,
though even then the infection found its way in.

Anne could not tell in which direction they were walking. Mistress Langwith surged on. Not far, she said, as they came out
into Candlewick, then up Budge Row and Soper Lane to Cheapside. Anne knew that she had been to Bulstrode the draper's in

Candlewick; now she could not even recognize the shop in the crush. Budge Row had a distinctively rancid, foxy stink which made the skinners' shops uninviting. Bundles of furry shapes with heads, legs and tails still on hung on hooks in the doorways, with dried sightless eyes, wrinkled like raisins. Until they emerged into Cheapside, Anne might have been walking through a maze. It seemed a long way, for she was unused to walking far in pattens.

Down the broad highway of Cheapside Anne had ridden in King Edward's triumphal procession, a prisoner, while the Jesus bells of St. Paul's had pealed for her humiliation. Now the street was its everyday crowded self, jammed with wagons, the shops no longer decorated in the King's honour. Cheapside, though far from being paved with gold, came very near to being walled with it. There were getting on for fifty goldsmiths' shops lining the street between the water conduit at the Standard and St. Paul's, all with open fronts where mounds of shining plate were always on display. Here the nobility came to buy. Some of the younger, more raffish of them were buying now, and causing a disturbance in the street. The wheels of two wagons had managed to become locked in the press, and the carters had climbed down to abuse each other and sort out the tangle. They got in the way of the lordly party sauntering past the shops, and foul language passed freely between everyone.

Anne glanced fearfully in their direction. The roistering young lords looked too elegant to set foot in a London street, but their language matched the draymen's. Their arrogance and ill manners were not much different at the King's court.

"No better than guttersnipes!" Mistress Langwith said, as they made a detour to avoid the incident. Anne glanced at her and saw her contempt. She did not volunteer the information that one of them had been the Queen's son.

"Not far now, my dear," Mistress Langwith said, slowing her pace to accommodate Anne's flagging steps. "Just passing into Bread Street Ward, where I live."

They had come to Friday Street and turned down it, behind the goldsmiths' shops, when her new mistress grasped Anne's arm and hustled her past the entry to an alley, urging her to look the other way. It was too late; she had already seen. A woman, ragged and filthy, was lying on the ground in the alley mouth, groping feebly, as if to catch at the legs of passersby. Black vomit drooled down her chin. People had begun to die of plague in the streets, even behind the houses of the great merchants, the rulers of London.

Mistress Langwith hurried on, saying nothing. In a gap in the house roofs, Anne saw the spire of St. Paul's again, rearing so high in the sky that the gilded weathercock on top might have been ready to fly in at the gates of Heaven. It was familiar, but not reassuring. Here in the hot, disease-afflicted city, Anne felt very helpless and alone.

Pentecost Lane

July — November 1471

Then went I forth by London stone,
Throughout all Can[dle]wyke streete;
Drapers mutch cloth me offred anone;
Then comes me one, cryed, "hot shepes feete".
One cryde, "mackerell"; "Ryshes grene", another gan greete.
One bad me by a hood to cover my head;
But for want of mony, I myght not be sped.

John Lydgate, *London Lickpenny* (15th century)

"Brawn!" The woman's face as she shrieked was the exact mottled colour of it. She yelled for the cook. "You call that brawn? I'd make a better brawn out of my backside. What is it then? Eyes, ears, arseholes and whoreson great gobbets of fat—that's what it is, and I'm not having it. You give me my money back!"

The housewives of London were not shy of making complaints, or of what they did in protest! This very forthright one had dumped the offending commodity upon the shop counter, sliding it out of its mould so it stood wobbling, pink and unwholesome, like bad legs, for by the time it had made the journey back to the shop in the woman's basket it was far from fresh.

The cook looked and sniffed. "Never known brawn that wasn't," he said with superiority. "Honest pigs' heads, ears and all. Never use anything but the best. Not bought yesterday either. Lady, I'm not giving back money on stale food I sold as fresh."

"I'll report you to the Common Council!"

"You'll get yourself fined for making false complaints!"

Anne Neville, after two months of observing London house-wives, still marvelled at their outspokenness. She still could not understand their quick, vulgar speech. "Answer up according to your size, dear," friendly people said to her. But she was too shy to pit herself against their wit. The men seemed to be a constant threat to her virtue, and the women a censorious, jealous crowd, who mocked her behind their hands. She scarcely dared to speak to her employer, the master cook, yet his customers abused him freely. Her employer! That the mighty Earl of Warwick's daughter came to be employed in a London shop, selling cooked food to those who had no hearth at home or no time to cook, was in-credible even to herself.

Within a week of Anne's escape with her into the streets of London, Mistress Langwith had died of plague, and her sister, the cook's wife, had given succour to several of her servants, though many would not have done so, for fear of infection. Somehow, in the cook shop, they were all still in health, and Anne's own fear of the disease had been overtaken by many other fears. Now that cooler weather had come, things were safer.

At least the cook and his wife kept an orderly house. Anne's ignorance and blunders exasperated them, but her obvious gen-tility gave them a certain status. Though they could not hope to rival the big inn just round the corner, the Bull's Head, which catered for much of the traffic entering or leaving London by Aldersgate, at least they had a serving maid who was something of a lady. For this reason, they had kept her on.

Pentecost Lane lay in the parish of St. Nicholas Shambles, north of St. Paul's, east of Newgate, and south of Aldersgate. The front of the house and the open part of the shop faced the narrow street; the rear had a yard which backed on to the wall of the Greyfriars' garden. The lane itself led off Blowbladder Street, where the butchers' market was, and made a dog-leg, with a dead end up against the wall enclosing the precinct of St. Martin-le-Grand. This was the wall of the sanctuary, behind which even now a few remaining supporters of the Earl of Warwick found refuge. At first, it had occurred to Anne that she might seek sanctuary there, but she knew that sometimes the King seized people from even such protected places. The Duke of Exeter, who had been carried to Westminster sanctuary more dead than alive after Barnet, on King Edward's orders had been removed to the Tower, before he was even fit to leave his bed. In any case, you needed money to live decently in St. Martin's; if you had none, you would have to hide like a rat in a thieves' hovel with murderers and whores.

The month of August had come and gone, and then September, without the signs Anne was desperately waiting for. It had now seemed certain that she was carrying, though there was no swelling of her belly that she could detect. All her few moments of inactivity were filled with dread. More than ever it was necessary to avoid discovery by the King, though discovery by the cook's wife of her condition was nearly as much of a threat; she might well throw Anne out onto the street. No servant girl, living among so many others, could keep a pregnancy secret for more than a couple of months. There was no one in whom Anne might confide. Even God seemed far away, as if He did not know the ways of cook shops.

Among all the other things there were to be afraid of, was that she made so inept a servant that suspicions would be aroused. The tendrils of the grapevine of gossip reached from Westminster to London daily, from the highest to lowest, and there must be plenty of rumours of the disappearance of the Duchess of Clarence's sister.

But the cook and his wife would have been hard to persuade that Anne was indeed the missing great lady. The mere notion that such a person would willingly seek employment, or have landed up in their shop, was so manifestly absurd that if Anne had confessed to it on her knees, they would have laughed and assumed that she was touched in the head. Her vague explanation of a secluded upbringing in a country convent, the hint of her being a gentleman's bastard, were enough to allay suspicions, if not to deflect their impatience of her shortcomings.

The cook's wife had luckily assumed at the beginning that a girl whose trade was fine sewing was unsuitable for kitchen duties. She saw in Anne a useful maid for serving customers in the shop. When it became clear that Anne had never served anyone across a counter in her life, had apparently never handled the coin of the realm, had never answered back to the aggressive, they were merely irritated and told her that she would have to learn to do all these things quickly, if she were to stay with them.

The amazing thing was that Anne had managed to learn enough to induce her employers grudgingly to keep her. Anne was continually surprised at herself, meekly providing customers with their wares, picking out the small change from bewildering rows of coins. She had even begun to feel some satisfaction at not making the same mistake twice. Her mistakes had been many. She had found it impossible to tell the different foods apart, not knowing that a pie of one sort was immediately distinguishable from another by its shape, finish and garnish. The mint sprigs proclaimed the mutton and the sage the pork, scallop shells the fishy items. Customers cheerfully or irately instructed her.

Every day the cook himself decorated the big counterfront of his shop with his wares to tempt customers, while his servants stood respectfully by. Pyramids of food, flourishes of herbs, coloured pastes and painted shells, created pictures which looked like shrines. The shop did a good trade; even some of the sanctuary men at St. Martin's sent out their servants to buy food, steaming stews in coffins of pastry, pitchers of broth, roasted joints and fowls, brawns and pies.

The cook had arrangements of convenience with certain butchers in the Shambles. Anne had only once been to the butchers' market. If Hell had streets, surely they would be inhabited by butchers. All those gaping carcasses, the trays of livers and lights flopping about, the head with hairy ears still on, the maggoty horrors hiding forgotten in corners, and all the flies in London feasting there. The stink—years of accumulated stink —was enough to knock anyone down. It had got into the walls of all the houses round about; in summer the cook shop not only reeked of food, but was enveloped in the stink of the Shambles.

Even the church of St. Nicholas, and the fine house of the Grey-friars, must live eternally in the stink.

In the house in Pentecost Lane, Anne shared a tiny attic with three other girls. It was at the back, above the kitchen, and always smelt of cooking food, stale fat, and onion-scented breath. This ordinary crowded living with other people had been as difficult to get used to as the serving in the shop. Worst of all were the endless prying questions of the girls, whose curiosity was aroused by the simplest errors. Anne had very seldom in her life had to dress herself in the morning, or to remove her clothes at night, and she tried to hide her fumblings, in case they betrayed her. She was regarded as a harmless freak, or a foreigner; friendly gestures were not lacking, among the laughter and teasing, and spitefulness was confined to one girl only, who could be ignored. But Anne was cut off from her companions both by her class and the constraints imposed on her by fear of discovery.

When, on the arrival of the month of October, Anne found herself visited by her monthly courses in the usual way, she had no room in her mind for wondering why this had happened, or why it previously had not, her relief was so great. That morning, huddled up and aching as she always was at such times, she sat on her bed and laughed and cried both at the same time, until the others thought she had gone crazy. The cook's wife, who had begun to cast her suspicious looks, smiled at last, reassured of her maid's respectability; now she would not have to have a word with the parish priest about her doubts. Safe from instant dismissal from the shop, Anne also realized that her importance to the King was now greatly diminished though, of course, he could not know it.

Soon after, a chance remark by one of the customers aroused Anne's fear all over again.

"All arse over head they were at the Bull's Head yesterday!" a gossip had clucked, leaning her basket on the counter and addressing everyone else. "A Royal Person came down here—imagine—just round the corner, and was asking all these questions about the Earl of Warwick's daughter, the Prince of Lancaster's widow. Something about abduction—it seems the King's looking for her all over London."

"What Royal Person?" another woman said, hoping for a good long gossip.

"No less than the King's brother!"

"Holy Virgin! Which one?"

"The younger one."

"The Duke of Gloucester? Here? Himself?"

"In person."

Anne piled veal patties into the cloth her customer had provided, with trembling hands. Her cousin Richard, the King's henchman, no more than a few yards away at the end of the street, searching for her. Surely the King must put the price on her head very high, if his brother were willing to come to the City in person. She felt unreasoningly afraid of them. There was only one thing she could do, and that was to stay in the cook shop, never to go out, and to pray that for lack of success, the hunt might at length be called off.

King Edward looked like Jove ordering a parliament of the gods. It was Christmas night and he was King of England again, wearing his crown and presiding over the feasting in his palace of Westminster. Richard thought that he looked more magnificent than he ever had done before, all eyes in the White Hall followed him in fascination. Richard deliberately kept his own eyes away from the almost equally dazzling figure of the Queen. Elizabeth Woodville sparkled and shimmered like one of the tinsel-decked players, who had just performed the interlude, only every single stone of her glitter was worth its weight in pounds sterling, not halfpence. It hurt the eyes—in more ways than one—to gaze on her unblinking. Her six months' pregnancy shone in rounded unmistakable glory in front of her, and her unbound hair spread like silver gilt tissue down her back. Any other woman of her age would not bear close inspection—she did. She had even bestowed a gracious little smile on Richard that evening, cut short his kneeling time, and asked him if he liked the north. She was probably hoping that he would stay there.

The Queen's greeting to her brother-in-law Clarence had been in contrast noticeably chilly, and his disdain all the more marked. Clarence was in favour with no one. In the last weeks,

Richard had only just been able to restrain himself from bodily assault upon his brother. On his return from the north at Martinmas, he had found the brief period of cordiality between Clarence and the King at an end. Richard, when greeted with the news of Anne Neville's disappearance, had lost his temper and accused George of deliberately hiding her, so that he might not have the opportunity to marry her. King Edward had ended the scene by shouting louder than them both and sending them out of his presence like two noisy schoolboys, though afterwards he had assured Richard of his support. But his consent to the marriage had come too late; Anne Neville could not be found.

George swore repeatedly that he knew nothing of her whereabouts, until Richard was inclined to believe him. He seemed so angry at her disappearance himself, as if she had thwarted him in some way. For nearly two months, Richard had searched London for her, though he did not even know for certain that she was still in London, or even in England. He planted his servants where he could in every district, he visited every religious house or place of refuge himself and even sent men to all the best-known brothels and taverns. Every day Anne was constantly in his mind, as she would perhaps not have been had she not been in such trouble.

Now, on Christmas night, Richard's fears were redoubled. Surely this was the worst time in all the year to be in trouble and alone. The feasting in the hall had reached the stage where the noise was unendurable, the air stifling, and the company full of wine, making a spectacle of themselves in the dancing. Richard had been trying to have an interesting conversation with Lord Howard, about the east coast ports and the Iceland trade, but even with Howard at bellowing pitch, they had been obliged to give up.

He had almost decided that he could stand it no longer, and was about to make his excuses to the King and leave, when he felt someone pluck at his sleeve.

"Your Grace, excuse me—but I have news." They pushed towards the doorway, battling with noise and too many people.

"Of the Lady Anne?"

"There's word about a maid servant in a cook shop—

somewhere near Aldersgate, a street called Pentecost Lane. They have a girl who was once in the Duke of Clarence's household. She was taken on as a maid sometime this summer. That is about all we know at present, your Grace."

"It's enough. I'll go there myself. Get a horse ready and a pair of boots and a warm cloak."

"Now, your Grace?" The man stared at his master in surprise.

"Now. And about a dozen men, I think. But mind, not bristling with arms. It is Christmas night, and we may be disturbing honest citizens for nothing."

The doors of the shop in Pentecost Lane were bolted against uninvited guests, but chinks of light showed through the shutters and sounds of noisy merrymaking came from within. Richard's men banged on the door. There was no response. Probably they were all making too much noise to hear, and three parts fuddled. It was late, and dancing seemed to be going on inside, to judge from the thumping, and the shuddering of the entire building. A determined hammering on the shutters did better, for after a little, a man opened them wide enough to allow him to put out his head.

"We would like a word with the master of this shop. We are on the King's business and believe that he may be able to help us. There is nothing to fear if he answers us honestly."

The head was withdrawn and the shutters inhospitably bolted again. One of Richard's men swore.

Richard said, "No good servant will allow strangers inside at night without his master's permission." They waited. Presently the door opened. The servant appeared to fumble for words. A little too much strong ale had widened the gap between his thoughts and his tongue.

"Sirs," he said carefully, "will you step inside. Christmas night, and we feast here as well as all the dukes in the kingdom. My master will speak to you over a cup of ale."

They followed him towards the back parlour where the noise was coming from. Even on the entrance of a dozen strangers it was slow to die down. Several couples were leaping up and down to the accompaniment of clapping and stamping, while somewhere a whistle pipe and a small drum struggled for a hearing. A fat woman, wobbling like a vast jelly, was prancing and showing her best white stockings and fancy garters. Her partner's points were undone at the back, like a ditch digger's, so his shirttail flapped. Another man was jiggling on a table, wearing a sort of mask with a red nose, like fools use. With the extreme care of the drunk, he was fastening the ribbons of his codpiece into bows. Holly and ivy decorated the door lintels, rosemary the windows and a kissing bough hung in the middle of the room. Apple bobbing had been enjoyed—there was water all over the floor and down the fronts of many guests.

Richard's men could have put a stop to all this racket at once, but he did not wish them to enter like a raiding party of sheriff's men. A short, enormously fat man and similar woman were pushing across the room towards them—the master cook himself, and his wife.

Richard's eye had scanned the whole room in the first moment, but he could not see Anne among all the people, and his hope began to fade once again. The smells of roasting and stewing, boiling and baking, were overlaid by onions, garlic, beer and sweating people of varying degrees of cleanliness. The rushes on the floor were fairly fresh. To judge from the demolished ruins of the feast, the cook's family, friends and servants had eaten and drunk very well indeed. The room was as hot as Hell's own kitchen.

Richard slid off his cloak and his servant took it. This unintentionally created an effect equal to an appearance of Beelzebub in a pulpit. It silenced the revelry more quickly than could shouts, or drawing of swords. At Westminster, he had been just one gorgeously dressed male among a throng of others; here he was an apparition from another world.

The women goggled and the men gaped. They were all full of ale and wine, and each hesitated to ask his neighbour if he saw what confronted them, in case he were scoffed at for seeing alehead visions. Such jewels and cloth and style had never been seen at close quarters, let alone walking in among them. Rich stuffs graced the backs of the Mayor and aldermen of London but nothing remotely like this. The young man who had so strangely interrupted their Christmas feast, winked and sparkled

as if he were covered in chips of coloured glass with the sun
shining behind them, though the obvious, and unbelievable fact
was that they were genuine precious stones. His doublet seemed
to be more shining gold stuff than cloth, though figured with velvety patterns in dark blue, the jewels forming the centres and
stems of flowers. The shoulders were about four times as wide as
the waist. More gems sparkled on his fingers, and surely he was
more clean and scented than was Godly, he was shaved smoothly
and his fingernails were spotless and his hair shining. His hose
were shimmering blue silk, the kind which need lining with
satin, and tight! Well, the doublet was so short—any son of the
house would have been thrown out on his ear for indecency.

Most of the stares took in nothing lower than this, but the
master of the house did. He did not notice the elaborate gilded—
or gold?—spurs, or the boots of soft blue Spanish leather; but his
visitor had a band of velvet, also blue, buckled round his left leg,
just below the knee. Diamonds blinked on it. The cook's face,
competing with the roast beef in colour, took on the hue of veal
in milk. There were only about a score of lords in the kingdom
who wore the Garter, and here was one of them in his back
parlour, wanting words with him.

At the sight of blenching fright descending upon their host,
the company all lapsed into motionless silence. The lady showing
her own garters had given a shriek and let her skirt fall. The
cook's wife stood stoutly at her husband's side, puffing, her great
shelf of bosom heaving up and down.

Richard spoke to her first, gently, but loud enough to ensure
that everyone else heard what he said. "Madam, I have reason to
believe that in July last you employed a servant of your dead
sister, Mistress Ellen Langwith—a young girl from the household
of the Duke of Clarence. . . ." This was enough to produce a response more immediate than he had hoped for.

Before the cook's wife could answer, all heads turned towards
a place at the far end of one of the benches at the other side of
the room, where the servants were. Prepared, indeed expecting,
hoping, to find her, as he was, the sight of Anne Neville sitting
there, very still, so shocked Richard, that all he could do was
stare at her. Though she scarcely moved a muscle, she seemed to

cower and shrink away. As the watching company began to notice her fear, their faces changed from wonder and amazement
to suspicion and hostility. Richard saw them change. Anyone
would think he was about to do something highly dishonourable,
to sling her over his shoulder and carry her off, as the Romans
did the Sabine women.

Richard turned to the cook's wife again. "Madam, your maid
Anne is the Earl of Warwick's daughter, whom the King is
seeking."

A large elderly lady at the back promptly blew a raspberry for
comment. "And I'm the Pope's grandmother!" she snorted, and
everyone shush-shushed.

One of Richard's men put his hand towards his sword. Richard
gave him a warning look. To exert naked authority would not
gain anything. If these people were entirely sober, then they
would be easy to intimidate, but as it was their blood was up,
and a nasty brawl might ensue.

He stepped forward among them and sat down in a vacated
place on one of the benches. "Let me explain," he said. The
cook's wife, who had collapsed on the nearest seat, fanning her
face, found herself sitting next to a real lord, and almost fainted
away. When she recovered, she was utterly disarmed by the way
he talked to them, as if they had as much right in the matter as
he did. She saw that he was young, not much more than twenty.
He had crooked up one knee, the one with the Garter, over the
other, and she stared fascinated at the shining stones. Those hose
were tight enough to split, but there didn't seem to be any danger, or he wouldn't move so freely.

"In July, this lady was living in the house of her sister, the
Duchess of Clarence. . . ." There were oos and ahs at this. "I
believe Mistress Langwith, who does fine sewing—your sister,
madam—helped her to find work. I believe neither you nor your
sister had any inkling of who this lady was?"

The cook's wife was distraught. "Mother of God! My Lord,
she told me her husband was killed at Tewkesbury and . . . I
. . . My poor sister, God rest her, was taken by plague before I
could hear any such tale. As for the Duchess of Clarence . . . !"
She was quite speechless. Anne's sister a Duchess! In the house

of the King's brother! It was more than she could stand on top of
the Christmas pie and a pint too many.

The cook himself made a strangled noise, and his face became
a congested puce colour. His wife gathered herself together first.
"Who are you, my lord?" she said fearfully, looking sideways at
Richard. To her surprise he smiled at her. One of the men with
him spoke for him. "This is the King's other brother, the Duke of
Gloucester."

The whole company in the room gasped loudly, and goggled
even harder. The cook seemed about to flop down on his knees.

"Stand up, man," Richard said. "I don't hold you responsible.
That lies with others. I can see you tell the truth, and you have
not harmed the lady."

"Never! Oh, no, your Grace, your Highness. . . . This is a re-
spectable house. . . . B-b-but she's been my servant! Merciful
saints, your Grace, if I'd known . . . if only I'd known . . . !"
His eyes were popping and glassy with shock, like a cod's on a
slab.

"Richard!" Anne had somehow found her voice and her courage, and the Christian name escaped her unthinkingly. "They did
not know. They've done no harm."

Everyone stared in unbelief at the girl. The cook's wife had
scolded her for giving wrong change in the shop and for being
clumsy in cutting parsnips into straws, and here she was addressing the royal Duke as if he were her brother. The cook had once
threatened to beat her because she let a customer carry off a
good crock without a deposit. He broke into a sweat at the
thought.

"Why does the King want me?" Anne asked in a small,
wretched voice. She would not come up close to speak to Richard.

"For no more reason than to see you are treated according to
your rank. I don't want you to come with me, and I think you
would rather not be in the King's custody. Would you like to go
to the sanctuary at St. Martin's for a while, until . . . you can
take a house there and live quietly for a little, until you decide
what you want to do."

"My mother . . . ?"

"Your mother is still at Beaulieu Abbey. I've looked for you all over London for two months—I'd have looked longer if I hadn't been in the north. I thought I'd never find you."

"Now you have." Anne sounded far from glad about it. She stood nervously where she was, approaching no closer, her eyes downcast, pale as a waterlily, except for two spots of colour in her cheeks from the heat of the room. She was dressed in the sort of gown servant girls wore, drab-coloured and coarse. There was a fade mark where she had been constantly wearing an apron. It had been brushed and neatened, and her linen cap and cuffs, obviously added for the evening, were crisply white. There was not a hair straggling out over her forehead, and nothing awry anywhere, unlike many of the cook's guests, who were dishevelled and overheated.

Richard watched her. He was deeply disturbed by finding Anne in this situation apparently of her own free will, and at her hostility to himself. She seemed to accept the suggestion of moving into the sanctuary as a defeat, and she did not regard him as her friend, that was certain.

"Have you anything to take with you?" he said abruptly.

"I have no possessions."

"The lady came here with nothing but what she stood up in, my lord," said the cook's wife anxiously.

Richard said nothing. The cook's wife noticed how his face hardened in expression, and was afraid. Now that she had begun to gather her wits, she remembered some of the things she had heard about this young man—he was not afraid to spill blood by all accounts, and his power and might were next only only to the King's own. The thought gave her the shakes, and she fanned herself again, gasping. He was civil enough, more courteous than could possibly have been expected, but God knew what might happen afterwards.

"Madam, will you give Lady Anne my cloak to wear if she has none? It's cold outside." His manner towards her was as polite as towards his own mother, she thought, and wanted not to be afraid of him, but could not quite manage it.

"I don't have a cloak of my own," Anne said briefly. "I did not go out much."

Thus exonerated from keeping her servant short of clothing,

the cook's wife took the Duke's cloak from his servant and with trembling hands put it round Anne's shoulders, while the girl stood still as a block of wood. The cloth was soft and heavy wool, with a sheen like silk—there couldn't be many merchants in London who dealt in fine chamlet of that quality—very dark green in colour, and lavishly lined with blue velvet. It was just the right size for Anne. The Duke, the cook's wife noticed for the first time, was short, and of very slim build. That he had given her the garment to slip on Anne was odd, as if he thought it better not in any way to approach or touch her. The next thing he said seemed to confirm this impression.

"Let mine host and his lady come with us to St. Martin's. I should like them to witness that I do not abduct this lady against her will. I am her cousin."

As if in answer Anne moved towards him a little. He turned towards the door. The cook's wife and various women in the company rushed to fetch their cloaks, agog to witness this amazing event. "Watch out for the mistletoe, lovey," one squawked tipsily and was quickly stifled, with giggles, by the others.

Anne walked through the door into the street as if in a dream. The cold night air struck her face. Richard's cloak was so warm— she had forgotten the feel of rich materials, the caress of velvet across her knuckles that smelled nice, of perfumed clothes chests and cleanliness. Her own clothes smelled of food, however clean she tried to keep herself under them. Outside in the street in his jewels and gold, Richard looked quite extraordinary. He seemed older, grander and less known to her than when she had last met him. She followed him now without thought. She was beyond asking questions or volunteering information.

The horses seemed to take up most of the street. If it had been daylight, horses so fine would have drawn a crowd, even without their riders. A grey turned a pale, enquiring face towards them. Richard himself unhitched its reins and looped them over his arm. "Get up, Lady Anne," he said, and made a step for her with his hands and lifted her up to sit sideways in the saddle. Then, though his servant would have done it, he led his horse down the narrow, rough cobbled length of Pentecost Lane and out into the wider street. The sound of its iron shoes echoed loudly between the houses, followed by all the others, and people might have stuck their heads out from their shutters to see if an army had invaded them, if they had not been either still celebrating Christmas or sleeping it off.

The south gate of St. Martin's was closed in the winter from nine in the evening till six in the morning. It took a few minutes to knock up the porter, but when he did appear and discovered who the latecomer was, men began scurrying in all directions. It was arranged that Anne should be admitted to one of the sanctuary houses immediately, and report to the Dean's clerk the next day in order to have her name written in the register of persons seeking refuge in the precinct. A woman servant would look after her needs. Anne did not question who would pay for all this, the house rent, her food, servants. Either the King, or Richard, it made no odds. All she wanted to do was to lie down and sleep, and see no more of anyone.

The Turning Wheel

December 1471 — September 1472

She saith that she hath seen hit wreten
That seldin seen is soon forgeten;
  It is not so,
For in good feith, save only her,
  I love no mo.

Wherefore I pray bothe nighte and day
That she may cast alle care away,
  And leve in rest,
And evermore wherever she be
  To love me best.

Now Wolde I Faine. . . .
(15th century)

When Richard had ridden back from St. Martin's to Westminster on Christmas night, he found the King still up, but in his bedgown and probably off to some assignation. King Edward was no longer entirely sober, but he had a phenomenal capacity for wine and was able to pay reasonable attention to what Richard had to say. He was not pleased to have his young brother erupt into his presence at three in the morning, with a story so fantastic it could have been made up by the most incapable drunk in the palace—and there were plenty there that night. There was nothing he could do but listen.

Richard was unusually voluble, angry and upset. When he had finished his outpouring, the King said, "Dickon, I've followed your tale as far as I can, and I feel much as you do, but my head won't go beyond that now. I'll be better at seeing the reason later in the morning, after a brief encounter with my bed. I've a feeling our brother George is the stirrer behind all this, and it's an ugly thought I'd rather postpone for an hour or two. As long as the young lady is safe. . . . You did the best thing possible, to take her to St. Martin's—only George is likely to accuse you of abduction! Now, get to bed. We'll begin the explanations tomorrow—later today. . . ." He yawned hugely; with his chestnut hair tousled and his arms stretched above his head and the meaty paws clenched, he was more than ever like a big, sleepy lion.

Richard had to be satisfied with that, but he did not get any sleep that night. In the morning, before dinner, he went again to the King and found that Clarence had already arrived. George's greeting to him was to snap out accusingly, "You've been meddling, I hear!"

"Hold your tongue!" growled the King, who had already had words with Clarence, and could have been feeling fresher and better tempered.

"Meddling! If that's what you call it!" Richard was in fully as volatile a state as George. "Warwick's daughter, *your* sister-in-law, hiding as a poor servant in a cook shop—a *cook shop!*—within a stone's throw of Cock Lane—and it's your fault, George! I wouldn't put it past you to have sold her to a Cock Lane brothel . . . !" he yelled.

"Richard!" roared the King. He grabbed both their shoulders and pushed them apart just as they were facing up to each other like fighting cocks. "You're behaving like brats, the pair of you. Sit down with the table between you, and we'll begin the explanations. Open a window, I need air," he said to a page, and settled himself in a position where he could grab his brothers again if necessary.

"It is *not* my fault . . . !" George began.

"Quiet!" King Edward's temper was not improving. "I am going to ask the questions. I'd be obliged if you'd let me speak before giving answers—both of you.

"Now, I've heard Richard's tale of how Anne Neville was

found, and I've already heard yours of how she disappeared
from your house in July. She has told Richard that she was not
abducted but ran away, with the knowledge of no one but herself and a seamstress. What I should like to know, George,
is why Warwick's daughter—little, timid, white mouse Anne,
should dare to run away into the cesspit of London city at a
time of plague—and to *not* dare to appeal to any one of us who
might have helped her? She ran out of *your* care, George, yours
and Isabel's. Explain yourself."

"I've told you already, I don't know," George slung at him.

Richard opened his mouth, but before they could start shouting at each other again, the King said calmly, "Oh, yes, you do
know. Was she afraid of you, of her own sister?"

"No, she was not. She was afraid of you—of being clapped in
the Tower with that mad hag Margaret of Anjou."

"I see. Afraid of me? Poor little Anne. Since I sent Margaret to
Windsor within weeks of her capture, as you very well know,
George, and Anne is not stupid and knew I had no reason even
to confine her, you'll have to think up another story."

George was on the hook and struggling to get off it.

"I'm waiting," the King said.

Richard watched in silence, wondering if George would come
out with the truth. He was not entirely certain himself of what
the truth was.

"Why was she afraid of me?" the King said again.

"Ask yourself!" George was, as usual, overstepping the mark.
There were some ways one might answer a brother, but not the
King.

"I'm asking you."

"For the same reasons that her mother is afraid, I suppose."

"George, I'm losing patience." King Edward leaned back in
his chair and glared at the sullen, prevaricating Clarence. Then
he said, "You told me, back in July, that there was no possibility
of your sister-in-law being *enceinte*, and that your wife had
made certain of it. I'm beginning to wonder, George, whether
I've been told everything."

"What do you mean?" Clarence had adopted an aggrieved,
misunderstood air, to conceal his evasiveness.

"If you don't understand my meaning, I suggest that you leave my presence now, give the matter some thought, and speak to me again when you are disposed to be more civil. One of these days, George, you'll cause me severe displeasure. It could be today."

When Clarence had flounced out, the King said to Richard, "Our brother is lucky to have made a mistake. If you had found poor little Anne eight months gone, he'd have had a great deal more to answer for. There's no sign of anything, I suppose?"

"No! Christ, if that had been the case. . . . I wouldn't like to answer for my actions, though he is my brother."

"Then all three of us, and the girl, are lucky. Try to handle George with as much tact as you can muster, Richard, to make my life easier."

"He meant to cause you more trouble than he is doing now." Richard had not yet reached a stage where tact could override his anger.

"Hmm. Do you see yourself as a peerless knight rescuing the lady from among the pie dishes?"

"She doesn't see me in that role." Richard coloured a little.

"I've no doubt not. A little tarnished and blood-stained and too much of my henchman?"

"Yes."

Despite this undoubted coldness on her part, Richard felt that he should go to see Anne again that day, in the hope that she might be willing to tell him a little of what had happened to her.

Anne had found herself the centre of attention at St. Martin's. The canons could not do enough for her—because Gloucester had spoken for her, and because the Dean, Bishop Stillington, was the King's Chancellor. That afternoon men came with bolts of cloth, and sewing women expecting orders. Furniture mysteriously arrived, plate and linen, and a rather unwise combination of a singing bird in a cage and a tiny kitten. Last, but best of all, came Alice. Alice, who had been to Anne both ruler and devoted slave in her nursery days, and whom she had never expected to find again in London. Alice had in recent years gone to the household of the Duchess of York, where Richard had found her.

Anne did not give much thought to how or why he had thought of this—it was enough to see Alice, who had been the real mother of her childhood.

Late in the afternoon, when darkness had fallen, Richard came again to see her. She felt a little resentful at the sight of him, knowing that he would ask questions, and report what he had heard to the King. By this time, after all the hubbub of the afternoon, she was feeling tired and unwell, as if she were going to have a bad cold.

"I came to see if you had everything you wanted."

"Oh, yes, everything."

There was a silence. Richard perched on the arm of a chair and swung his foot. The kitten pounced for the toe. He scooped it up and put it on his knee, where it sat, blinking at both of them.

"You've lived for five months under the very walls of St. Martin's, why in Heaven's name didn't you seek sanctuary there in the first place?"

"What happened to the Duke of Exeter, who was carried to Westminster sanctuary after Barnet?" came very tartly.

It made Richard both angry and uneasy to admit that Exeter had been removed to the Tower and sanctuary broken, on the King's orders. "Your case is scarcely to be compared with Exeter's. You are a completely innocent party."

"What is innocent? What crime had King Henry of Lancaster committed?" Her words, and her eyes, her father's eyes, pierced Richard like swords. He felt all the blood drain out of his face. If she really knew, had seen himself that night, giving the order for the quick crack over the skull, climbing the stair, kneeling by the body . . . No one but his brother could have got him to do such a thing, and he had accepted the cold-blooded logic of it without a murmur.

There was a long, wretched silence, in which Anne would not look at him, and he dared not look at her.

"Surely you didn't think you could stay in a cook shop for the rest of your life?" he asked at length.

"I couldn't think beyond the hour."

"You must have thought of some things you risked happening to you."

"Some of them."

"Yet you were still brave enough to take that way out?"

"Not brave."

"Hmm." Richard looked at her. She did not look brave, or remarkable in any way, more like a wilting flower than anything else. She made him feel ashamed, though he kept telling himself he had nothing to be guilty about—at least, not as far as she was concerned. She had been so easily cast aside and injured in the game of war, yet was so resistant to his own efforts to make reparation. Filled with sudden gloom, he wondered why he was contemplating marriage to her; it would be a mistake to bring up the subject now.

"Why didn't you send to me, or to my mother?"

"You?" She looked at him in astonishment, as if he were the last person she would have turned to. "Because I thought you did the King's bidding in everything."

This was the first barbed remark she had ever made to him, and it struck home.

"You think I'd be better for not doing it—like Clarence?" he said angrily.

She withdrew visibly at the change in his tone of voice. "No-o. You are the King's brother." There was a pause. He got up to go, tipping the cat off urgently onto the floor. Then she said, "I was wrong to say that, when you stood by him." She sounded so miserable, putting down her defences like that.

"Was there no one to turn to?" he said, very gently, this time.

"All my Neville relatives are beholden to the King now."

The bleakness of this statement killed any further conversation.

"I'm tired," Anne said wearily.

"I'll go."

Anne said nothing. She did not want to talk to him, to anyone. She let him go without thanking him for sending Alice to her, which she had meant to do.

Richard found that he had even less interest than usual in the next eleven days' feasting. He was not normally ill-tempered or

morose, but now the sight of his brother Clarence, peacocking
about as if he had nothing to be ashamed of, reduced him to a
state of surliness which, of course, gave George every opportunity for baiting him.

"Brother long-face!" Clarence jibed when they met.

Richard ignored him, and turned his back to hide his fury.

"So she sent you off with a flea in your ear!" crowed George,
who could never make do with one remark when he had two on
his tongue.

"Thanks to you!" Richard snarled and walked quickly away
before he could do Clarence some physical damage. George was
well able to provoke a saint to madness.

"It serves you right, for being greedy for her lands!" was his
parting shot.

The story of how Lady Anne Neville, the Prince of Lancaster's
widow, had been found in the disguise of a maid in a London
cook shop, provided the court with a Christmas feast of gossip.
Bets were made on whether the King would favour his brother
Clarence or Gloucester in the matter, though not many were
willing to venture money on Clarence. Richard knew all eyes
were upon them, waiting to be scandalized by some misbehav-
iour on their part.

The hard task of peacemaker fell to King Edward, to his great
annoyance. He waited until after Epiphany, wishing to enjoy the
first Christmas after his homecoming in peace before tackling the
quarrel between his brothers.

Meanwhile Anne Neville fell ill, and was unable to see anyone, or to put forward any wishes of her own. Richard was
forced to admit that he had not mentioned the subject of marriage to her, and that he could not visit her at present to do so.
Clarence laughed in his face and told him the whole project was
impossible. What the girl wanted was immaterial. It was clear
that Richard was only determined to have her in order to grab
what he could of George's, or Isabel's property. In any case, it
would take a king's ransom to persuade the Papal Curia to grant
a dispensation for such a marriage, which Richard was in no position to provide. Why, it would be trebly within the proscribed
degrees of consanguinity. It would be illegal under canon law.

"Since you got a dispensation by bribing our Papal legate . . ." Richard reminded his brother.

"Only after months of trying," George shrugged. "And it was the same with Lady Anne's marriage to Lancaster. King Louis had to borrow money to pay for that one. You've got both difficulties to contend with."

"Hang the dispensation!"

"What?! You want a clandestine marriage—children who cannot inherit? You've got enough bastards—another on the way, I hear!"

"Damn your prying!" How could George have found that out? Richard had thought his misdeeds sufficiently distant from London to be concealed.

"The dispensation is irrelevant at present," King Edward said, silencing them. "What I want is to see that Richard is not denied a reasonable request by your covetousness, George. This time I am not deceived. You want to bully Lady Anne into entering a convent, so that she may relinquish all her worldly goods to Isabel. All the inheritance for you and your wife. Well, I'm not having it. If Richard wants the girl, he has my consent. I want you to come to some agreement with him."

It was a month before Clarence would concede anything, even grudgingly. After Shrovetide, the court moved to Sheen where the Queen could quietly await her lying-in, and with the benefit of the general absolution of sins at the beginning of Lent, George and Richard might patch together some agreement. The King called a council meeting, and made his brothers explain themselves, saying afterwards that they were as full of wily agreements as a couple of attorneys, and that it was a pity their talents were not better employed. At the end of it all, Clarence, making as much show about it as if he were conceding England to France, said, "My brother may have the lady my sister-in-law, for all I care, but don't expect me to divide the inheritance with him!"

This was not enough. At length, driven by exasperation, the King forced a makeshift settlement upon the unwilling Clarence. Even then, George did better than Richard who, in an attempt to pacify him, surrendered to him the Great Chamberlainship.

By Easter, Richard was obliged to go north again. Before he left, Anne Neville was enough recovered from her illness to see him, though he found her so white and wilting and listless of speech that he wondered if he had chosen an opportune moment to make a proposal of marriage. He found Anne sitting close by the fireside, her feet on a hot brick wrapped in flannel, a book and the kitten on her lap. She was reading, and he came into the room quietly, so she did not look up.

"What are you reading?" he said, for want of anything else.

Anne looked up quickly, like a creature frightened by the sound of a human voice. Then the expression of wary surprise on her face was replaced by even warier, and chilly, politeness.

"The Visions of St. Matilda," she replied, like a child answering a schoolmaster. She had been thinking, recently, that it might after all be best if she did enter a convent.

"I have the King's permission for . . . I . . . If you are agreeable . . . Lady Anne, would you consider becoming my wife?"

Anne was so startled that she lost her place in the book and almost let it slide off her knees. "You?" she said, in just the same way that she had when he had suggested that she might turn to him for help—as if the mere suggestion were preposterous.

"I don't want to press you for an answer now," he said hurriedly, then paused. "Will you consider it, Anne?"

"Oh yes, yes, of course," Anne said faintly. She could think of nothing further to say. She still felt weak, her legs made of paper and her mind unequal to the task of thinking about the future. Marriage was the last thing she wanted, yet without marriage a woman had no status in the world. She longed to go out of the world, longed for a refuge. A convent—Syon, maybe—the King would have no objection to paying her corrody, if he saw it as a means to be quietly rid of her. Such high walls enclosed the life of the religious. . . .

"I had thought of being professed . . . ," she said lamely, then realized that this was a churlish thing to say after receiving an offer of marriage. But Richard had very little to lose; he would probably get most of her property anyway. If only she could be certain of what he really wanted; she did not dare hope that it was herself.

"You must do as you please, of course," he said stiffly. Then, "I am leaving London soon, to go north. I intend to make my home at Middleham whenever possible. I've always liked the place more than anywhere else. Probably I shall come back to London during the summer. May I see you again then, Anne?"

"Yes."

When he had gone, Alice appeared, and it was clear that she had heard every word. She brought another hot brick for Anne's feet.

"Not that I couldn't see that coming months ago, when he first asked me to come to you," she said smugly, as if granted some divine foreknowledge.

Anne glared at her. Elderly women often talked like this to young girls. "I am nothing but a chattel to be haggled over by the King and his brothers. That trio! They are dividing the spoils after my father's fall. My mother is to be treated as if she were dead, and all the Beauchamp and Warwick lands taken by the King to provide for his brothers. If I were to marry one of them, I'd be living off what my mother has lost. And my sister of Clarence is as greedy as any of them. I hate them all!"

"The ways of men and Kings and power are not designed to take account of us women. He's not so bad; better than many I'd say. Your mother won't die a pauper. You may say no now my lady my pet but you wait a little while. . . . By the summer you'll feel differently. You see, by Christmas there'll be a wedding."

"There will not! Alice, you're a wicked old match-maker. I *won't* marry Gloucester, I tell you. They all caused my father's death, all of them. I won't have him!"

Anne seemed so provoked to anger that Alice smiled. It was the best sign of recovery that she had seen so far.

"Oh yes, you will, my love," she said infuriatingly. "You've just had the best offer a young lady could have, short of the King himself. He will be the wealthiest young man in the realm after your sister's husband, and twice as powerful. Think what he can offer you before you refuse him. If it wasn't for him you might have ended up marrying a greasy cook. Why, he wants to take you home to the north, where you were children together.

I'd say he was more honest than most—didn't he stand by his brother the King as a brother should do—unlike some we could mention! And there was a time when he thought as much of your father as you did—and a time when you would have liked to marry him—I know!"

"Go away, Alice," Anne snapped. She did not wish to hear a catalogue of Richard's virtues. She did not want to think about him at all; it hurt. Alice, apart from her remarks about his wealth, was being romantic. There was nothing romantic in the affair, nothing at all.

"He's been paying the rent of this house for the last nine months!" Alice said, round the door. Anne kicked the hot brick out from under her feet, and began to cry.

Richard, as he rode north, thought with gloom of the problem which he left in London, and with guilt of the one which awaited him at Pontefract. In the castle of Pontefract the steward's daughter was eight months gone, with his child. It had happened at some village festival the previous August, when he had first gone north with Fauconberg. He had been rather drunk, and highly irresponsible. The girl professed to love him, but he thought it was his rank and repute which entranced her. A suitable marriage would have to be arranged. That was easy. But his guilt was aroused because he found it uncomfortable to cast off a woman, especially if he had misused his privilege in the first place. If Anne were told of it, she would be sure to refuse his offer. He would have to wait for her answer now, until he returned to London at Michaelmas.

On the morning after his arrival back in London, he went to St. Martin's, unable to wait any longer. Anne got up late, these days. She slept a great deal because there was nothing else to do.

Richard, seeing the windows of her rooms open, called her gently. She came to the window. She still held a comb in her hand, surprised in using it by his call. The window was small; a vine grew up the surrounding wall and over the lintel, pinned onto a wooden trellis. Long, dry, trailing stems dangled down, brushing the girl's hair. The vine held bunches of grapes, small green ones which would not make wine.

They stood looking at each other seriously, she a little downwards, because the garden was at a lower level.

"I came to London for your answer."

"Where from?"

"Carlisle." He was aware that this sounded impressive.

It was a very long way to come for an answer. A messenger riding post night and day took four days. Richard must have been on the road a week. Perhaps he had come to see to some business also. He was very brown from the sun. Anne suddenly envied him his summer in the north. She hated London. He did not seem to have a great deal to say, but then he had never been a babbler. He had eyes that looked straight at one, though it was hard to read what thoughts lay behind the look. If they had known it, their serious expressions reflected one another.

A strand of her hair flopped over the window sill and swung like a silk tassel, tickling his hand, which he moved away instantly. He had never tried to touch her in any way, the usual ploy of a wooer. This had been a great relief to her. The reason, of course, had been that he did not want her to see how the most casual touch could explode desire in him like gunpowder and perhaps frighten her again. By now, and especially now, it was becoming unbearable to want someone so much. No one else would do.

Anne watched the man who had asked her to marry him with a new curiosity. His hand resting on the window sill was even browner than his face. The fingers were thin, and on one was a ring he must wear all the time because there was a band of untanned skin under it. Nice hands—she disliked podgy paws and hairy fingers. Looking at him closely for the first time in several years, she realized that he had grown. Absurd thought! She had begun to think of him as being years older than he was.

He ducked away suddenly, and if he had not been the self-assured young man who had replaced the boy she used to know, she would have thought him seized by shyness. It was a novel experience, to have this effect upon someone, when usually afflicted oneself. He bobbed up again, closer this time. He had picked a sprig of rosemary from a bush growing under the window. He handed it to her.

"Rosemary for remembrance," he said, looking at her without smiling, but then, he was not one for smiling every few moments for no special reason.

Anne fingered the green needles of leaves, releasing their aromatic scent. She sniffed it with pleasure, loving the herb's pungency. "Remembrance of what?" she said soberly, thinking of her father, of all the things which were past, which Richard had helped to take from her.

"Of times that we shared, that you might remember kindly."

Anne bent her head and lowered her eyes, so that he could not see her expression. She looked the prettiest thing in the world standing there. Well, no, she was not really pretty, Richard thought, but there was something about her . . . more than enough. He could have wished that picture of her preserved forever in his memory; the girl with unbound hair, framed by the window and the trailing vine, the soft September sun gilding her a little, making her look prettier than she was. It was so different from the sober, unhappy young widow of the winter, reading by the fireside.

Quite suddenly, without thinking, Anne put out her hand and touched Richard's face, very lightly and shyly. "Come in by the door," she said, her gravity broken by a smile, which dimpled her cheek and made the pink lips curl upwards at the corners; it was quite the most marvellous thing he had ever seen, because it had been so long a shadow of itself. Also, she had touched him entirely of her own free will, as if she at last wanted to know what he felt like. The fear had gone. At this stage he dared not let the triumph in him burst its way out. He hoped, as he walked through the door, that his face bore no evidence of the hugeness of his delight. He could have bounded through the window itself in one leap.

Once inside, his way was barred by Alice. "No visitors until the lady is properly dressed to receive a gentleman—your Grace." She spoke to him exactly as she had when he had been ten and doing something he should not. He smiled, because old nurses always took such liberties.

"Hurry, Alice," he said. "I have something to give to Lady Anne, if she'll have me." He showed her the ring on the palm of his hand. Alice looked at it and a huge beam of pleasure and approval spread over her face. She took hold of his other hand and kissed it.

"Oh, your Grace, this is a happy day, to see my lady restored to where she ought to be. . . . If you had taken her no for an answer, she would have broken her heart, poor lamb. How could she have known her own mind, after everything she'd been through? Legalized in church or not—and in a funny French church at that—nothing more nor less than rape in my opinion!" Alice snorted with indignation. Richard wisely concurred in this by keeping silent. That she expressed her opinion so forcefully, and seemed so pleased at the hoped-for engagement, was a measure of her esteem of him. Besides, what she said was a revelation, that Anne had wanted to be his wife all the time, and had held back only out of fear and mistrust.

When Alice had disappeared into Anne's room to finish dressing her, he wondered what they said to each other, who were so different in age and rank but, being women, close in understanding. It was gratifying that Alice had taken his part.

Anne came out to greet him with her hair put away decently under velvet and wire and gauze which was disappointing—he hated women's headgear, the more fashionable, the more unbecoming. Anne had resumed her serious expression.

They both opened their mouths to speak at exactly the same moment. "Did you . . . ?" This made them both laugh, which was the best way of beginning things.

"It's a long way to ride from Carlisle," Anne said.

"Yes. But I prefer to live in the north."

"Home."

Richard turned abruptly from her side and walked over to the window, where he stood with his back to her, apparently studying the Dean's garden outside. He said, with the worst effort at casual enquiry she had ever heard, "Yes. Have you considered my offer, Anne?"

"Oh, yes, of course."

Richard did not turn round to face her. He did not want her to see his expression, the bleak disappointment if the answer should be no. There was silence in the room, except for the tick of the table clock he had given her, remorselessly stealing away the moments of their lives. These might be the last ones they would spend together.

"Richard?" Anne spoke his name very softly.

Oh, God, he thought, put me out of my misery quickly. His own voice in reply to her sounded quite unrecognizable to him, loud and echoing round the walls, as if everyone in St. Martin's might hear. "Anne," he said in a quick burst, "will you have me?"

The silence nearly burst his eardrums and seemed to last forever. He did not hear her move. Suddenly he felt a touch on his sleeve, and jerked his head round to find her close, looking straight into his face.

"Yes," she said. For a second he could not remember what the question had been and stared, ashen-faced and dumb at her. Then he woke up and the expression changed, as if someone else's face had been put there in its place, to amazement and delight. At the same moment, Anne began to laugh. It was the first time he had heard her laugh properly for years, and she was laughing at him, with pure amusement and happiness. He gaped at her like a love-lorn idiot.

"I say yes," she gurgled, "and you look at me as if I'd sentenced you to death! Richard, what do you want?"

"You!" he said promptly. He realized that he must be grinning like a lunatic and that his hands were shaking. He suddenly remembered what he was doing and held out one hand, unclenching the fingers from the ring he was still holding. He held it out to her. She stared, then smiled very sweetly and held out her own hand, instead of taking it from him. She wanted him to put it on. He did so, though he was shaking so much he was frightened of hurting her. When it was on, he held her hand between his own, flat between his palms. It was the first time he had touched her.

"I've no ring to give you," Anne said.

"Time for that later. Time for everything."

"Yes."

His mind began to think rationally again. "Parliament sits next week," he said, "and the session is bound to be a long one.

I'm stuck in London for the winter, Anne. In the spring, I'll take you home."

"Home to Middleham?"

"Yes, as soon as I can. You know we're cousins, we need a dispensation—it may take a long time to persuade Rome to give us one. Maybe nearly a year. Will you wait, Anne?"

"Will you?"

"Not too long. If it does not arrive by next Easter, we'll marry without it and receive it later. There's been too much waiting and wrangling already."

They were still standing just as they had been, her hand between his. The cat rubbed round their legs, jealous of the attention given to her mistress.

"Kiss me?" Richard said, like a suppliant. He shut his eyes and heard her move, then felt a touch on his cheek like a butterfly's feet gingerly walking. "Mmm," he said, and turned his head slightly so that he met her soft, shy, hovering lips just where he thought he would, with his own. Just a touch, but enough. He drew away first, before he was overcome, and grabbed her and kissed her as one should kiss a lover. As it was, he was breathing like a broken-winded horse and shaking like a virgin under assault. Anne seemed not to notice. For a widow of sixteen she was remarkably innocent and desperately timid. He recognized that when they were married—and please God let it be soon— that he would have to go very carefully indeed. She had been frightened badly in so many ways, of wedding, bedding and childbirth. He hoped that he would be able to withstand the strain self-restraint imposed. He would have to be everything to her, husband, father, mother, brother, lover—she had no one else.

"I'm sorry," she said, contrite as an erring child, "that I set my mind against you for so long. I had no right to reproach you."

He silenced her by taking the hand he was still holding and placing her own fingers against her lips. "Hush!" he said. "What's past is past. Think of our future."

For answer Anne took his hand and kissed it, as if she had cause to be grateful to him. Before, she had not thought she had a future. "Take me home," she said.